Wielder's Rising

ok 2 of the Wielder Trilogy

By T.B. Christensen

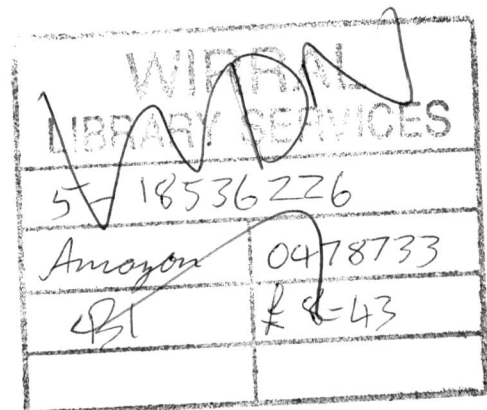

Cover art by Elise Christensen

Copyright © 2012 T.B. Christensen

All rights reserved.

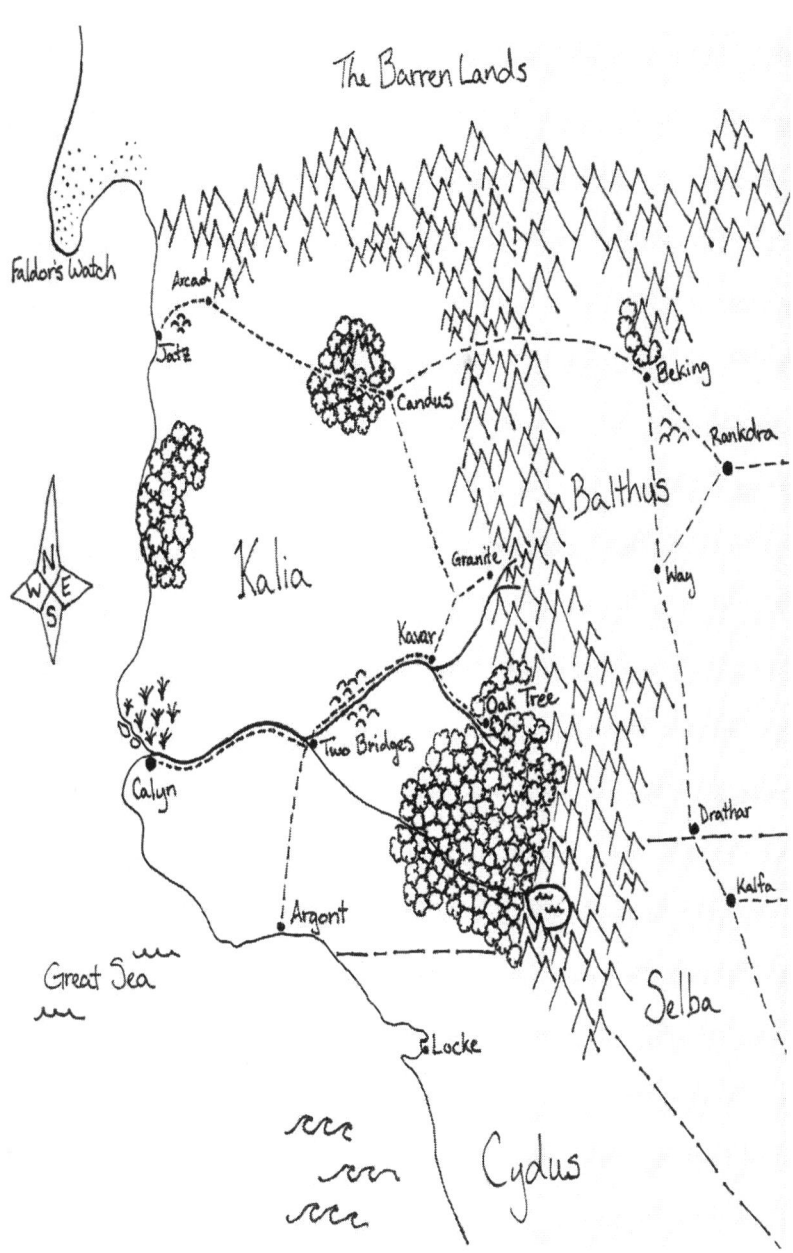

Prologue

Kadrak smiled as the once great queen of Balthus brought in a steaming cup of spiced wine. At first she hadn't rendered proper obeisance to him, but that had soon changed. She had learned that her former position didn't matter in his presence. She was a servant like all the rest in the palace. She would be rewarded for her service and not for what she used to be. He took the wine and smiled as the queen backed out of the room making low bows.

He walked over to the window and peered to the west. The high mountain pass that provided the only highway into Kalia for hundreds of miles was still buried in snow. The winter had been colder than usual and had deposited an immense amount of snow in the mountains. While spring had already arrived in the lowlands, winter still had a hold on the mountains. Kadrak had hoped to be able to move his army into Kalia early in the spring, but it appeared that he would have to wait at least another month to move through the mountains and into the neighboring kingdom.

He knew that the Kalian Army was on the march. The second segment of the army had set out from Calyn several days ago. It was unfortunate that the main body of soldiers would be in position to challenge him near Candus before the pass was clear. He supposed it didn't really matter. By the end of summer Calyn would be his, regardless of where he defeated the High King's Army. When the pass was finally clear he would meet the Kalian Army, wherever it happened to be, and destroy it.

Soon he would be seated on the throne in Calyn with the crown of the High King of Kalia atop his noble brow. His dreams had confirmed it. The vividness of them proved of their truth. It was a fascinating thing to be able to know of one's future success. His victory would be soon, and the outcome was certain once he marched against the neighboring kingdom.

The invasion of Kalia would have to wait for the pass to clear. However, there were other matters that couldn't wait. The young wielder in Calyn needed to be taken care of. Kadrak didn't know what the boy knew of the ambience, but he could tell that the boy was strong in it. It worried him that the young man was staying in Kalia's Royal Palace. Did the High King think to match the boy against the great wielder Kadrak?

He shook his head as he turned away from the window and walked across the room. While it would be more satisfying to kill the young wielder personally, he wanted the boy taken care of long before he moved his army into Kalia. He didn't like unexpected surprises when advancing his plans. Unfortunately, he would have to delegate the killing of the boy to someone else.

He exited the lavish room and walked down the hallway to the stairs. He wondered who Shadow had picked to accompany him on this assignment. He knew that Shadow wasn't happy about having a companion on his mission, but Kadrak didn't want to leave anything up to chance. Wraith had failed to kill the boy, and he did not want the failure repeated. Shadow was smart enough to accept his instructions to choose a partner without complaint.

Kadrak was soon on the other side of the palace and heading down into the dungeons. Fire flickered across his path from the torches set into the stone walls as he descended below the palace. The dungeons were quite spacious and quite empty. He had no use for prisoners. All those who opposed him were killed. Why waste precious resources to sustain enemies? It was as simple as that. As he reached his destination, he waved his hand in front of him. The dungeon door creaked open to reveal a large room. Shadow stood patiently waiting with another man. They both knelt as their master swept into the room.

"Rise, my servants," Kadrak said immediately. Shadow was an incredible assassin and had served him well in the past. The strong, dark man gazed back with anticipation to set out on an important assignment once again. Kadrak turned and focused on the tall man who rose next to Shadow. He recognized him as one of Gilrod's close associates. Gilrod was Kadrak's right hand man and had offered the use of his vast spy network when he had entered his service. If this man was a close associate of Gilrod, it meant that he was used to spying and could avoid attention. That would be good. He did not want the two of them seen until after they had finished off the young wielder. It would be best if the young man was taken completely by surprise.

"This is Rolt," Shadow mumbled as he cocked his head toward the tall man next to him. "Gilrod recommended him." Kadrak studied Rolt closely for several moments before speaking.

"So, Gilrod recommended you," he stated flatly. "Why did he pick you?"

"I have always served Gilrod faithfully, and now I live to serve you, Master Wielder." Rolt swallowed uncomfortably under his intense stare. This man would do.

"You just said exactly what I wanted to hear," replied Kadrak. "I'm currently in need of someone who indeed lives to serve me. I am also in need of someone who is willing to sacrifice for me." He paused to let what he was hinting at sink in. "Are you willing to sacrifice for me, Rolt?"

"Yes, Master," Rolt said. He remained composed, but Kadrak could see a lessening of color in the man's face. "I am willing to sacrifice my life, Master Wielder!"

"Oh, I'm not asking for that," Kadrak said with a chuckle. "I'm asking you to sacrifice your humanity." He smiled at the confused look on the man's face. "You will not be accompanying Shadow in your current form. You will be given a great blessing today, Rolt. You will become something with more power than you've ever dreamed of having. I will give you this gift because of your loyalty. Other men will fear you from this day forward."

Kadrak motioned for Shadow to leave Rolt's side and guard the entrance to the dungeon room. Shadow inclined his head, assured him that no one would disturb them, and stepped out of the room, shutting the door behind him. Kadrak turned back to the tall man whose legs didn't seem as solid as they had earlier. He took a deep breath and cleared his mind. He had attempted this before on small animals and had an idea of what was possible and what was not. However, he hadn't tried what he was about to do on a human. Perhaps he should have tested it on someone else first, but he didn't want to repeat the effort more than he needed to. The transfiguration would take a great amount of power and concentration to accomplish. It would leave him incredibly weakened.

"I see that you are slightly worried," he began. "That is okay, Rolt. I believe this may be somewhat painful, but the pain will be worth it. When I'm done, you will be incredibly strong. Others will fear you. Others will tremble at your presence." Kadrak slipped into deeper concentration as the elements in the air of the chamber began to solidify in his mind's eye and swirl around the nervous Rolt.

* * * * *

Shaman Azulk looked out over the land of the humans from his high perch upon the mount. In the distance he could see the remains of the once great city of Beking. The broken city that Kadrak had left behind was already starting to fill with humans once again. They had begun to rebuild it once the army had moved on to Rankdra. The shaman wondered if they would be so eager to move back into the city if they knew what was waiting for them in the shadows of the nearby mountains. Would they still be rebuilding or would they be fleeing south in fear?

The Wielder Kadrak had done a surprisingly good job of crushing any resistance as he had marched with his army to Beking and conquered it. Rankdra had fallen with even less resistance once it was clear that they couldn't stand against a mighty wielder and his army.

It was unfortunate that the mountain pass to the west was still impassable. Azulk was eager for Kadrak to continue into Kalia. He had no doubt that Kalia would offer greater resistance than Balthus had. It had the most disciplined army in the land of the humans and had to be somewhat aware of what it would be facing. The Kalians would have heard reports of a wielder leading the Balthan Army. Surely they had been preparing carefully through the winter to meet this wielder's army in the spring.

As soon as the pass was open, Kadrak and his army would pour through it into Kalia. A tremendous battle would commence when they met the waiting Kalian Army. The fighting would drag on for awhile. The Royal Army wouldn't crumble under Kadrak's attacks. A lone wielder could only do so much when faced with such a large, disciplined army. Kadrak would have his moments, but Azulk knew all too well of the limits of the ambience. A wielder could only use so much of it for so long before being drained of all physical strength. Even with the increase of troops from Rankdra, the Kalian Army would hold firm against the invading army. Kadrak's army would be greatly weakened by the time they defeated the Kalian Army, if they were even able to.

Soon the time would be ripe for his own race to take back what they had lost. Kadrak wouldn't be able to stop him when the galdaks marched with the Great Shaman Azulk at their lead. A pleasant rumble purred up from the shaman and into the still air. After countless generations of waiting, the galdak's vengeance was almost at hand. Soon his hopes for his race would finally be fulfilled. The Great Shaman Azulk would sit on a human-made throne and rule over all of the lands! He knew it would happen. His dreams certainly foretold it.

Part One: Searching

1

Traven had no idea where he was. He hadn't been in this room in the palace before. The ceiling was extremely high and plaited in gold. Two stories up a balcony wound its way around the entire room. The balcony's edge was lined with small white columns and a railing that would allow onlookers to peer over and down at the room below. He was sitting in a tall chair on a raised dais with the open and empty room stretching out in front of him. The glassy tiles of the floor gleamed around him as he shifted in his chair trying to figure out where he was.

Glancing down he realized that he wasn't just sitting in any chair, he was sitting in an ornately decorated throne. Traven jumped to his feet with a start. He realized what room he was in. He was in the High King's throne room and audience chamber. He wasn't sure how he had gotten there, but he did know that he did not want someone to find him sitting in the High King's throne. Looking around for an exit, he was startled to see that there were no doors leading out of the room. He knew that didn't make any sense, but as he scanned the far walls he couldn't find an exit of any kind.

"Traven, sit back down. They will all be here soon." He jerked around at the melodious voice and found the High Princess Kalista standing right behind him at the edge of the throne. Where had she come from? He was too stunned to do anything but comply as the princess reached up, grabbed his shoulder, and gently pushed him back down onto the throne.

He smiled in spite of himself. Her delicate hand felt warm against his shoulder, and she left it there even after he was firmly seated back on the throne. She stepped around in front of him with her hand still on his shoulder and smiled at him. She was breathtakingly beautiful, and he soon found himself lost in the endless pools of her blue eyes. She somehow seemed more real than anything else in the room. Traven watched, mesmerized as she lifted her other hand towards his head. In it gleamed the High King of Kalia's crown. It seemed to pulse as the princess lifted it up and set it carefully on his head. She then set her other hand down on his other shoulder and drew herself closer to him.

Traven didn't know what to do. What was going on? He should not be here alone with the princess. She was engaged, and he had no right to be in the High King's throne with the crown of Kalia on his head. He could be put to death for such an act. Kalista leaned toward him and kissed him gently on the forehead. She then whispered in his ear.

"Don't forget me."

* * * * *

Traven awoke with the sun streaming into his eyes and a smile on his face. It was the third time that he had dreamed of the princess and the crown in the last week. The princess and the crown were always there, but the details surrounding them had changed with each dream. This was the first time the princess had done more than place the crown on his head. She had asked him not to forget her, and he didn't want to. However, he knew that she would soon be married to Commander General Gavin.

It would be best to forget her. It troubled him to be having such vivid dreams about the crown of Kalia and the engaged princess, but he definitely preferred them to the nightmares of the cave and the serpent that had plagued him before.

Traven turned over in the luxurious bed one last time and stretched. He then rolled out of the bed and began to get ready for the day. He had been in the palace for just over a week. The first two and a half days he had been unconscious. After finally regaining consciousness he had been nursed back to health. It had taken another two days before he was up and walking once again. He was still not back to full health, but he was feeling much stronger. He hadn't been able to figure out what exactly had happened to weaken him so badly. He knew that it had something to do with his father's stone exploding, but other than that he couldn't explain it.

The might stone was no more now. It lay shattered across the floor of an ancient room deep in a cave in the marshes north of Calyn. He planned on returning to the ancient room someday but didn't have time for it right now. Two days prior he had watched from his palace window as a procession left to lead the second part of the Royal Kalian Army east to Candus. There they would prevent the rebel army in Balthus from advancing into Kalia. Despite being a soldier, he hadn't marched east with the army. Instead, today he would be leaving on a ship heading north.

He felt as though he should be marching with the army. He had been training hard for the impending war and would have felt more comfortable marching with the other soldiers. He was a soldier after all and should be fighting with his comrades. However, Professor Studell had different ideas.

Upon waking to find himself in the palace, Traven had been given the golden chest that was found in the ancient room among the ruins in the marsh. He had somehow been able to open the box when no one else had succeeded. Inside there had been several jewels, two might stones, and a map. The map had ancient writing on it and supposedly stated that whoever opened the chest must follow the map to a place called Faldor's Keep. Nobody seemed to know of such a place, and Traven was fairly certain that by now it must be ruins like those of the ancient city in the marsh.

However, the philosopher felt that it was incredibly important that he travel to this place. He had discussed this with the

High King while Traven was still recovering and convinced the High King to give Traven the special assignment of going to Faldor's Keep to search for anything that might help in the coming battle with a wielder.

Traven wasn't sure if Professor Studell really thought there would be something there that would help in the war or if he just wanted to go searching for more ancient writings and artifacts. Regardless of Studell's true intentions, the High King had granted the professor's request and sent a letter to Traven informing him that his assignment would be to accompany the professor to Faldor's Keep instead of marching with the Royal Army to Candus.

He supposed he should be excited to see something new and have more adventure. But after his last experience with adventure, he wasn't sure if he wanted any more of it so soon. He hoped the trip to Faldor's Keep wouldn't be too eventful. With any luck they would quickly find whatever Studell was looking for. Then he could catch up with the army in Candus before the battle began.

Traven finished getting dressed in a new set of his black clothes that the royal tailor had made for him. He then buckled on his belt and grabbed the bundle at the base of the wardrobe. It contained the golden chest, which had the two might stones and some of the jewelry still inside. The day before, he had sent a couple of pieces of jewelry to be delivered to his grandparents. He had also written a letter describing his current circumstances and mission. He wondered how they'd react to the gifts and news. No doubt they would be surprised. He smiled at the thought of what they might say when they received his package.

He turned his thoughts back to the golden chest. He had wanted to leave it in the palace. It would be hard to travel with and could attract unwanted attention. He had originally only planned on bringing the chest's contents. However, Studell had been adamant that he bring the actual chest. Traven hoped that he would be able to find out what the might stones were for while they journeyed. The extra jewels he could sell if he ever ran out of money, but he doubted that would happen. He had plenty of gold tallies. Professor Studell had already taken possession of the scroll.

After gathering all of his things, Traven left the palace room and headed down to the stables. He found Pennon already saddled and ready for the journey. He slipped his bundles into Pennon's saddlebags and pulled himself up with some effort. It amazed him how weak he still was after having rested for a whole week in the palace. He thanked the stable hand who had prepared Pennon and headed out of the stables, through the palace gate, and into the great square. He turned around for one last look at the Grand Palace of Kalia. It was still as awe inspiring as it had been the first time he had seen it.

He had never imagined when he first arrived in Calyn that he would see the inside of it and had never dreamed that he would actually be a guest in it. He sighed as he turned his back to the grand palace and nudged Pennon forward. He would never be welcomed back into the palace as a common soldier. He didn't expect to be. He knew that his place was not in the palace. Nonetheless, it had been an incredible experience to be there for the past week. Traven tried to put thoughts of the palace and the princess behind him as his horse trotted towards the docks. He knew that the ship would be leaving soon, and he didn't want to be late.

His senses were assaulted with new sights and smells as he made his way out of the city and onto the docks. Huge boats lay anchored in the harbor, towering above him. He had never seen boats so large. Despite their size, the open ocean behind dwarfed them. The scent of the docks was far from pleasant. It smelled of rotten fish and salt water. He watched as men from different lands moved around busily. After asking a few different people which ship was the Arrow, a dockhand directed him to where it was anchored.

Traven slid down from Pennon and led him towards the large ship. There were many ships that were larger, but the Arrow was still bigger than half of those in the port. He looked the large vessel up and down. It was narrow with a long pointy front that would cut right through the water. He watched as sailors on the ship hustled back and forth preparing the ship to sail. He took a deep breath and led Pennon forward.

He walked up the wooden plank carefully, trying not to think of the water swirling below on either side. Once he was on the ship he didn't feel much better despite its large size. He glanced around at the sailors scrambling across the deck tightening ropes and preparing to shove off. They all seemed perfectly at ease. Traven wondered how someone could feel at ease when there wasn't solid ground beneath his feet. A sailor hurried towards him and Pennon.

"Are you Traven?" the gruff man barked.

"Yes, I am," he replied.

"I'll be taking your horse below if you don't mind. We need to get him below and secure so we can push off." Traven thanked the sailor and handed him Pennon's reins. He glanced around the deck as Pennon was led away by the gruff sailor. On the other side of the deck he could see Philosopher Studell excitedly looking out to sea. Traven carefully walked over to join him.

"Isn't it a great day for sailing?" Professor Studell exclaimed when he stepped up beside him. The philosopher was extremely excited to be going on the journey. He had been ready almost from the moment he had first read the scroll. He had impatiently been waiting over the last few days while the preparations for the voyage were being finalized.

"I guess it's as good a day as any," Traven replied. "Does the boat always rock this much?"

"This is nothing," Studell answered. "Wait until we get out on the open sea. The waves are much higher away from the docks and out of the harbor. That's when sailing gets fun!"

Traven steadied himself against the side of the ship and tried not to think about the boat rocking more than it already was. Though he had been told they would only be on the ship for five or six days, he already knew it was going to feel much longer. At least they would make it all the way up the coast in a mere fraction of the time that it would take traveling on land. He thought he might even be able to beat the Royal Army to Candus if Studell found what they were looking for quickly enough.

"Prepare to shove off!"

He turned to see a large, scruffy man standing at the helm of the ship. He had bushy red hair, a sunburned face, and a stance that said he was in charge. The sailors instantly began to untie ropes and wind them. Traven watched with a little regret as the ramp was pulled up and the boat lurched away from the dock. It was too late to turn back now.

"What's wrong?" Studell asked with concern. "Did we forget something?" Traven realized how pitiful he must look and traded his frown for a smile.

"Oh, it's nothing," he replied as he glanced at the open sea.

Studell shrugged and turned back to stare out to sea as well. The vessel slowly made its way through the other ships and out into the harbor away from the docks. Traven took a few more deep breaths as the boat got further and further from land. He didn't understand how everyone else on ship didn't seem to mind. Finally the Arrow was past all of the other ships in the harbor and picking up speed as it headed out into the open ocean.

He turned back and watched Calyn grow smaller and smaller. When he had first seen the city with the ocean behind it, he had never dreamed that someday he would be sailing out of the city and onto the never-ending blue expanse beyond. As they got further away, he noticed an increase in the swaying of the boat. Studell had been right about the rocking, but Traven was happy to find that it didn't bother him as much as he had thought it would. Perhaps the rocking of the boat wouldn't be too bad after all.

"And we're off and racing." Traven turned and saw the large, scruffy man who had been at the helm of the ship walking towards them. "Sorry I didn't get a chance to introduce myself. I'm Captain Willie of the Arrow, the fastest ship in the sea!" Traven accepted the captain's outstretched hand.

"It's good to meet you," he replied. "I'm Traven."

"Now that we have the formalities out of the way, I'll let you know how this trip is going to work. I normally don't accept passengers on my ship, but I couldn't refuse a request sent from the High King, may he live long and prosper. So I ask that you stay out of the way of my sailors, and we'll stay out of your way. You'll find a guest cabin at the bottom of the stairs to the left. It is small but cozy." The large captain's face broke into a smile as he mentioned the room. "We'll follow the coast north and should be in Jatz in four or five days depending on the wind. We'll dock there, unload our goods and restock our supplies. We'll then sail you to wherever you want on the coast of Faldor's Watch." The captain paused for a second and then went on. "What are you doing there anyway? There's nothing up there but sand and rocks."

"We are following a map to Faldor's Keep," Professor Studell declared as he slipped the ancient map out of one of his large pockets and waved it in front of the captain's face.

"Oh, you're treasure hunters," Captain Willie chuckled. "With all due respect, I think you'd have better luck finding gold around the mines of Arcad than the barren deserts of Faldor's Watch."

"We are not searching for gold, my good captain," Studell fired back. "And we are not treasure hunters. We're on a mission in search of knowledge and understanding."

"Whatever you say," Captain Willie said with a shrug. "We'll have you there within a week, and then you can do whatever you want. We'll see if you have anything when we return to pick you up sixteen days after we drop you off." Traven could tell that the captain still thought they were foolish treasure hunters.

"Thank you," Studell said to the captain. "Now if you will excuse us, we will retire to our quarters." Studell turned from the captain and beckoned to Traven. "We have some important things to discuss." Traven followed the professor to the stairs and down below deck. Behind him he could hear the scruffy captain chuckling to himself.

At the base of the stairs there was a long narrow hall. Studell opened the first door on the left. Traven had to duck through the doorway to walk into the room. Once he straightened back up inside, he decided it really wasn't a room at all. It appeared to be more of a closet. Captain Willie's comment and smile about the room being cozy now made sense. There were two small bunks attached to the right wall for sleeping in and about three feet of space between the beds and the left wall. The room made him feel claustrophobic. His saddlebags were already in the back corner along with several bundles that he assumed must be the philosopher's.

"I can't see anything in here," Studell proclaimed. Traven noticed a small lamp attached to the left wall and lit it. "Much better, much better!" Studell blinked and looked around the small room. "It is quite small, isn't it?" Traven nodded in agreement. "Oh well, we won't be spending that much time down here anyway. I enjoy being on the deck. But for right now I think it best that we have some privacy while we discuss our plans."

Traven stepped to the side as Studell reached past him to shut the door. Studell then sat down on the bottom bunk and motioned for him to sit next to him. Traven sat down but had to remain leaning forward so he wouldn't hit his head on the upper bunk. Studell pulled the scroll back out from his pocket and began to open it. Traven was excited to finally see what it looked like. Studell had been studying it ever since he opened the golden chest, and as far as he knew, the philosopher hadn't let anyone else look at it.

Traven's eager gaze fell upon the ancient scroll. The map was an outline of Faldor's Watch and the western coast of Kalia. The only thing marked on the map was a single dot near the southern tip of Faldor's Watch. Below the map were a bunch of ancient symbols that Studell had called the old tongue.

"That's where we're going?" Traven asked as he pointed to the dot.

"Exactly," the philosopher said with excitement. Traven's hopes of finding the ruins disappeared as he looked at the small dot. If there were ruins right on the coast, he was sure that plenty of ships would have seen them before.

"Don't you think others would have already found these ruins if they're right on the coast as this map suggests?"

"What are you talking about?" Studell exclaimed as he stared back at him. "Faldor's Keep is not located on the coast. It's at least a few days' journey inland." Traven took another look at the map and then glanced back at the philosopher. He pointed at the dot once again with a questioning look at Studell.

"It looks like it's right on the coast." Studell looked from Traven to the map and back to him.

"That's not where the ruins are," he said with exasperation. "That's just the starting point. The map explains where to go from there. Can't you read the directions?" Studell paused as if waiting for him to answer and then started laughing. "Oh, sorry. What am I thinking? Of course you can't read the directions. They're in the old tongue."

Traven was reminded again of Studell's interesting personality. The man often forgot that others didn't know as much as he did when it came to history and other academics. He also seemed to expect others to know exactly what he was thinking without having to explain anything.

"Perhaps you could read the directions to me," Traven said, smiling. "I would like to know where we'll be heading once we land."

"Of course, of course," Studell replied. "Sometimes I just think too far ahead. That's why I brought you down here to the cabin. I wanted to discuss the map with you where others wouldn't be able to overhear. You can never be too careful you know."

Traven leaned back over the map as he waited for the philosopher to begin reading. He had been anxious to find out specifically where they would be traveling and what they were supposed to find at the ruins of Faldor's Keep.

"The map has the starting point fixed here as you can see," Studell began while pointing at the southern tip of Faldor's Watch. "These first symbols state that the one who opened the chest must follow this map to Faldor's Keep where he will find 'what he has been searching for'. I'm not sure what that necessarily means, but I suppose we'll find out when we get there. Below that are the directions for getting to Faldor's Keep from the starting point that is marked on the map.

"First we must find the exact spot to start from. The directions state that it will be a small cove near the most southerly tip of the peninsula. There are two large rocks that jut out of the water several spans out in the ocean in front of the cove. This is how the cove is to be identified. Once we leave from Jatz, we will have the captain sail to this point and look for the two rocks. When we find them, he can drop us off at the cove and our search for the keep will begin!"

Traven wrinkled his brow in thought. The map didn't indicate what was at the keep. It left him wondering what it was that he was supposed to be searching for. The only thing mentioned on the scroll was that at the keep he would find 'what he was searching for'. What was he searching for? Perhaps he was looking for a weapon that could be used against the wielder leading the Balthan

Army. At least that's what Studell had convinced the High King of. The vagueness of the statement of what would be found at the keep concerned him. It basically meant that anything could be waiting at the ruins of the keep; if in fact anything was there at all. He turned his attention back to the philosopher as the scholar continued reading the directions.

"From the small cove we will need to journey along the coast for about a day until we reach a break in the cliffs that we can follow up into the desert beyond. We will follow the break until we reach the 'shimmering hills' of the 'Dune Sea'. From there we continue due north for a set amount of time until we come to the 'Keeper's Staff'. It will be a tall rock formation that reaches up into the sky. Just north of the 'Keeper's Staff' will be a small spring were we can replenish our water supply. At the spring we turn east towards the 'Twin Guards', two similar mountains right next to each other. From there we will head due north again to the 'Blood Mountains'. In the midst of the 'Blood Mountains' lies Faldor's Keep!" The philosopher turned an excited look towards Traven. "Fascinating, isn't it?"

He didn't know if that was the word he would use to describe it. He knew from his time at the merchant academy that the only thing on Faldor's Watch was one huge desert. He wasn't certain that he wanted to venture into it with only vague directions to follow. However, he supposed it would have to do since the directions on the scroll were all they had.

He could only hope that with some luck they would find the ancient ruins. Who knew, maybe they actually would find a treasure hidden there.

2

Traven sat up and hit his head with a loud crack. He groaned and let himself fall back onto the small bunk. He had jerked awake as the boat lurched suddenly and sat up without thinking about where he was. He rubbed is head and hopped down off the upper bunk. The rocking of the boat had actually helped him to fall asleep the previous night, and with sleep his dreams had come once again. He didn't mind his dreams of the Princess Kalista and the crown of Kalia, but he was left wondering once again why they occurred so often and what they might mean.

The last time he had a recurring dream it had led him to the cave in the marsh and ultimately to the golden chest. He still couldn't figure out how he had dreamed of an actual place he had never seen before, but somehow he had. Was it possible that his new recurring dream would lead him to something else important? If so, he had no idea what it could be. He couldn't understand why the crown of Kalia would have any importance in his life.

He quickly dressed himself and grabbed his sword as the boat lurched once again. He hoped he would be able to get some exercise and sword practice in before it got too busy on deck. Studell was still snoring quietly as he slipped out of the room and went up the stairs. The sun had not yet cleared the horizon, and there were only a few sailors up and about. He breathed in the fresh ocean air deeply with a smile. The small sleeping quarters had been stuffy and stale.

He almost lost his balance as the boat lurched once again. He noticed several sailors standing together looking to the northwest. He followed their gaze and immediately felt uneasy. Angry looking black clouds boiled in the far distance. Large waves were rolling towards the ship from the approaching storm. He wondered if they would have to find a place to dock the ship before the storm hit. At least the storm appeared to still be fairly far away.

He loosened himself up and started to exercise on an empty section of the deck. Soon he had his sword out and was methodically going through his forms. It felt great to be doing them again. Over the last several days, as his body had slowly regained strength, he had been working his way back up to the intensity of his practices before the kidnapping and rescue. He was happy to see that his body finally appeared to be close to full strength. He was very grateful for the strength he had regained, especially with the search and journey that lay ahead of him. He let his mind rest as he continued through his sword forms. Soon the sun was peeking over the ocean and gleaming off of his swirling sword.

"What have we here?" boomed the voice of Captain Willie. Traven turned towards the captain and sheathed his sword.

"Just practicing my forms," he muttered to the scruffy captain.

"I can see that," Captain Willie exclaimed. "You look like you're quite good with that sword."

"Thanks," he replied.

"Now I don't feel as bad putting you and the philosopher on shore alone at Faldor's Watch. I've heard tales of the beasts that wander the desert there. At least now I know the philosopher will have some protection."

Traven hoped there weren't dangerous beasts roaming the desert. He would prefer not to have to use his sword. The memory of his most recent sword fight with the thieves was still fresh in his mind. The captain turned to look at the approaching storm and shook his head.

"It looks to be a nasty one," he stated.

"Are we going to dock on shore before it hits?" Traven asked.

"Nope," the captain responded. "There's really nowhere to dock until we get to Jatz. Besides, we're safer out here in the open water than near the rocky shoreline."

Traven looked from the dark storm clouds to the approaching waves. He didn't feel safe out on the open water with the storm approaching but tried to quench his fears by telling himself that the captain knew more about a ship on the ocean than he did. He was sure of one thing; the lurching of the ship that had been happening all morning was not going to get any calmer as the storm got closer. He was already beginning to feel queasy and wasn't looking forward to more movement.

"Don't worry about it," Captain Willie said slapping him on the back. "We've been through plenty worse with the Arrow. The only thing this storm is going to do is give us a ride and put us about half a day behind schedule." The captain started to walk away but stopped and turned back to face him. "You might think I'm crazy for asking, but can I take a quick look at your sword? I swear the stone in its hilt is twisting the light."

"Oh, you're not crazy," Traven said as he unsheathed his sword and carefully handed it to the captain. "The stone in the hilt somehow sucks in light."

Captain Willie took the sword and began to stare at the dark stone in its hilt. Traven followed as he walked over to the side of the ship to get a better look at it in the morning sun. The captain leaned over the railing of the ship and held the sword up. Traven could clearly see the glint off the blade of the sword appear to be streaming into the dark stone.

"If that ain't the strangest thing I ever saw," Captain Willie muttered as he turned the sword slowly in his hands. "I've never seen a jewel that did such a thing."

"It's not just some jewel. It's a stone." Traven turned and saw Philosopher Studell coming over to join them. "A might stone to be exact!"

He smiled as the philosopher burst into an explanation of what in fact the captain was holding in his hands. Traven touched his chest gingerly. His cuts and burns still hadn't completely healed. It was strange not having his father's stone around his neck anymore. Ever since waking up from the horrific event, he had felt the loss of the stone. It left him feeling strangely exposed. However, it also left him feeling freer. He couldn't explain why, but somehow he felt incredibly different without his father's might stone around his neck.

"No!!!"

Traven was jerked from his thoughts as Studell let out a scream. At first he didn't know what had upset the philosopher so much. Both Studell and the captain were staring over the side of the ship.

"What have you done, you big oaf?" Studell screamed as he shook his finger at the large captain.

"What have I done?" Captain Willie yelled back. "You're the one who tried to grab it out of my hands!"

Traven stared aghast at the deep blue water as the realization hit him that neither the philosopher nor the captain was holding his sword. They had dropped his sword into the depths of the ocean! He watched as the ship sped away from where the sword had been dropped. In despair he stared at the patch of water as he felt the sword stop falling and come to rest on the ocean floor. What was he going to do without his sword? It was his most valuable and useful possession. Not only had it been wrought by the ambience, but it was his main form of protection. It had felt so natural in his hands. No other weapon had ever felt the same. He needed the sword!

He gave a start as he felt the sword growing closer. He wasn't sure how he knew it, but somehow he could tell that it was. As the feeling increased, Traven stretched out his hand, willing the sword to come to him. Suddenly the sword burst out of the ocean in a spray of water and flashed through the air into his open hand. His mouth dropped open as he stared at the dripping sword. Both the philosopher and the captain looked on with disbelief as the ocean water continued dripping off the raised sword and onto his sleeve.

What had just happened was impossible. He didn't want to believe what he had seen. Was he going crazy? He knew of no way to explain what had occurred, but he had seen it with his own eyes. He could feel the hilt molding once again in his hand and could see his awestruck expression reflected back at him in the shining blade. His sword had returned to him.

"What in the . . ." the captain sputtered. "How could . . . I can't believe it!" he exclaimed as he finally finished a full sentence.

Traven felt the same way as the captain sounded. He began to feel slightly unsteady on his feet, and it was more than just the increasing consistency of the large waves.

"I think I'll take Traven back to our quarters to get some more rest," Studell announced as he grabbed his arm and began leading him back to the stairs. Traven let himself be led down the steps and into their small cabin as Captain Willie continued to stare from behind them. Studell helped him sit down on the bottom bunk with his hand still tightly gripping the sword. His lightheadedness started to dissipate as he closed his eyes and rested. Even with his eyes shut he could tell that the philosopher was pacing quickly back and forth in the cramped room. He rubbed his head with his free hand. He wondered if the philosopher might have an explanation for what had just occurred.

"Philosopher Studell," he began, "what just happened?"

"What just happened?" the philosopher asked quizzically. "You tell me, young man. You did it!"

Traven glanced down at the stone on the hilt of his sword. It must have had something to do with the might stone. There was no other explanation. The stones had magical properties. What he couldn't figure out is why nothing like this had ever happened before with the sword.

"Light the lamp," Studell demanded. Grumbling, Traven got off the bed to light it. He had been enjoying the dimness of the room. It didn't bother his head as much.

"Not like that! Sit back down. I want you to light it using the ambience." Traven sat back down leaving the lamp unlit.

"I don't think the stone works that way," he responded.

"Don't use the stone. I want you to light the lamp by yourself."

"I can't do that," Traven said in frustration. "I don't have any magic. This is reality, not some legend from one of your old scrolls."

"Oh, then maybe you can answer a few questions for me," the philosopher began. "How did you save the princess from that monstrous serpent? How did you open the golden chest when no one else could? How in the world did you get your sword back after it had fallen into the depths of the ocean?"

He opened his mouth to respond but realized that he didn't have answers for any of the questions. He supposed they all had to do with the might stones somehow, but he couldn't prove it.

"See, you don't know, do you? Now light that lamp!"

Traven let out a frustrated sigh. Studell wasn't going to give up. He decided that he might as well try and prove the philosopher wrong. It had nothing to do with him. It was the might stones. He glanced at the hilt of his sword and then stared at the lamp. When nothing happened, Studell began to mutter under his breath impatiently.

"Well, what did you expect?" Traven asked.

"I expected you to light that lamp!" exclaimed the philosopher.

Traven turned back to the lamp, frustrated. He focused on it and wondered how it would feel to use magic. Slowly the lamp began to fill his vision, and Studell's mumbling and the rocking of the ship faded away. The air around the wick of the lamp seemed to be thickening. He could almost see a flame. He shook his head and stared back at the lamp. He couldn't really see it, but he felt that it was there. The thickened air slowly began to swirl inside of the lamp, gaining speed as it moved around the wick. There was a flame there! He could feel it even though he still couldn't see it. He could feel it with his mind. The flame felt like it was just beyond sight. He concentrated on the flame and pulled on it. The flame burst into sight, lighting the lamp, and Traven blacked out.

He came to as Philosopher Studell excitedly shook him awake. He sat up groggily with a splitting headache. He watched silently as the philosopher kept looking between him and the lighted lamp with a silly expression on his face. What had just occurred slowly came back to him as the fuzziness left his head. The last thing he remembered was the flame suddenly appearing. Had he really created it?

"How long was I out?" he mumbled.

"Only a few moments. I saw the lamp burst to life! When I turned to congratulate you, you were slumped down on the bed, so I shook you awake. This is amazing!"

Traven looked back at the lamp. Had it really happened? He wanted to deny it, but Studell had witnessed it as well. He had somehow lit the lamp without physically touching it. He had somehow used the ambience. That in itself troubled and confused him. What worried him even more was what had happened to him as a result. He had blacked out and now had a splitting headache. It appeared that it was dangerous to tamper with magic. He wondered if it would be bad enough to do permanent damage or even kill him if he meddled in things that he didn't understand. He slumped back onto the bed, with his head in his hands and his eyes closed.

"Do it again," Studell said excitedly as he blew out the lamp.

"No," Traven mumbled from the bed with his eyes still closed and his head still reeling.

"What do you mean no?" Studell demanded. "You can't just do something as amazing as that and then stop. Light the lamp again!"

"It's too dangerous," Traven replied. "You saw what just happened. I blacked out after lighting the candle. And if I really did somehow use the ambience in the cave as you suggested, it left me almost dead. I shouldn't be tampering with something I don't even understand."

"Well, you'll never learn to control your power if you don't practice it. Besides," countered the philosopher, "I have never read anything about the ambience being dangerous to a wielder."

"Then how do you explain what just happened to me?" he asked. Studell threw up his hands in exasperation.

"Sometimes you must sacrifice for knowledge," he exclaimed.

Traven took a deep breath and sat back up. He'd try one more time and see what happened. If he blacked out again, he would stop this nonsense until he could learn more about the ambience and wielding it.

The lamp filled his vision. He concentrated on lighting it. Once again the air seemed to thicken and circle around the point where the flame should be. He could feel where the flame was just out of sight. He reached for it with his mind and pulled it into reality.

The lamp once again burst to light with a flame seemingly appearing out of thin air. Traven put his hand down on the bed next to him and steadied himself as he dizzily closed his eyes. The feat had increased the intensity of his headache, but at least he hadn't passed out this time. The use of the ambience definitely had a negative effect on his health, but maybe it would not always be as bad as he had feared.

"You are definitely a wielder!" exclaimed Studell excitedly. He was looking back and forth between the lamp and Traven with a silly grin on his face. "What else can you do? How long have you had this power? Oh my, it's true! There really were wielders! Of course I already knew that but when you see something like . . ."

Traven shut out the philosopher's ramblings and laid back down on the bed. He rubbed his head and neck, trying to soothe the pounding. He felt incredibly drained as if he had done a whole day's work of hauling logs.

"Oh, sorry," Studell apologized. "I'll let you have some rest. Later we'll get some more answers!"

"Please don't say anything about this to anyone," Traven mumbled as the philosopher opened the door to leave. Studell paused before closing the door.

"You're right, young man. It would be unwise to let it out that you are a wielder until we know more about your power. I'll try and smooth over the sword incident with the captain."

Studell then closed the door, leaving him alone. Traven sat back up and blew out the lamp before slowly pulling himself up onto his bunk. He wanted to think about all that had just happened, but his head was still pounding and he was too tired. He soon drifted off to sleep in the small, cramped cabin as the ship continued rocking back and forth.

3

Traven woke up with his head feeling better but his stomach feeling worse. The ship was lurching back and forth, not gently rolling on the water anymore. He got off his bunk and stretched, placing his hand against the wall to steady himself. As he stood in the dark, he thought of everything that had happened to him that morning. Apparently he really was some kind of wielder. He, of all people, somehow had the ability to manipulate the power known as the ambience. The thought brought with it a mixture of both excitement and fear.

He wondered what all he could actually do with his powers. If he could light a lamp, he could definitely do other things. But how would he learn how to do them? He knew that there was danger in using the ambience without knowing more about it. How could he be safe and learn to wield the ambience without some kind of guidance? He supposed that Studell probably knew as much about it as anyone alive that wasn't a wielder himself. Perhaps if he was very careful he could experiment a little and learn how to safely use his newfound power.

Traven smoothed out his clothes and headed up on deck. He hoped the fresh air would help to calm his stomach. He was met by a stiff wind that blasted him in the face as he stepped outside. Above, the sky roiled with ominous gray clouds. The sailors were running around, finishing taking down the sails and cleaning up the deck before the storm broke. Traven located Studell at the front of the ship and made his way over to him. As he passed by the sailors, he noticed them giving him sidelong glances. Some looked with interest while others glanced with fear. He finished walking to the philosopher's side, feeling very uncomfortable.

"I thought you were going to sleep all day!" Studell exclaimed when he suddenly noticed Traven standing next to him.

"I didn't sleep that long, did I?" he asked as he glanced up at the sky. It was impossible to tell what time of the day it was with the dark clouds overhead.

"It's the middle of the afternoon," Studell replied. Traven was surprised that he had slept so long. At least his headache was gone.

"So how did things go with the captain? The sailors are giving me strange looks."

"I tried to smooth everything over by telling the captain that the sword came back because it has a magic stone and that it had nothing to do with you. I don't think he believed me." Studell glanced backwards over the ship and over the various sailors. "The captain wasn't the only one that saw it. Some of the sailors think you practice black magic and that it is bad luck to have you onboard. They want to throw you overboard."

"They what!" Traven exclaimed looking at the choppy water.

"Oh don't worry. The captain won't let them," replied the philosopher. "However, I do think they will all be happier once they deliver us to our destination and you are off the ship. I believe it would be best if you didn't do anything else like that in sight of the crew."

A wry smile crossed Traven's face. He definitely wouldn't be wielding the ambience in sight of the others. He wasn't even sure if he would be wielding it at all. He glanced up as he felt a drop of water splatter on his hand and suggested they go below deck before they got soaked. Studell agreed, and they hurried down below as it started to rain.

The next couple of days were spent below deck as the storm continued to pound the ship. They remained in their cramped cabin during most of the tempest, but they also spent time with the captain and first mate. Studell quizzed them on the exact type of terrain they would be facing when they landed on Faldor's Watch. He got as much information from them about what type of supplies he and Traven would need as he could. After wringing every last drop of information out of them, he was satisfied that they would be able to get everything they needed when they stopped in the port of Jatz.

Without room to practice his sword forms below deck, Traven spent much of his time practicing lighting the lamp with the ambience. He also figured out how to extinguish the flame with a mere thought. At first he had been hesitant to wield the ambience when Studell insisted that he keep practicing. Luckily, each time he did it, it seemed easier to do and had less of a negative physical effect on him. By the end of the second day below deck, he could light and extinguish the lamp several times in a row without getting a headache or feeling very tired.

Thankfully the storm dissipated on the third day and the sun returned to the sky. Traven excitedly stretched and went through his sword forms on deck. He tried not to notice the growing crowd of sailors watching him and focused on his forms. The fresh air and sunlight were more than welcome after so much time below deck in the cramped ship. The captain had said they would dock in port around midday, and Traven was excited to have solid ground beneath his feet once again. After practicing his forms, he got ready for the day and had some breakfast. He then returned to the deck and eagerly watched as they slowly sailed closer to the strip of land in the distance.

When they finally slipped into the bay, Studell came over to him, weighed down by a small but heavy brown bag that clanked as he walked. He had an excited smile on his face and stared at the port city of Jatz.

"The captain says the ship will leave early tomorrow morning to take us the rest of the way. This afternoon the sailors will be unloading the ship's cargo and restocking for the return journey to Calyn. That should give us plenty of time to purchase everything we need." Studell patted the bulging sack at his waist and smiled. "Tomorrow we will begin to follow the map. How exciting!"

Traven smiled and watched as the ship slowly made its way to the large dock. He was more anxious to have solid ground under his feet than he was for anything else. Once the ship was solidly attached to the dock by several ropes, the gangplank was lowered. Traven hurried down it as Studell slowly followed. He took a deep breath of relief once they were off the dock and he was on solid earth. He had gotten somewhat used to the ocean but still felt much more comfortable on firm ground.

"Shall we?" Studell invited as he made his way past him and into the city.

Traven followed happily. The city of Jatz was very different from Calyn. The buildings were not built for beauty but for functionality. The people that walked the streets were also a rougher looking sort of people. Almost everyone carried a sword, even some of the women. Their clothes were not as fine as those in Calyn, and Traven felt out of place in his fancy, dark clothes. Several people gave him an appraising look as he walked past, making him feel slightly uncomfortable.

After walking a short distance, they found a cluster of shops that appeared to have what they needed. The captain had said that the best gear for traveling in the harsh desert was robes and head wraps. It sounded strange to be wearing so much in such a hot place, but the captain was insistent that it was the best way to be protected from the sun and sand. Traven and Studell turned into a clothing shop and were happy to find that among the sturdy clothing available, there were robes and head wraps. They each selected a robe and a head wrap and took them up to the shopkeeper.

"So you're heading north are ya?" said the rotund shopkeeper as they approached him.

"As a matter of fact we are," replied the philosopher. "How much for the clothes?" The shopkeeper stated a price, and Studell dug into his bag of coins and paid the fee without haggling at all. Traven thought the price was way too high and tried to stop him, but the philosopher assured him loudly that he had plenty of money to cover whatever they needed.

"Are you sure you don't need anything else?" the shopkeeper asked with a greedy gleam in his eyes. "It might be best to have an extra robe or two."

"No thank you," Traven replied as he hurriedly led Studell from the store. He could feel the shopkeeper's eyes boring into his back as they exited the shop. The shopkeeper's eyes had said that he wanted more than to just sell them some extra clothes.

"You need to be more careful with your money," Traven told Studell once they were out of the shop. "This city seems a little lawless, and I think it's unwise to mention to strangers how much money you're carrying."

"No one would dare rob us in the light of day," Studell said dismissively.

Traven hoped the philosopher was right, but he noticed that the shopkeeper was watching them from the window of his shop as they made their way down the street and into another store. There they purchased several large water skins. The captain had been adamant that there wasn't any water to be found on Faldor's Watch. Studell said that the map showed where they could get water, but Traven didn't want to stake his life on an ancient map. He wanted to carry as much water with them as they could. After getting the water skins and a few other supplies, they headed deeper into the city to find some food for the journey.

They found a shop where they bought some bread, cheese, and dried meat. At the suggestion of the shopkeeper they also bought a large quantity of nuts and dried fruit. They then searched for a shop where they were able to purchase extra feed for their horses.

When they finally had all of the provisions that they would need for the journey, they started to return to the docks. They had quite a load to carry with them, and after a couple of blocks the philosopher was winded and breathing heavily. Traven relieved him of most of the supplies that he was carrying, and they continued on. The sun would be setting soon, and he didn't want to be left wandering the streets of an unfamiliar town in the dark.

Studell suggested that they take a shortcut down a small side street to save time, and Traven followed him. Halfway down the street Traven heard footsteps behind them. Glancing backward he could see that a man was indeed hurrying to catch up to them. He urged Studell forward at a quicker pace. It looked like they could reach one of the larger avenues of the city before the man caught up. He wasn't too worried about one person following them but would rather avoid any confrontation. Studell began complaining that he couldn't keep such a quick pace but continued onward at Traven's urging.

Traven glanced over his shoulder again. The man was much closer now but was not coming quickly enough to catch them before they made it to the larger avenue near the docks. Traven let out a sigh of relief as they made their way out of the small side street and into the avenue. Studell stumbled across the road and slumped down against a building on the opposite side, out of breath. Traven set their purchases down beside the philosopher and smiled. He could see the ship from here, and there were plenty of people traversing this street. They could rest here for a few moments before returning to the ship.

He glanced back to the side street and watched as their pursuer emerged into the avenue. He was surprised to see that instead of stopping or merging with the people on the street, the man kept walking straight towards them with a menacing grin. Halfway across the avenue the man unsheathed his sword and pointed it at Traven and the philosopher. Traven could hardly believe what was happening. He was amazed that the man would be so brash as to attack them in full sight of so many people. Some in the crowd stopped to watch the scene unfold, but the majority of the people just continued about their business, giving Traven and the man a wide birth.

"Hand over all your money, old man," the thief growled at the philosopher. "And you hand over your sword boy, and I'll let you both live." Traven stepped between Studell and the would-be-thief, shaking off his initial surprise. He cleared his mind. Out went the surprise, out went the fear, out went the excitement. He was focused and ready for whatever might happen.

"You might want to reconsider this," Traven stated quietly as he waited for the other man's move. The man stared at him for several moments before suddenly lunging at him.

Traven's sword leapt out of its sheath and easily parried the attack. He continued to block the next several slashes with a minimal amount of movement. The attacker paused and took a couple steps back. He then lunged again with an increased amount of vigor. When Traven continued to block all of his attacks easily, the man disengaged and backed into the middle of the avenue, sheathing his sword.

"I now see why the old man was so loose with his tongue." Their attacker then bowed respectfully towards Traven and disappeared back down the side street.

Traven looked around the crowd, confused. Many of the onlookers nodded to him approvingly before turning and continuing on their ways.

"Amazing," Studell exclaimed, breaking the relative silence. Traven just shook his head as he sheathed his sword and offered the philosopher his hand to help him to his feet.

"What a strange city," he muttered as he reached down to pick up their purchases. "See what I meant about guarding your tongue?"

"I think I agree with our attacker," the philosopher said excitedly. "With you around why does it matter what I say? With your skills with the sword and your other unmentionable skills," Studell said with a wink, "I think we are quite protected from anything." Traven let out an exasperated sigh. "Okay, I guess it is better to be careful," Studell conceded. "But, oh my, that was exciting!"

Traven tried to not let the philosopher's praise and excitement have any effect on him as they continued on their way to the ship, but he couldn't help cracking a smile. It felt good to be able to thwart attacks with such ease. It had seemed, to him, that he knew where each slash of the attacker's sword would land before it actually happened. Maybe he was just getting to the point where his subconscious could tell by an opponent's slight movements what would happen next. Blaize had always said the more he practiced and concentrated, the easier it would get to predict an opponent's next move.

Then again, perhaps there was more to it than that. Ever since he had started practicing wielding the ambience, he had begun to sense things more acutely than he had before. He wondered if his increased skill with the sword was also a result of his newly discovered power.

His smile got bigger once they were safely back on the ship. His practicing with the ambience was going well. Using it to light a candle was no longer a challenge. He wondered what he would be able to do once he had as much practice with the ambience as he had with the sword. What would be possible?

4

Traven shielded his eyes with his hand as he glanced north in the early morning light. He could see the coast far in the distance. That would be the beginning of their real journey. The lookout still hadn't spotted land, but Traven guessed it would take them a couple of hours to arrive at the coast. He smiled at the thought of being on solid ground again and headed below deck to his room. He finished packing his belongings as Studell began to wake up.

While Studell blinked away the sleep from his eyes, Traven sent the lantern bursting to light with barely a thought. He was happy to note that he didn't feel any side effects at all from the now simple task. Studell grinned like a fool as he always did when Traven lit the lantern with magic. Soon he would be alone with the philosopher and would have the opportunity to practice more. He looked forward with both excitement and trepidation at the chance to experiment with the ambience and see what all he was capable of doing.

He informed Studell that land was in sight and set down his packed bags. Studell jumped up excitedly and began to get ready for the day. Traven headed up on deck to check the ship's progress. He could see their destination more clearly now and stared at the coast, searching for the two jutting rocks that would mark the starting point of the map.

"Land ho!" the lookout finally yelled.

Traven was soon joined by several other sailors and the captain in staring north towards the distant shore. As they sailed closer, he saw the two rocks. He had been worried that they might be hard to find, but was pleasantly surprised to discover that they were hard to miss. Both rocks jutted high out of the ocean. Beyond them he could clearly see the small cove that would be the beginning of their journey on land. Studell was soon on deck and excitedly pointing out the two rocks to Traven. He smiled and took a deep breath. As the ship grew closer to the rocks the captain turned to Studell.

"We'll have to ferry you to the beach from here," he announced. "The water is too shallow for us to safely steer the ship closer. You're sure this is where you want to be dropped off?"

"Positive," replied Studell.

"I still think this is foolish," muttered the captain. "We can take you back with us to Calyn if you want."

"We've been through this before, Captain," Studell replied with a smile. "You can't dissuade us. We must do this."

"Okay, but no one can say I didn't try to stop you. Lower the boat!"

Traven watched as the small rowboat was lowered into the water. He was glad there was only a short distance to the shore. He didn't want to be in something so small surrounded by so much water for very long. Thinking about the small size of the row boat made him wonder where the horses would fit.

"What about the horses?" he asked.

"We'll tie them to the row boat, and they'll swim to shore," replied the captain. "It's not very far."

Traven now understood why they had told him not to saddle Pennon or load up the pack horse. Once the rowboat was in the water with two sailors to row them to shore, he tossed down all of the gear and supplies. After thanking the captain for their safe passage, he climbed down into the rowboat and helped Studell in. As soon as they were settled, the three horses were put into the water and the sailors began rowing to shore. Traven was happy to see that the horses didn't appear to be struggling as they headed for the beach.

He looked past them and began to study the shore. Immediately behind the narrow strip of light, sandy beach, enormous cliffs rose straight up for several hundred feet. As far as Traven could see in both directions the cliffs continued along the coast. As they rowed closer, the cliffs swallowed more and more of the sky.

The horses were soon rising out of the water and were no longer swimming but walking. The horses shortly began pulling the rowboat forward. The sailors smiled as they rested their paddles. After a few moments the boat slid to a halt on the soft sand. The sailors immediately jumped out and pulled the boat all the way up onto the dry sand of the beach. Traven got out and gave Studell a hand as the old philosopher climbed onto the beach. The sailors helped as he and Studell saddled their horses and began loading their extra supplies on the packhorse.

As soon as everything was unloaded, the sailors wished them luck and headed back to the ship in the small rowboat. Traven stood on the shore, watching them row away. With the waves lapping against the beach and the imposing cliffs rising behind him, he wondered if the philosopher and he were making a mistake. As uncomfortable as he had felt on the ship, he felt even more uncomfortable watching the rowboat leave them on a deserted beach far from any civilization. The captain had promised to sail by this point in sixteen days. If Traven and Studell had any hope of returning, they needed to find what they had come for and be back on the beach before the sixteen days were up.

He hoped that the philosopher had indeed calculated the distances and times correctly on the map. If they weren't back on the beach at the right time to catch the ship, there was no telling when they would ever make it back to civilization. In fact, if they missed the ship they might not make it back to civilization at all. He tried to shake the worrisome thought from his head and focus on what needed to be done.

He turned from the ocean and stared up at the enormous cliffs. They continued in an unbroken line as far as the eye could see in both directions. The steep cliffs looked impossible to scale. They would effectively keep anyone from leaving the beach and heading into the interior of the land. Traven wondered how long they would have to walk along the beach before finding the supposed break in the cliffs that would allow them through.

"And so it begins!" Studell announced excitedly.

Traven turned to see the philosopher holding the map high over his head as if it was a grand prize. Traven smiled in spite of himself as the philosopher lowered the scroll and carefully began to unroll the map. He walked over to the philosopher's side to study it once again. The surrounding landscape put the directions on the map in a whole new perspective.

"We follow the coast to the west until we reach the break in the cliffs," Studell said. "If I calculated the distance correctly, we'll get there sometime tomorrow morning. From there it appears to be about a five day's journey to the ruins of the keep. Let's get moving!"

After finishing loading up all of their supplies, Traven helped Studell onto his horse and then mounted Pennon. He wasn't looking forward to camping on the beach, trapped between the cliffs and the water. As they began down the coast, he listened to the rhythmic lapping of the waves and the calls of the birds that soared overhead in and out of tiny nooks in the cliffs. It was an interesting feeling to have the vast ocean stretching out to the horizon on the left and the towering cliffs rising unbroken to the right. He definitely felt trapped between the two.

They made good progress throughout the day as they followed the coast. Studell appeared to be deep in thought, so Traven let himself fall into somewhat of a trance as the horses plodded along and the water lapped against the shore. The day passed slowly as they continued down the thin strip of beach. It became wider, then smaller, then wider again. The cliffs marched on with their majestic height, leaving no breaks to reveal the dry desert beyond them. The only sounds to be heard were the waves and the birds. It was peaceful but monotonous.

As the sun set and the sky slowly began to darken, Traven instinctively began looking for a spot to set up camp. He decided that it really didn't matter where they stopped for the night and chose the next stretch where the beach widened. He would feel best sleeping as far from the water as possible. As he pulled up, Studell's mount automatically stopped alongside Pennon.

"I think it's time to make camp," Traven said.

"At last," Studell mumbled with a grateful sigh. The elderly philosopher carefully slid off his horse, grateful to be done riding for the day.

Traven hopped off of Pennon with a smile and walked a little further up the beach to gather some driftwood for a fire. Glancing back at the philosopher gingerly walking, he was reminded of his first full day of traveling in a saddle. After gathering sufficient driftwood to last the night, he returned to the small camp that Studell was slowly setting up. Traven helped unload the horses and get everything ready for the night. After a quick dinner, he built a small fire as the philosopher nodded off to sleep. He lit it with the ambience and smiled at how easy it would be to light a fire from now on.

He laid out his bedroll and stared out over the ocean. He hoped that the philosopher would be able to hold up okay on the rest of the journey. The half day's ride today had been almost too much for the aged man. Traven laid down to think but was soon fast asleep as the waves continued their rhythmic lapping along the shore.

Traven arose early and practiced his sword forms, thankful to be doing them on solid ground. However, the sand of the beach caused a certain amount of resistance to his routine which left him more winded than usual. As the sun broke the horizon and shone over the water, he made his way back to the small camp. Studell was still fast asleep, so Traven added the last pieces of driftwood to the glowing embers of the fire. He sat quietly, staring as the new pieces caught fire and began to burn.

As the flames grew bigger and bigger, he wondered how large of a flame he could make using the ambience. He had only tried making a small flame up until now. He was nervous to try something new but also excited. He stood up and walked over to a piece of driftwood that had landed on shore near their camp overnight.

Traven cleared his mind and focused on the wet piece of wood. He envisioned in his mind's eye a flame about twice the size of the ones he had created in the past. The air seemed to thicken and swirl around the large piece of wood. He could feel the flame just beyond sight and was about to pull it into existence but stopped. It seemed as easy to form the larger flame as it had been to form the smaller ones. He decided he might as well increase the size of the flame some more. He allowed his mind's eye to let the flame grow larger and larger until it enveloped the entire piece of wood. The substance of the air began to swirl faster and faster around the imagined flame. He concentrated and pulled the flame into existence.

Traven stumbled backwards with a yelp of surprise as the entire piece of wood burst into flame with a loud whoosh. He hadn't expected it to happen so suddenly. He plopped down on the sand feeling too exhausted to walk back up the beach to the camp and stared at the roaring flames at the water's edge. The bright, flickering light hurt his head and he closed his eyes. He wasn't sure whether to be excited by his success or disappointed in himself for causing a headache so early in the morning. He kept his eyes closed and laid back on the sand to rest for a moment, hoping the pain in his head would dissipate.

"Did you sleep down here all night?" Studell asked as he trudged down the beach towards Traven.

"No," he replied with his eyes still closed. "I'm just resting."

"Resting! Resting! You had all night to rest," the philosopher exclaimed. "We need to get moving. There's a lost keep to find!"

Traven pushed himself up with a groan and followed Studell back to the camp. Obviously the philosopher felt refreshed from his good night's sleep. After eating breakfast, Traven felt a little better. His headache was only minor, but he still felt as if he had been practicing his forms all day. He was reminded of how much it had drained him the first time he had lit a candle with the ambience. He would need to be more cautious when experimenting.

"Hopefully we'll reach the break in the cliffs by midmorning," Studell announced when they started along the beach to the west.

As they made their way, boulders jutting out of the ocean along the beach became more numerous. The soft lapping of the waves turned into loud crashes as they slapped against all of the rocks. The boulders continued to grow larger as the morning progressed. Traven could see why the starting point of the map had been further to the east. There was no way a ship could navigate these waters without hitting the rocks. As midmorning neared, he began eagerly watching the cliffs for a sign of the fissure that would allow them passage into the interior of the land. The beach became rockier and the cliffs appeared to diminish slightly in size. Just after midmorning he spotted the break in the cliffs.

5

Traven watched at first with eagerness and then with disappointment as they drew closer to the break. It was a large gash in the previously unbroken cliffs. Instead of a sheer wall, it appeared that part of the cliff had fractured and collapsed. The resulting rock slide extended all the way from the top of the cliffs to the beach at its base. He had hoped that there would be an easy path through the fissure and into the desert beyond. However, the path before them looked anything but easy. It appeared steep and treacherous. He pointed out the spot to Studell who squinted into the distance trying to pick out the break in the cliffs. When the philosopher was finally close enough to see it, he too grew concerned.

"How are we supposed to get up that?" he inquired.

Traven shrugged in response. He wasn't sure. They continued riding towards the fissure. As far as he knew this would be their only chance of climbing through the cliffs and continuing further inland. He hoped that their journey wouldn't be cut short so soon.

When they finally arrived at the break, Traven pulled up on Pennon's reins and studied the ascent more closely. The path along the fissure and up to the top of the cliffs looked difficult but not as bad as he had at first feared. The base of the narrow break in the cliffs was covered with sand and medium sized rocks that continued all the way up to the top of the cliffs. The ascent would be fairly steep, but as long as the rocks were solid, there should be enough footing for the horses to make it up. He suggested that they eat their lunch and give the horses a rest before attempting the climb.

"I agree," replied Studell. "We want the horses rested. I'm still not even sure we will be able to make it to the top."

"The horses can make it," Traven assured him. "We just need to take it slow and be careful."

After eating lunch and watching the waves crash against the rocks jutting up out of the ocean, they decided it was time to make the ascent. Traven led the way. Pennon was surefooted and was able to pick out a safe path for Studell's mount and the packhorse to follow. Traven kept his eyes on the rocky rise before him. Not because his mount needed any help picking out a safe path, but because he didn't want to think about how high they were getting. They paused about halfway up to give the horses another rest.

Traven glanced downwards toward the shore. A wave of dizziness swept over him, and he turned away to look at their path once again. He tried to get the image of the steep drop out of his mind. He reminded himself that the horses hadn't had any trouble so far and would be fine, but he knew he wouldn't feel completely comfortable until they reached the top. When the horses were ready, they continued on. There were a few instances where one of the horses stumbled slightly, but all were able to quickly regain their footing. As they neared the top of the cliffs, Traven let out a sigh of relief and loosened his white-knuckled grip on Pennon's reins. With one last heave, his mount crested the top of the cliffs.

Traven stared in awe as Studell's mount and the packhorse climbed up next to Pennon. As far as the eye could see there was nothing but waves of fine sand, rising and falling in giant swells. No wonder it was called the 'Dune Sea' on the map. He shielded his eyes from the glare of the sun off the endless desert that stretched before him. He could also see why it was referred to as the 'shimmering hills'. The air seemed to waver slightly, causing the sand to look like it was shining in the bright sun. A hot blast of dry wind and sand blew against them as they stood staring. He turned away from the desert, rubbing his eyes as Studell began coughing.

"Isn't that something," Studell said in between coughs. Traven agreed. The desert had a stark beauty to it, but the heat coming off of it was not welcome.

"It's amazing how hot and dry it is up here with the ocean so close," Traven observed.

"It is quite different from being down on the beach," Studell replied. "My mouth is dry just looking at that endless stretch of barren wasteland."

Traven agreed. He looked out over the ocean, being careful not to get too close to the edge of the cliffs. He wished he could still feel its cool breeze. He turned away from the sea and studied their new path. As uncomfortable as he had felt trapped between the cliffs and the ocean, he would take the narrow beach any day over venturing out into the desert that stretched before him. Studell suggested that they change into their desert gear before heading inland. They donned their robes and head wraps and gave the horses some water.

Traven watched with concern as the horses lapped up the precious liquid. He knew the horses needed it as much as he and Studell did but was worried that there wouldn't be enough for all of them. Staring out over the endless hills of sand, he hoped that the map was correct and there truly was a spring halfway to the ruins of the keep. If not, they would have no chance of making it to the ancient keep and back alive. When the horses were finished, the two men remounted and set off into the desert.

The rocky ground at the edge of the cliffs soon gave way to the fine desert sand of the dune sea. Traven led them along the tops of the soaring dunes making his way due north. After only an hour of plodding along into the desert, he wondered if they were making a huge mistake. The heat rose in shimmering waves around them as their mounts trudged forward. He was dripping with sweat and wanted to take his robe off for relief but knew that although the robes kept his body heat in, they also protected him from the blazing sun.

Traven glanced back at Studell often and could tell that the elderly man was faring even worse than he was. After another hour of monotonous plodding through the shimmering sand under the sweltering sun, he decided that it would be best if they stopped to rest. The philosopher had almost fallen out of his saddle several times, and Traven was worried that if they continued on any longer the philosopher might pass out.

"Let's stop here and take a rest," Traven said. "We'll set up a little shelter and wait out the hottest part of the day."

Studell nodded in agreement and slipped down off of his horse. Traven hurried to set up a small shelter to block out the blazing sun. He then helped Studell out of his robes and under the lean-to. The philosopher was flushed and obviously struggling in the heat. Traven offered him some water and suggested that they try to sleep a little and then continue on once it wasn't as hot. Studell agreed and was soon asleep.

Traven glanced out from their shelter at the shimmering air that appeared to be rising off of the sand. In all directions he saw nothing but sand and more sand. At first he had thought the shimmering distortion in the air was water in the distance, but after traveling so long without seeing any sign of it, he had realized that it was nothing more than an illusion created by the rising heat.

He and the philosopher had greatly underestimated how hot and dry the desert would be. It had been unwise to set out across it in the middle of the day. He was tempted to suggest heading back to the coast but knew that the philosopher was set on finding the ruins. Traven had to admit that he also wouldn't give up on their task so easily. He decided that their best chance would be to sleep during the hottest part of the day and travel as much as they could at night. That would allow them to conserve their small supply of water and prevent the philosopher from passing out from the heat.

Traven laid down to join the philosopher in sleep, but just as he started to nod off the horses began to get agitated. He thought nothing much of it and tried to rest. However, when they started to neigh loudly and dance around in place he began to wonder what was bothering them so much. He looked out of the small shelter to see what the problem was and found them staring to the west with wild eyes. He followed their gaze and gasped.

There was an incredibly tall roiling wall of dark brown racing towards them. At first he had no idea of what he was seeing but suddenly realized that it was a giant wall of sand. Soon the sun was blotted out. He wasn't sure what to do. There was no way they could outrun it. He knew that whatever he needed to do, he must do it fast. He instinctively threw blankets over the horses to protect them from the sand. He then threw himself under the lean-to and pulled it down on top of the philosopher and him just as the wall of sand slammed into their impromptu camp.

"What's happening?" the philosopher mumbled, disoriented in the dark with the screaming wind all around him.

"It's a sandstorm!" Traven yelled back. "Just stay still."

The two of them waited under their shelter, holding the blanket down as tightly as they could, trying not to let any sand in. The wind outside continued to howl as it rushed over them, blasting everything with sand. Traven wondered how long it would last. The blanket kept getting heavier and heavier as the storm deposited more and more sand on top of them. The stuffiness and darkness made it hard not to imagine that they would suffocate. He tried not to think about it. Instead he attempted to make out any sounds from their horses, but he could hear nothing above the screaming of the wind. He hoped that their mounts would be okay and that none of their gear would be lost.

He was stunned by the suddenness and fierceness of the sandstorm. He had never seen anything like it. It went on and on as it swept over them. Just when he began to wonder if the storm would ever let up, it abruptly stopped. The silence seemed more acute than normal after the incessant howling of the wind. Traven pushed himself up on his hands and knees and heaved the sand covered blanket off of him. The brightness of the sun temporarily blinded him, and he blinked away the tears that sprouted in his eyes. He pulled the blanket the rest of the way off of the philosopher and helped him to his feet. They both drank in the fresh air as they surveyed their surroundings.

Traven was relieved to find the horses in exactly the same position he had left them in with the blankets still covering them. He hurried to pull the sand covered blankets off of them and allow them to also breathe in the fresh air. The horses proceeded to shake the rest of the sand from their bodies as they snorted.

"Well now," Studell said as he stared to the east and brushed the sand off of his shirt and pants. "I felt like I was being buried alive. How exciting this trip is turning out to be!"

Traven shook his head at the philosopher's excitement. The man could have suffocated in the sandstorm moments ago and yet now he was as giddy as a little kid on his birthday. He joined Studell in watching the diminishing wall of sand speed away to the east. He hoped that they wouldn't run into any other sandstorms. He anxiously checked their gear and was pleasantly surprised to find that it was all still securely tied to the horses.

Deciding that it was still too hot to travel, Traven put their makeshift shelter back up, and they rested for a few more hours. When the sun began to get low on the horizon, they ate a small dinner, packed up their camp, and continued north. It was still warm but not as oppressively hot as it had been earlier. They talked of the sandstorm and the sand dunes that looked like the waves of the ocean as their horses plodded along in the soft sand.

As the sun began to set, the heat began to fade more quickly. By the time night fully arrived, it was actually cool enough that Traven was grateful for the thick robe. The coolness soon turned to cold. He was taken aback by the dramatic change in temperature. He wondered how it could be so hot during the day and yet so cold at night.

"It's the dry air," Studell explained. "There's not enough moisture in the sand or the air to retain the heat from the sun. Once the sun has set, the heat rapidly rises back into the sky leaving it cold."

"I wish the temperature wouldn't change so much," Traven stated.

"That's how deserts are, extreme heat during the day and extreme cold at night. I expect it will get even colder before the night is over."

Traven hoped that the philosopher was wrong but knew that he was probably right. Luckily the dry, clear air also allowed the stars to shine brightly down on them. There was no moon, but the bright stars gave off plenty of light for him to lead them north across the now cold desert. Several hours later it had indeed gotten colder. Traven wrapped his robes as tight as he could, but still couldn't keep from shivering. Looking back he saw that the philosopher was shaking even more than he was.

He wished that there was wood or something else to burn. A warm fire would definitely be welcomed. It would be good to give the horses a break and to warm up a little. Traven scanned the barren landscape in vain for anything that would burn. However, he knew that it was hopeless to look. He hadn't seen anything but sand since venturing into the dunes. As the cold continued to seep in, he wished he had thought to bring along some of the driftwood from the beach. He could easily create a flame with the ambience and start a raging fire like he had that morning.

He suddenly had an interesting thought. He didn't need wood to produce a flame with the ambience. He only needed wood to keep the flame burning. Or did he? Was it possible to keep the flame burning without wood? A fuzzy memory of flames floating in the air came back to him. Where had he seen that? He tried to remember but couldn't. Perhaps it had been in a dream. Regardless, he decided that he might as well try.

He focused on the air in front of him and concentrated on creating a flame. He then pulled it into existence. The small flame burst into life, shining brightly in stark contrast to the dark desert night. Pennon reared in surprise, and Traven almost fell off. The flame immediately winked back out, and Traven worked to calm his surprised mount.

"What was that?" Studell questioned from behind. "Did you run into something?"

"No, I just made a flame with the ambience and surprised Pennon," Traven replied. He decided that if he was going to experiment, they should probably stop. "Let's take a short break. I want to try something."

They both dismounted, and Traven walked a short distance away along the ridge of the dune. He knelt down in the starlight and thought about what he wanted to do. He obviously could make a flame appear easily, but could he keep it burning? He had never tried to hold the flame once he'd created it. He took a deep breath and attempted it. He pictured the flame and concentrated as the air thickened and swirled around it. He focused on keeping the flame in his mind's eye as he pulled it into reality.

The flame burst into life and continued burning in front of him at eye level. Traven smiled with excitement, and the flame began to sputter. He quickly regained his focus on the flame, and it burned brightly once again. He wondered if he could make it larger and proceeded to picture it growing. The fabric of the air spun faster around the flame and it slowly began to grow. It grew and grew until it was the size of his head. He focused on it, keeping it steady and bright. He smiled as he warmed his hands under it and felt the heat from it warming his face.

However, his smile faded as he began to feel the strain on his body. He broke out in a sweat from the effort and started to feel sleepy. A dull throbbing also began in his head. He knew if he held onto the flame any longer it would only get worse, so he let the flame disappear. He took several deep breaths as he waited for his eyes to adjust to the darkness that once again surrounded him.

"That was amazing!" Studell exclaimed from behind him. "Do it again. I definitely wouldn't mind warming my hands over a nice, hot flame."

Traven rubbed his temples trying to massage away the dull headache. He wondered how bad it would get if he tried to recreate the flame for Studell.

"I'll try to do it again," he said. "But I probably won't be able to hold it very long. Using the ambience in such a way drains me quickly."

Traven concentrated on a spot in front of Studell and pulled a large flame into reality. The philosopher jumped back with a surprised gasp but then grinned and stepped towards the bright flame. He only had a chance to rub his hands in front of it for a few seconds before it disappeared. Traven walked back over to the philosopher and the horses. He was breathing hard and the extra effort had caused him an even worse headache. He was grateful for the dark night and cool air that wouldn't agitate his pain. He heaved himself up onto Pennon's back.

"We better keep moving," he said quietly. "That took a lot out of me. I'd like to ride as far as we can before it gets too hot in the morning."

Studell agreed and thanked him for creating the flame. Their horses were soon once again plodding through the soft sand along the ridges of the dunes in a northward direction. As the night wore on, Traven's headache slowly began to fade. When it was finally no more than a dull ache, he began searching the far horizon for the next marker along their journey, the Keeper's Staff.

He wondered how close they would have to get to the tall rock formation to see it in the dark. He kept scanning the horizon hoping to see it soon. If they weren't able to locate the formation, they wouldn't be able to continue following the map to the ruins. About an hour later Traven noticed a thin, dark line rising up from the horizon. He couldn't see it well enough to guarantee that it was the formation known as the Keeper's Staff, but he changed their course slightly to the west so that they would be going directly toward it.

He smiled with relief as the sky finally began to lighten ever so slightly, foretelling the coming of dawn. With the extra light he could tell that it was indeed a tall, crooked rock formation rising up out of the desert. Studell still couldn't see it but trusted Traven's declaration that they were indeed going in the correct direction. Within a short time, their surroundings began to change. The high sandy dunes began to get smaller and smaller, and rocks began to poke through every so often.

Just before sunrise, the horses' hooves left the soft sand of the dunes and began to clink against the solid rock of the changing landscape. It was still as barren and void of life as the sand dunes had been, but the flat landscape was interspersed with boulders and small rock formations. The single, most prominent formation of them all was a tall, narrow rock configuration that made its way crookedly up towards the sky. Even though it was still a ways into the rocky terrain, it was now clearly visible to the philosopher as well.

"You've got good eyes," he said to Traven as they continued riding towards it. "I would have to say that is definitely the Keeper's Staff."

The sight gave hope to Traven that the map truly was accurate. He hoped more than anything that the spring on the far side of the Keeper's Staff still existed and would be easy to find. They paused, as the sun was rising, to eat breakfast and refresh themselves. Then they made their last push towards the Keeper's Staff. They wanted to get as far as they could before stopping to sleep during the hottest time of the day. The warmth of the sun was welcome after the chill of the night, but as they continued onwards and the temperature continued to rise, Traven was reminded of why they had decided it was best to travel at night.

By midmorning the heat began to bother the philosopher, and they decided to stop and sleep. They were both exhausted from the lack of rest during the night. They set up a quick camp in the shadow of a tall boulder and collapsed onto their bedrolls. Despite the hard rockiness of the terrain, they were both soon fast asleep.

6

Traven woke up in the late afternoon feeling much better. His headache was completely gone and much of his weariness had been chased away by the sleep. He mostly just felt hungry and very thirsty. He took a sip of water and began munching on nuts and dried fruit. Beside him, the elderly philosopher continued snoring quietly. Traven was happy to see how well the philosopher had held up so far. What he lacked in physical stamina, he had made up for with his enthusiasm for adventure. Traven decided to let him sleep a little longer before waking him. It was still too hot to travel.

He stood up and watered the thirsty horses. He watched with a grimace as they greedily lapped up the water he offered. He worried that the water might not even last them to the spring, if the spring even existed. He shook his head trying to erase the depressing thought from his mind. He had to believe it existed where the map said. If not, their journey would be over. He knew that if the spring wasn't there, they might not even be able to make it back to the coast alive. He glanced at the crooked formation rising up out of the desert to the north. Hopefully they would reach it sometime during the night.

He didn't think Studell would wake up for awhile, so he reached into one of his saddlebags and pulled out the golden chest. He opened it and pulled out the two might stones. He had been meaning to study them again since he had discovered that he was a wielder. The stones' magic no longer seemed as mysterious as they had the first time he had seen them. He took the two stones and sat back down in the shade of the small shelter.

He set the orange one down and focused on the green stone. He turned it over several times in his hands. The light green might stone was interspersed with veins of yellow that were moving. He stared at it for awhile, mesmerized by the movement. It was so strange and different from anything he had ever seen. He wondered what special powers the stone possessed.

It didn't glow like his father's might stone had, but it did feel like it gave off a small amount of heat. He closed his hand around it and shut his eyes. He could feel warmth emanating from it, and it made his hand tingle slightly. As he continued to hold it and concentrate, he felt a wave of energy wash over him. His eyes snapped open. He wasn't sure what had just happened, but he had immediately felt refreshed and anxious to get moving. He looked at the stone and smiled. Perhaps he would have to hand the stone to the philosopher the next time he wanted to rest and see if it had the same effect on him.

Traven set the green stone down beside him and picked up the other might stone. It was a deep orange that glowed slightly. He cupped it in his hands and put his eye up to it. It didn't seem to give off any heat, but it definitely gave off light. He pulled it away from his eye and turned it over several times in his hands. He then closed his eyes and focused on it like he had the other. He didn't notice anything different and reopened his eyes. He had no idea what powers the stone might possess.

He picked the other one back up and got to his feet. He put them both back in the golden chest and returned the elaborate box to his saddlebag. Maybe when he learned more of how to use the ambience he would be able to study them better and figure out what they were for.

Traven walked back to the small shelter and gently shook the philosopher awake. Studell blinked and swiveled his head from side to side, looking disoriented. After a moment his eyes lit up and a grin graced his face as he remembered where he was.

"Is it time to continue on?" he asked. "How long before we reach the Keeper's Staff? Let's get moving."

"You probably want to eat something first," Traven said with a smile. "If we start heading for the formation right after you finish eating, I think we should reach it sometime in the middle of the night."

Studell ate a quick meal and guzzled down some water. Traven wanted to advise him to go easy on the water but knew the elderly philosopher needed it. They put on their head wraps and took down the camp. Then they set off for the Keeper's Staff. It wasn't long before the late afternoon heat had them dripping with sweat. Traven was glad that the sun would be setting before too long. As much as he disliked the cold of the desert nights, the cold was easier to travel in than the heat of the day.

As they got closer to the tall formation, signs of life began to appear. Dry looking scrub bushes could be seen here and there along their path. Traven also noticed a lizard or two scampering behind the bushes as they passed. By the time the sun set, he was feeling much more optimistic about the journey. This part of the desert was obviously not completely devoid of moisture. Hopefully the spring really was nearby.

With the setting of the sun, darkness began to creep over the desert once again. As the temperature began to drop, Traven was happy to see that there were plenty of scrub bushes around them. It would be easy to get a small fire going to warm them up when they stopped for a break. The darkness eventually took over and thousands of stars began winking in the night.

They continued in a straight line towards the tall rock formation mostly in silence. Something about the darkness and the immense dome of stars looking down on their small party made them content to keep their conversations to a minimum. As they got closer to the formation, it appeared to reach higher and higher into the heavens. Sometime around the middle of the night, they reached its base.

Despite how thin it had appeared from far away, the base of the Keeper's Staff was actually incredibly wide. It looked as if it was at least fifty arm spans across. Studell commented on how small he felt with it rising above them, blotting out a large swath of stars. Traven agreed with him and went to collect enough of the scrub bushes to get a warm firing going. When he had gathered plenty, he put several together and lit them with the ambience. They burst into flames, burning much faster than he had anticipated. He gathered a few more bushes and sat down next to Studell to warm himself by the fire.

The heat of the fire was welcome and quickly dispelled the chill from the night. Traven and Studell munched on some of their food and took several sips from the last full water skin.

"I hope this spring of yours is close," Traven said. "If we are careful we might be able to make this water last through another day."

"It will be there," Studell replied. "Everything else has been right where the map said it would be."

Traven didn't have a problem trusting the map. After what they had seen so far, he believed that the map was accurate as far as how things used to be. However, just because a spring existed in ancient times when the map was made didn't mean that it still existed. He tossed the last of the dry bushes into the fire and tried to relax.

The crackling of the fire was distracting and reminded him of his journey to Calyn with Blaize. How many fires had he shared with the grizzled warrior on their journey to the capitol of Kalia? He missed the talks they had shared and the stories Blaize had told. He supposed that now he would have some stories of his own to share with Blaize once they met up again. Hopefully they really would find some interesting treasures amongst the ancient ruins. Then he would have even more to talk about when he eventually met back up with the army.

As the fire began to die down, they remounted their horses and made their way around the base of the Keeper's Staff. They continued north towards where the spring should be. Traven kept a sharp lookout for the spring, but after a couple of hours they still hadn't found it. To the east he could see the outlines of the mountains known as the 'Twin Guards' that would lead them on their way to the ruins of Faldor's Keep.

The spring should be somewhere close, but he couldn't see any sign of it. After another long stretch of night without seeing it, he began to get really worried. The horses had needed a lot of water thus far. He knew that realistically their meager supply wouldn't last another full day. His lips were cracked and his throat was dry. If they didn't find water soon, they would all eventually die. Traven tried not to panic as he continued to scan their surroundings for any sign of the spring. He was afraid that he might miss it in the dark and wondered if it would be wiser to wait until the morning to look for it. He once again wondered if it even existed anymore.

Perhaps it would be wise to suggest that they should turn back. As he considered how best to explain his thoughts to the philosopher, he noticed something different on the horizon. He strained to see what it was but couldn't tell. As they got closer, he realized that the shapes were trees. His heart leapt at the sight. If there were trees, there was water. He happily pointed them out to the philosopher. Despite the man's assurances earlier, Traven noticed a visible relief wash over him upon hearing the news. It was not long before Traven could clearly make out the small oasis.

There were seven trees and a spattering of bushes clumped in a small, tight circle. The trees looked like none he had ever seen. The trunks were tall and skinny. The numerous green branches at the very top of the trunks fanned out in all directions and drooped slightly.

As they rode closer, Traven searched for the spring. As hard as he looked, he couldn't make out any sign of water. He hoped it was just hiding behind some of the bushes, but once they arrived at the small cluster of trees, his hopes were crushed.

They dismounted and searched the small concentration of foliage but found nothing other than dirt. They searched the entire area several more times but to no avail. Traven noticed a distinct change in the philosopher's countenance as they continued looking. The man's shoulders slumped and the enthusiasm with which he had faced previous obstacles was completely gone.

"I've doomed us," Studell said sadly as he collapsed to the ground at the base of one of the strange trees. "My foolishness has led us to our deaths. I let my excitement get in the way of my reason. I knew that springs come and go. Some springs last for years and then suddenly disappear. I should have planned for the possibility. I should have . . ."

Traven shut out Studell's ramblings as the philosopher continued to lament about his foolishness. It wasn't the elderly man's fault. Traven had known the risk before they had begun traveling across the desert. He cleared his mind and tried to focus on what needed to happen next. Their water supply would run out the next day. Perhaps they could make it back to the beach if they turned around immediately. They would have to ration the remaining water and only travel during the night. They would have to leave any unnecessary supplies so as not to burden their mounts anymore than was necessary.

Even as he began planning for the return trip, he knew that they probably couldn't make it back across the desert. There just wasn't enough water left. He might be able to survive without water for a day or two, but he knew that the elderly philosopher could never make it. Their other option was to continue following the map, hoping that they found water somewhere else. But where would they find water in the middle of a desolate desert? Perhaps there was a water source near the ruins of the keep, but that was still a couple days away as well.

For all he knew there might not be water anywhere in this blasted desert. However, he knew it wasn't true. He had seen signs of life and these trees and bushes had to have water to survive. Their leaves were lush and green. There was water somewhere. He paused as the answer hit him. It was just below the ground! Traven hurried to the pack horse and pulled out the small shovel that the philosopher had brought. He looked around and chose a spot in the center of the clump of trees. He took the shovel to the small clearing and after taking a deep breath, began to dig.

He was thankful for the cold night air as he began to sweat with the effort of digging. He removed his robe and continued to methodically thrust in his shovel and create an ever growing hole in the sandy dirt. His muscles eventually grew tired from the effort and screamed for him to take a break. He stopped to rest but resisted the urge to drink any water. Studell had come over to see what he was doing and reached down into the hole.

"The dirt does seem a little damp," he said dejectedly. "But there is no water. You could dig for hours and not reach the source. We're doomed. How foolish I am! What was I thinking? Ohhh."

Traven watched as the distressed philosopher made his way back to the tree and collapsed. He dropped the shovel and hurried over to the elderly man. Luckily, he was just sleeping. The strain of their journey and current predicament must have finally been too much for him. Traven balled up his robe and put it under the philosopher's head, trying to make the elderly man more comfortable.

He then returned to the hole and continued digging. It was now obvious to him that the philosopher wouldn't be able to make it back to the beach unless they found water. He made the hole wider and deeper, but there was still no water. His muscles again screamed for him to stop and his parched throat called for water. He took a small sip to wet his throat and collapsed at the side of the hole.

He knew that he couldn't keep digging much longer. He had already exhausted himself to the point where he could barely lift the dirt out of the hole. They had plenty of food left, but what he needed was more water to keep going. He stared at the hole with frustration. What more could he do? The philosopher had been right. There was no way he would be able to dig deep enough. The dirt was definitely moist at the bottom of the hole, but that was all.

Traven put his face in his hands in exasperation. There had to be some way to get to the water. If only he could make the hole bigger and deeper with his mind like he had done the night before with the flame. He paused as the thought took hold. Maybe he could. He let his hands fall back to the ground and took a deep breath.

He stared at the hole, trying to picture it bigger and deeper, but nothing happened. He blinked several times and concentrated harder. The air started to thicken and time slowed, but still nothing happened to the hole. As hard as he struggled, his efforts were in vain. No change occurred. He closed his eyes in frustration. Why couldn't he enlarge the hole like he had the flame? He tried to block out the pain of his sore muscles and cracked lips as he searched his mind for an answer.

In his focused state, the faint memory of a lightning bolt flitted at the edge of his memory. Had he really created one? If he could make a bolt of lightning again, perhaps he could blast the hole deeper. He decided that it was worth a try and opened his eyes. His strength was nearly gone, and he couldn't think of any other options.

He looked up pleadingly and reached towards the night sky. He concentrated and slowly began to form a lightning bolt. He began shaking with the effort, but continued forming it in his mind's eye. After struggling for several long moments, he managed to direct a sizable bolt of lightning down from the clear sky and directly into the center of the hole. He expelled an exhausted breath as he focused on the imagined bolt. It was there, just beyond sight. Without stopping to think further, he used the last of his strength and yanked it into existence.

The extreme force that accompanied the blinding flash of light knocked him backwards through the air and into a tree. He slid to the ground and lost consciousness as a deafening boom washed over him.

* * * * *

Studell bolted upright with a ringing in his ears. The horses were neighing and rearing in panic to his right. He shook his head trying to stop the ringing in his ears. What had happened?

In the dark he could just make out the form of Traven sleeping a little ways to his left at the base of one of the palm trees. Whatever had made the sound had not disturbed the young man. He must have been exhausted. Studell remembered watching the young man digging before he himself had fallen asleep. Traven must have finally given up and decided to sleep as well.

He frowned sadly. There wasn't any hope of finding water. They were going to die. Dying of dehydration would be a horrible way to go. His hopeless thoughts were interrupted by the horses. They were no longer rearing in fright but struggling against their ropes to get to something. He peered into the darkness but couldn't tell what they were so anxious about. He stood up and walked toward where the horses were straining to get to.

He took several more steps forward and stopped in amazement. He couldn't believe his eyes. He rubbed them and stared. The philosopher had never seen anything so wonderful in his entire life. Directly at his feet was a pond full of glistening water!

7

Traven awoke at dawn with a splitting headache, a sore back, and a parched mouth. He slowly pushed himself up into a sitting position and blinked in the bright dawn light. He closed his eyes and rubbed the back of his neck. He let out a groan as he stretched. He felt horrible. He reopened his eyes and located the philosopher.

Studell was already awake and splashing water on his face. Water. Where had it come from? He ran his dry tongue over his cracked lips at the thought of water. He got to his feet and hobbled over to Studell. The philosopher was standing right next to a small pond.

Where had the pond come from? It hadn't been there the night before. Traven didn't care. He fell to his knees at the edge, leaned over, and slurped up the water. It was the sweetest thing he had ever tasted. After getting his fill, he laid down on his back with a sigh.

"Isn't it wonderful," Studell said cheerfully. "We're not going to die." Traven smiled and then winced again at the pain in his head. "How long did it take you to dig it?" the philosopher asked.

Traven pushed himself up and looked at Studell, slightly perplexed. He saw the small shovel at the edge of the pond and remembered his fruitless digging during the night. Then it all came back to him, and he remembered blasting the hole with an ambience-created bolt of lightning. He must have blacked out right afterwards, because he couldn't remember anything after seeing the bright flash of light. He stared at the sizeable crater, now full of water.

"I blasted the hole with lightning," he mumbled.

"You what!" Studell exclaimed.

"Well, I got too tired to dig anymore, so I decided to see what else I could do." Studell looked back and forth several times between Traven and the pond.

"Wow! I wonder what all you're capable of?" he said thoughtfully.

Traven looked at the pond and shrugged his shoulders. He didn't know how to respond to the philosopher. What all was he capable of?

They had a nice breakfast beside the pond and drank as much water as they could. They then filled up all of their water skins and watered the horses. Traven took one last long drink before they headed away from the small oasis and toward the twin mountains.

He felt better knowing there would be plenty of water for their return journey back to the coast when they were done. Much of the worry that had accompanied their journey thus far was now gone. Other than his pounding headache and sore back, he felt very upbeat. Two more days and they should arrive at the ruins. After a day or two of searching for anything important or useful, they would head back to the small oasis and return to the coast. There they would be picked up by the captain of the Arrow and return to a milder and more civilized climate. Things would work out just fine.

As they made their way towards the two mountains, the lighter rock and dirt began to give way to rock that was black. The dark rocks soon completely took over the landscape. By midmorning the heat was almost unbearable. It felt hotter than it had at any other point along the journey. After an hour they made camp and waited to continue until evening.

"Those two mountains are volcanic cones," Studell began to explain as they sat under their small shelter. "All of this black rock is the dried lava flow from those volcanoes."

"What's lava?" Traven asked.

"It's the molten rock that spews from volcanoes," the philosopher replied. "It bursts forth from the opening at the top and runs down the sides and all over the countryside. As it cools, it gets hard and becomes this black rock. The lava from those two volcanoes is what caused this sweltering, barren wasteland that we are currently sitting in."

Traven looked up at the Twin Guards and wondered what it would have looked like to see lava spewing from their tops. As far as he could see in every direction the ground was black. There must have been an incredible amount of lava that came from the two volcanoes to cover such a large area.

They talked, slept, and rested until the sun was low on the horizon and then continued on with their journey. The sun set and night fell as they continued making their way towards the two volcanoes. The Twin Guards truly looked majestic against the night sky. Traven wondered what they were guards of. Was it of the treasures that were waiting amongst the ruins of Faldor's Keep?

When they arrived at the base of the volcanoes they turned left for the last stretch of their journey. There was a sense of excitement as they rode due north across the hardened lava flows.

"Do you really think there will be something special in the ruins? Will our journey through this barren desert be worth it?" Traven asked.

"Well, it depends on what you mean by special," the philosopher answered. "I believe that the ruins themselves will be special. Can you imagine walking among the crumbled walls of an ancient castle where no one has walked for centuries? I believe that in itself will make this journey worth it."

"So we've risked our lives to walk around some crumbling walls?"

"I didn't say that," Studell replied with a smile. "I hope we find much more. If these ruins really are connected with the ambience and the wielders of ancient times, we may find some writings or artifacts that tell us more about their history. Who knows? We may even actually find another might stone or some other magical object that will help the Royal Army."

Traven wondered what kind of magical object could help the Royal Army. Would they truly find some kind of weapon? If they did, he could take it with him when he went to rejoin the army. If the rogue army truly had a wielder leading it, it would be good to have some magical weapon to fight back with.

For the first time, an interesting thought made its way into his mind. He was a wielder. He had magical abilities. Was he a weapon that the Royal Army could use in its fight against the rogue army? The thought brought with it a mix of emotions. Could he really make a difference? If the rumors he had heard about the wielder leading the rogue army were true, he was very powerful. If the High King learned that Traven too was a wielder, would he expect him to confront the rogue army's leader? He doubted he could last very long against a powerful, experienced wielder. He would rather face an opponent with steel than with magic. He knew how to fight with a sword, but he had no idea how to fight with the ambience. If he were forced to face the Balthan wielder, he would be destroyed.

He shook his head. Why should he worry about this now? First they needed to find the ruins and see if there was anything useful there. He would have plenty of time to think about the future on the journey back. Maybe he would even have enough time to develop his newfound power and be ready to face the Balthan wielder.

"Is it okay if we stop here and sleep for the remainder of the night?" Studell asked. "I haven't gotten nearly enough sleep on this trip and want to have my wits about me when we get to the ruins."

Traven looked around. He had been so engrossed in his thoughts that he hadn't been paying any attention to his surroundings. The Twin Guards were now distant silhouettes to the south. To the north, he could just make out some mountains on the far horizon. He supposed it probably would be wise to get a half night of sleep before finishing their journey to the ruins. It would be best to search them in the daylight. He looked around to see if there was any type of natural shelter nearby. Seeing nothing but the flat, black surface of the hardened lava flows, he decided here was as good as anywhere.

"Sure, let's stop here. We can finish making our way to the Blood Mountains and the ruins early tomorrow morning before it gets too hot."

As they made camp and snacked, they talked of the coming day and what they hoped to find. Both were excited for what lay before them, but both were also tired. They soon settled down on their bedrolls and drifted off to sleep.

8

They arose before dawn and broke camp. Traven wanted to be as close to the mountains as they could get before the sun rose. They made good time and were only a short distance away from the base of the mountains when the sun began to peek over the horizon.

The sight of the mountains in the morning sun left both of them speechless. The mountains shone a brilliant red above the dark black lava fields. Traven had never imagined that rock could be so vibrant. As he rode closer and closer he became more and more awed by the bright red rock. The black lava flows had been diverted to either side of the clump of red rocks and mountains. As they crested a hill in the midmorning light, they stopped and stared in amazement, forgetting the oppressive heat that was beginning to beat down on them. Out of the dark lava flows, sharp, red fingers of rocks stretched up towards the sky. Sheer cliffs shot up behind the skinny formations of rock, towering above them. Behind the cliffs rose a small cluster of tall red mountains.

Mesmerized by the sight, Traven and Studell guided their mounts quickly down the hill and towards the base of the rock formations without talking. They left the hard, black lava flows behind and stepped onto the fine red sand at the base of the finger-like formations. They dismounted in the shade of one of the wider rock towers and watered their horses. They welcomed the shade as they ate an early lunch.

"So we're here," Traven said with relief. "Where are the ruins?"

"Oh, we're not quite to the ruins yet," Studell replied. "We still have a little ways to go."

"I thought this was the ending point on the map. It can't be much further to the ruins." Traven looked around searching for any signs of the ancient keep. At least there was plenty of shade amongst the tall formations and cliffs. They wouldn't have to search under the unrelenting sun.

"Now is the tricky part," the philosopher announced.

"What do you mean?"

"The back of the map includes additional directions," Studell said as he pulled out and unrolled the map. "They tell how to get through the maze of canyons and to the actual keep."

"Well, if there are directions it should be easy," Traven said as he noticed for the first time that there were multiple canyons that gave entrance into the cliffs and beyond.

"The instructions aren't straightforward like they have been up until now. They seem to be in riddles. Either that or I'm not translating them correctly," he said with a frown. "Oh well, we'll just have to follow them the best we can.

"Why didn't you say anything earlier?" asked Traven.

"I guess it was because I wasn't really sure what they all meant. It makes more sense to me now actually being here and seeing what is in front of us."

"Let's hear the rest of the directions," Traven sighed. He was anxious to know how much further they needed to go.

Studell stared at the back of the map for a few moments in silence. He then cleared his throat and read the directions.

"Into the maze, between the two towers;
Don't leave the way, until you see flowers.
Deeper you go, follow the new path;
Stay to the sides, or face the sand's wrath.
Into the valley, beautiful and sweet;
Prepare yourself, for those you will greet."

"That's everything?" Traven asked confusedly when Studell stopped reading. "What does it even mean?"

"That's why I didn't bring it up earlier," the philosopher said while shrugging. "Of course, looking at what lies before us, I think I understand what 'Into the maze' means. Perhaps the other parts of the riddle will make sense as we get closer to the ruins."

The philosopher was probably correct. However, he thought it strange that the directions had been so clear and easy to follow until now. Why would the last part of the directions be so confusing?

They remounted their horses and started making their way through the maze of narrow red towers towards the base of the cliffs. Neither of the narrow canyons that led into the cliffs near them had 'two towers' by their entrances, so they followed the base of the cliffs towards the east.

They passed numerous columns of the bright red rock as they continued eastward along the cliff face. After passing several more openings without any towers, they finally found an opening into a very narrow canyon that fit the description. On both sides of the opening, a slender spire shot up into the sky, reaching even higher than the tall face of the cliffs.

"This must be it," Studell exclaimed as they stood staring at it.

Traven agreed. At first he had worried they wouldn't know which canyon to follow, but after seeing the two grand spires, he was convinced that this was indeed the canyon that the riddle described. Perhaps the last set of directions wouldn't be too hard to follow.

They looked at each other with grins and headed into the canyon, excited for what they might soon find. The shadowed canyon was nice and cool. Traven was grateful to be out of the sun and heat but felt slightly claustrophobic in the narrow canyon. It was only a couple of arm spans wide and reached high into the sky.

Looking straight up, he could barely make out a sliver of the bright blue sky. He stared up at it as Pennon continued through the canyon. Every once in a while a wispy cloud would make its way across the thin sliver of blue. Traven shook his head and looked back down. The movements of the clouds crossing the sliver of sky created the illusion that the canyon walls were moving and not the clouds. It left him feeling slightly dizzy.

The horses appeared happy to be in the cool shade as well and contentedly walked along the fine red sandy floor of the narrow canyon. As the day wore on, they passed several side canyons but saw no signs of any plants at all, let alone flowers. There was only red sand and the towering rock walls on either side. Traven finally pulled up.

"I don't know how we are going to find any flowers," he muttered. "There's nothing alive in these arid, sandy canyons."

"I've been thinking the same thing as well," Studell added. "These rock formations would still be the same centuries after the map was made, but for all we know, there might not be flowers anywhere in these canyons now."

Traven sighed with frustration. He wished that the final directions had included measurements of distances like the first. He wondered how long they should keep following the main canyon that they were traveling in. After yet another hour, and having bypassed several more side canyons, Studell suggested that perhaps they should turn around and explore the side canyons that they had already passed. Traven was about to agree, but then he heard a faint sound in the distance ahead of them.

"What is it?" Studell asked when he noticed Traven listening intently to something.

"I'm not sure," he replied while trying to make out what it was.

"It is probably just the wind. Let us turn around and explore the side canyons."

"No," Traven replied. "I'm not sure what it is, but I do hear something. Let's continue on a little further. I want to find out what it is."

As they continued onward, the sound slowly grew louder. Soon the horses' ears were also twitching, listening to the faint noise. Finally Studell heard it as well. By then it was almost a roaring in Traven's ears. He urged Pennon into a trot, eager to find the source of the noise. It almost sounded like rushing water. As they came around a bend in the canyon, the source of the sound was revealed.

Water came crashing down into a small pool of water. They looked up at the waterfall in awe. The water tumbled over the top of the cliff, falling from an immense height. Traven's mouth broke into a grin as his eyes returned to the crystal clear pool of water. The edges of the pool were teeming with small white flowers. And just as the riddle had suggested, there was a narrow side canyon that opened up in the canyon wall opposite the flowers.

They both dismounted and refilled their water skins. The mist from the waterfall felt great on their dry skin after having traveled in the arid air of the desert.

"Isn't it strange that no river flows from the pool," Studell said as they relaxed in the cool mist. Traven realized that the philosopher was right. With all of the water pouring down from the waterfall, one would expect to see a stream flowing away from the pool. The water had to be going somewhere.

"The pool must be connected to an underground river," Studell concluded. "We thought there was no water in this arid desert, but it seems that there might be more under our feet than we realized."

After eating some dried meat and fruit, they remounted their horses and prepared to enter the side canyon. It was actually slightly wider than the one they had been following and looked as though three horses could easily traverse it side by side. This canyon led deeper into the center of the mountain range and was obviously the 'new path' mentioned on the map.

However, the next part of the riddle gave them pause. It had stated to 'stay to the sides, or face the sand's wrath'. Neither of them were sure what the 'sand's wrath' was, but since the directions had led them so well thus far, they decided to follow them exactly.

Traven led the way into the side canyon keeping his mount as close to the left side of the canyon as he could without scraping against the rock wall. Studell's mount and the packhorse followed directly behind him. As they made their way through the winding canyon, Traven kept alert, scanning the canyon for any signs of danger. However, he didn't notice anything out of the ordinary.

The new path did make him feel more claustrophobic than the other one had. At its base it was wider, but the upper reaches of the canyon were closer together. At times it almost felt as if they were traveling through a tunnel as the sky would disappear altogether. Riding in the dim light of the shadowed canyon left him feeling tired. He tried to stay alert, but his eyelids kept drooping closed. After following the winding trail for awhile and seeing no signs of any danger, Studell rode up next to Traven.

"I hope we get to the valley soon," the philosopher said. "This canyon feels like it's closing in on me. I don't know how much more of this I can stand."

Traven agreed with Studell as he rubbed his eyes. It would be nice if they reached the valley spoken of in the riddle soon. He took a deep breath of air, trying to stay awake. He noticed a slight change in the air. He took several more deep breaths. The dry, musty smell of the canyon was now sometimes interspersed with brief whiffs of a soft fragrance that he couldn't identify. Perhaps they were getting close to the valley after all.

Suddenly Studell yelped and his mount screamed. Traven whipped around to find the horse buried up to its chest in the sand. He vaulted from Pennon's saddle and rushed to Studell's side. He watched with horror as the horse continued to quickly sink. He grabbed the philosopher, yanked him forcefully out of his saddle, and tossed him up against the canyon wall. He was careful to stay on solid ground as he tried to help the terrified horse out of the sinking sand. When it became apparent that the rescue of the horse was hopeless, he quickly cut off Studell's saddle bags and cut the rope that led to the packhorse before Studell's mount completely disappeared beneath the sand.

Traven stared at the now bare spot of sand with a mix of sorrow and amazement. His heart sank with the thought of the poor animal's fate. He couldn't believe that the horse had just completely disappeared below the surface. The spot of sand looked almost identical to the rest of the sandy floor of the narrow canyon, giving no hint of the hidden danger lurking beneath the ground. He turned and helped a still stunned Studell back to his feet.

"I guess that's the sand's wrath," Traven muttered still in awe. "We better make sure we stay as close to the side of the canyon as we possibly can."

As soon as Studell got over his shock, he promised Traven that he would not go anywhere near the center of the canyon. The philosopher was still pale, and Traven told him to go ahead and ride Pennon. He would walk in front and carefully lead the horses. They definitely couldn't afford to lose another horse if they hoped to be able to return to the beach in time to meet the Arrow. As it was, one of them would be riding without a saddle.

Traven tied Studell's saddle bags to the packhorse and tied the packhorse's reins to Pennon. He then helped the philosopher up onto Pennon's saddle. Once he was sure that Studell was calm enough to stay in the saddle, he carefully made his way around the horses. He took hold of Pennon's reins and carefully led the horses onward, staying even closer to the canyon wall than he had previously.

He kept a wary eye for any patches of sand that would be dangerous and was fairly sure that he identified several more patches in the center of the canyon that would prove deadly if wandered onto. By late afternoon, a soft, sweet breeze began to blow. Traven smiled at the sweet smell and hoped that they would soon be out of the maze of narrow canyons. The path suddenly made a sharp turn to the left and opened up into a small valley.

They both stared out over the valley, stunned at the beauty of it. The valley was full of lush green foliage that created an eye popping contrast against the red stone cliffs. Several waterfalls cascaded down the steep cliffs that surrounded the entire vale. Traven could see no other entrances or exits from the valley except for the canyon that they had just emerged from. After so many days in the barren desert, the sight was almost too much to believe. It was awe inspiring!

Studell dismounted and came to stand next to Traven as he stood gazing over the valley. The valley truly was beautiful and sweet. Some type of plant or flower in the vale gave off a sweet and calming aroma. After several moments of silence to appreciate the scene, they began to scan the valley for any sign of the ruins of Faldor's Keep. The vale wasn't very big, and Traven could easily see all the way across it. The trees in the valley weren't very dense or tall and didn't look as though they could hide anything. He was surprised he couldn't see any signs of the ruins whatsoever.

The map had most certainly led them to this very spot, but the ruins of Faldor's Keep were missing. Was the map some kind of joke? There should be some sign left of the ancient keep. If it truly had been here, it seemed unlikely it could have disappeared without a trace. Traven hoped they hadn't come all this way for nothing. He took a few deep breaths of the sweet, calming air.

Maybe if they headed down into the valley they would find something. As they began walking away from the mouth of the canyon, Traven suddenly had the uneasy feeling that they were being watched. He scanned the valley below but saw no signs of life. As they continued forward the feeling grew stronger. He tried to figure out where the uneasy feelings were coming from but couldn't. He stuck out his hand to the side and stopped Studell.

"What are we waiting for?" the philosopher said excitedly. "We're here. Let's get down in the valley and find the ruins."

"I feel like we're being watched," Traven stated uncomfortably. "Can't you feel it?"

"No," he replied. "Maybe you just got so used to the narrow canyons that the openness of the valley leaves you feeling exposed. Now come on. I want to see what's down there."

Traven wished that it was as simple to shake the feeling as Studell made it sound, but it wasn't. The more he focused on the feeling, the more he was certain that whoever was watching them was only several arm spans in front of them. He knew it seemed impossible, but he could undeniably feel a presence directly in front of them. He wondered if he was going crazy, but then he noticed that Pennon was getting slightly skittish as well. The harder he stared in front of them, the more he was sure something was wrong. The air almost seemed to have a slight shimmer to it.

"We're not alone," Traven whispered to the philosopher. "Stand behind me." Studell looked at him disbelievingly, but seeing that he was serious, the philosopher moved behind him.

Traven began to feel that the threat was growing and felt strangely exposed. He slowly unsheathed his sword as he looked ahead at the spot in front of him where he felt the threat coming from. He lifted his sword at the ready for whatever might occur next. Nothing happened, and he wondered once again if he was somehow imagining it.

Suddenly four cloaked figures stepped forward out of thin air directly in front of him. All four had bows raised and arrows pointed at Traven's chest.

9

The two men disengaged and studied each other for a few moments as they caught their breath. Both were sweating heavily in the cool morning air. When they were once again ready, they raised their swords. They then reengaged, and the swords began to swirl and crack. Finally, Gavin began to gain an advantage. He pressed the advantage as he sensed the tiring of his opponent. Soon he had landed several glancing strikes. With a quick burst of speed, he lunged forward and landed a killing stroke.

A soft applause rose from the onlookers as Commander General Gavin reached down and helped his sparring partner back up onto his feet. The two men exchanged a few words and a clap on the back. Gavin then turned and made his way back up the hill towards his beautiful fiancé, the High Princess Kalista.

Kalista smiled as she watched Gavin making his way up the hill toward her. He was still breathing heavily, and his warm breath created puffs of mist in the cold morning air. He looked stunning despite his worn sparring attire and the sweat that dripped from his brow. She was reminded again of how lucky she was to be engaged to such a dashing man.

"My dear," he said as he reached her and kissed her hand. "Did you enjoy watching the match?"

"I suppose so," she replied.

"You suppose so?"

"You won for the fourth day in a row. You are definitely improving, and it isn't quite as exciting when I know you are going to win," she smiled. "Perhaps you should recruit a new sparring partner."

"Are you suggesting that you want to see me lose?" Gavin asked.

"No," the princess answered with a mischievous grin. "I was just thinking it would help you keep getting better. You did say you wanted to be able to lead your men with the sword if you had to, didn't you?"

"I did say that," he said while nodding. He paused for a moment before continuing. "Okay, I will have General Blaize pick out a new sparring partner who is more skilled with the blade. Now if you will excuse me, I am going to get cleaned up and change into my uniform. We need to get marching soon if we want to reach Kavar by the end of the week." He then gave her a wink and headed off to his tent.

Kalista let out a contented sigh as she watched him walk away. She loved it when he winked at her. She turned away from him as he entered his tent and looked out over the encampment. The soldiers had already broken camp and were preparing to march. It always amazed her to see how fast such a large group of soldiers could set up camp and then take it down again in the morning. They had been making good time and were already five days past Four Bridges. They should reach Kavar in another five days.

It had been nice to stay in the city of Four Bridges, and she was looking forward to staying in Kavar for a night. While her tent was much nicer and bigger than those of the regular soldiers, it would never be as good as sleeping in an actual room at a fine inn. A comfortable bed was not the only perk of staying at an inn. She reminisced on the delicious dinner and breakfast she had while at the inn in Four Bridges. As the princess, she did have her own chef and ate better than the soldiers. However, she still didn't get to eat a large variety of food and more often than not it wasn't very fresh.

She turned from watching the soldiers prepare to march and made her way back to her tent. It had already been emptied, and her servants were beginning to take it down. She sighed and leaned against the side of her horse. She wasn't looking forward to another full day in the saddle. She didn't even want to consider how many more days there were until the army would finally reach Candus.

The only thing that made all of the hardships of the journey worth it was that she was able to ride beside Gavin. It had allowed her to continue to grow closer to him. She was able to see more of him now than she was ever able to when they had been back in Calyn. Despite the deprivations of the journey, she didn't regret her decision to come on the march.

She watched her servants as they finished taking down her tent and deftly packed it away. She was glad she didn't have to set up and pack her own tent everyday like the soldiers did. She supposed she shouldn't feel like the journey was overly difficult for her, but it was definitely more physically demanding than life in the palace.

Two short blows on a trumpet announced that all the soldiers needed to move to their proper places in their ranks. They would begin marching soon. Kalista pulled herself up into the saddle of her horse and waited for Gavin to come join her. They would then make their way to the head of the column of soldiers and begin the day's march.

She watched as a young soldier hurried by in front of her as he ran to get into position. He looked younger than many of the other soldiers. He must have been as young as Traven. She smiled at the thought of him. She wondered how the young man who had rescued her and saved her life was doing. She knew he had been commissioned by her father to sail north. He was traveling with a philosopher to look for something among some lost ruins. She wondered if Traven and the philosopher had found what they were sent to look for.

"Hello, my Princess," Gavin said as his mount made its way to her. "What are you thinking about? You have that faraway look in your eyes."

"Oh nothing," Kalista replied shaking her head. "Are we ready to start the march?"

"Yes," Gavin said as he reached out and squeezed her hand. "Another exciting day in the saddle."

Kalista smiled as they made their way towards the front of the column of soldiers. Her guards immediately fell in place beside her. Even in the midst of an army, they were always nearby. Ever since her abduction, her guards were never very far away, no matter where she was or who she was with. She supposed it was safer this way, but it annoyed her to always have so many people following her. The only time she could feel alone was in her own tent. Even then she knew the guards were posted all around the outside of it.

Kalista and Gavin were soon at the front of the column and in place. Three sharp bursts of a horn were sounded, and the entire company of soldiers surged forward. Another full day of marching had begun.

* * * * *

General Blaize gazed back over the ranks of the soldiers behind him. The formations were tight, and the soldiers were marching in time as they should be. The army was on schedule to arrive at the pass with plenty of time to prepare for the coming battle. He turned and looked forward.

It still felt strange to him to be a general and riding at the head of the Royal Army of Kalia. What was even stranger was that he wasn't even a Kalian. He was a Balthan. He found it ironic that they were marching to fight the army of his own country.

He reminded himself that it wasn't the Balthan Army they were going to fight. Even though the Balthan Army had been incorporated into the rogue army, it was led by the Wielder Kadrak. It was the wielder's army, not the army of Balthus. Blaize felt no qualms fighting against a tyrant who was trying to subject the world to his will.

In fact, the reports of the destruction that Kadrak and his army had caused to the cities of Rankdra and especially Beking, gave him motivation to avenge the wrongs committed against his fellow countrymen. Blaize was happy to be leading an army that was fighting to protect the citizens of its land and not fighting to gain power.

He glanced back again at the soldiers, approving their disciplined march. They would need that discipline when they faced the Wielder Kadrak. At first he had been hesitant to believe an actual wielder was leading the invading army, but after hearing so many reports, he now had to believe it. Supposedly the wielder could call down lightning and fire from the sky. The soldiers would need to be disciplined in order to hold their positions if such an unnatural onslaught was sent against them.

However, he was confident that the Royal Kalian Army would be able to repel the attack. They had plenty of soldiers, intelligent commanders, and a cause worth fighting for. The Wielder Kadrak might turn out to be a formidable opponent, but he was only one man. Blaize knew all too well that no matter how strong someone may be, one could only do so much against numerous opponents.

Many of the soldiers in the ranks were young recruits without experience. They had been taught discipline, and he hoped that discipline would keep them firm when facing actual opponents. They had been informed that there was indeed a wielder that they would be facing. He knew some still didn't believe it, but at least they had been warned. Hopefully that would help them react with less fright than the soldiers who had been guarding Beking and Rankdra.

He hoped that the youth of his soldiers would also lend them courage and stamina. The battle wouldn't be won quickly unless they were able to capture or dispose of the Wielder Kadrak. As long as the wielder was leading the rogue army, the Balthans would keep fighting. The battle might turn out to be long and drawn out.

His thoughts turned from the ranks of soldiers following him, to a young soldier that wasn't even with them. Traven was someone he knew he could trust with his life. The young man had grown to be an expert swordsman and had proven his courage and loyalty by saving the princess when she had been abducted. Blaize certainly wouldn't mind having him fighting at his side.

He hoped that Traven's search for the 'secret weapon' as the philosopher had called it, was going well. As he understood it, Traven had headed north by ship to Faldor's Watch. He would be searching among the ruins of an ancient keep for something that might help them against the Wielder Kadrak. He then would try to meet up with the army near Candus. The army could definitely use any help they could get when facing a wielder.

He looked forward to seeing Traven again. He was the closest thing Blaize had to family, and he missed their early morning training and talks. The young man had grown so much since he had first pulled him out of the river not far from where the army was currently marching. He hoped to meet up with him soon.

Turning his thoughts back to the present, Blaize went through a mental list of the soldiers under him. Earlier in the day, Commander General Gavin had asked him to choose a new sword sparring partner for him. He needed to choose a soldier who was a good swordsman but not so good that the commander general would always lose to him. The soldier also needed to be mature enough to practice with Gavin without trying to show off.

Blaize continued down the list in his mind until he settled upon a good swordsman that he thought would work out. He summoned a messenger to him and told him to go and inform the soldier that he was being assigned to train with the commander general. The messenger then hurried down the column of soldiers to deliver the message. Blaize smiled. One more assignment was out of the way.

*****

Kalista watched as the two men began to spar. This was definitely more exciting than riding in the saddle all day. Gavin was facing a new opponent. General Blaize had said this soldier was very skilled with the sword and should be a harder challenge.

The general had been correct. She could tell that the soldier was easily blocking all of Gavin's attacks. Once the soldier counterattacked, Gavin didn't last very long and was soon on his back. She watched as he pushed himself up from the ground, and after taking a moment to catch his breath, began sparring again. He was soon once again on the ground, this time rubbing his arm where he had been struck by the practice sword.

She expected him to be done for the day, but instead he rose once again and engaged the soldier in another round of attacks and counterattacks. She admired Gavin's determination. It was one of the traits that made him such a great leader. After a slightly longer sequence of sword work, Gavin was struck once again.

She really didn't enjoy seeing him lose to anyone, but she knew it would help him continue to improve. Gavin did not like losing, and it would drive him to push himself harder in his practicing. She wanted him to excel in all of his endeavors.

She hoped when the battle commenced east of Candus he wouldn't have to use his sword fighting skills at all. He should be safely at the rear of the army, far from the front lines, directing the battle from a distance. His leadership ability would be of more worth from a tactical standpoint than from a fighting standpoint on the front line. However, if for some reason he was ever drawn into actual combat, Kalista wanted him to be able to come out of it safely. The better he was with the sword, the better the chance he would escape unscathed. She was pleased he was taking the opportunity to improve his skills now while he had the chance.

She tried not to worry about his safety in the upcoming battle. At least she knew that not only would he have his own fighting skills to protect him, he would also have a contingency of highly skilled guards. They would all give their lives to protect their commander general. The guards who were chosen to protect their commanders would be some of the best soldiers in the army; soldiers who could take on multiple opponents at once, a soldier like Traven.

Another smile flitted across her face at the memory of the young soldier. He could definitely take on multiple opponents at once. She remembered how he had easily disposed of her three kidnappers and later how he had bested multiple thieves when they escaped. He had even held at bay five thieves in his weakened state when guarding the entrance to the cave.

Traven would certainly be someone that she would like near Gavin if he were threatened during battle. She looked back at Gavin as he shook hands with his new sparring partner. Maybe someday Gavin would be good enough with the sword to spar with Traven.

10

Kadrak spread out his arms in wonder. How had the boy done it? He was nowhere to be found. Had he died in the blasted desert? While that would take care of the problem, he somehow doubted the boy, with so much power in the ambience, could have died so easily. Perhaps he had figured out how to block others from seeing him. That would make things more difficult. He would have to trust that Shadow could track him down and take care of him.

Kadrak had been checking on the whereabouts of the boy every few days. For some reason he had headed north by ship instead of heading east with the High King's Royal Army. The boy had landed on Faldor's Watch and then set out across the desert. He had been very curious as to what the boy was up to, but now it appeared he might never find out. He knew that the boy still had to be somewhere in the desert, but he couldn't locate him anymore.

He didn't like not knowing what the boy was up to but knew that he couldn't do anything about it for now. He would forget the matter and focus on what he could do. That was part of being a good leader. One had to know what he could change and what he couldn't and move on.

Preparations were currently underway to move his army towards the pass. The snow was finally beginning to melt and the pass would soon be clear. His first assistant Gilrod had done a good job incorporating the rogue army into the Balthan Army. The army would be ready to march towards Beking by the end of the week.

Kadrak planned to restock supplies there and then continue his army's march to the mountain pass. By the time they reached the pass, he hoped the snow would be gone. He didn't want to have to wait any longer to begin his campaign into Kalia.

He knew that the main body of the Kalian Army would be in place at the other side of the pass long before he arrived with his army. What he hoped to avoid, however, was allowing the reinforcements of the opposing army to arrive and supplement the army's strength. Hopefully he would be able to finish off the main body of the Kalian Army before the reinforcements arrived.

However, before his army marched, there were a few things that Kadrak needed to take care of. He left the dark room where he had been screeing and headed to another part of the dungeon. Two guards straightened visibly when they heard him coming. Both bowed slightly as he passed and followed as he made his way deeper into the dungeon. These guards, like most in the palace, had learned who their new emperor was. A few, though, had chosen to stay loyal to the previous Empress of Balthus.

A week ago, the traitorous guards had helped to smuggle her out of the palace. The empress still hadn't been found, but he was sure that sooner or later Gilrod's spies would find her. They had already received a few leads. The former empress would have to be dealt with harshly and in a public manner once she was caught. Kadrak's subjects must understand that none would be allowed to act against his will.

The guards who had helped her escape had already been identified. They would be dealt with now. Kadrak continued down the dark hall until he reached Gilrod. The cunning man had quickly been able to determine which of the palace guards had helped the former empress flee. Some had initially denied any involvement, but most of them had defiantly expressed their loyalty to the empress and the royal family of Balthus.

"I've questioned them all multiple times and believe I have gleaned as much information as I can from them," Gilrod said. "Several have been in contact with certain factions within the city that are planning to take back power as soon as we leave with the army."

"How large of a threat is it?" Kadrak asked curtly.

"It appears to be fairly sizeable," Gilrod replied. "However, if you would like, I believe I can round up most of the leaders of these rebellious factions over the next day or two. From there I can most likely root out some more dissenters before we march to Beking."

"Please do what you have to," Kadrak said with a sigh. "You know that you have as many men at your disposal as you need."

"Yes, Master," Gilrod said with a bow. "I will clean up as much of this as I can before we leave. I would also suggest leaving a small contingent of some of your more loyal troops here to stop anyone else from getting any ideas."

Kadrak shook his head in disgust. It was frustrating to have to worry about people trying to take power away from him once he had seized it. He supposed that he would have to become accustomed to it. The more cities and lands he conquered, the more opportunities would arise for others to try to steal power from him. The key to keeping things under control was to carefully select those who would rule under him. He was glad he had chosen Gilrod from the beginning.

"I agree," Kadrak stated. "I would like you to choose a loyal and capable soldier and elevate him to the level of a governor. He will remain in Rankdra with a few thousand troops to maintain order here."

"As you wish," Gilrod replied.

"Now go," Kadrak said. "I will finish up things here. I want the traitors that are hidden in the city found and disposed of publicly before we march."

Gilrod made a low bow and quickly walked away down the hall. Kadrak watched him go. The man truly was a valuable asset. He always took care of things just as he was supposed to. Kadrak was glad that he wouldn't need to worry about Rankdra while he was gone. Gilrod would root out the trouble makers and appoint someone capable to maintain the capitol.

Maintaining a firm hold on Rankdra would be essential when he marched with his army to Kalia. He would need the city's material support. It would be advantageous to have a steady stream of supplies flowing from the capitol to support his army.

Kadrak turned his thoughts to the real reason for his visit to the dungeons. Punishments needed to be dealt out. He pushed open the cell door that Gilrod had been standing outside of and walked into the dark room. A glowing orb of light appeared in the center of the large cell, bathing the eight prisoners in a pale blue light. They all rose to their feet and after adjusting to the light, stared back at him defiantly.

The two guards who had followed him stepped into the room behind him and closed the door. He had brought them along to witness the fate of the disloyal guards. He wanted the news spread of what happened to disloyal subjects.

Kadrak smiled at the defiant prisoners. He had no problem with them looking at him the way they were. In fact, he was happy about it. He wanted them attentive for the show he was about to put on. He raised his hands above his head as his eyes tightened. Lightning and fire began to lance near the ceiling of the room, above the treasonous guards' heads.

They all looked up with wide eyes at the unnatural display. Kadrak could see the fear shining in their faces. Where was their courage now? He was glad the prisoners were all coherent enough to witness the show. It would be the last thing any of them would ever see.

Part Two: Training

11

Traven stood frozen in place with Studell slightly behind him. Studell's mouth was gaping open. Traven could hardly believe his own eyes. The four men had appeared out of thin air. One second there had been nothing and the next second there were four figures standing in front of them.

All four wore dark brown cloaks with deep hoods that partially hid their faces. The two in the middle were a head taller than the other two and appeared to be slightly taller than Traven. Within the shadows of the two taller men's hoods, he could make out angular features and piercing, bright green eyes. It also looked like both had a black streak slashing down over their left eyes. There was something strange and slightly off about the two men, but he couldn't put his finger on what it was.

The other two men had hard jaws and dark eyes. They were of a much stockier build and appeared very solid. Traven noticed that besides the bows and arrows pointed at him, all four men had swords belted at their waists. By how they stood, he was sure they knew how to use their weapons.

He nodded towards the four men and slowly sheathed his sword. The sun glinted off his blade and disappeared into the dark stone at its hilt as he slid the sword into its sheath. One of the men in the middle shifted slightly, and Traven knew that he had noticed the odd phenomenon.

What Traven couldn't figure out was why four men were out here in the desert and how they had suddenly appeared. He wondered if they also had a map and had beaten Studell and him to any treasures left in the ruins of the keep. After a few more seconds of tense silence, one of the tall men in the middle lowered his bow and took a step forward.

"What business do you have here?" he asked sharply.

Traven detected a hint of a strange accent in the man's voice but couldn't place it. He debated what to say to the cloaked men. He didn't want to say anything about the map and Faldor's Keep if they didn't know about the ruins. Then again, their sudden appearance out of thin air led him to believe that they were more than simple travelers hiding out in a hidden valley in the middle of the desert. He suddenly remembered the last line of the map's riddle; 'Prepare yourself, for those you will greet.' It was crazy to think the riddle could have predicted that there would be people here.

He knew that he would be no match for the four armed men. He could make up a story as to why he and the philosopher were here, but he didn't see how it would help their current situation. Instead, he decided that he might as well be honest as to why they were in the valley.

"We came looking for Faldor's Keep," he replied to the cloaked man. A glance passed between the cloaked men, and Traven knew that they recognized the name.

"What makes you worthy to enter the keep?" the tall man asked.

He wasn't sure how to answer a question like that. What was the man talking about? Why would it matter who entered the ruins of the keep? Behind him, Studell finally recovered from his shock and walked over to Traven's saddlebags. He fished out the golden chest that contained the two might stones and the jewelry. He then stepped past Traven and held the chest towards the cloaked man.

"We are returning what was taken," the philosopher stated.

The tall man took the chest and looked inside. Traven wondered what Studell was thinking. What did he mean by handing over the stones to the strangers and saying that they were returning what had been taken? A look of recognition and surprise passed over the sharp face of the tall man as he looked in the chest and then closed it. He handed it back to the philosopher.

"Follow me," he said. With that, he turned around and disappeared into thin air. Traven and Studell just stood in place staring at where the man had been. The remaining men chuckled.

"Well, get a move on it. We're not going to stay here all day," one of them said.

Traven looked at the remaining three and then at the spot where the fourth had disappeared. He took a deep breath and grabbed Pennon's reins. He walked slowly towards the point where the man had disappeared. The philosopher followed close behind, not wanting to be separated.

When Traven reached the spot, he sensed something directly in front of him. Reaching his hand forward, he felt a chill against his skin and watched as his hand disappeared. He took another deep breath and stepped forward. His entire body was immersed in cold, and then he was through. The tall cloaked man was there waiting for him. Behind him in the distance rose a dark stone structure.

The valley looked the same as it had from the other side of the barrier; the same fine red sand, green foliage, and meandering streams. However, now signs of civilization could be seen as well. Cultivated fields were visible in several areas at the base of the valley and well worn paths radiated from the dark stone keep.

Faldor's Keep looked nothing like what he had been expecting. Instead of being a bunch of ruins, he was surprised to find it in perfect condition. The keep was positioned in the very center of the valley. Its black stone walls contrasted sharply against the red sand and green foliage surrounding it. The walls rose straight and smooth several stories into the air. The structure appeared to be a precise square with a small tower at each of its four corners. Despite the age of the ancient keep, it appeared brand new.

Traven tore his gaze away from the keep and looked back through the barrier. The barrier itself was faintly visible as a slight shimmering in the air, but he could still see everything on the opposite side of it. He watched as Studell passed through it and gasped from the cold shock. The professor's eyes grew large as he too saw the keep in the distance. It was obvious that Traven wasn't the only one feeling a sense of awe.

He wondered how one could see out of the barrier to the cliffs but couldn't see through it when looking towards the center of the valley from the outside. He asked the tall man about it as the other three cloaked men passed back through the barrier.

"It was set up long ago by Faldor," he replied curtly. "It was to protect the keep and its defenders from unwanted eyes. Now let's get a move on it. You can direct any more questions to the keeper."

The man turned, having said all that he was going to. He began towards the keep as the other tall man hurried to fall in step beside him. The two stockier men took up positions behind Traven and Studell. Traven exchanged a look with the philosopher and followed the two cloaked men towards the keep.

As they drew closer, he couldn't believe Faldor's Keep was not only in such good shape but that people were actually living in it. He scanned the vale as they continued on towards the keep. The keep was still a good distance away, but the temperature wasn't nearly as harsh amongst the green foliage of the valley as it had been in the barren desert. The several streams that meandered across the vale also made the air slightly humid. The change in climate was a welcome relief after the arid desert. He was still amazed that such a valley as this could exist in the middle of the desert.

By the time they reached the keep, the sun had disappeared behind the high cliffs that surrounded the valley. The path they had been following led right up to the south side of the keep. A massive portcullis stood at the entrance of the keep, blocking access into it.

Through the grate, Traven could see that the path continued through the thick walls of the keep and ended in a large courtyard.

At the portcullis, the two cloaked men in the lead pulled back their hoods and turned to face them. Studell gaped openly at the sight, but Traven managed to appear calm except for a slight widening of his eyes. He had already noticed their eye tattoos and the sharpness of their features from within the dark confines of their hoods, but he hadn't been prepared for this. They were not human!

As similar as they looked to humans, they were also distinctly not. While their angular features and long flowing hair could pass for human, their ears and eyes couldn't. Their ears rose to form distinct peaks at the top and their eyes shone slightly with a metallic gleam. What were they?

"Elves," Studell muttered in awe.

Traven could hardly believe what he was seeing and hearing. Elves? In the stories they were always ugly, mischievous, and deadly creatures. While their appearance was striking, they definitely weren't ugly. Their appearance was in fact very regal. However, he was sure they were deadly. From the fluid grace of their walks, he could guess at their skill in fighting.

He glanced behind him at the other two cloaked figures. Both had also dropped their hoods and both were clearly just human. The presence of the two men left him feeling slightly more at ease. The elves smirked at the surprise their features had caused.

"Welcome to Faldor's Keep," the lead elf said. "Before you enter, you must surrender your weapons."

Traven glanced at Studell nervously. He was reluctant to give up his sword. He didn't feel comfortable entering a strange new place surrounded by deadly elves without a sword for protection. The lead elf noticed his hesitation.

"There is no honor in attacking an unarmed opponent," he stated flatly.

Traven could tell his hesitation had offended the elf and decided it would be best to do as the elf had requested. He deftly unbuckled his sword and handed it to the other elf whose hand was outstretched. The elf gave a low whistle as he inspected the magnificent weapon and caressed the might stone embedded in its hilt. Traven knelt and retrieved the dagger from its hiding place inside his boot. The lead elf gave a nod of approval as he also handed the dagger over.

"Please bring the chest and follow me," the lead elf said as he motioned and the portcullis began to lift. "Mill and Jasper will see to your horses."

Traven and Studell followed the two elves as they led the way under the grate. Behind them the two humans took the reins of their horses and slowly followed. The elves led them down the long tunnel-like hallway and into the large courtyard in the center of the keep. The courtyard was surrounded by the tall walls of the keep with numerous windows looking down upon it.

Traven glanced around at the various windows and wondered how many people there were in the keep. He was still in awe of how new it looked and wondered if perhaps this was not the original keep but a newer one that had been built over the ruins of the original. The large courtyard was empty except for a stable at the far end and three large stone pillars in the center that all curved to meet together at the top.

The elves led them across the courtyard to a set of large wooden doors that led into the keep. They stopped in front of them and waited as the doors slowly swung open. From inside the keep an extremely old man dressed in the same brown robes as the others shuffled his way out into the courtyard. He had a tall, white staff that he leaned upon heavily as he came forward to meet them. The lead elf stepped forward and whispered something to the elderly man. When the old man's eyes widened in disbelief, the elf nodded and stepped back.

"That is the box," the old man exclaimed pointing at the chest that Studell was still holding. "You have returned Faldor's chest?"

"Yes," Studell replied.

"Please bring it here," the old man said with excitement.

Studell stepped forward and handed the golden chest to the lead elf. The old man motioned, and the lead elf opened the ornately carved chest and held it forward for the old man to look inside. He quickly studied its contents and returned his gaze to Studell.

"Excuse my lack of manners," he said. "It has been so long since we have had any visitors." He then pushed himself up and stood a little straighter. "My name is Eldridge, and I am the keeper of Faldor's Keep and the secrets it contains. Are you the one who unlocked the chest?"

"Oh my no," Studell replied with a chuckle. He turned and pointed to Traven. "Traven is the one who unlocked the chest." Eldridge quickly turned his focus to Traven and looked him over appraisingly.

"So young," he muttered in awe. "I had expected him to be older," he said to the lead elf. "No matter," he said as he shrugged. "If you unlocked Faldor's chest, you are the one!" The keeper turned back to the elves and told them to show the guests to their proper chambers where they could wash up before dinner. "After dinner I will be ready for the ceremony," he announced to all of them. Having made the announcement, Eldridge smiled and shuffled back into the keep.

What did the elderly man mean about being ready for a ceremony? What would be taking place tonight? The lead elf gave Traven a long and calculating look, interrupting his thoughts. He then called to the two men who were taking care of their horses to bring their bags.

"My name is Darian," the lead elf stated tersely. "Follow me."

Traven and Studell hurried to follow as Darian swept into the keep. The two other men followed closely with their bags. The other elf slipped away as they followed Darian up the large stairs that rose from inside the entryway of the keep. At the top of the stairs Darian turned left and led them down a hall. The walls of the hall were covered in bright tapestries. They depicted scenes of wielders of old doing amazing things with the ambience. The tapestries' colors were so bright and vibrant that the scenes seemed to leap off the fabric. Traven stared at them with wonder. Half way down the hall Darian stopped and opened a door. It led into a modest sized room with a large bed, wardrobe, sitting chair, and washbasin.

"The guest chamber," the elf announced. He turned to Studell. "This will be your accommodations while you remain at the keep."

"Perfect, perfect," Studell declared as he walked into the room and looked around.

Having shown the philosopher his room, Darian beckoned Traven to continue following him down the hall. Traven glanced back to see Studell's belongings being carried into his room. He expected Darian to stop at the next door, but the elf walked right past it. They passed another door and then another. Traven followed, walking past all of them with confusion. He wondered where the elf was leading him.

When they finally reached the end of the hall, Darian stopped in front of a large door. He turned and gave Traven another long, calculating look. The elf finally gave his head the slightest of shakes and opened the door.

"The master wielder's residence," he announced. "This is where you will be staying while you remain at the keep."

Traven's mouth fell open as he stepped into the room. It was enormous! There was a large antechamber that was bigger than his grandparents' entire home. It contained furniture as fancy as any that he had seen in the royal palace. At the far end a pair of doors was open to reveal a large bedroom with a giant bed. His bags were carried through the antechamber and deposited on the bed. As he continued looking around the room, Traven noticed another door that led from the antechamber to somewhere else.

"Someone will be up in about an hour to lead you to the dining hall," Darian said curtly. He then paused for a moment before continuing. "No one has stayed in this room since Faldor himself. You will respect this chamber and all of its contents."

The elf then closed the door and left him alone in the room. Traven stared at the closed door. It was obvious that Darian wasn't exactly happy that he would be staying in this suite, and the elf's last statement had been a threat to be careful with the contents of the room or face consequences. Traven could also tell that the elf had something against him but didn't understand why. He had just met the elf and hadn't done anything to warrant the dislike.

Traven shrugged it off and turned from the door to stare at the room once again. Why had they put him in the master wielder's suite? What were they expecting from him? He was just a guest like Studell. As he looked around the room at all of the fine furnishings, he knew he would have felt more comfortable in a small, simple room next to the philosopher. He walked across the antechamber and into the bedroom. He was happy to see that his sword and dagger had been deposited on the giant bed with the rest of his belongings.

He plopped down on the foot of the bed and looked around the room. There was an enormous wardrobe intricately carved with battle scenes, a large desk and chair, and a door. He got off of the bed and opened it. It led to a large balcony that overlooked the courtyard. He closed the door and returned to the bed. He was excited to explore his new surroundings but also tired from the long journey. He laid back and rested for awhile. The bed felt so soft and the thought of sleeping on a comfortable mattress after sleeping on the ground for the past week was almost more than he could resist. However, he forced himself to stand up.

He wasn't sure what Eldridge had meant by saying that there would be a ceremony at dinner, but Traven wanted to look presentable for whoever would be there. He had already made a bad impression on Darian and didn't want to make a bad impression on anyone else. He changed out of the dusty robe that he had worn on his journey through the desert and put on a set of his new black, silver embroidered clothes. He looked at himself in the large mirror that hung in the room. He tried to smooth out the wrinkles in his shirt as best he could but could only do so much for a garment that had been packed away for the last week.

He then slipped his dagger back into his boot and debated whether or not to strap on his belt and sword. They had returned it to him, but he didn't want to risk offending anyone. He decided it would be best to put it inside the wardrobe with the rest of his belongings. Looking in the mirror once again, he determined that he was as presentable as he was going to get and left the bedchamber to get a better look at the front room.

He soon discovered that the antechamber also had a large balcony that overlooked the courtyard below. He was about to go out on it, but his eyes were drawn to the small plain door on the opposite side of the room. He walked over to it, wondering what it led to. He pulled the door open and was met with a burnt and musty smell.

Directly behind the door, stairs spiraled upwards to a higher level. His room must have been right under the northwest tower of the keep. He looked up the stairs wondering what he would find in the tower. He started forward but stopped when he heard a knock at his door. He quickly shut the door that led up into the tower and made his way over to the door that led to the hall. He opened it and found the man who had helped him with his baggage.

"Dinner is ready, Master Wielder," he said politely. "Please follow me."

Traven stepped out into the hall, closed the door, and followed the man. In his head, he mused over how the man had addressed him. Did they really think he was a 'master' wielder? They hadn't even seen him do any magic yet. In fact, he wasn't sure how they even knew he was a wielder at all other than he had been the one to open the chest. While he was a wielder, he was definitely not a master of anything but the sword. He suddenly felt very foolish for allowing them to put him up in the master wielder's chamber.

For some reason they thought he was something that he wasn't, and without realizing what he was doing, he had gone along with it. He began to dread what would soon take place in the dining hall. Most likely everyone in the entire keep would show up at dinner to see a master wielder. He would then have to confess before all of them that he was nothing more than a simple soldier who could light candles with the ambience.

He continued following, feeling slightly sick to his stomach, as the man led him back down the stairs and to a large set of doors that no doubt led into the dining hall. Traven took a deep breath as the man pushed open the doors. The dining hall was huge, but to his surprise, he found that it was also completely empty but for one person.

The old man, Eldridge, sat on the far end of the hall at the center of a long table. The table was positioned so that all those seated behind it could look out over the entire dining hall. The old man smiled as Traven was led past the empty tables and to the very front of the hall. He nodded a welcome as Traven was led to the chair at his right. Traven sat down next to Eldridge and surveyed the large hall. It looked like it could easily seat several hundred people. He sat nervously, wondering when the others would be arriving. He recognized that his seat would effectively be putting him on display for all those who came to dine.

He watched uncomfortably as Studell was led through the doors and to a chair near the head of the table that sat perpendicularly in front of him. At least the philosopher would be nearby. The philosopher smiled excitedly at Traven and sat down. Next walked in three robed elves and one robed man. All four sat down next to the two men who had brought Studell and him into the dining hall. Traven saw Darian but not the other elf from earlier. He also noticed the two new elves and the new human casting quick and calculating glances at him. Then another elf and human slipped into the hall and sat down just inside the doors.

Eldridge smiled and carefully stood up, using the table for support.

"Thank you all for being here and preparing everything on such short notice," he announced. "It has been a very long time since a Master Wielder graced the halls of Faldor's Keep. We are here to celebrate this momentous occasion. Let the feast begin!"

The elf and human by the doors got up quickly and left the dining hall. They returned almost immediately, carrying trays of soup and bread. Traven looked around the large room confused. Where was everyone else? The elf and human with the food first served the keeper, Traven, and Studell. They then sat down with the other robed men and began to eat dinner.

Traven ate his dinner in silent confusion. The warm soup and bread tasted delicious after the dried food the philosopher and he had been eating, but it was hardly a feast. It also almost seemed ridiculous to be using such a large dining hall for only eleven people. The entire group in attendance consisted only of the keeper, Traven, Studell, four elves, and four humans. He realized that he hadn't really seen anyone else since arriving, not in the halls or in the courtyard. It was hard to believe that such a large keep was only home to five men and four elves.

When everyone had finished their soup and bread, the elf and human who had served them got up and cleared away the empty bowls. They returned a few minutes later with plates of roasted chicken. It was as good as the soup and the bread had been but definitely not gourmet.

There was a sense of nervousness and tension in the air that also didn't make it feel like a celebratory feast. The meal was eaten in silence except for the snatches of whispers that Traven's ears picked up. He overheard the robed men saying things like ". . . don't know . . . do you really think . . . all these years . . . fraud if you . . . so young . . ." He tried not to think too much about the snatches he heard. He was grateful when the meal was finished and all of the platters had been cleared away.

As much as he was not looking forward to confessing that he wasn't a master wielder, he hoped that he would have the opportunity to find out what was going on. He had just eaten a meal in a keep that should only be a bunch of ruins. On top of that there were elves, creatures that shouldn't even exist, staring at him. He kept wondering to himself if it was somehow a dream. He had had plenty of dreams in the past year that were very lifelike. He was pulled from his thoughts as Eldridge stood up and addressed the small group.

"Tonight is a momentous night," he began. "Our long wait and the even longer wait of those before us have not been in vain. Once again a master wielder roams the halls of Faldor's Keep!" Traven shifted in his chair uncomfortably as the keeper continued. "The years of solitude, preparation, and caretaking all now have meaning. The vision of Faldor has proven to be correct. Our sacrifices have been justified!"

Traven watched the excitement on the faces of the four humans and one of the elves. The other three elves just kept looking back and forth skeptically between Eldridge and him. The keeper turned to Traven and laid a hand on his shoulder.

"The keep is yours, and we are at your disposal," he stated. "I offer all of my knowledge and the guardians of the keep offer their protection and service."

Traven sat quietly, trying to process what Eldridge had just said. Was the elderly man serious? It must be some kind of mistake.

"Just a moment," Darian said as he rose from his table. "We have sworn to take care of and protect the keep, but as for serving this human boy, to that I have not agreed."

"Faldor's vision clearly stated that the heir of the keep would return the chest and be a master wielder," one of the humans interjected. "Now I know he appears young, but that is hardly a reason-"

"Quiet, quiet," Eldridge said softly, effectively cutting the man off. The two stopped obediently and waited to hear what the keeper had to say.

"Master Wielder," he began while smiling at Traven, "please stand and give us an example of your power. We have waited long to see someone actually wield the ambience. Perhaps if you indulge us with a demonstration, those of us who are slow to believe will be placated."

Traven stood up slowly, wondering what he should do. He thought of telling them that he wasn't really a master wielder, but the keeper had expressed so much confidence in him and looked so eager. He didn't know how to let those who believed in him down, so he decided to do the only thing that he really knew how to.

He stuck out his hand in front of him and concentrated. Everything grew quiet around him. The air began to thicken and swirl. He carefully visualized a small flame above the palm of his outstretched hand. He wrapped the air around the flame and pulled it into reality.

There were several gasps as the flame winked into existence. Traven looked around and found the keeper and many of the guardians with large smiles. Several, however, including Darian, looked less than impressed. For some reason Darian's disapproval upset him the most. Did the elf think he could do any better?

Traven focused on the small flame with increased determination, and it slowly began to grow in size. As it grew bigger, he realized that he could somewhat control its shape. He wrapped the flickering flame into a ball and felt it become hotter and hotter. It continued to grow larger, a roiling ball of flame until it was bigger than his head. Darkness began to edge in on his vision, but he resisted and willed the ball of intense heat to continue to grow. In the distance he could feel his legs weakening and a burning sensation on his palm.

His reflexes suddenly took over, and he jerked his hand back. He immediately began to collapse, all of his strength gone. Just before blacking out, he watched as the large ball of flame fell right through the table and splashed onto the stone floor beneath it.

12

Traven woke the next morning in an incredibly soft and comfortable bed. The light coming through the windows of the room agitated his headache, so he kept his eyes closed and enjoyed the comfort of the large bed. He knew he was in the master wielder's suite but couldn't remember how he had gotten there.

As he lay in the bed relaxing, his memory of the previous night returned. He must have looked like a fool, passing out while giving a demonstration of his power. He supposed Darian had been proven correct. He definitely was not a master wielder. However, even if he was weak in the ambience, at least he could wield some of it.

They had left him in the master wielder's suite after his performance, and he hoped that was a good sign. He finally propped himself up on his elbows and sat up, deciding to brave the light. The bedroom doors were wide open, and he could see Studell sitting and reading a book in the antechamber. Traven got out of bed and changed into some fresh clothes. He then left his bedroom and walked into the antechamber. This room was even brighter than his bedroom had been, and he had to squint against the light.

He rubbed his temples and slowly made his way over to the chair that Studell was sitting in. The philosopher was so engrossed in whatever it was he was reading that he didn't notice Traven standing at his side. Traven cleared his throat, and Studell jumped in surprise with a gasp.

"Why'd you sneak up on me like that?" he exclaimed. "You could have given me a . . ." he trailed off as his breathing began to slow down. After a few deep breaths he said, "Oh well. It doesn't matter. I'm fine now." He then broke out in the biggest grin that Traven had ever seen. "You won't believe the size of the library here! The books contain so much information that has been lost to the rest of the world. It's amazing!"

Traven couldn't help but smile at the philosopher's excitement. The man glowed with the joy of finding new knowledge and had a far off look in his eyes as he was no doubt reliving in his mind his visit to the keep's library. He looked so happy that Traven hesitated before interrupting him. However, he really wanted to know what had occurred the previous night.

"What happened last night after I passed out?" he asked.

"Last night?" Studell asked with confusion as he was pulled from his thoughts. "Oh yes, last night. That was quite the display you put on. I didn't know that you could even do that. Anyway, those elves with the skeptical faces sure changed their minds once your flame began to spin and turn into whatever that thing was you made. Even that Darian's eyes got wide." Studell paused and smiled at the memory.

"Then what?" Traven asked, urging Studell to continue.

"Well, then you had to go and pass out. That surprised everyone and caused a lot of discussion among the guardians. Eldridge had one of them carry you up to this room. I followed along, and the keeper asked me how long you had been wielding the ambience. When I told him for only a few weeks he looked very surprised. After we left you in your bed, Eldridge was nice enough to show me to the library."

Traven stood in silence. At least his display of the ambience had impressed them. However, he wasn't sure if it was worth the headache that he had woken up with. He looked down and interrupted Studell as the philosopher began to read again.

"Why did you hand them the chest yesterday?" he asked. "How did you know it was from the keep?"

"That's what the map said," Studell said without looking up.

"You didn't say anything about that before," Traven stated.

"I know," Studell said as he set the book back down. "The map said that whoever opened the chest was to return it to Faldor's Keep. I assumed there wasn't a keep left standing to return it to, so I didn't mention it." Traven wished the philosopher would have shared everything with him from the beginning. He wondered if there was anything else Studell was holding back.

"Did the map say anything else?" he asked.

"No," the philosopher replied. "If you want to know anything else, I suggest you ask the keeper. He said he would be up to your room this morning to talk to you."

As if Studell's words had been a signal, a knock came at the door. The door opened to reveal the bent over form of the keeper.

"Ah, you're both here. I'm glad to see you up and looking so well," he said to Traven. Eldridge pulled some bread and cheese from under his robe and handed them to Traven. "I assumed you would be hungry since you didn't make it down for breakfast."

Traven gratefully accepted the food and began to devour it as Eldridge took a seat next to Studell. Traven sat down in one of the chairs that faced them.

"I guess it's true," Eldridge said as he chuckled. "The use of the ambience takes a lot of physical strength and leaves the wielder hungry."

Traven looked down at his hands in embarrassment. Had he really eaten all of the bread and cheese that fast?

"Oh don't worry, my boy," the elderly man continued. "It is fascinating for me to see the things that I have studied all these years come to life right before my eyes." He then paused for a moment with a thoughtful expression. "As for you not being a master wielder . . ."

"I'm really sorry that I didn't say anything about it right away," Traven said. "I should have let you know from the beginning that I wasn't anything special."

"Nothing special? Nonsense," Eldridge stated firmly. "You may not be a master wielder yet, but you will most certainly become one."

Traven didn't necessarily believe the keeper, but he was glad that the elderly man wasn't upset.

"You see," Eldridge began, "I interpreted the language of Faldor's vision incorrectly. Faldor stated that the wielder who was to be led to the keep would 'be' a master wielder. I thought it meant that you would already be a master wielder when you arrived, but now I see it meant that you would be a master wielder in the future." Eldridge paused and broke out in a large grin. "It actually makes a lot more sense now, why Faldor did what he did."

Traven was trying to take in everything the keeper was saying but was having trouble following the elderly man's ramblings. He jumped from thought to thought like Studell often did without fully explaining anything. He had heard Faldor's vision referred to the previous night and now it was being referred to again. How could Faldor have known the future? Who was he and what had he done?

"I can see that you have questions," the keeper said while studying Traven's eyes. "I will try to start from the beginning. Hopefully what is happening will then make more sense."

Traven settled down in his chair and got comfortable. He could tell it would be a long story. He listened intently as the elderly keeper unfolded the story of Faldor.

"Faldor was a master wielder that lived nearly a thousand years ago. He was not only a master wielder but also one of the most powerful and certainly one of the wisest and most accomplished of the wielders of old. When the Wielder Wars began, Faldor became very worried.

"A large group of powerful wielders had joined together and were intent on subjecting all of the lands to their rule. Each one would have the kingdom of his choice to rule when they were finished. In the past there had been plenty of wielders who had tried to take power by force but never before had such a large coalition of powerful wielders joined together.

"As the war began, Faldor chose to remain neutral. He refused to join the coalition of power hungry wielders but also refused to join with the wielders who were trying to protect the freedoms of the individual kingdoms. He watched it all from a distance, hoping the conflict would end quickly. However, it soon became apparent that the war would continue to grow worse. There was warring between the different factions, warring within the factions, and constant betrayal and switching of factions.

"The war continued as whole cities and whole armies were destroyed. Slowly, many wielders also began to be killed as the more powerful ones destroyed those who were weaker in the ambience. Faldor recognized that many of the advances and much of the knowledge of the ambience were also being destroyed. Each time a wielder was killed in battle or by assassination, more knowledge died with him.

"Faldor realized that he had to do something more than just watch these events from a distance. He decided to leave his keep and gather as many wielders as he could in an effort to preserve the current knowledge and secrets of the ambience. He had visions of a world without wielders in the near future and worried that all knowledge of the ambience would be lost. He slowly was able to convince a number of wielders to return with him to his keep.

"These wielders wrote down their knowledge of the ambience, preserving the secrets of the disciplines of the ambience that they had mastered. The wielders also experimented together, discovering even more of what the ambience was capable of. It was a great time of learning and archiving the grand knowledge of the ambience.

"Unfortunately, despite the renaissance occurring within Faldor's Keep, outside things had continued to get worse. Three of the most powerful dark wielders formed an alliance and succeeded in destroying all of the other wielders in the land. In their wake they left many destroyed cities and hundreds of thousands dead. Seeing the great destruction, even the elves who had loyally followed the three dark wielders became disillusioned and hid from the world of men.

"The three dark wielders now had complete control of all that was left in the lands except for one place, Faldor's Keep. Knowing that there was a group of wielders there together and afraid of what they could do, the three dark wielders gathered together a large human army and began their march for Faldor's Keep.

"The wielders of what had become known as Faldor's council were worried that all they had accomplished in the past few years would be destroyed. Many of them were well advanced in years, and they knew they would be no match for the three dark wielders in their prime with their large army. The council turned to Faldor for guidance. Although he was younger than most of them, he was also powerful, wise, and had been the one to gather them all together.

"As Faldor contemplated on what they could do, he began to have visions of ten stones. At first he had no idea what the visions meant. However, slowly he pieced together the importance of what he was seeing. Several of the wielders had been attempting to create with the ambience objects that would not only last forever but that would also be imbued with magical powers. They had not been able to create anything with magical properties yet, but theorized that it would be possible if a wielder's life force was intertwined with the object.

"They knew that some of the dark wielder's had created monstrous beasts by wrapping the elements around live souls. Some of the council believed that a similar thing could be done to imbue inanimate objects with magical properties. No one had been eager to test this theory as it would mean giving up their life. However,

Faldor's visions led him to believe that creating these magic stones was incredibly important.

"Faldor worked hard to convince the other wielders of the importance of creating the stones. With the impending invasion of the dark wielders and their army, the council and all of their hard work would be destroyed. None of the wielders wanted to die, but they were slowly convinced by Faldor that if death was imminent, it was better to choose the time and place and in so doing preserve their legacy. Wouldn't it be better to sacrifice their lives creating something incredibly special that would last forever, than to be murdered by an attacking army? At first only a few wielders were willing to try, but eventually the others were convinced that creating the stones was the best course to follow.

"The next step was to actually test the theory. One of the younger wielders who was far from the strongest but one of the sharpest in intellect volunteered to do it. He spent the next few days preparing for the important task. When he was ready, all of the council gathered in the great hall to witness his sacrifice and learn if their plan would work. They all looked on as he slowly created a small blue stone with the ambience. When it was completely formed but not quite solidified, he took a deep breath, and closing his eyes, let his life force be swept from his body and into the stone.

"The blue stone lit up a brilliant, glowing amber before it faded back to blue and the master wielder fell to the ground lifeless. The other wielders watched in amazement. They paid their respects to the wielder for his sacrifice and then carefully approached the stone. As they approached it, it turned back to amber and began to glow slightly when they drew closer. Faldor picked it up and felt the heat emanating from it. It was no ordinary stone. The experiment had worked. The stone contained magic of its own!

"The council called the stone a might stone and studied its properties. Upon learning the power that it held and understanding how important the stones could be in protecting the keep from the advancing army, the rest of the council decided to make the ultimate sacrifice. However, one of them would have to stay behind to use the stones and safeguard the keep.

"They chose Faldor, he being the youngest of them and the wisest. Faldor's apprentice was also chosen to stay behind and support him in defending the keep. The next day the remaining nine wielders gathered in a large circle in the great hall and created the other nine might stones, giving up their lives.

"Faldor and his apprentice gathered the might stones and studied their magical properties. Several turned out to not be of any use in protecting the keep, but several others proved to be invaluable. With the help of the might stones, Faldor and his apprentice were able to protect the keep against the invasion and even kill the three dark wielders. With their leaders dead, the army returned to their lands, leaving Faldor's Keep, with its treasures of knowledge, untouched.

"Faldor and his apprentice were left as the only known wielders in all the land. Faldor knew that although they would have longer life spans than most, they would not live forever. Knowing of the importance of having the keep protected after he died, he devised a plan to preserve it. His visions foretold of a time in the far distant future when a wielder would return to the keep. He felt that it was essential that the keep be preserved until then.

"Faldor wanted to enlist the help of both humans and elves in protecting the keep. To accomplish this, he fashioned special gifts using two of the might stones. First he crafted a beautiful sword using the ambience. In its hilt he set the 'loyalty stone'. This stone would return to a wielder who called it. In the hands of a regular person, the stone would allow the sword to mold to his grasp and become almost an extension of him. Faldor then made an armband with the ambience. He set in it the 'stone of endurance'. The endurance stone had allowed Faldor to continue wielding the ambience against the keep's attackers long past the point where his normal strength would have given out. On the arm of a non-wielder, it would give the wearer greater strength, endurance, and longevity.

"With these two special gifts, Faldor left the keep in his quest to enlist the help of both humans and elves. He first traveled to a small, remote village at the base of the Parched Mountains. He met with the village council and formed an agreement. The village would send four men to be guardians of the keep. For their service, Faldor gave the village the 'loyalty sword' that he had crafted.

"He then left the village and journeyed to the base of Mount Morian. There he sought out the king of the elves. The king was very reluctant to continue any dealings with the humans after the great loss of his people in the Wielder Wars. However, he could not deny that Faldor's cause was a noble one. He committed to send four elves to the keep to be guardians and accepted the 'armband of endurance' as a token of their agreement.

"Faldor returned to the keep, passing the village along the way and bringing the four chosen young men with him. They would spend their time training and studying. After they had served as guardians of the keep for twenty years, they would return to their village and four other men would journey to the keep to take their place. In ten years, four elves would arrive at Faldor's Keep and follow the same type of twenty year cycle as the four humans. Thus, there would always be eight guardians, four of which would have at least ten years of experience in protecting and maintaining the keep.

"The first four guardians trained extensively in all manner of arms. They also spent time every day learning with Faldor as he studied. When the first four elves came to join their fellow guardians ten years later, the human guardians had become skilled warriors and disciplined in the mind. The elves soon acclimatized to the routine of the guardians of the keep. Faldor's wish of having eight guardians to safeguard the keep was realized.

"Faldor also devised another way to protect the keep and the writings that it housed. He chose three might stones that he felt would be of the most worth to the keep and to those who remained within its grounds. In the center of the keep's courtyard he built three stone pillars and melded them together at the top. Towards the top of each pillar he embedded one of the might stones. The first would give longer life to all within its range. The second would cast a cloak of invisibility over the keep and its inhabitants keeping them safe from unfriendly eyes. The third would amplify the effects of the other two.

"Once his monument was completed, Faldor left the keep in the hands of his apprentice and the eight guardians. He ventured back into the outside world in search of a human who was devoted to learning and could take care of the keep's library. He found someone worthy and returned with the keep's first 'keeper'.

"However, to Faldor's dismay, his apprentice had left the keep, taking six of the might stones with him. Two of the guardians had discovered Faldor's apprentice at the top of the monument prying out a might stone. When they confronted him, he had killed them. By the time the other guardians discovered the foul deed, it was too late. The apprentice had fled the keep with Faldor's golden chest and six might stones. Only the two remaining stones in the monument were left.

"The betrayal angered and hurt Faldor deeply. The remaining guardians wanted to go after the betrayer, but Faldor knew that his apprentice would be too powerful with the six stones in his possession. He convinced the guardians that it would be best to stay and protect the library of the keep. That was the true treasure they had been enlisted to guard. Faldor spent the next twenty years teaching and training the keeper.

"He then prepared himself to make one last journey. Before he left, he let the keeper and guardians know that he had a vision that made it clear to him a wielder would someday come to the keep and return the golden chest. When this happened, the keep would serve its purpose of expanding the knowledge of the ambience in the land once again. Faldor then left his keep, never to be seen or heard from again."

Traven and Studell sat in silence as the keeper finished his tale of the great wielder Faldor. Traven didn't know how to respond. The story had answered many of his questions but left many more unanswered. In fact, the tale had created numerous new questions in his mind that he hadn't even contemplated before. Eldridge smiled at the two of them.

"So here I am today, the eighth keeper of Faldor's Keep," he stated.

"The eighth?" Studell exclaimed in surprise. "But you said the first keeper was here nearly a thousand years ago."

It took a second for Traven to realize why Studell was so surprised. Then it dawned on him. If Eldridge was only the eighth keeper that would mean that each keeper had been at the keep for over a hundred years! People didn't live that long. The oldest person he had ever heard of was in his eighties. Often people would live into their late sixties and early seventies. Some lived to their early eighties but to live beyond that was unheard of.

"You heard me correctly," Eldridge said with an even bigger smile. "I am one hundred and forty years old."

Traven and Studell cast unbelieving glances at one another. Was that even possible?

"You have no doubt heard that the wielders had longer life spans than regular humans," the keeper continued. "Some of the greatest wielders lived to be almost two hundred years old. When Faldor created the monument in the courtyard and embedded the 'longevity stone' in it, it created a time womb around the entire keep. Those of us who live within its reach somehow only age one year for every two that pass by. I was brought to the keep when I was thirty years old. Since then one hundred and ten years have passed by, and I have only aged to the ripe age of eighty-five. Unfortunately, I don't believe I will live much longer."

Traven just stared at the ancient man in silence. It was difficult to imagine that someone could live so long.

"I think it is well past the time for me to find my successor," Eldridge muttered. He then turned a penetrating look directly at Traven. "I feel incredibly blessed to be the keeper to see Faldor's vision fulfilled."

The keeper's intense gaze made Traven feel uncomfortable. He still didn't understand what was expected of him. Eldridge thought he was this master wielder that Faldor had seen in a vision a thousand years ago. While he was a wielder, he was definitely not a master wielder. In fact, it seemed as though he could hardly wield the ambience at all without passing out.

"I'm sorry," Traven replied while shaking his head. "I wish that I was this master wielder that Faldor said would come to the keep, but I'm not. I don't think I'll ever be a master wielder. I can't do much more than create a flame without blacking out."

"Nonsense boy, nonsense," the ancient keeper said. "You don't have a clue as to what you are talking about. Professor Studell told me last night that you haven't even been wielding the ambience for more than a few weeks. Do you realize what you created in the great hall last night?"

Traven just stared back at the keeper. He had passed out in the great hall the night before. That was what he had done.

"You created a ball of liquid fire!" Eldridge seemed incredibly excited about that fact, though Traven didn't know why. "Only very powerful wielders could create something with substance and hold it for as long as you did. And even those powerful wielders wouldn't have been able to do what you did without months of training first. Sure, you did pass out, but first you created something incredible."

Traven wondered if it was true. Did he really have the ability to become a master wielder? If what he had created the night before was as difficult to create as Eldridge had suggested, perhaps there was hope for him. However, it was always hard for him to do anything more than create a flame. When he created other things, he was always left exhausted or would pass out.

"Why do I keep passing out?" Traven asked.

"The ambience draws upon the strength of the wielder. Wielding the ambience is in a sense like using a muscle. You have to exercise a muscle in order for it to grow stronger. The more you wield, the stronger your ability to wield the ambience will become. For now, it will be best for you to practice on things that are not too demanding."

"That's the problem," Traven responded, slightly frustrated. "I don't know what I'm doing. I don't know what's supposed to be easy and what's supposed to be hard." Eldridge let out a chuckle.

"That's why you are here Traven. While you could probably learn best from a fellow wielder as his apprentice, I am the next best teacher. For over a hundred years I have been studying the books in the keep's library that explain what the ambience is, how to control it, and what can be done with it. I know all of the theories and specifics of how the ambience is supposed to work. I will train and guide you." He paused and looked into Traven's eyes, very directly once again. "I will guide you, giving you the knowledge I have been entrusted with. This keep and the sacrifices of the council that once resided here will fulfill their purposes. You will become a master wielder!"

All three sat in silence once again as Eldridge finished speaking. Traven still had his doubts, but now there was also a growing sense of excitement welling up inside. He would soon be able to understand the power that resided within him. He would learn to control a magic that most people didn't even believe existed. He would learn to wield and control the ambience.

13

"When would you like to begin your training?" Eldridge asked.

"Why not right now?" Traven responded eagerly. The keeper began laughing.

"How about after lunch?" the elderly man said. "Meet me in the great hall at midday. After we have eaten, your training can begin. For now, I think it best that we rest."

Traven stood up to show that he was strong enough to start immediately. He kept a straight face, refusing to cringe at the pounding in his head.

"I'm fine," he said. "We can start right now."

"I wasn't as worried about you as I was about myself," the keeper replied with a small smile. "I'm a fairly old man. After telling such a story I need a rest." Traven's face reddened as he helped the ancient keeper to his feet.

"Midday it is," he said with an apologetic smile.

He followed Eldridge to the door as the keeper shuffled out of the room. He then closed the door and slumped back down in a chair with his eyes closed. He hoped the headache would go away soon. He wondered if Eldridge might know how to take care of the headaches. That was one of the first things he should ask about when they started to train. For now, he would do as the keeper had suggested and rest.

"It's all just so fascinating!" Studell exclaimed, startling Traven. "It really is all true. I knew it. I always knew it! We are so lucky to have found Faldor's Keep. Do you have any idea how much lost knowledge there is in the library here?"

Traven smiled and opened an eye. It was obvious that the excited philosopher was eager to get back to the library and look through the books there.

"There's no need for you to wait here with me," Traven told him. "Go ahead and go to the library."

"Oh that sounds like a great idea," Studell said as he hopped up and headed to the door. "I'll see you later."

Traven smiled to himself as the door shut. It appeared that Studell's dreams had come true. He had found a treasure trove of knowledge. He had found the treasure he had been looking for. Traven was happy for the philosopher.

He closed his eyes again and leaned back in his chair, pondering his situation. He was excited to learn how to use the ambience but still confused and nervous about what the future held for him. A year ago he had been nothing but a simple woodcutter living with his grandparents in a tiny village at the edge of Kalia. He had been nothing special, just a commoner trying to earn a living. Over the last year he had traveled across Kalia, fought bandits, become an excellent swordsman, had brief stints in a merchant academy and the army, rescued a princess, and found out that he was a wielder. Just recalling all that had happened in the past year caused his head to swim.

Who was he really? He still often thought of himself as a young, simple woodcutter experiencing the world outside his village for the first time. For awhile he had thought of himself as a student and most recently as a soldier. Now he wasn't sure what to think. He had found out that he was a wielder only a couple of weeks ago. Now he was being told that he would become a master wielder. He wasn't certain if that would happen or not, but what if it really did?

He supposed now he would begin training in the ambience and learn what he was truly capable of. It appeared that he wouldn't be returning to Calyn on the Arrow or joining back up with the Royal Army any time soon. Instead of standing on the beach waiting to be picked up in a week, he would be learning an all but extinct form of power.

So who was he now and what would he become? What would be expected of him as a wielder? He wondered if he would end up spending years studying in the keep, mastering different aspects of the ambience. He could make Faldor's Keep his new home. Eldridge had said that he was the heir to the keep. Did that really mean it was now his? He dismissed the thought. It was no more his than it was the keeper's or the guardians'. It was merely a place to house those guarding the secrets of the ambience and those learning the secrets.

How long would he be a guest here? He could technically spend the rest of his life within its walls growing in knowledge. However, he knew that wouldn't happen. He would learn to control his newfound power and then leave when the time was right. How long that would be, he didn't know. But he was sure of one thing. When he did leave the keep he wouldn't be leaving it as a commoner or a simple soldier. He would be leaving it as a wielder of the ambience.

He shifted in the chair and tried to get comfortable. He also tried to clear his racing mind. His headache had not gotten any better, and he wanted to rest before he began his training. He hoped sleep would relieve most of the pain. He thought of getting up and lying down on his bed, but before he made the effort to do it, he was fast asleep in the armchair.

Traven woke up several hours later without a headache but feeling famished. He looked outside and saw that it was just past midday. He hurriedly straightened himself up and made his way down to the great hall. He looked through the large open doors and saw Eldridge sitting towards the front, already eating. He hurried across the hall to join him but paused when he saw the table behind the keeper. There was a huge hole in the middle of it and an indentation in the solid stone floor underneath. He flushed with embarrassment at the vague memory of his ball of liquid fire dropping through the table and crashing to the ground just as he had passed out.

"No more liquid fire in the keep," Eldridge announced with a large smile, seeing what Traven was staring at. "If you want to practice that, you better do it outside."

Traven was relieved to see that the keeper wasn't upset about it. He would need to remember to be more careful no matter what situation he found himself in.

"Hurry up boy," Eldridge said. "Your food is getting cold."

Traven quickly sat down next to the keeper and began eating the lukewarm soup and the large hunk of bread that were waiting for him. Eldridge finished his meal before Traven, having already eaten most of it before he had arrived.

"I've been thinking about where to start," Eldridge said while Traven continued eating. "I should probably start with an explanation of what the ambience is. What do you know of it?"

"Not much," Traven replied between mouthfuls. "All I really know is that it's magic. I've heard some stories of how powerful it can be, but that's about it."

"Fascinating!"

"What?" Traven asked confusedly.

"You don't really know anything about the power you have, and yet you are able to wield it anyway. Most wielders had to be taught how to use their power by someone who already knew. However, you, like some of the greatest wielders of the past, have taught yourself."

"Not really," Traven answered as he finished up his meal. "I don't really know what I'm doing."

"What you mean is that you don't understand what you are doing," the keeper corrected. "You know what you're doing. I'm fairly certain you meant to create the flame last night and meant for it to grow into a ball of liquid fire. You have incredible instincts. Let me try and help you understand how you do what you do."

The ancient man pushed the bowls aside and turned to face Traven. His excitement to finally be able to share his knowledge was easily recognizable and made him seem younger than he was.

"The power and ability to wield the ambience is something that certain people are born with. The ability is not entirely random. The children of wielders were more likely to possess the ability than children of non-wielders, so there is some type of inheritance to it. However, no one knows for sure who will end up with the power and who will not. The power is not manifest until sometime near adulthood. The dormant power that the wielder was born with unexpectedly bursts to life. The wielder suddenly notices a difference in the world around him. He sees sharper, hears better, and is stronger. All of his senses are enhanced. When this change occurs, it signals that he can now wield the ambience. This change is known as the wielder's awakening.

"When the wielder's awakening occurs, the power to wield the ambience is no longer dormant. The wielder has the 'power' to manipulate the world around him using the ambience. However, the actual 'ability' to wield the ambience needs to be learned. Otherwise, a wielder may never use the special power that he has been born with. If the power is not used, it begins to fade over time until even the wielder's passive abilities of heightened senses and longevity fade to almost nothing.

"However, if the power is used often, it will continue to grow stronger and stronger until the wielder's power eventually peaks. Every wielder peaks at a different level of power in the ambience. Some will have great power when they reach their peak while others may only be able to ever perform the most simple of tasks."

Traven thought back over the last year wondering when his awakening had occurred. Had it been when he saved the Princess? He remembered feeling his senses heightened when he had woken up after the incident in the cave. It was from that moment on that he had started to use the ambience. However, thinking back further, he realized that his senses had been heightened even before the incident in the cave. In fact, he had felt different ever since the day he had left home for the merchant academy, ever since he had suddenly blacked out. Eldridge hadn't mentioned anything about blacking out when the awakening occurred.

"Do wielder's usually black out when the awakening occurs?" he asked.

"No," the keeper replied. "I've never heard of a wielder blacking out when his awakening occurred. It is usually a very exciting experience. The wielder is suddenly filled with energy and vitality, and the world opens up to him like he has never experienced it before. Isn't that how it was for you?"

"Not even close," Traven answered. "I blacked out and fell off my horse." Eldrige gave him a very confused look.

Why had it not been such a great experience for him? Why had he passed out when other wielders hadn't? He did remember feeling different when he woke up and got back on his horse, but he hadn't been filled with energy and wonder. His senses had been heightened, but that was all that had happened except for his father's stone changing from blue to amber.

Thinking of the stone, he was reminded of the keeper's earlier story about the creation of the might stones. The first might stone ever created had been blue. Eldridge had said when the wielders had approached it, it had begun to glow an amber color. It seemed that his father's might stone and the stone from the story were one and the same. What had the stone ever done for him but burn him on multiple occasions? What special magic had the stone had?

"Eldridge," Traven began. "I used to have a might stone that turned from blue to amber the day my awakening occurred. It remained amber for the remainder of the time I had it. I was wondering if it was the first might stone created and what powers it had."

"The stone you are referring to is the 'protection stone'. It is the only might stone that changes from blue to amber. You had it in your possession?" Eldrige asked.

"Yes, I used to wear it on a cord around my neck."

"No wonder you blacked out when you had your awakening," Eldridge chuckled. "It all makes sense now." The keeper shook his head, laughing for a few moments before going on. "The protection stone was one of the most useful stones in defending the keep from the dark wielders. It was found to negate the ambience. Whoever held it could not be touched by the ambience. Of course, it worked in reverse as well. Whoever held the protection stone couldn't wield the ambience either." Eldridge paused to let Traven realize the implications of the stone's power. "When you had your awakening, the stone immediately began blocking you from using your new power. That must have been the reason you blacked out."

At least that explained some of what Traven had experienced after his awakening. He was relieved to know it was the might stone that had caused him to pass out and that there wasn't necessarily anything wrong with him.

"The stone also burned me several times," Traven said. "What would cause it to do that?"

"The protection stone gets hotter and glows brighter as it takes more and more of the ambience into itself. That is how the stone negates the effects of the ambience," the keeper explained. "So my guess would be that the stone could burn the bearer of it if they were trying to use the ambience or perhaps if someone was trying to use the ambience against them." He stopped and thought about something for a moment. "You mentioned that you used to have it. Where is the protection stone now?"

"It was destroyed."

"Impossible," the keeper stated.

"It's true," Traven replied. "I was wearing it around my neck when it exploded. It almost killed me." The keeper sat in stunned silence for several moments before continuing.

"Might stones are indestructible," Eldridge said slowly. "At least that is what the writings say. You are certain that the protection stone was destroyed?"

Traven responded by pulling up his shirt and pointing to the scars that crisscrossed his chest. The keeper's eyes grew wide.

"This is what happened to me when the stone exploded," he explained. "I'm sure the stone was destroyed. How it happened I still don't know. I think maybe it had something to do with me creating a lightning bolt while I was wearing it."

"You were able to wield the ambience while wearing it?" Eldridge exclaimed. "That shouldn't have been possible. Then again, the stone shouldn't have been able to be destroyed either. The stone must have gotten so hot trying to contain the ambience that you were attempting to wield that it burst. This is amazing!" The keeper stared excitedly at Traven as he pulled his shirt back down and tucked it in. "You truly are someone special to already have so much strength in the ambience. I can't wait to see what you will be able to do when you peak!"

It bothered Traven that the keeper kept referring to how great in the ambience he would eventually become. For now, he still couldn't do much without passing out. He had almost died when he created the lightning bolt to save the princess.

"So why do I keep passing out?" he asked.

"I'm sorry," Eldridge said, calming down. "I am getting carried away. A wielder passing out when trying to wield more of the ambience than he is ready for is common. Let me go back and explain what the ambience is.

"To understand the ambience you must also understand the world around you. Everything around us does not just spontaneously occur. There is order to how things are made and how things grow. Everything is made up of smaller and smaller pieces. For example, this keep did not just appear here. It was built from thousands of stones, pieced together to form this structure we now live in.

"It is roughly the same concept with the ambience. You do not just suddenly create something out of nothing. You start with the smallest of pieces and organize them into something larger. Does that make sense?"

"Kind of," Traven replied. "I understand how a building is formed from many smaller pieces. However, I don't remember 'building' the liquid fire I made last night from smaller pieces. I just pictured a flame in my mind and then pictured it growing and spinning."

"When you picture a flame, what happens to the air around it?"

"I guess to me it seems like it is thickening and spinning around where the flame will be," Traven said sheepishly. "I know that sounds a little crazy since the air is nothing, but that's what it seems like to me."

"Oh that's not crazy at all," Eldridge replied. "The air is in fact full of what you need to create things. I will try and describe what all happens when you create a flame using the ambience. Hopefully it will make sense to you as you think back to what happens when you make a flame.

"A wielder has the ability to focus his mind to such an extent that he can focus on a single moment in time. He then has the ability to control what happens in that moment. That is why it may seem to you that time freezes when you wield the ambience. As a wielder focuses on that specific moment in time, the air appears to thicken and move. The reason for this is the wielder is not just focusing on the air but all of the tiny particles in the air. Tiny particles that the human eye can't see swirl around everything constantly as they float through the air. These particles are the smaller pieces that make up everything else in the world. They only need to be brought together in the correct pattern in order to create things."

"That sounds really complicated," Traven interjected. "How would I know how to put all of the particles together in the correct patterns?"

"That's one of the things that makes wielders so special," Eldridge continued. "They cannot only control these physical particles, but they can also control much finer, ethereal particles. They can see beyond our physical realm and into the ethereal one. The wielder, using his mind, forms in this ethereal realm the thing that he wants to create. Once the wielder has sufficiently formed this image, collecting the necessary ethereal particles, the correct physical particles will begin swirling around it, waiting to create physically what the wielder has created in the ethereal realm. When the wielder pulls the object into the physical realm, the particles in the air instantly adhere to it in the correct pattern, and the object is created."

Traven sat back with wonder, contemplating how he had created the flame. It made so much more sense now. He was excited to finally somewhat understand what it was that he was doing when he used the ambience. The keeper's explanation wasn't exactly how it happened when he created a flame, but he didn't think there really was any better way to describe the process.

"Why don't you go ahead and create a small flame," Eldridge said. "Just a small flame mind you, and think about what I just said while you are doing it."

Traven agreed to do it and concentrated on a spot just in front of him. He noticed the world grow still as he focused on the specific moment in time. He also noticed the air begin to thicken right before his eyes and began to pick out the individual tiny particles that could be used to build things. As he studied the air, he began to think that he could even tell slight differences between the particles. Some types were larger than others and some types were much more numerous than others.

He then focused on imagining a small flame. He could clearly see it in his mind's eye, just outside of the physical world. He now knew that he was seeing it in the ethereal realm. He slowly pulled the flame to the barrier between the ethereal world and the physical one and stopped. He watched with fascination as certain types of particles in the air separated and rushed to begin spinning around the exact spot where the flame would be pulled into existence. He carefully slipped the image of the flame through the barrier between realms and into reality. The particles instantly collapsed inward and a small flame leapt to life.

Traven let the flame disappear as the sounds, smells, and feel of the normal world rushed back around him. He turned and found the keeper grinning from ear to ear.

"It's so amazing," Eldridge said. "I know I already said this, but it's so gratifying to finally see the ambience in use after all these years of studying about it."

Traven couldn't help breaking into a large grin as well. He felt even more excited than the keeper. He finally had someone to guide him as he practiced wielding the ambience. He would no longer have to be afraid of using his power. As he learned more about it, it would be easier to control.

"How long did it take me to create the flame?" Traven asked curiously.

"It appeared almost instantly after I asked you to create it."

Traven shook his head in amazement. It was hard to fathom that his mind could move so fast as to notice and think about everything he was doing while creating the flame, all in a single moment. The ambience truly was an amazing thing.

"Now let's try something else," Eldridge suggested. "Try to make a drop of water."

Traven concentrated, the world froze, and the air thickened and swirled. He imagined a small droplet of water and noticed that a different pattern of particles rushed to form the droplet of water as he pulled it into existence. The small droplet hung suspended in midair for a few moments while he stared at it, mesmerized. It then dropped to the table with a tiny splash. Traven shut his eyes, trying to rid himself of the small twinge of a headache that was beginning to appear.

"That sure would have been useful while we were crossing the desert to get here," he said as he opened his eyes.

"I imagine so," the keeper replied with a smile. "Of course it would have been a lot harder to make a droplet of water out in the arid desert than it is to make it here in the valley."

"Why would it be any different?" Traven asked.

"When a wielder forms something using the ambience, it is created physically by the particles swirling around nearby. Out in the arid desert there aren't many water particles in the air. You would have to pull them from quite a distance to create a meaningful amount of water." Eldridge paused to let what he was saying sink in. "You can still do it of course. It just takes more skill and more energy. A wise wielder takes into consideration his surroundings when using the ambience. By creating things that have plentiful amounts of the necessary particles nearby, the wielder is able to conserve his strength and energy."

"Is that why I pass out sometimes?" Traven asked. "Am I using too much of my energy?"

"Correct," Eldridge replied. "A wielder gets headaches and can even lose consciousness when he wields more of the ambience than his body can handle."

"I guess I'm not very strong," Traven muttered. "I almost always end up with a headache."

"You might not be strong now, but I believe you will grow to be quite strong," the keeper stated. "All wielders begin weak in the ambience. The more they use it, the stronger they become. It is through continual practice that wielders are eventually able to reach their full potential."

"So what makes you think I will be so strong in the ambience?"

"The liquid fire you created last night. Many of the less powerful wielders were only able to create something like liquid fire after they had reached their full potential. Seeing that you can already create it, having had so little practice, leads me to believe that your potential is very high. I assume your power will peak as high as some of the greatest wielders did." Eldridge paused, and Traven could see that he was pondering something. "Of course, if I was a wielder myself I would know more easily."

"What do you mean by that?" Traven asked.

"When wielders look at other wielders, they can see a glow around them. Depending on how strong the wielder is and will become, the aura will be brighter. It is not exact by any means, but it does show roughly what the potential peak of a wielder is." Eldridge chuckled. "It's kind of amusing how it works. A wielder cannot see his own aura even if he looks at himself in a mirror. He can only see the auras of other wielders. Therefore, he can't compare himself against others. He can only judge between the strengths of other wielders and has to rely on their judgments as to how strong he will be."

Traven sat in silence for awhile as Eldridge finished. It was a lot of information to take in. It was so different hearing about the ambience from the keeper than it had been hearing about it from Studell and others. Before, it had always just been stories or assumptions. Now it was facts supported by explanations. It made him more eager than ever to practice the ambience and learn more. The hesitation he had felt previously was gone. In its place was excitement and wonder.

"So when can I try more?"

14

Traven spent the next few days learning more of the ambience and practicing wielding it relentlessly. The more he did, the more other possibilities were opened to his mind. He soon fell into a routine that allowed him to learn and advance in the ambience as fast as possible.

He would get up early, exercise, and practice his sword work. He would then practice wielding the ambience, eat breakfast, take a short nap, and practice wielding the ambience again. When lunch time came he would eat ravenously, take another nap, and practice wielding the ambience again until dinner. The only time he rested during the day, other than for his short naps, was during his short sessions with Eldridge when the keeper would explain more of the ambience and offer suggestions about how to do new things.

Traven spent the first week doing simple things over and over again. Eldridge had assured him that this would help him build his strength in the ambience. He continued practicing making fire and water. He also would make wind and occasionally lightning. After a few days, Eldridge explained how to make ice by pulling cold wind around water. Traven had fun making different shapes out of ice. He also mixed water and fire to make bursts of steam.

As the week went on, he practiced making the elements appear near him and far away on the opposite side of the courtyard. He would also create things high overhead. At first, many of the guardians would gather to watch him practice. But they soon grew used to seeing him wield the ambience and returned to their normal routines of practicing with arms and maintaining the keep.

When Traven got bored of the repetition, he would practice moving and manipulating the elements that he had created. At first everything but the ice would disappear almost instantly. However, with more practice and some suggestions from Eldridge, he began to be able to hold his creations together for longer periods of time. The trick had to do with a more precise imagining of the object and a slower and more focused creation of it when pulling it into the physical world.

Eldridge also assigned him to start meditating every day. By doing this, Traven began to hear, see, and more than anything, feel things that he had never consciously noticed before. He began to feel the flow of the particles around him and around other objects at increasingly further distances. By the end of the first week he could sense when anyone entered the courtyard, even if his back was turned to them.

The new awareness of the world around him was exciting and invigorating. He had never felt so alive. He even began to feel what kinds of particles were in the air around him and instinctively knew what would be easiest to create under the given conditions. The week flew by with Traven lost in his new awareness and power.

At the beginning of his second week in the keep, he suddenly realized that he hadn't talked to Studell or anyone else in the keep besides Eldridge for over a week. All he had done for the last week was think of, wield, and dream of the ambience. Each day seemed like years as he learned and grew in the ambience. It had all passed by in a blur, yet looking back, it was hard to even remember all that had occurred when they had first arrived at the keep merely a week before.

He finally managed to pull himself out of the new world that he had been lost in. He decided that he needed to take a small break from his training in the ambience. After practicing his sword forms in the morning, he went looking for Studell. He thought it would be nice to have a chat with him before breakfast. He also wanted to see how the philosopher was doing and what he had been up to all week.

He stopped by Studell's room but found it empty. It was still so early that Traven was surprised to find the philosopher already up. Then an idea struck him, and he headed to the library. Sure enough, he found Studell soundly asleep in an armchair surrounded by a scattering of books. He could tell by the philosopher's disheveled appearance that he hadn't made it to his bedroom the night before. It appeared that Traven was not the only one who had gotten lost in this new world of magic and knowledge.

He walked over to Studell and gently shook him awake. The philosopher slowly opened his eyes and looked around in confusion.

"Where am I?" he asked sleepily.

"In the library," Traven said with a smile.

"Why am I in here? I should be . . ." Studell frowned as he looked around. He then suddenly smiled as his eyes fell upon a certain book. He picked it up and handed it to Traven. "This is the most fascinating book that I have ever laid eyes on!"

"What's it about?" Traven asked, indulging the philosopher.

"Take a look at it," he said eagerly. Traven glanced at it and then handed it back.

"You know I can't read the ancient script."

"Oh yes. Quite right. Sorry." Studell stared at the book in his hands. "This book is the history of Faldor's Keep!"

"Eldridge already told us the history," Traven responded.

"Yes, but he left out so many details. This book contains everything that happened. It mentions the greatest accomplishments of the wielders who had gathered here. Last night I was reading about all of the specific might stones that were created. It was just so interesting that I couldn't put the book down."

"Tell me about them," Traven said. He was very interested in knowing about the stones, especially the ones he had in his possession.

"Well, as you already know, there were ten might stones created. Each stone had some connection to the wielder who created it and imbued it with power. The first stone created was the 'protection stone'. The wielder who gave his life for it had spent his life focusing on ways to use the ambience in defense of others. Of course, that is the stone that you had and destroyed in the cave. The other stones that are currently accounted for are the loyalty stone, the invisibility stone, the longevity stone, the energy stone, and the healing stone.

"The loyalty stone is in the hilt of your sword. The invisibility stone and the longevity stone are still firmly in place in Faldor's monument. The energy stone and the healing stone are the two that we found in Faldor's chest. The other four stones could be anywhere. They are the endurance stone, the deceit stone, and the two seeker stones. I suppose the endurance stone could still be in the possession of the elves, but who knows where the others are."

"I've seen one of the others," Traven stated. "It was black and turned red when in the presence of the ambience. The assassin that kidnapped the princess and me had it."

"One of the seeker stones!" Studell proclaimed. "I guess if the elves really do still have the endurance stone, then there are only two might stones that are unaccounted for. I find that fascinating. After all these years most of the stones are still accounted for."

"I wonder where the other two stones are."

"Who knows?" Studell replied. "I bet Faldor's apprentice sold some of them for money. Valuable objects like the might stones have a way of switching hands many times over the years and traveling to all parts of the world."

Traven wondered once again how one of the might stones had wound up in the possession of his father. Had it been inherited? It seemed like his father would have never had enough money to buy such a precious stone. Perhaps it had been passed down from father to son over the years until it ended up with him. He wondered how long the protection stone had been in his family. Was he the descendent of someone wealthy who had bought the stone, or worse, was he the descendent of Faldor's treacherous apprentice?

"What have you been up to?" Studell asked, interrupting Traven's thoughts. "I haven't talked to you in over a week."

"I've been practicing wielding the ambience every day," Traven replied. "It's been getting easier and easier. I hardly get headaches anymore."

"That's great," Studell replied. "I've been spending all of my time reading books. I could read them all day everyday for the rest of my life and never get through them all."

"I'm glad you're keeping busy," Traven said as his stomach grumbled. "I think it's breakfast time. Would you like to join me?"

Studell thought it sounded like a good idea and pushed himself out of the chair. They left the library and headed to the dining hall. Eldridge was there eating, and after grabbing their food they went and sat next to him.

"Good morning," the ancient keeper greeted them.

"Thank you for suggesting that last book," Studell said in reply. "It was truly fascinating."

"I'm glad you liked it," the keeper replied. "It's fortunate that you know the ancient script and can take advantage of the books here in the keep's library." The keeper then turned to address Traven. "What will you be up to today?"

"I guess I'll just keep practicing," he replied.

"I've been watching you," Eldridge said. "I think you have mastered wielding the simpler spells. I've been surprised by how much your strength in the ambience has already grown. If you would like, I think we can begin working on some more complicated combinations."

* * * * *

Studell watched as Traven followed the ancient keeper out into the courtyard. The young man was definitely learning fast. Whenever the philosopher needed to rest his eyes, he would leave the library and walk to a window where he could look out over the courtyard. Over the past week he had seen Traven repeatedly create flames, water, wind, and even ice. The young man worked as hard as anyone he had ever met. If he continued practicing the ambience with such diligence, Studell had no doubt that he would grow to be a master wielder like those he was reading about.

He turned and headed for the library. It was so exciting to be involved in this new world of magic. He felt privileged to have had a part in guiding Traven to the keep. When he had originally insisted that the two of them follow the map, he had never imagined that they would find more than a few old artifacts or perhaps some scraps of ancient writing.

As he walked back into the library, he stopped and stared once again at the numberless books that lined the walls of the large room. He had seen libraries that were much bigger, but never had he seen so many books full of knowledge that was lost to the rest of the world. He smiled with satisfaction as he sat down and picked up the book he had been reading. This was the life. He imagined that he could live out the rest of his days in Faldor's Keep and never get bored.

* * * * *

Traven stood next to Eldridge near the center of the empty courtyard. He was eager to learn something more complicated and challenging.

"One nickname of old for the wielders was 'Wind Whisperer'. This was on account of the wielders being able to, in a sense, send their voices on the wind to people far away. Obviously the further you try to send it the harder it is, but I think the idea behind it is simple enough. Do you want to give it a try?"

Traven nodded in response. It would be fascinating to be able to talk to others that were far away. He wondered how far he could really send his voice and listened carefully as the keeper began to describe the process.

"First you create a sphere directly in front of your mouth surrounded by swirling particles. Just swirling particles, mind you; nothing solid. The only part of the sphere that should be open is the part that is directly connected to your mouth. You clearly speak a word into the sphere and immediately close up the opening. You then create wind and use it to guide your sphere of swirling particles to the chosen location. When it reaches the correct spot, you let the sphere disappear, releasing your word. Does that make sense?"

"I think so," Traven replied. "Let's try it!"

Eldridge shuffled over to the far end of the courtyard, and Traven began to focus. Once the keeper was in place, Traven fell into his trance. The world slowed and the particles swirling around in the air became visible to him. He tried to move the particles into a spherical pattern but found that he had no control to directly move them at all. Contemplating on his problem, he realized that he never actually moved the particles himself. The particles would move of their own accord to create whatever it was that he imagined in the ethereal realm.

He decided to imagine a hollow sphere of ice. Sure enough, the correct particles began to swirl tightly in a sphere right in front of his mouth, ready to form a ball of ice. He spoke the keeper's name into the small opening and immediately imagined it closed. With the swirling sphere of particles in front of him, he created a breeze to blow the sphere to the edge of the courtyard. However, as soon as the breeze hit the sphere, the particles scattered in all directions.

Traven paused, thought for a second, and started over. This time he made a conscious effort to remain focused on his ethereal ice sphere as he pushed the particles forward on a light breeze. When the ball of swirling particles reached the keeper, he let it disappear and smiled. However, the smile slowly vanished when he saw no change whatsoever in the keeper. He obviously hadn't heard anything. Traven quickly tried it again with the same result, or lack thereof. He tried it once again, using a stiff wind to carry the sphere faster. When it reached the keeper, the ancient man perked up.

"Did you hear it?" Traven yelled excitedly.

"No," Eldridge yelled back. "But I felt a stiff wind in my face."

Traven threw up his arms in frustration. What was he doing wrong? Eldridge shuffled back across the courtyard so they could talk without having to yell.

"Explain to me exactly what you did," the keeper instructed. Traven obliged him by giving him a detailed description.

"Perhaps you should try it again," the keeper suggested. "You can't expect it to work on your first try."

"I already sent it to you three times," Traven replied.

"Oh, I forgot how fast you can do things." The keeper paused and thought for a few moments. "Perhaps your particle sphere isn't tight enough," he suggested. "Perhaps the sound slowly escapes before it reaches me."

Traven thought about the possibility and decided that it made sense. It was worth another try. As soon as the keeper had returned to the far end of the courtyard, he tried again. He focused on keeping the particles tighter and found that the only way to do it was to come closer to pulling the ice sphere into existence without actually doing it. This time when he sent the word to the keeper, the particle sphere was much tighter. When he released the sphere, the keeper smiled.

"I heard something," Eldridge shouted back to him. "I couldn't make it out, but I definitely heard something."

Encouraged by this, Traven tried again. Apparently for this to fully work the particles would need to be even tighter. He tried again, slowly pulling the ice sphere closer to the physical world. He pulled it so carefully and so slowly that when it came against the barrier that separated the two realms it didn't burst through. It merely pushed against and bent the divide.

Fascinated, he kept pulling slowly as the divide stretched even further without breaking. Wondering how far it could stretch, he kept slowly pulling.

"Ahh!" he shouted as the ice sphere broke through the barrier and appeared directly in front of him. He jumped backward as it fell to the ground and shattered, just missing his foot.

"What happened?" Eldridge shouted.

Now that he knew where the breaking point was, he formed a hollow ice sphere ethereally, pulled against the divide, and spoke the answer to the keeper's question. The particles were now as tight as they could get without actually creating the sphere of ice. He sent the answer to Eldridge's question on the wind and held his breath as he released the particles. The keeper immediately stumbled backwards with a look of surprise. Traven quickly ran over to him.

"It worked," Eldridge said excitedly. "Suddenly it was as if you were standing right in front of me. I distinctly heard the word 'accident' out of the thin air." Traven smiled. It felt great to have succeeded in sending a message on the wind.

"Let's climb up to one of the towers and practice this a little more," the keeper said with a mischievous gleam in his eye.

As they walked through the keep and up to one of its towers, Traven practiced keeping a new sphere tight and sailing right in front of them. When they finally reached the balcony he let it go. Eldridge jumped in surprise at the sudden sound. Traven frowned at the garbled mess.

"I wonder why my message ended up sounding that way," he mused. He knew that he had kept the swirling particles as tight as before.

"Did you try to say multiple words?" the keeper asked as he worked on slowing his breathing.

"I said a phrase," Traven replied. "But I don't see why that would be a problem."

"For some reason, if you try and use more than one word they all just get mixed together. If you want to send multiple words, you have to send them separately."

Traven nodded in understanding. He wondered how many spheres of particles he could create at once. Up on the balcony, he looked out over the entire valley. In the distance he could see several of the guardians tending some crops.

"Do you see anyone out there?" the ancient keeper asked.

"Darian and two other guardians are over there," Traven said while pointing at them.

"I can't see them," Eldridge said while squinting. "But I trust you're right. You are a wielder and have advanced vision. How about you try and send a message to those guardians?"

"Do you think I can send it that far?"

"I don't see why not," the keeper replied. "If you can see them, there's no reason why you can't direct your words to them."

He supposed that Eldridge was correct in his assumption. He thought for a few moments about what he wanted to say. He then took a deep breath and tried sending several words in succession.

* * * * *

Darian rose back up from the ground and tossed another vegetable into the basket. He wiped his brow with the back of his hand. Even though he had been trained as a warrior, he didn't mind doing the domestic work of gardening. He even found it somewhat relaxing.

At times, while he methodically took care of the crops, he dreamt of traveling to lands far away and also of his elven home in the mountain forest. He had been a guardian of the keep for over sixteen years now and looked forward to the time when he could return home. However, until then he would be satisfied guarding and maintaining the keep. He knew his duty. He smiled as a cool breeze touched his face.

"Darian . . ."

He jumped, looking around in confusion. The sound had not come from either of the two human guardians working alongside him. They too were looking around in confusion. Darian hadn't heard anyone approach, and quickly scanning the trees, he didn't see anyone else nearby.

". . . thanks. . . for . . . your . . ." There was an even longer pause and then a barely audible whisper, ". . . service."

He looked around in surprise, unable to determine the origin of the voice. It seemed to be coming straight out of the air in front of him. Was it a message from his ancestors in the great realm beyond? His two companions continued looking around nervously, seeking for the source of the message. He continued scanning the valley. As his keen elf gaze swept over the keep it stopped. Standing on the balcony of the northeast tower, looking in his direction were the keeper and Traven.

"Wind Whisperer," he muttered. Turning to his two companions he pointed at the keep and let them know the message had been carried on the wind and was from Traven. The three guardians all had a good chuckle at their jumpiness and went back to work.

Darian glanced at the keep again before leaning back over. The boy was definitely not a master wielder yet, but his progress had been rapid. He had seen the boy do amazing things while practicing in the courtyard, and now Traven was whispering on the wind. He began to somewhat understand why his ancestors had chosen to bind themselves to and follow the master wielders of old.

* * * * *

"Did they hear it?" Eldridge asked eagerly.

"Yes," Traven replied, trying to keep from laughing. "They all jumped and were nervously looking around for the source of the message until Darian spotted us up here."

"How wonderful," Eldridge said clapping his hands.

Traven's smile got even bigger as he began to think of all of the fun he could have with what he had just learned. He tried not to dwell on the mischievous side of his thoughts and instead concentrated on how useful it could be in relaying important messages and information.

"How far away can I send a message?" he asked the keeper.

"Well," the keeper said while scratching his head, "theoretically, as far as you can guide it. Of course the further the message has to go and the longer it takes to reach its destination, the more diluted the word will become. Keep practicing," he said with a smile. "After lunch I will teach you to scree."

Traven nodded as the ancient man shuffled away. He had no idea what to 'scree' meant but was excited to find out, especially if it was anything like whispering on the wind. He turned away from the keep and looked out over the valley. He began sending messages out over the valley to no one in particular. He continued practicing, and the task became easier and easier.

The more he practiced, the less thought it took to keep the particles tight enough to contain the words. He soon had numerous words floating to the edge of the valley in rapid succession. At first it was difficult to hold them steady for such a distance, but as he continued doing it over and over and as he began to alter the shapes of the word containers, it became increasingly easier. By midday he was able to easily send whole messages in a row out over the tops of the mountains that surrounded the valley without much thought.

Wielding the ambience was surprisingly similar to practicing his sword forms. The more he practiced something, the easier it became. It became almost automatic as his mind became accustomed to the task. The things he practiced the most, he could create almost instantly with the slightest of thoughts.

He finally stopped practicing whispering on the wind and headed down to the dining hall for lunch. He smiled at the progress he had made. At first he thought he wouldn't be able to control the words as they got further away, but he had found all he had to do was concentrate a little more. He was sure that he could send the messages even further if he could only see further. It was too bad his ambience enhanced sight could only penetrate so far into the distance.

15

The horses' hooves made sucking noises as they plodded onward through the mud. It had been raining for almost two entire days. It was more of a drizzle now than rain, but it was still miserable. Kalista felt especially bad for the foot soldiers. Marching in the mud had without doubt slowed the army's progress. It would take longer for them to reach Candus than they had hoped.

They had left Kavar two days ago but hadn't made nearly the progress they had wanted to. Oh how Kalista longed to be back in the city. She had enjoyed the comforts of the lavish inn that she had been put up in. Her only regret was that she had only been able to stay there for one short night. She had almost felt as if she were back in the palace.

She had enjoyed a delicious dinner, a hot bath, and an extremely comfortable bed. Breakfast had been just as good the next morning, and she had been tempted to send the army on without her. Of course, that would have meant parting with Gavin, and she couldn't do that. Being with him for practically the whole day, every day for the last three weeks made the thought of being apart even harder to bear.

After two days of slogging through the rain, however, she was beginning to second guess her decision to not stay at the inn in Kavar. At least the march for the day was almost over. It was hard to judge the time without any sign of the sun, but the growing darkness was evidence enough that night was fast approaching.

Soon the signal was given, and the soldiers stopped. Kalista made her way off the road as the soldiers hurried to set up camp and get out of the rain. She sat on her horse, next to Gavin's, holding her cloak tight against the cold dampness as her servants quickly set up her tent. Gavin's tent was being set up nearby with the command tent next to it.

As soon as her tent was up, she slipped off her mount and hurried inside. She shook the water off of her cloak at the entrance and moved to the middle of the tent. Soon a fire was going, and she let her cloak fall as she walked over next to it to warm up. Water fell through the small opening at the top of the tent, sizzling as it hit the flames. She waited contentedly by the fire while her servants finished setting up the inside of her tent. They brought in several chairs for the front part that she was currently in, and brought in her chest of clothes and her bed for the back, private section of the tent.

She focused on the warm flames of the fire as her servants finished making everything ready for her. She knew they would lay out a nice dress for her to change into for dinner and would warm some water for her to freshen up in. Her tent soon contained all of the necessities, but it was still a far cry from even a room at a modest inn. The walls of the tent were tightly stretched against the ground, and she knew that the damp grass in the back section of her tent had been covered with a dry rug, but neither gave the illusion that she was in a solid room instead of a flimsy tent in the middle of nowhere.

She sighed as she left the fire and parted the dividing flaps to enter her room. As a servant helped her change out of her riding clothes and get prepared for dinner, she wondered how much more she could take. Once again she questioned whether or not it had been a good idea to come along. She had never thought of herself as necessarily soft, but after another rainy day of marching she was almost ready to stop.

Of course the idea was ridiculous. They were in the middle of nowhere. They really wouldn't come upon another city until they reached Candus. She realized it was probably good that the rain had not begun until yesterday or she would have been even more tempted to stay put in Kavar. Now, she really didn't have a choice but to continue on to Candus.

When she finished getting ready, she took a long look at herself in her mirror. She supposed she was holding up fine, and when she smiled at herself, she could almost imagine that she was back in the palace getting ready to attend dinner with her father. However, she did determine that on the way back to Calyn she would be riding in a plush carriage and not traveling on horseback with the Royal Army. She would then have the liberty to travel at her own pace and choose where she wanted to stop and rest and for how long.

She tried to smooth out her hair, and then headed into the front room of her tent. Gavin was already there, quietly waiting in one of the chairs for her. He rose as soon as she entered and gave her a small bow.

"You look lovely as always," he said with a smile. "Would you care to accompany me to dinner?"

"Yes I would," Kalista said as she took her fiancé's arm. "Having dinner with you is about the only thing that I have to look forward to these days."

They ducked out of her tent and quickly made their way through the misting rain and into the command tent. It was larger than her tent with several different partitioned rooms. The front room had a large table in the middle of it surrounded by chairs. It would be used for planning once dinner was over, but for now the room was empty except for Gavin, her, and a few servants.

Gavin pulled out a chair for her and carefully pushed it in as she sat down at the table. He then sat down next to her and clapped his hands. Two servants immediately appeared with plates of food that they set on the table.

"Doesn't this look delicious?" Gavin said with a charming smile. "We'll have to send our compliments to the chef."

Kalista shook her head as she looked at the plate of food. It wasn't much different than what they ate every night. Gavin must have sensed her mood and was trying his best to cheer her up. She really didn't feel like playing along tonight. She picked up her spoon and took a taste. She then covered her mouth with the back of her hand and coughed as if the food was making her choke.

"You must be eating something different than I am," she said with a scowl. "I think we ate this a few days ago. Is it the leftovers?"

"Well, I . . ." Gavin began to say before he started laughing. He quickly got himself under control. "Okay, it's not that great. But I'm hungry enough that most anything looks good."

"I wish I were as hungry as you," she replied. "Then perhaps I could make myself finish this." She pushed the plate away from her. "I hope the chefs in Candus are better than the army cooks."

"The chefs in Candus are some of the best in the world," Gavin said as he put down his fork. "I guarantee that there will be no complaints once you have tasted the delicious creations of our palace chef. You will most likely think your first meal in Candus is the best you have ever eaten." He paused, trying to keep a straight face. "I can guarantee this because after eating this for another two weeks almost anything will taste gourmet."

"I guess I will have to eat my dinner so as to dull my taste buds enough to not make you a liar when we arrive in Candus," Kalista said.

She finally gave in and smiled. The food they had was not that bad. They definitely ate better than the soldiers. She pulled the plate back towards her and finished her dinner. Despite what she had said, she was hungry after such a long day. They both finished their meals in silence. When they were done eating, Gavin turned to her and held her hand.

"I am sorry about the rough traveling conditions," he said. "Perhaps I should have insisted that you ride in a coach."

"It's not your fault," Kalista replied. "I am the one that insisted on riding by your side. Most days aren't bad. I just hope this rain clears up by tomorrow."

"I am sure it will. These spring storms never last more than a day or two. We'll be in Candus in another twelve days and then you can relax, comfortably as the High Princess of Kalia deserves. Did you know they are planning an engagement celebration for when we arrive?"

"What?" she responded with surprise. She hadn't heard anything about an engagement celebration. "They're planning a celebration with a hostile army at their doorstep?"

"Of course," Gavin replied. "They are not going to let our arrival pass by without celebrating the union of the baron's son to the Princess of Kalia. Besides, after such a long march it will boost the troops' morale. It will remind them of what they are fighting to preserve."

Kalista supposed it made sense. The celebration would not only be an opportunity for the city of Candus to pay its respects to the crown but also be an opportunity to lift the soldiers' spirits and prepare them to defend their homeland. And now she had something to look forward to as well.

"That is good news," she said with a smile. The only bad part was that there would be another twelve or so days of marching before they even reached Candus.

The servants cleared away the dinner plates and brought in some candied fruit for dessert. Kalista smiled in surprise at the variety and the sweet smell. They had only eaten desserts when they had stopped in the cities. She wondered where it had come from. She was almost certain that the army cooks didn't normally have such delicacies with them.

"I had some picked up when we were in Kavar," Gavin said nonchalantly. "I had planned on waiting a few more days before having it served, but after such a long day of riding in the rain I thought you might appreciate it."

"I do appreciate it," she said with a smile that was continuing to grow larger. "You think of everything, don't you?"

"I wouldn't say that I think of everything," Gavin replied. "Then again, I didn't say it. You did. I don't want to argue with someone as intelligent and beautiful as you, so I will concede that you are right and I think of everything."

She grinned and shook her head as she popped a piece of candied plum into her mouth. She closed her eyes and savored its sweetness. It was delicious. She felt Gavin leaning in towards her, and her eyes slowly opened. His face was only a few inches away from hers.

"In all honesty," he said softly. "I really do not think of everything. Most of the time, I am only thinking of you."

Her fiancé then gently touched her chin and lifted it towards him. He finished closing the distance between them and softly kissed her lips. Butterflies flitted through her stomach.

"Things will work out just fine my Princess," he said as he settled back in his chair. "Soon this march and the skirmish at the borders will all be distant memories. We'll reminisce on our little adventure when we are older and think of the fun time we had together."

"Perhaps I'll reminisce on our time spent together as fun," Kalista replied as she turned back to her dessert. "But I will definitely never think of riding through the cold rain and mud as fun."

They chuckled as they continued savoring the candied fruits. Kalista was thankful for Gavin's optimism and thoughtfulness. He would make a great husband and king. As soon as they had finished dessert, the two generals and some of the captains began to arrive at the command tent. Kalista stood up and allowed Gavin to help her into her cloak.

"Are you sure you don't want to stay?" he asked.

"Of course," she replied with a smile. "I do not want this night's happy memory tarnished by talk of war."

"As you wish," he said.

They both ducked out of the command tent, and Gavin escorted her the short distance back to her own tent. She was happy to notice that it was no longer raining. Perhaps tomorrow they would even be greeted by the sun.

"Thank you for a wonderful dinner date," she said with a grin. "Please give my compliments to the chef." Gavin smiled back at her warmly.

"Sweet dreams my Princess," he said as he gently squeezed her hands. "I shall try to survive the night away from your presence." Kalista reached up and brushed his lips with a kiss.

"Hopefully that will make your night easier," she said teasingly.

With that, she turned and entered her tent. She sighed as she let her servant remove her cloak. The day had not turned out to be as bad as she thought it would. She would follow Gavin's last suggestion and have sweet dreams, dreams of an early summer wedding.

16

"Screeing is something that has fascinated me ever since I first read about it," Eldridge said with excitement. "I think it will be incredibly useful to you. Screeing is the ability to see things that are far away, things that would be impossible to see even with ambience enhanced vision like yours."

"How far?" Traven asked, full of curiosity.

"As far as you want," the keeper replied. "I suppose you can imagine why this fascinates me so much. I love being the keeper of Faldor's Keep, but I haven't been outside the keep for over six years. And even then it was only to bring the new human guardians to the keep from their small village at the base of the Parched Mountains.

"I often wonder what is going on in the world outside. What changes have occurred? What is the same? To be able to actually see the outside world while safely in the keep, doing my duty, well that would just be, it would just be . . ." Eldridge paused. "Incredible," he finished. "Enough of that, I'm sure you are anxious to learn how to do it."

Traven was indeed anxious to learn how to scree. It did sound fascinating. Looking around the dark room, he wondered how it would be possible. They were back in the same tower they had been in earlier in the day. However, instead of out on the balcony, they were in the center of the tower room with all of the windows and doors shuttered. He wasn't sure how they would be able to see much of anything in the dimly lit room.

"I must admit that I wanted to teach you this from the beginning, but I knew that you needed to learn more of the basics first. Screeing includes doing several different things with the ambience all at once. After your success this morning, I don't think it will be too hard for you to figure out how to do it. Come over here."

Traven walked to the center of the room and stood opposite the keeper. In between them there was a small table. On the table sat a shallow dish filled with water. He looked down at the dish and smiled back at the dim reflection of himself in the water. He then looked back at the keeper.

"Why is it so dark in here?" he asked. "If we want to see something far away, don't we need to be outside with a lot of light?"

"Oh no," Eldridge replied. "Screeing is much easier in the dark. At least that's what the texts say. It is easier to see the image when it is contrasted against the dark in the room. You won't be straining your eyes like normal to see a distant image. Screeing involves bringing the image to you."

Traven frowned, not understanding how it would be possible.

"This screeing dish is the only tool you will need," the keeper said while pointing at the dish of water. "The image will be reflected on the surface of the water, just like your current reflection. However, the image you will soon see will not be from within the walls of this room but from somewhere outside."

Traven still didn't have any idea how he would be able to do it, but he was excited to learn how. The keeper had been very adept at explaining new concepts to him thus far, and he had full confidence that this time would be no different. It would be amazing to be able to pull up images of things that were far away.

"Explain to me what I need to do," he said eagerly.

"In a way it is like sending a message," Eldridge began. "However, instead of sending sound away from you, you will be pulling light towards you. You will need to create a conduit of particles that rises from this dish up into the sky. At the far end of the conduit, you will need to create a smooth sheet of water. It is imperative that this sheet of water be completely smooth and still.

An image will reflect off this sheet of water, travel down the conduit, and appear on the surface of the water here in the dish. Once you get the hang of it, we will be able to look at anything that you choose right here on the glassy surface of this water dish."

"Okay," Traven replied while thinking of the concept. It didn't seem too difficult. It was just like reflecting an image from one mirror to another. He glanced up from the dish towards the ceiling and frowned. "How am I supposed to form a conduit that goes out of this room?" he asked. "You have all the openings shuttered." The keeper looked at him with a confused expression for a moment and then smiled as he realized what Traven was asking.

"You don't need any large openings. Just form the conduit straight up through the ceiling."

"But it's solid rock," Traven replied. "I can't form anything through solid rock, much less pull light down through it."

"It's not really solid," the ancient keeper stated as he took on a lecturing tone. "The particles that make up the stone in this keep or anything else that appears solid, have tiny spaces in between them. With the ambience you have the ability to exploit those tiny spaces and form things through supposedly solid objects. In the case of screeing, you can use the tiny spaces in the stone to pull light through it. Fascinating isn't it?"

Traven nodded, thinking about what the keeper was saying. He knew that there were particles in the air all around him even though there appeared to be none. Why not air in what appeared to be solid objects? He focused and looked at the solid rock above him. He wondered what would be the easiest to imagine in order to form a conduit from the room up into the sky. All he could think of was a lightning bolt, but he was hesitant to try and form one through the ceiling. If he pulled on the ethereal image too hard he could accidently blast a hole in the ceiling of the keep. He would have to be very careful.

Time slowed, and he formed an image of a lightning bolt very slowly and deliberately. As the particles in the air swirled to form around the expected bolt, he was startled and pleased to find that even though he couldn't see the particles in the ceiling and beyond up into the sky, he could feel exactly where they were and what they were doing. It was almost as if he could see right through the solid rock.

This realization caused new excitement. He began to wonder what he could do with the ambience by sensing things but not necessarily seeing them. Suddenly Traven felt static in the air and jerked his attention back to the task at hand. He let the ethereal bolt back slightly away from its strained push against the barrier to the physical world. It had been way too close. He had almost pulled the bolt into existence without thinking. He made an increased effort to focus on the task at hand.

Concentrating on the bolt, he let his mind travel up its length, through the ceiling, and up into the sky until he reached its top. At the top he concentrated on creating a thin sheet of water. It was tricky to get it perfectly level and smooth, but after struggling with it for a few moments, he managed to stabilize it. He then willed light to travel from the sheet of water down the bolt and into the screeing dish. He kept his hold on the water and the ethereal bolt and glanced down at the dish of water.

He smiled as small flashes of light began to dance across the surface of the dish. Unfortunately, the small flashes never sharpened to create a specific image. Eldridge stood across from him, glancing at the dish excitedly. After a few moments he glanced up at Traven. Traven gave him a shrug and a questioning look. The ancient keeper thought for moment before speaking.

"Is the conduit perfectly smooth?" he asked. Traven shook his head no. "Try making it smooth"

Traven put extra focus on the bolt again. It was anything but smooth, having all of the jagged lines associated with a bolt of lightning. Slowly and carefully he imagined the jagged edges becoming smooth. To his delight, the bolt melted into a perfectly smooth cylinder shooting straight up to the heavens.

He focused on pulling the light once again, and slowly a fuzzy image formed across the entire surface of the dish of water. He smiled at it and then frowned once again. There was definitely an image being reflected on the water, but it was too fuzzy to make out. He allowed his thoughts to run over his smooth bolt and up into the sky. The bolt was still perfectly smooth. However, as his thoughts reached the sheet of water, he realized he had allowed his hold on it to slip. He concentrated on making it completely smooth again and looked down as Eldridge let out an excited gasp.

The image in the dish had sharpened clearer than Traven would have ever expected. It looked as clear as anything he would look at with his own eyes. It glowed slightly, giving off light of its own.

It only took a moment for him to realize what he was looking at. It was a bird's eye view of the entire Blood Mountains. Almost directly in the center of the tight range of mountains was a small, green valley, in stark contrast against the red rock. No keep could be seen in the green valley, but he was certain that if the might stone hadn't been shielding it, Faldor's Keep would be visible as well.

He continued staring at the image in wonder. He had seen several maps before, but none had come close to comparing in detail to what he was now looking at. Studying the image, he found the path that Studell and he had taken to arrive at the valley. He stared with wonder at the maze of canyons that zigzagged through the mountains. Without directions, they could have explored the maze of canyons for weeks and never made it to the secluded valley in the center.

"Are you up to trying to move the image?" Eldridge asked excitedly but with a hint of caution. Traven was beginning to feel tired, but he supposed he could maintain a firm hold on the ambience for a little longer without doing any damage to his body.

"Sure," he replied. "What do I do?"

"First of all, by making your conduit reach higher into the sky you can see a greater area of land. Some of the master wielders of old were strong enough to see the entire land at once! However, I think you should wait to attempt to make your conduit higher until you have rested. Right now let's just try moving the image. The trick to moving the image is forming a second conduit that proceeds downward from your sheet of water in a direction different than your current conduit of particles. Wherever the second conduit is pointed is where you will be screeing. If you increase the length of the second conduit towards the ground, you can enlarge anything that you want to take a closer look at. Does that make sense?"

The idea seemed simple enough, so Traven responded by carefully forming a second, very short conduit that extended from the sheet of water slightly to the south. The image in the dish changed to show two mountains rising side by side. He recognized them as the Twin Guardians. They looked different from the higher angle. Both had craters at their peaks that he hadn't been able to see from below.

He stared at the two volcanoes in wonder. Sweat broke out on his forehead as he made his second conduit slightly longer. The two volcanoes grew in size to fill the screeing dish. He slightly shifted the conduit and made it even longer as he peered into one of the craters. The gaping hole at the top of the volcano was deeper than he expected. He lengthened the conduit even further as he tried to peer into the crater's depths. A bead of sweat dripped off his forehead and landed with a small splash in the dish of water, distorting the image.

"I think we better take a break," Eldridge said as he looked up from the dish and at Traven's face. "You are looking a little pale."

Traven let go of his hold on the ambience, and the image disappeared. The keeper was correct. He needed to rest. There was an intense throbbing in his head, and he felt exhausted. He probably should have stopped earlier, but the screeing had been so exciting. He was looking forward to practicing again when he was fully rested. The wonders of screeing amazed him.

17

The throne room was full of people. All were paying the proper respect to the next High King of Kalia. Some were bowing and others were kneeling. Traven sat in his throne uncomfortably, waiting for the crowning ceremony.

He looked around the room, searching for those he knew. In the back he saw his grandparents. Professor Studell knelt near them. To his right Blaize towered above the others, even while on his knees.

Traven continued looking over the respectful crowd. He saw some of his old classmates from the academy as well as some of his old professors. He also recognized several of the generals from the Royal Army. He kept looking, searching the crowd for someone in particular.

Someone important to him was missing from the crowd, but he couldn't remember who it was. Even with those in the crowd that were closest to him like his grandparents and Blaize, he still felt alone. How could he rule Kalia without the most important person in his life at his side?

He thought as hard as he could, trying to recall who it was that was missing. Slowly, deep blue eyes and long blond hair flitted across his memory. A gorgeous smile and a delicate hand flitted though his mind next. A memory of a soft, warm cheek against his shoulder. Kalista!

How could he have forgotten her? She was the single most important person in his life. It was she who would guide him when he was the High King. It was she who knew him better than anyone else. It was she who gave him a reason to keep going when things seemed impossible. It was she who he would lay down his life for.

Where was she? He needed her soft, firm hand on his shoulder now more than ever. He needed her strength and her comfort. Perhaps she was merely finishing preparing for the ceremony.

He tried to calm himself, taking deep breaths as he waited. Behind the closed doors of the throne room he could hear the echoes of steps approaching down the hallway. The steps stopped at the door. He let out a relieved breath as the large doors began to swing open. Now he remembered. The princess would be the one to crown him. It was her whose footsteps he had just heard. She would be entering the room, bearing the crown.

However, his hopes were dashed when the opening doors revealed the bearer of the crown. It wasn't the Princess Kalista with her mesmerizing eyes and comforting smile. The bearer of the crown was merely a page. Traven watched as the boy approached carefully with the crown pulsating on the pillow that he carried in his hands. The page stopped directly in front of him and knelt respectfully.

Traven sat still as the pulsating crown was lifted from the pillow and carefully placed on his head. The crowd rose to their feet cheering. The room was instantly full of celebration and excitement for the new High King of Kalia. Everyone in the crowd appeared overjoyed to have him as their new king. He wished that he felt the same excitement. He wished that his heart could soar with those in the crowd.

Unfortunately, he only felt sad and empty. What did any of this matter if the princess wasn't at his side? What did the pulsating crown on his head even mean to him? The only thing that mattered to him at the moment was the princess. Where was she?

* * * * *

Traven awoke feeling incredibly distressed. He tried to shake the feeling but couldn't. The feelings of emptiness and hopelessness that the dream left him with were much stronger than they should have been. He didn't even really know the princess. It was true that she had been a constant fixture in his dreams for the past few weeks, but why should her absence from his dreams leave him feeling the way he did?

He tried in vain to shake the dismal feelings as he got up and went down to the courtyard to exercise and practice his forms. Part way through his routine, one of the human guardians asked if he would like to spar against him. Traven hadn't sparred with anyone for a while and gratefully accepted the invitation, hoping that the distraction would help him forget the distressing dream. He forced a smile as one of the other human guardians handed him a practice sword.

"My name's Jorb and this is Ethan," he said pointing to the guardian who was going to spar with Traven. "You've been so busy with the keeper that we haven't really had an opportunity to introduce ourselves and get to know you."

"It's nice to meet both of you," Traven replied. "I feel bad that I haven't had a chance to meet all of the guardians. I think it's amazing what all of you do to maintain and protect the keep."

"Well I don't know that we really do much to protect the keep," Jorb replied. "In fact, when you and the philosopher showed up last week you became the first unexpected visitors to Faldor's Keep in the past five hundred years."

"He's right," Ethan chimed in. "Mostly the guardians have just maintained the keep over the years and taken care of the keeper. You have no idea how exciting it is to have a wielder at the keep. The elves try to play your appearance down, but it's just for show. It makes all of our sacrifices seem like they are worth something having you here."

Traven smiled back at the two guardians. It still made him feel a little uncomfortable having such importance placed upon him, but he was glad that his arrival at the keep had helped lift the guardians' spirits. He could only imagine how hard it would be to give up family and home to be a guardian at the keep for twenty straight years.

"Are you ready?" Jorb asked. "Ethan and I have admired the sword forms you go through each morning. We have a little wager on whether you are as good with the sword as you appear to be."

"I'm ready," Traven said with a smile. "However, I've seen you all practicing as well and feel at a slight disadvantage. I haven't sparred with anyone for awhile. I'm sure Ethan has a lot more training and practice than I do."

"True," Ethan said as he took his position across from Traven and readied his sword. "We've been training longer, but you are a wielder after all."

He wasn't sure what being a wielder had to do with sword fighting but didn't have time to think about it. He threw up his practice sword and blocked Ethan's swipe as the guardian attacked. Traven cleared his mind and focused on the sparring match. Ethan was good but no match for him. The fight felt the same as when Studell and he had been attacked in Jatz. It was as if he knew where each of Ethan's sword strokes would fall before they even occurred.

He methodically blocked the guardian's attacks for awhile and then went on the offensive. The guardian held him at bay at first, but as soon as Traven picked up his attack, the fight ended quickly. Ethan was soon lying on the ground in the dirt with a sore thigh where Traven's practice sword had struck him.

"I told you," Jorb said while chuckling. Traven reached down and helped Ethan to his feet. "Looks like you'll be weeding the beets today."

Traven smiled as Ethan rubbed his thigh. He now knew which of the two had bet against him. Ethan continued rubbing his thigh as he scowled at Jorb. Traven wondered how Ethan compared to the other guardians in his talent with the sword.

"Would you like to spar next?" Traven asked Jorb.

"No way," the guardian said with a chuckle. "Ethan's the best swordsman out of us human guardians. You made beating him look too easy. I wouldn't last against you for more than a few seconds."

"You should try fighting Darian," Ethan said. "He's the best swordsman here. Even the other elves never beat him." Ethan looked around the courtyard. "He should be here any second. Here he comes now. Hey Darian!" Ethan shouted. "Traven wants to spar with you!"

Traven watched nervously as Darian and another elf approached them. He had seen the elves practicing and knew that they were quicker than the human guardians. After the way Darian had treated him when he had first arrived, he supposed the elf would enjoy beating him with the sword.

"Why don't you spar with him?" Darian responded to Ethan. "You're always bragging that you can beat any human."

"Can't you tell by the dirt all over his clothes he just got beat?" Jorb said with a large smile.

"Thank you, Jorb. Thank you!" Ethan said as he brushed the dirt off his clothes.

Darian looked back and forth between the two guardians and then looked directly at Traven. He gave him an appraising look for a second.

"So the master wielder is also a master swordsman," the elf said with a hint of a smirk. "Are you ready to cross swords with an elven blademaster?"

Traven wasn't necessarily eager to fight Darian, but he was ready. He wondered if the elf was in fact a blademaster. He had seen the elves' quickness and knew that if Darian was truly a blademaster, it would be an incredibly difficult match. However, he had practiced against some of the best swordsmen in the army and was interested to see if he could hold his own against the elf.

"I'm ready when you are," Traven replied.

"Let's spar then," Darian said as he snatched the practice sword out of the air that Ethan tossed towards him. He took several steps backwards and faced Traven with a grin. He waited a few moments and then attacked.

Traven stumbled backwards as the elf attacked with amazing quickness and skill. He hadn't been prepared for how quick the elf would actually be even after seeing him practice before. He quickly fell back into complete concentration and let the surprise disappear as he continued blocking the elf's lightning quick slashes.

He had to push his body to its limit to match the speed of the elf. However, once he adjusted for the elf's speed, he was able to block all of the elf's attacks with ease. Darian's smile turned to a frown as Traven switched from defense and began to attack. The elf grimaced as he was pushed backwards. He was then once again on the attack.

The fight continued on and erupted into an intense battle with Traven and the elf taking turns attacking and defending. As the fight progressed, Traven found that as long as he concentrated he could deflect any attack that Darian brought against him. As had been the case when fighting Ethan, he could tell where a stroke was going to come from just before it happened. The realization that he could hold his own against the elf encouraged him to pick up his attacks.

He watched for any weaknesses or holes in Darian's defense and was surprised to find none. He continued to wait patiently like Blaize had taught him. There was no need for him to take a risky chance and leave himself exposed. His new awareness would allow him to keep blocking Darian's attacks as long as his strength held up. As the fight continued on and on, he began to wonder if the elf ever really would show a weakness. He also began to wonder if the elf's stamina would be greater than his own.

The fight continued on. Perspiration dripped from his brow and his clothes felt drenched. Seeing that Darian was perspiring and breathing heavily as well gave him hope. Perhaps he could wear the elf down. However, his hope was soon dashed. The elf's eyes took on a gleam and with a burst of speed, Darian attacked with more ferocity than Traven would have thought possible. He was able to hold the elf at bay for awhile, but his muscles were tiring. Even though he knew where the elf's strokes would land, he was having a harder and harder time getting his body to react fast enough.

Crack! Traven fell backwards as he brought his sword up too slowly and Darian's practice sword slammed into his ribs. He lay on the dirt floor of the courtyard, holding his side and trying in vain to catch his breath. He stared up at the elf, who was also breathing heavily and staring down at him with the same gleam in his eyes. He watched as the strange gleam left Darian's eyes and the elf's gaze took on a measure of respect and something else that Traven couldn't place but left him feeling uncomfortable.

Darian stepped forward and offered him his hand. Traven accepted it and allowed the elf to pull him up to his feet. The elf bowed respectfully and then turned abruptly and walked quickly away, vanishing into the keep.

"Incredible," Ethan mumbled under his breath. "In all my life I've never seen a swordfight like that."

"I can't believe you lasted that long," Jorb said with amazement.

"How long were we fighting?" Traven asked, still trying to catch his breath, as he looked up at the sky.

"I don't know," Jorb replied. "At least half an hour." Ethan nodded in agreement. The elf who had accompanied Darian tipped his head towards Traven.

"You didn't mention that you were a blademaster as well as a wielder," the elf said. "I believe we will all have even greater respect for you now, especially Darian. The legends tell of few wielders who bothered to develop their skill with the sword. They were the ones that lasted the longest when the Wielder Wars came. It is wise to be able to defend yourself without the ambience and conserve your magical strength for when it is most needed. I salute you Traven." The elf tipped his head again toward him and then disappeared into the keep just as Darian had.

"Wow," Ethan said as soon as the second elf was out of sight. "You probably don't have any idea of how great a compliment those two elves just gave you."

"What do you mean?" Traven asked. His breathing was close to normal, but he was exhausted and ravenous.

"The elven guardians almost never compliment humans," Jorb explained. "They think they are superior to us. And I guess if you take into account their physical prowess and abilities, they are superior in that sense. Out of the four elven guardians here, I would say Darian is the most proud. He bowing to you was almost as amazing as your sword fight." Jorb paused and shook his head. "Then Elial saying he salutes you topped it off. When an elf says that, he means he sees you as an equal."

"I don't see why they were so impressed," Traven said slowly. "I did lose after all."

"You don't understand," Ethan said. "I might be good with the sword for a human, but all four of the elven guardians could beat me in their sleep. The elves send their bravest warriors to be guardians of Faldor's Keep. If you believe what they say, Darian has never lost a swordfight since he was a teenager. I doubt anyone has ever lasted against him as long as you just did."

"Ethan's right," Jorb agreed. "That was truly an amazing display of sword work. Now let's go celebrate by eating breakfast. I'm starving."

* * * * *

Darian walked quickly up the stairs and into his chambers, slamming the door behind him. He stared at himself in the mirror as his mind raced and his breathing slowed. He could hardly believe what had just happened, and it was harder still to believe how he had reacted to it.

He had always found the stories of his race anciently binding themselves to master wielders to be ridiculous. How could an elf follow an inferior human? How could he disgrace his proud race and do the will of a mere man? He had always believed that only the weakest of elves would have bound themselves to a wielder.

However, now his convictions were being tested and his emotions were reeling. He knew what it was. All elves knew of the 'devotion'. He just couldn't believe that it was happening to him. He had felt it slightly upon seeing the wielder create liquid fire and had felt it slightly upon realizing the wielder could whisper on the wind.

However, not until now, after having sparred with him and almost losing, had the 'devotion' begun to rage within him. With the feeling came emotions and longings that he was fighting to suppress but couldn't. He understood now why the elves in the past were referred to as 'Children of the Wielders'.

As he stared into his eyes, which were glowing brighter than normal, he wondered what was happening to him. He felt a strong desire to do something that he had always looked upon with disgust. What should he do? Should he fight the desire or should he give in? He wondered if the other elven guardians felt even a little of what he was feeling. He tried not to scream as he studied in detail his honor tattooed over his eye. He couldn't believe that he was seriously considering doing it. The implications of the choice he was about to make would forever change the course of his life.

18

Traven woke with a start. He could have sworn that he had heard a scream, but all was now silent. He decided that it must have been the remnants of yet another bad dream. He shifted in his bed and stared up at the ceiling in the predawn darkness. He felt like he hadn't gotten any rest all night.

Yesterday had drained him, and he had been looking forward to a good night's rest. After his two sword matches the previous morning, he had spent the entire day practicing wielding the ambience. He had started by practicing wielding fire, wind, water, and lightning. He had then spent the rest of the afternoon and evening practicing whispering on the wind and screeing. By the end of the day, he had been able to scree the path that he and Studell had taken all the way from the coast.

Screeing took more energy than he would have expected, but it was so exciting to him that he had kept practicing into the night. It was amazing to see something far away from above and then be able to magnify it. He had gotten to the point where he could focus on a single sea bird and follow it in its flight. By the time he had finally stopped and gone to bed, he had a throbbing headache.

The peace and rest he had hoped to find in sleep had never come. Throughout the entire night he had continued to dream over and over about the crown of Kalia and the absence of the Princess Kalista. The details of the dream always changed except for the crown always being present and the princess always being absent. He would awake at the end of each dream with a sense of hopelessness and loss.

Despite all of the distractions the day before, he still had not been able to completely shake the depressed feelings he had felt the previous morning. He was not looking forward to carrying the same feelings with him throughout the coming day. He found it strange that the dreams could affect his mood to such an extent. The princess had been in his dreams almost constantly for the past few weeks, but he never imagined her absence would leave him feeling empty inside.

He didn't know if it was the vividness of his dreams or something else. Perhaps Eldridge would have some advice for him. His dreams had previously led him to the cave in the marsh. Perhaps his current dreams meant something as well. He had never been overly superstitious, but having such vivid dreams and strong emotions related to them left him wondering if his dreams did indeed mean something important.

Traven determined that he wasn't going to get any more sleep and left his room. After going through his morning routine, he returned to his room and freshened up. It was still too early for breakfast to be served, so he decided to practice screeing in his wash basin.

The keeper had mentioned that if a wielder created his conduit high enough, he could see all the land at once. He decided that he might as well give it a try. So far he had only tried to view the desert and the coast nearby. Time slowed as he created his conduit and sent it reaching for the heavens. He pushed it as high as he could, faintly feeling the end of it somewhere far overhead. He created his sheet of water and pulled down the faint light of dawn.

At first he was confused and didn't understand what he was looking at. Studying the image, he finally realized what it was. He was seeing the entire land of Kalia! He was able to make out the western coast all the way to the towering mountains on the eastern edge of the kingdom.

He stared at the image in awe. He had no idea that he would be able to get the conduit high enough to see so much of the land at once. He followed his journey to Faldor's Keep in reverse as he gazed over the map. His eyes traced a line down the coast to where he suspected Jatz was and from there to where Calyn was. He then traced a line back along the river to Four Bridges and then to Kavar. From there he traced a line back into the woods to his home village of Oak Tree. It was just like following his path on a map, but the image before him wasn't a map. It was real! Everything he saw was actually there.

Could he really look anywhere in Kalia he wanted to? The thought intrigued him greatly. Not only would he never need a map or get lost again, he would be able to check on places he was nowhere near. He concentrated and formed a second conduit down from the top of the first. He was soon looking at an image of only the eastern part of Kalia. He lengthened the conduit even more and was soon looking at a familiar forest and then at the village of Oak Tree. He located his grandparents' home on the outskirts of the village and focused on it. Soon his grandparents' small home filled the dish.

Traven's mouth fell open in surprise. At the side of the house, his grandfather and grandmother were weeding the garden. He was flooded with emotion at the sight of his grandparents. He hadn't realized just how much he missed them until now. A tear fell from his eye and splashed into the basin of water, distorting the image. He stared at the dish and waited for the image to become clear again.

He knew that screeing let him see exactly what was happening, but for some reason he hadn't thought he might see his grandparents. He took several deep breaths as he calmed his emotions. The water in the dish soon cleared, and he resumed gazing at the two wonderful people who had raised him and allowed his dreams to flourish.

He was delighted to see that they appeared healthy and happy, working together in the early morning spring sunlight. His thoughts had been turned to them after seeing them in his dream the other night. It gave him a certain amount of peace to see that they were well. Perhaps he would have the chance to visit them once the battle with the army from Balthus was over. They would be so surprised to learn that he was a wielder.

Thinking of his grandparents and the love he had for them led his mind to think of someone else that he had strong feelings for, the Princess Kalista. Of course, the feelings he had concerning her were from his dreams and not from reality. He wondered where she was and what she was doing. If he could scree his grandparents, why couldn't he scree an image of the princess?

He smiled at the image of his grandparents one more time and let the image fade away as the eastern part of Kalia came into focus. He knew that the Princess Kalista was traveling with the Royal Army on its march to Candus. He stopped and thought about where the army would be. They had left from Calyn almost a month ago. He supposed the army would be somewhere near Kavar. As he made the image move closer to the city, he noticed a smudge to the north. As the image got closer to the smudge, he was happy to see that it was indeed the Royal Army.

He continued magnifying the image until he could make out the individual soldiers in the army. They were marching northward in a long column. He supposed that he would find the princess towards the head of the column and moved the image along the column of soldiers until he reached the front. He then magnified the image even more.

He smiled to himself. The princess was indeed at the head of the column along with Commander General Gavin and Blaize. The sight of his friend at the head of the army brought a large smile to his face. However, his gaze soon left the warrior and rested upon the graceful figure of the princess. While he watched, Commander

General Gavin leaned towards her and whispered something in her ear. She tilted her head back towards him and laughed as she looked up at him adoringly.

A pang of jealousy emerged within Traven's chest. He quickly tried to suppress it. He wouldn't deny that he found the princess attractive, but he had no reason to feel jealous of her attention towards the commander general. Gavin was her fiancé after all. He took a last look at the Princess Kalista and let the image fade. Having seen her again had done nothing to alleviate his sadness. In fact, the longing to see her again in person was now even stronger.

He once again tried to shake off the feelings he had awakened with but had no success. Glancing at the window, he supposed it was late enough now that he could get breakfast and look for Eldridge. He was anxious to ask the keeper about his dreams. He left his room and made his way to the dining hall. As he descended the stairs his ears picked up some commotion at the other end of the keep, but he couldn't make out what was being said. The keep was always so silent that the noise seemed out of place.

He entered the dining hall and was excited to see Eldridge already sitting and eating his breakfast. Traven was so anxious to ask the keeper about his dreams that he started walking towards him before he realized he hadn't grabbed his breakfast yet. He turned around, picked up his breakfast, and quickly walked over to the keeper to eat.

He tried to wait patiently for Eldridge to finish his meal but without much success. He shoveled his own food down rapidly and sat fidgeting as the ancient man slowly continued to eat his breakfast. Finally the keeper set down his spoon and looked at him with a hint of a grin.

"It appears that you are anxious to say something to me," he said. "I suppose I am done with my meal. What's on your mind?"

"Dreams," Traven replied.

"Dreams," the keeper mused. "I was wondering when you might ask me about them. However, I don't think you really mean dreams. I think you want to know about visions."

"What do you mean?"

"Dreams and visions are two very different things," the keeper continued. "Everyone dreams while they sleep. Sometimes dreams are happy, sometimes they are sad, and sometimes they make no sense at all. However, visions are something totally different. Only wielders have them, and not all wielders, only some. Apparently you are a wielder that has visions while you sleep. Am I right?"

"I guess so," Traven replied. "I've been having dreams that seem more real than normal, and I often have a variation of the same dream over and over."

"You are describing visions, not dreams," Eldridge reminded him. "I guess I will start by explaining what visions are. From there we can analyze your vision and see what we might be able to discover.

"A vision is like a dream in that it normally occurs while you are sleeping. Though, some wielders had visions while meditating as well. Visions have a purpose. Dreams don't really mean anything. They are just the mind sorting information. However, visions tell truths. Sometimes they point out important things that the wielder needs to think about and sometimes they show the future.

"The tricky thing about visions is they are not necessarily straight forward in their meaning. Visions usually contain important symbols. Most of the vision is unimportant and will change from night to night. However, the important symbols will not change. They are what must be focused on in order to understand the meaning of the vision. Even then it is tricky to ascertain the true meaning of the vision. Many a wielder misinterpreted a vision with disastrous results. One must be careful when trying to gain meaning from a vision. Does that all make sense?"

"Yes," Traven replied as he pondered what the keeper had just told him. Thinking back over his repetitious dreams, he was now certain they were visions. There was always something, a symbol, that stayed the same.

"Now let's analyze your visions," Eldridge said with a hint of excitement. "When did you first start having them?"

Traven thought back to when he first remembered dreaming about the cave that held Faldor's chest. It had been almost a year ago, just a little before he had his awakening.

"Almost a year ago," he replied. "I believe I had my first vision before I even had my awakening. Is that possible?"

"Yes," the keeper said while scratching his head. "It is rare to have them before the awakening, but it is not unheard of. I believe Faldor began having visions before his awakening. And do you still have the same vision?"

"No. I stopped having my first vision after I found Faldor's chest. It was the vision that led me to the cave where the chest was hidden. I had been dreaming continually of the entrance to the cave."

"Fascinating," Eldridge said with a large smile. "So in a sense, it was your vision that ultimately led you here."

Traven thought about it and nodded. If not for the vision that had led him to the cave, he would never have found the map to Faldor's Keep.

"And now you are having a different vision?" the keeper asked. Traven nodded once again.

"I began having this new one right after I found Faldor's chest. It didn't really bother me until two nights ago. The dream, I mean vision, changed. The last two mornings I have woken up feeling disturbed."

"Like I said earlier," the keeper began, "Visions will change often. It is the symbols that always stay the same."

"I think that's what's bothering me," Traven replied. He hadn't known that there were symbols in his visions until the keeper had mentioned their importance, but now looking for them in his visions, it was easy for him to identify them. "The vision was always different, but there seemed to be two symbols that always remained the same. Two nights ago, one of the symbols vanished."

"Hmmm," Eldridge mumbled. He sat thinking for several moments before continuing. "Perhaps if you describe the visions to me, I can help you decipher a possible meaning."

Traven looked around uncomfortably. He wasn't eager to share either of the symbols from his vision. It embarrassed him to have to admit out loud that he was dreaming of the crown of Kalia and the Princess Kalista. However, he knew that he needed to be honest with Eldridge if he wanted the keeper's help in deciphering the meaning behind the two symbols.

"Well," he began nervously. "I've been dreaming of the crown of Kalia. It's one of the symbols. In all of my visions it's either being placed on my head or it's already on my head." He paused, gathering the courage to share the other symbol.

"Go on," the keeper said encouragingly.

"The other symbol that was in all of my dreams until two nights ago was the High Princess of Kalia." He could feel his cheeks burning as Eldridge stared at him intently.

"Those are two very interesting symbols indeed," the keeper noted. "I was not expecting two symbols with such obvious importance. You are sure that those are the two symbols in your visions?"

"Yes," Traven replied. "They are the constants. They seem more real than anything else in the visions and seem to pulse with energy. Even once the princess vanished from the visions, I always knew during the vision that something was missing that should be there."

"I believe you're right then," Eldridge said with conviction. "Those are the symbols. Now we need to decipher them and understand what they mean."

Eldridge sat quietly for awhile, pondering the possible meanings. Traven sat silently as well, feeling awkward to have his visions of the crown and the princess out in the open. He wondered what the keeper was thinking about him. The ancient man shook his head several times as if dismissing certain thoughts, but finally cleared his throat to speak.

"Let's begin with the crown," he said quietly. "The symbol of the crown could be either literal or symbolize something else. So a very literal translation of your vision would be that you will be crowned the High King of Kalia. I highly doubt that is what the vision means, but it could mean that. I would suspect that it symbolizes power. Perhaps it means you will gain immense power or you will seek power to rule over others. This slightly worries me, for the desire for power was how the Wielder Wars began."

"I don't want to rule over anyone," Traven cut in.

"Oh, I'm not saying you do. You are not a symbol in the visions, so it really doesn't matter that the crown always ends upon your head. It could have nothing to do with you whatsoever. I would guess that the vision most likely symbolizes that something will happen to dramatically change who has power in the land. That is easy to believe, given that a wielder has gathered an army and is marching to challenge the High King of Kalia.

"It is your second symbol that really had me thinking. Not only is the symbol a person, but you mentioned that the symbol disappeared. I would say that you will cross paths with the princess in the future or that she will have an important part in the change of power in the lands. That being said, I wonder why she disappeared. Do you think she could have been killed?"

"No," Traven replied. "I just screed her this morning."

"You screed her this morning?" the keeper asked with surprise. "Never mind that question. If she is still alive then that theory is wrong. Hmm, do you think it means she will die soon?"

As much as Traven wanted to deny what the keeper had just said, it rang true to him. As Eldridge had posed the question, the feelings of loss and sadness instantly washed over him as strong as they ever had in the last two days. The princess was in trouble. He felt certain of it. He had to help her. In his previous visions she had often asked him not to forget her. But how could he help her? She was on the far side of Kalia. The only way he could protect her was if he was with her. He suddenly knew what he needed to do.

"I think you're right," he said to the keeper. "I must leave the keep and go to her. I need to protect her from being killed."

"Let's not get carried away," Eldridge said with a chuckle. "There is much for you to learn before you head back into the outside world. We don't even know if that is what your vision means."

"No," Traven stated. "I believe that is exactly what my vision means. If I had a vision of the princess, there must be a reason. If I can do something to prevent her death, I have to do it."

"I don't know that I agree with your decision," Eldridge said. "Where is the princess?"

"She's on the other side of Kalia, marching with the Royal Army towards Candus," Traven replied. "I kind of feel like that's where I belong anyway," he mumbled.

"You want to be in the middle of a war?" the keeper asked. "Are you seeking for power and fame? A war is not a place you want to be."

"I don't want to be there," Traven said firmly. "But I do feel like that is where I should be. I am a soldier in the Royal Army. The Balthan Army has a wielder at its head. As a wielder myself, I feel like I have a responsibility to help the Royal Army."

Eldridge stared at him earnestly. Traven returned the keeper's gaze, refusing to flinch. The more he thought about going to join the army and protect the princess, the more right it felt. He didn't want to leave the keep with so much left to learn but knew that even if he left now he might not reach the army in time to help with the battle or protect the princess. He felt the same sense of urgency that he had felt in his dreams. He needed to find the princess, and he needed to find her soon.

"You are determined then?" Eldridge said it more as a statement than as a question. Traven nodded in reply. The ancient keeper let out a sigh. "I suppose it is as it must be. How soon will you be leaving?"

"I feel I must leave immediately in order to have any chance at catching up to the princess in time," he replied.

"I thought so," Eldridge answered with a defeated shrug of his shoulders. He then grew firm as he looked directly at Traven. "However, one thing I won't let you do is leave without being taught how to use the ambience in defense. I will not have you die in battle because I didn't teach you how to defend yourself. Do what you must to prepare for your journey, but meet me in the courtyard in one hour. I will be ready to teach you what I can."

The keeper then rose and walked from the dining hall. Traven sat in place, digesting everything that had just happened. Was he crazy? He had just decided to leave the keep and journey across the entire length of Kalia because of a dream. He felt that he needed to do it, but he also felt foolish for abandoning the keep so early in his training with the ambience. He felt ungrateful and fickle to just abandon the keep and the keeper so suddenly.

As he made his way back to his room, he tried to think of a way he could show his thanks to the elderly keeper for all he had taught him in such a short period of time. He reached his suite and opened the door. He glanced around the room and realized it wouldn't take him more than a few minutes to get all of his things together. He thought about taking a quick nap, but his eyes were drawn to the door that led up from the antechamber of his room.

He had never had a chance to see where it led. He supposed he had plenty of time before he needed to meet with Eldridge, so he walked over to the door, opened it up, and looked up the stairs. They spiraled upwards into what had to be one of the keep's towers. He began climbing the stairs, curious as to what he might find in Faldor's personal tower. As he ascended, the musty and burnt smell that he had noticed when he had first opened the door grew stronger.

He reached the top of the stairs and looked around but couldn't make out much in the darkness. There were piles and stacks of things everywhere, but he couldn't tell what they were. He carefully made his way over to one of the windows, unlatched it, and pulled it open. Light and fresh air streamed into the forgotten room.

Traven stared at its contents with wonder. The entire room was full of strange objects. There were books, models, instruments, and all manner of other objects that he couldn't identify. There were chemicals and powders in small jars. He could also see where the burnt smell had come from. There were scorch marks all around the room.

Apparently Faldor had used this tower to experiment. He carefully rummaged through some of the objects on the various tables. He couldn't even begin to imagine what half of them were for. He wondered what the ancient wielder had discovered while working in this very tower. What types of discoveries had the wise wielder achieved?

His gaze finally fell upon a small model that looked familiar. He picked it up and carried it to the window. Looking down at the courtyard, he compared the model to Faldor's stone sculpture. It was an exact match, except that the model still had all three stones in it. He glanced at the model as an idea came to him.

He put the model back down and closed the window. He then descended the stairs and returned to his room. As he packed his few belongings, he set aside the golden chest. He could certainly leave it in the keep. It was Faldor's chest after all. He opened it and looked at the two might stones. Grabbing the energy stone, he smiled. He knew what he could do to show his gratitude to the keeper and the guardians.

19

    Eldridge looked out from his window at the courtyard below. He was deeply saddened by Traven's unexpected and rash decision to leave the keep. He had been looking forward to continuing teaching and training the young wielder. The young man had been at the keep for less than two weeks but had already grown in the ambience immensely. Still, the young wielder was only beginning to scratch the surface of what he was capable of. There was so much more for him to learn, but he was already preparing to leave.

    The keeper shook his head. He couldn't really blame Traven. Visions were said to evoke strong emotions in the wielders who had them. If Traven really felt that he needed to protect the princess, the feeling would not go away. The young wielder was only doing what he felt he had to.

    What worried Eldridge the most was Traven's youth and inexperience. He believed the young man had a good heart and hoped that he would not let his new found power corrupt him. Of more concern to him was the safety of the young man. Professor Studell had shared the reports of what the wielder in Balthus had done when conquering major cities. If the rumors were true, Eldridge was afraid that Traven was not yet prepared to face him.

    The keeper could only hope that Traven's life would be spared, and he would be able to return to the keep and continue his training. Traven had so much potential but such limited training. He hoped the young man would be safe at the battle front. To lose one so young and so full of potential would definitely be a tragedy.

    Eldridge was pulled from his thoughts as he watched Traven enter the courtyard. The young man walked directly to Faldor's monument in the center of the courtyard and looked up at it. After a few moments, he wrapped his arms around one of the stone pillars and began to climb up. What was he doing?

When the young wielder reached the top, he straddled the stone pillar with his legs and began inspecting the two might stones that lay embedded in the solid rock. Eldridge's heart skipped a beat. He wasn't thinking of taking the stones was he? The keeper remembered all too well the story of Faldor's apprentice's flight a thousand years earlier. Was history about to repeat itself?

Eldridge watched with concern as two guardians entered the courtyard and looked up at Traven. However, the young wielder didn't reach for either of the two might stones. Instead he sat back and pulled something from his pocket. The ancient keeper strained his eyes to see what it was. In Traven's hand rested a stone. The stone appeared to be green with slight flashes of yellow sparking across its surface. It was the energy stone.

The keeper watched as the young man stared down at the empty socket where the might stone had originally lain. A flame appeared above the socket and began to spin in on itself. It spun faster and faster. Eldridge watched as it solidified into liquid fire. The liquid fire slowly descended to lay inside the shallow socket on the stone pillar. Traven watched it for a few moments as the liquid fire's intense heat caused the stone of the pillar to melt slightly. He then carefully set the might stone down into the glowing socket and jerked his hand back as it flashed a brilliant white.

The ancient keeper immediately felt a wave of energy wash through his body. He gasped at the feeling and stared at Traven, in awe of the young man. He felt guilty for his earlier suspicions. The young wielder had melded the might stone back into the column. He had restored Faldor's monument to its original glory. The monument would now give extra energy to all those at the keep. It would also strengthen the animals and plants nearby.

The young wielder would do just fine with his new power. He would be just fine.

* * * * *

Traven created a small ball of ice and held it in his right hand. It quickly helped to ease the pain of the slight burn on his fingertips. He had forgotten how hot liquid fire was. He tossed the ball of ice to the ground when his hand got too cold to hold it anymore. He glanced down at the might stone, newly embedded in the monument where it belonged. He created a small amount of water in front of him and doused the top of the stone column. He smiled to himself as the stone hissed and hardened around the might stone. He then turned around and slid down the stone column to the ground.

Two guardians stood at the edge of the courtyard staring at him. He had been so focused on setting the might stone into the top of the column that he hadn't even noticed when they entered the courtyard. They glanced from him to the monument and back to him. Both smiled, nodded to him, and then continued across the courtyard and into the keep.

Traven sat down and leaned back against one of the stone pillars. He was reminded of how much effort it took to create liquid fire. He closed his eyes and rested while he waited for the keeper to come and give him his last training session. He allowed his mind to open up as he tried to sense all that was around him.

He could feel a faint pulsing coming from the monument at his back and spreading outward in all directions. He could feel the currents in the air as they swept particles around the monument. He let his senses stretch further and could tell where the walls of the keep began as the particles in the air crashed against them and rushed up over and into the open valley beyond.

He found it fascinating that he could sense where things were with his eyes closed. It was his ability to sense the particles in the air that allowed it. Wherever the particles moved freely, he knew there was open air. If the particles went around something, he knew something solid was there. Eldridge had told him that if he meditated enough, he would get to the point where he would be able to sense everything around him whether he was meditating or not.

The particles in the air shifted, and he knew someone was entering the courtyard from the keep's main doors. He opened his eyes and was surprised to find Studell walking towards him instead of Eldridge. He pushed himself up to his feet to greet the philosopher.

"So you're leaving already!" Studell exclaimed before Traven had a chance to say anything. "We've only been here for about two weeks. I think if we spent the rest of our lives here we wouldn't be able to learn all of the knowledge that's stored here. Must you go so soon?"

"I don't want to go," Traven replied. "But I feel like I must." In his hurried decision to leave the keep he had completely forgotten about the philosopher. He imagined that Studell wouldn't be happy about leaving. "I'm sorry to drag you away from here so soon."

"Drag me away from here!" Studell exclaimed. "I'm not going anywhere. The keeper has offered to let me stay here until the day I die, and I think I might just take him up on it. Besides, I would just slow you down. If you're really going to try and catch up to the Royal Army, you are going to have to travel fast. Even so, I don't think you'll be able to catch up with them before they reach the pass."

Traven supposed Studell was probably correct. He just hoped that he would get to the princess in time to keep her safe. He assumed she would stay in Candus when the army continued on to the pass. There was no reason for her to be anywhere near the battle.

He hoped he would be able to at least reach Candus and the princess before the battle began.

"You do realize you've already missed the Arrow," the philosopher stated. "I'm not even sure how you're going to get away from this desert."

Traven stared back at Studell with worry. How was he going to get back? He supposed he could follow the coast, but it would take longer and be a difficult journey. The more he thought about the journey that lay ahead of him, the worse it looked.

"I suppose I'll have to follow the coast," Traven replied. "I'll be able to travel faster by myself, but I don't really like the prospect of traveling alone."

"You won't be traveling alone." Traven turned to see Eldridge listening from the front steps of the keep. "I have informed the guardians of your decision to leave and two have volunteered to accompany you. They feel a certain amount of responsibility to protect the wielder of this keep. They are preparing the necessary items for the journey."

Traven was relieved to hear that he wouldn't have to make the long journey alone. He wondered which of the guardians had volunteered. He watched as the keeper made his way down the steps and shuffled over to him.

"The guardians will lead you east along the route they use when coming to and returning home from the keep. They will also sail you across the gulf in one of our small ships. This will hopefully allow you to catch up to the princess and return to us sooner."

Traven let out a sigh of relief. Perhaps he wouldn't be too far behind the army after all.

"I see you have restored the energy stone to its proper place," Eldridge said with a smile, changing the subject. "For that I am very grateful. Faldor certainly would have approved of such an act.

"Now I would like to quickly teach you about defensive magic. The concept is simple and builds upon what you already know. One simple way to counteract anything a wielder casts at you is to form a particle sphere around yourself. Just as the sphere of particles you use to whisper on the wind doesn't let anything out, a tight particle sphere won't let anything in. Shall we practice?"

"Sure," Traven replied. He concentrated and instantly had a sphere of particles surrounding him.

"Have you created it?" Eldridge asked after several seconds.

"Yes."

"Then we will test it." The keeper carefully bent over and picked up a clump of dirt. He then threw it directly at Traven's face. Traven flinched in surprise, but the clump never reached him. It hit the invisible barrier and burst into pieces that all fell to the ground.

"Good," Eldridge said. "Now a few words of caution. If you hold the sphere for too long you will run out of air to breath. Also if the force of the attack against you is greater than your hold on the particle sphere, the sphere will either break or be thrown backwards. Either one could result in injury to you, so you must be careful. Oftentimes it may be better to create a flat shield of particles to deflect the individual attack.

"Another way to fight against attacks is by using the ambience to create something that will stifle the attack. For example, if a wielder throws a fireball at you, you can create water that will extinguish the flame. If an arrow is shot at you, you can use a gust of wind to alter its course. There are countless ways to counter an attack. I just wanted to mention a few to get you thinking. I wish I had time to teach you more but that will have to do for now. I expect you will practice all of these things along your journey so that you will be prepared when you reach your destination."

Traven assured the keeper that he would practice them. It seemed like it would not be much different than practicing wielding any of the other things he had learned. He figured that if he continued practicing wielding the ambience along the way to Candus, he would be much stronger and more skilled using the ambience when he reached his destination.

"Another useful trick is the ability to hide yourself from your enemies," Eldridge continued. "If this wielder in Balthus knows of you, he will definitely want to follow your movements. This trick will not only allow you to keep him from screeing you but will also allow you to stop those nearby from seeing you. A wielder hides himself by creating a particle shield around himself and then wrapping light around the shield. It takes practice to perfect, but I assume you could do a descent job of it right now if you wanted to."

Traven decided he might as well try it. He quickly created the particle shield around his entire body. He then pulled light around it. The keeper's eyes grew large and then he smiled as he shrugged his shoulders. Traven let the shield drop.

"Was I invisible?" he asked excitedly.

"Not exactly," Eldridge responded. "You were more of a shadowy blur, but with some practice you will be able to fully hide yourself. You already have the basic idea." Traven was a little disappointed at his failure, but eager to work on perfecting invisibility while journeying to Candus. Being invisible could definitely prove useful.

"There is one other thing that I wish I had time to teach you before you go," the keeper said. "Unfortunately, it's something that would take you years to master. It is the art of healing with the ambience. It is truly an amazing thing, but one must understand the body in precise detail or else he will do more harm than good. It would be very useful in the field of battle. However, since you do not have the time to learn it, you must make careful use of the healing stone. I presume you have it with you?"

"I do," Traven replied. He hadn't had a chance to learn how to use it but had hoped to discover its properties on the journey.

"It is simple to use," Eldridge continued. "You merely need to place it near a wound and feed it with energy. You will see certain particles rotating around the stone. You feed the stone by creating a flow of those particles from the air into the stone. The stone will absorb the particles and then transfer the energy into the person who is wounded. The stone will allow the wound to heal much quicker than it would by itself.

"However, if the wound is too severe the stone can do little to help the wounded. It would require much more energy than you could supply to it. The stone will drain your energy much faster than if you were healing a wound by yourself, but it eliminates the need for you to understand how to heal."

Traven pulled out the deep orange might stone and concentrated on it. Time stopped and the air thickened. He could readily see certain types of particles swirling around the stone. He guided them into the stone and watched as the stone let off light. The light began to change to white as he fed more energy into it. He stopped as he felt his strength being drained. The stone glowed for a few moments and then returned to its normal state. It seemed simple enough. He smiled and returned the stone to his pocket.

"That is all I have for now," Eldridge said. "I think you should finish preparing for the journey, and then we will have an early lunch before bidding you farewell."

Traven returned to his room with Studell tagging along and offering advice. Studell made him promise to deliver a message to the king about what they had found. He also made him promise to be careful so that he could return, continue his training, and tell him of his adventures. Most of all, he must not get killed. Traven readily agreed. Studell then bid him a safe journey and left for the library.

After Traven finished gathering everything he was taking with him, he paused to look around the room. It was hard for him to believe that he had only been here for less than two weeks.

Although the room still seemed too fancy and spacious for him, it somehow felt more like home than anywhere he had been since leaving his grandparents' house. He smiled at the room, hoping he would be able to return to it soon. He took one last look at the large comfortable bed and left. He knew for sure he would be missing it while he spent the next month or so sleeping on the ground.

When he arrived in the dining hall, he was surprised to find Eldridge already there along with seven of the guardians. Glancing at them, he realized that Darian was the only one missing. They all rose when he entered the room.

"We all wanted to be here to thank you and honor you for restoring the energy stone," Eldridge said. "We wish you a speedy journey, success in your endeavors, and hope you will return to the keep soon."

Traven was surprised by all of the ceremony. He had been there less than two weeks and hadn't done much for those at the keep at all. They had been taking care of him. He felt like he needed to give thanks to all of them. He thought for a moment and spoke to all in the dining hall.

"I would like to thank all of you for your hospitality and support," he said. "In the short time I've been here, I've come to feel like this is somewhere I belong. I hope to be able to return soon." All of the guardians smiled, and Eldridge nodded his head, seeming satisfied.

"Now let us eat," the ancient keeper said. "The sooner Traven leaves, the sooner he can return."

Traven sat down next to the keeper and joined the others in eating an early lunch. He was hungry after working the ambience earlier in the day and was glad for the meal. He ate his serving quickly and sat quietly waiting for the others to finish.

"Go ahead and eat Darian's meal," Jorb said as he pushed a full plate of food towards Traven. "He won't come down for some reason."

Traven wasn't sure if he should eat the elf's meal, but after assurances from several of the guardians that it was fine, he decided he might as well satisfy his hunger if Darian wasn't going to join them. He wondered if the elf was refusing to be present because he still held something against him. He felt bad if he had somehow offended the elf but tried not to worry. He finished his second helping and sat back contentedly.

"I think it's time for you to set off," Eldridge said as he stood up from the table. The guardians said their goodbyes to Traven and left for their various chores.

"Who will be coming with me?" Traven asked as he accompanied the keeper out of the dining hall.

"Jorb and Ethan volunteered to go with you," Eldridge replied. "They went to get the horses and supplies."

Traven was happy to hear that it was two of the guardians that he actually knew. The trip would be more enjoyable with the two of them. It would also be nice to travel with two others who were skilled with weapons. He didn't expect to run into any problems along the way but was glad for the two guardians' expertise just in case.

He waited patiently with Eldridge for the two guardians to bring the horses. He looked up at the clear blue sky and took a deep breath of the sweetly scented air. There was something undeniably special about this hidden valley. He truly hoped that he would be able to return soon.

"I cannot believe you did it," someone muttered from inside the keep. "You're really going to go through with this?"

"Where is your honor?" another voice asked tauntingly.

"You disgust me," a third voice stated vehemently.

Traven and the keeper turned around and peered through the open door of the keep, wondering what was going on. At the top of the stairs, a cloaked figure with his hood up began to descend. He had a pack slung over his shoulder and he walked with purpose.

Flanking him were three elven guardians. They all kept shaking their heads and expressing their surprise, horror, and disgust. It wasn't until the cloaked figure reached the bottom of the stairs that Traven realized it was Darian. He wondered what the elf had done to warrant all of the attention and derision.

He watched with interest as Darian left the keep and walked directly towards him. The other elves all stopped at the door. He stared with surprise as Darian walked right up to him and knelt at his feet. The elf threw back his hood and stared intently at him with burning eyes. The black slash of a tattoo over his left eye had been altered. Drawn delicately within the black were patterns of metallic silver that matched the patterns on Traven's own clothes. A gasp escaped from Eldridge.

"Master Wielder Traven," Darian began in a firm voice from his kneeling position. "I devote my life to you. I will live, fight, and die for you. I am yours to command."

Traven stared back at him in complete shock. What was Darian doing? He had no idea how to respond. He didn't understand what the elf was saying. Eldridge cleared his throat and leaned over to whisper into Traven's ear.

"The correct response is 'I accept your devotion'," he said quietly.

Traven wasn't sure if he wanted to say that or not. It made him feel awkward and uncomfortable. However, seeing the way that Darian was staring up at him, he decided that he should follow the keeper's advice.

"I accept your devotion," Traven repeated, still feeling uncomfortable. A wave of relief washed over Darian's face upon hearing the words. The elf rose to his feet, and after bowing to him, walked towards the stables.

Traven glanced at the other elves. All three gave him calculating looks before turning and walking back into the keep. He then turned with a questioning look to Eldridge.

"It is called the devotion," the keeper said quietly. "I never thought I would see it happen. I am especially surprised that it was Darian. I never would have expected him to chain himself to a human."

"What do you mean chain himself?" Traven asked worriedly.

"Not literally," Eldridge replied. He then took on a lecturing tone. "When an elf feels the devotion to a wielder, he makes an oath to do whatever the wielder asks of him. Elves are incredibly loyal to their oaths. They would rather die than break them. Darian will now do anything you ask of him, even if he doesn't agree with it. He would jump off a cliff if you told him to." The keeper paused and stared intently at Traven, making sure he understood what was being said. "Before the Wielder Wars, many of the elves performed the devotion ceremony and followed the more powerful wielders. For the last thousand years no elf has chosen to devote himself to a wielder, until now. Consider yourself honored."

20

    Kadrak finished his nighttime ascent up the gradual slope of the foothills. His army was camped outside of Beking and ready to march for the Pass of Banshi in the morning. He had climbed up into the mountains to visit with Shaman Azulk one last time before continuing his campaign into Kalia. He didn't fully trust the galdak leader and wanted to make sure that the shaman understood exactly what he wanted him to do.

    Kadrak stepped up onto a shelf of rock that offered a magnificent view of the land below. He glanced at the entrance of the cave that was set back against the mountain but sensed that it was empty. He turned from the entrance and looked out over the land below. In the distance he could see the city of Beking and just outside its walls, the many campfires of his army. All of it belonged to him. The country of Balthus had fallen even easier than he'd expected. The thrill of victory had left him anxious for more. Kalia would be next. Once it had fallen, he would turn his campaign to the southern countries. He wouldn't stop until he controlled all of the lands.

    He sensed a presence nearing the mouth of the cave. Turning away from the splendid view, he looked to the entrance of the cave once again. Soon he could see the lightly glowing yellow eyes of Shaman Azulk. The elderly galdak stepped out of the cave's shadow and approached him. His dark red skin was wrinkled and splotched, and his hunched form made him seem shorter than he really was. The shaman bowed deeply to Kadrak with the stones and skulls that dangled from his neck almost touching the ground.

"You wished to speak with me?" he said in a raspy voice as he rose from his bow.

"That is why I am here," Kadrak replied. "Tomorrow I will lead my army to Kalia. The Kalian Army is already in place at the western mouth of the Pass of Banshi and another contingent of troops will arrive there soon. The Kalian Army is rumored to be the most disciplined of any country's army. I expect that they will put up a decent fight."

He paused before continuing. He still debated whether it was the right time to reveal his army of galdaks, but he also wanted to be certain that the clash with the Kalian Army would end in a resounding victory for him. He didn't want to leave anything up to chance. He had made his decision already and would stick with it.

"I have come to make sure that your warriors are ready," he stated. "I believe I might have need of them soon."

"We have been ready for many years," Shaman Azulk whispered back in almost a hiss. "If I were to call them forth now, they would be ready to fight."

"Good," Kadrak replied with a smile. "I require that one thousand of your warriors be hidden in the mountains at the western end of the Pass of Banshi. They are to remain there, hidden, until I call for them."

"As you command," the galdak said. "They can easily be in place before your human army arrives. Are you certain that you only want a thousand?"

"Yes," he said. "Hopefully they will not be needed." He noticed a tightening around the eyes of the shaman. "The time will come for your people, Shaman. However, the time may not be here yet. We shall see."

"What signal should my warriors be waiting for?" the elderly galdak asked slowly.

"I will shoot three fireballs, straight up into the air. I will then create a lightning strike. Wherever the bolt strikes, that is where I want your warriors to attack. Do you understand my instructions?"

"I understand them perfectly," Shaman Azulk replied curtly. "My warriors will be in place and waiting for your signal. Should you call them, you will not be disappointed with their skill in war."

"Good," Kadrak stated. Having given his instructions, he was anxious to return to camp and get some sleep. "If your warriors prove useful, perhaps the time for the galdaks to avenge their wrongs will be at hand."

* * * * *

Shaman Azulk watched as the arrogant wielder strode away from him and began to descend the mountain. He clenched his fists tightly and tried to remain as calm as he could. His people had waited centuries to avenge themselves of the wrongs that had occurred at the hands of the humans. He would be patient. He would wait just a little longer. The time of the galdaks was swiftly approaching.

* * * * *

Kadrak swiftly descended to the lowlands and mounted his waiting horse. Every time he turned his back on the shaman, he wondered if the galdak would try and attack him. He supposed that Shaman Azulk tried to hide his distaste for him, but the elderly galdak didn't do a good job at it. It was easy to see that the shaman had no love for him whatsoever. He wondered once again how long he should allow the old galdak to live. The shaman was dangerous but smart enough to realize that Kadrak was his superior.

He grinned as his horse trotted back towards the army's encampment. The galdaks had already supplied him with a small fortune and now would guarantee him a victory against the Kalian

Army if he needed them. As long as he could control them, they would continue to be a valuable asset. It would be interesting to see how well they would obey his orders. If the galdak warriors proved that they could follow his instructions in the coming battle, he would have many other tasks for them to fulfill.

As he rode closer to the encampment, his mind turned from thoughts of the galdaks to thoughts of his human army. Combining the rogue army with the Balthan Army had worked better than he had expected it to. Gilrod had done an excellent job in appointing experienced leaders within the ranks. There were still more skirmishes and fights between the troops than he would have liked, but overall he was pleased with the integration.

The march from Rankdra to Beking had been much better organized than the previous march in the opposite direction. He hoped that things would continue to run smoothly. The army had a long way to march before they would reach their ultimate destination of Calyn.

Kadrak slowed his horse as he approached the encampment. He didn't want to have to kill any of his troops if he startled them and they accidently attacked him. As he entered the outskirts of the camp, his soldiers began to recognize him and bowed as he passed. Gilrod had suggested that he not go anywhere without an honor guard, but he had no use for one.

Everyone knew who he was. He didn't need pageantry to announce himself, and he didn't need any protection besides his own mastery of the ambience. When his people saw a tall, striking man with blond flowing hair, they knew who they were looking at. He would also often use the ambience to create a slight glow around himself at night. His soldiers could then easily see the power he possessed emanating from him. It affectively inspired awe amongst all who saw him.

He proceeded through the camp towards his tent as his soldiers continued to bow and show proper respect at his passing.

As a child he had been small and skinny. Many of those in his village at the southern reaches of Balthus had called him runt. No one would even consider calling him that now. When he had finally hit his growth spurt, long after the other boys his age, he had grown to be taller than most. He had worked hard on his parents' pitiful farm and had soon grown strong as well.

He then had paid every last one of the boys back for their teasing, taunting, and bullying of him. He smiled at the memory. Back then he had used the only two weapons he had, his fists. The boys of his village had steered clear of him after the beatings they had received. The following summer he had begun to realize that something was different about him. Soon he had begun to experiment with the power that lay inside of him.

His parents hadn't been pleased when he had showed them the tricks he could do. They were a superstitious lot and had banned him from using any of his magic. His father soon thereafter had caught him practicing making fire. He still remembered the look of anger on his father's face as he had thrown him out of the house and assured him that he would never be welcomed back.

Kadrak had made sure that no one would be welcomed back. Once his parents had left for the market the next day, he had snuck back into the house, gathered the supplies he would need for a journey, and set the place on fire. He had not looked back as he headed north with his childhood home burning to the ground behind him.

He wasn't sure what his parents had done after returning home to find their house destroyed. He had never worried or felt bad about it. They had gotten what they deserved. He had loved them and worked hard for them his entire childhood. How had he been repaid? He had been cast out.

He wouldn't repeat the same type of injustice against his followers that his parents had committed against him. Those who opposed him would be dealt with harshly, but those who respected and followed him would prosper under his rule. He would have plenty of power to share with those who were loyal to him. He would reward them generously.

Kadrak arrived at his large tent and brushed past the two guards standing at either side of the entrance. He had considered staying at the small palace in Beking for the night but had decided against it. When leading an army, his place was with the army, in the midst of his troops. He wanted his soldiers to know that he would be fighting with them.

He prepared for sleep and lay down on his soft bed. Although he would be sleeping in the midst of his troops, he wouldn't be sleeping on the ground like them. He needed to sleep well if he wanted to wield the ambience with as much strength as possible. He would go without certain things on the campaign into Kalia, but he felt no need to deprive himself of all luxuries. He had a nice bed, a sturdy desk, a skilled chef, and a special stock of his favorite foods.

A master wielder such as himself should be able to enjoy life no matter where he was. The long days of riding would be tempered by the small luxuries that he allowed himself. He closed his eyes and relaxed.

It would take nine days to reach the eastern edge of the Pass of Banshi. They would then march through the high pass in the mountains for five days until they reached the other end. There was currently still some snow in the pass, but he hoped it would all be melted by the time the army reached it. In fourteen days time, the Kalian Army would face the wrath of the Master Wielder Kadrak.

Part Three: Rising

21

Traven glanced out over the sea in the early morning light. The eastern coast of Faldor's Watch appeared much the same as the southern tip. However, the cliffs that rose up behind them here were much shorter than the ones further south and the beach was wider. Glancing south, he could make out several large rocks jutting up out of the water. Apparently, farther south in the gulf the rocks were extremely numerous. They made it all but impossible for a large ship to safely travel north. He supposed that was the reason the map had led them to the southern tip of Faldor's Watch and not further up its eastern coast.

The water of the gulf appeared fairly calm, but Traven was nervous about the prospect of crossing it in such a small boat. He glanced back at the guardians who were loading up their supplies and making the boat ready to set sail. They had assured him that it was a sturdy ship and not to worry, but the size of it still left him concerned. It looked as though it would barely be able to fit the four of them and their mounts.

It was long and narrow with a single sail. There were also oars for rowing. Jorb had said that if there wasn't much wind, they would still be able to reach land by nightfall if they all rowed hard. He hoped that Jorb was right. He didn't want to be out in the open water on the small boat any longer than he had to.

They had set out midmorning the previous day from the keep. It had taken all day and half of the night for them to reach the coast and the small cave where the keep's two boats were sheltered. The afternoon had been incredibly hot and draining, but luckily they had only had to endure the heat for one day. Traven was glad to be leaving the desert behind him and returning to a milder climate.

"Everything is ready." Darian said. "We should push off now if we want to reach the other side before dark."

Traven hurried over to the ship and helped the three guardians as they struggled to push the ship, now laden with four horses, off the sand and deeper into the water. After a few heaves, the ship broke loose and slipped fully into the water. All four quickly pulled themselves up and into the ship. Traven scooted to the center of the ship as Darian took his place at the rudder.

Traven glanced back at the elf. He was still in shock of what had happened the previous day. He never would have imagined that one day he would have an elf devoted to him. He still hadn't really had a chance to figure out their relationship. The human guardians treated him like a friend. However, Darian treated him differently. Throughout the previous afternoon, he was sure the elf had shot him multiple menacing glances. Then when they had stopped upon reaching the coast, the elf had politely offered to take care of Pennon.

At times he was sure that the elf was upset with him no matter what he did, and at other times the elf seemed to truly be devoted to him. He supposed that it had to do with Darian's own conflicts between his pride and choosing to serve a wielder. He hoped the elf would soon be able to reconcile his inner conflicts. Traven couldn't figure out how to act towards the elf until Darian figured things out for himself.

Traven looked at the coast and watched as it got further and further away. He tried not to think about all of the water underneath him. Luckily the sky was clear, the waves were small, and there was a light breeze. He hoped that the conditions would remain the same until they reached the opposite coast. He would handle the trip a lot better without large waves.

The boat continued onward at a fair speed as the sun broke the horizon. Traven had to shield his eyes against the glare of the rising sun off the water directly in front of them. Both Ethan and Jorb were silhouetted at the front of the boat. He got up and carefully made his way towards them. Both were looking forward with excited expressions.

"This is great," Jorb said excitedly. "Do you know how long it's been since I've been on the water?"

"I would say six years," Ethan responded. "The same amount of time as all of us human guardians."

"It was a rhetorical question," Jorb said rolling his eyes. "Traven, did you know that before I came to the keep I fished almost every day? My family and many of the people in my village have been fishers forever. I didn't realize how much I missed the sea until we got this boat out in the water. I guess six years in the middle of the desert makes you forget."

"It's true," Ethan responded. "You get so used to the routine at the keep that you kind of forget about everything else. I haven't thought about a smithy for years. I guess that's a good thing. It would be horrible to be longing for home every day for twenty years."

Traven hadn't ever thought much about what the guardians had been before they entered service at Faldor's Keep. He supposed they all had varied backgrounds. He glanced back at Darian and wondered what the elf had done before coming to the keep. He would have to ask him about it sometime.

"If this breeze keeps up, we'll easily reach the coast by nightfall," Jorb said. "I wonder if I can persuade Darian to let me steer for awhile."

Jorb left the bow of the boat and headed towards the elf. Ethan and Traven watched as he began pleading with Darian to let him take hold of the rudder. Ethan began chuckling as the elf refused to give up his spot and Jorb threw his arms into the air.

After a few more words, the guardian returned to the bow of the small ship.

"Darian is so difficult sometimes," Jorb said. A mischievous gleam then came to his eyes as he turned to Traven. "Can't you command him to let me steer for awhile?"

"What?" Traven said. "Why would he listen to me if he didn't listen to you?"

"That's obvious," Jorb said. "He swore his devotion to you. He'll do whatever you ask him to."

"I still don't understand how it works," Traven said. "Eldridge also said he would do whatever I tell him to. Will he really?"

"Yes," Jorb said. "At least I think he will. I don't suppose anyone living had seen an elf devote himself to a human before yesterday afternoon, so none of us are experts. However, from what we've read, the devotion ceremony is one of the most serious and sacred oaths an elf can commit. Darian may be difficult at times, but one thing he definitely doesn't lack is honor. I believe he really will do anything you ask him to."

The thought of the elf doing anything he asked him to made him feel uncomfortable once again. He would rather people listen to him because they wanted to, not because they had to. He almost didn't want to ask Darian to do anything for fear the elf would do it but be upset by the request. Traven wondered if there was a way for him to free Darian from the oath.

"Is there a way for Darian to be released from the oath of devotion?" he asked.

"The only way I know of is if you decide to reject him as a servant or if he dies," Jorb responded.

"Maybe I should reject him as a servant," Traven mumbled, thinking out loud.

"I definitely wouldn't do that," Ethan said quickly. "If a wielder rejects the oath of devotion, the elf is left disgraced. That might not sound bad to you, but to an elf it is worse than death. A disgraced elf has to tattoo a black spot on his cheek as a symbol of his worthlessness. All the other elves would refuse to associate with him. He would either have to live in isolation or be reduced to a beggar."

"Really?" Traven asked.

Both Ethan and Jorb nodded. It was hard to believe that such a small thing would lead to so much suffering. Then again, he supposed he didn't know much at all about the elf culture. They looked so much like humans that he forgot how different they might actually be. He would need to get to know Darian better soon. If the elf had chosen to be his servant, Traven wanted to know as much as he could about the elves.

"I think you're looking at this the wrong way," Jorb said. "You should be thrilled to have Darian as your servant. For starters, he's the best fighter I've ever seen. Who wouldn't want him watching their back?"

Traven had to agree with Jorb. To have such a skilled bodyguard was a blessing indeed. When he had traveled with Blaize, he had definitely felt a certain sense of security.

"And, he is much smarter than he looks," Ethan said with a grin. "He knows things that would amaze you. I guess when you've lived for over sixty years you can accumulate a lot of knowledge."

"Sixty years!" Traven exclaimed. He had guessed that Darian couldn't be any more than ten years his senior. He looked to Jorb, wondering if Ethan was joking with him. Jorb was smiling but nodded his head in agreement.

"Elves live longer than humans," Jorb explained. "Just like you'll live longer because you're a wielder. Even though Darian is over sixty, he's still in his prime."

Traven paused. He hadn't really thought about that. It did make sense. He had been told that elves had many of the same passive characteristics as wielders did. They had heightened senses, healed faster, and lived longer than humans. He supposed they would look younger for longer as well.

The thought of the elves' longevity led him to consider something else he hadn't really thought about until this moment. Wielders lived longer than regular humans. That meant he would live longer. Would he look as young as Darian when he was sixty years old? He had always expected to only live to be perhaps eighty. Now how old would he live to be? He made his way back to the middle of the ship and sat down.

He spent the next couple of hours in silence, contemplating the ramifications of living a longer life than those around him. On the one hand it was exciting. With extra time, he could see, do, and learn so much more than he would be able to otherwise. However, living longer also created problems. What would happen to his friends? They would get old and die long before he did. How would he deal with that? Would it be better to not get close to anyone at all? He shook his head. That wasn't a good answer. What would be the point of living so long if your days were full of loneliness?

And what of having a family? If he married, his wife would grow old and die while he remained young. He would also be forced to watch his own children grow older than him and die. He could only imagine the pain and sadness it would cause. Would it be better to avoid having a family altogether? He tried to shake the dismal thoughts from his head.

He glanced back at Darian. The elf had nothing to fear from his longevity. All of his people would live long like he. He wouldn't be left alone as he got older. His friends and family would age the same as he. Traven paused. He supposed another great benefit of having an elf as his servant was that they would age in the same way. He kept thinking about the implications of living longer as the boat continued slipping through the water towards their destination.

"Looks like we're rowing," Jorb announced with a groan.

Traven looked up. He had been so lost in his thoughts that he hadn't realized the boat had come to a stop. The sail hung slack in the still air. The early morning breeze had completely disappeared. Jorb and Ethan left the bow and picked up the long oars. Jorb handed one to Traven as Ethan walked one back to Darian.

"Hopefully the breeze will pick back up before too long," Jorb said. "However, if we just sit here waiting we won't make it to the coast before nightfall."

All four joined in rowing. The boat was soon moving along at a steady pace once again. Traven didn't mind it at first. It was good to have something to do besides just sitting and worrying about aging slowly. However, after awhile his arms were sore and his back ached. The air was still completely motionless, and the day was getting hotter. He paused in rowing and wiped the sweat from his brow. He wasn't sure how long he could keep doing this.

"Let's take a break," Ethan said while pulling up his oar. "My back is killing me."

They all agreed and pulled up their oars. Darian passed around some dried fruit and nuts, and they all took a long drink from their water skins. Traven stood up and stretched, trying to make his back feel better. He didn't want to row anymore but would much rather have a sore back than be stuck out in the sea on the open boat over night. He sat back down and picked up his oar with an audible sigh.

"May I speak freely?" Darian said quietly enough for him alone to hear. Traven nodded for him to go on. "Perhaps we might all be able to rest our muscles for awhile longer if you would deign to call up a wind to fill the sail."

Traven stared back at the elf feeling slightly foolish. Why hadn't he thought of doing that sooner? He had been practicing wielding the wind all week, and yet he hadn't even thought of using his new skill when the need was at hand. He looked up at the sail. It seemed like it would be easy enough to do. He would have to keep the wind sustained, which would eventually drain him. However, it would save his and the guardians' backs.

"I think that's a great idea," he replied to the elf. "I suppose I should have thought of it sooner." Darian stared back at him with a hint of a smile on his lips.

"Don't worry," the elf said. "You've only been wielding the ambience for a couple of weeks. It's still new to you as it is to all of us."

Traven glanced up at the sail and sky once again and time stopped. He pulled and pushed the necessary particles and soon a stiff breeze pushed the sails open and propelled the boat forward. Ethan almost fell over at the sudden lurching forward of the boat. He glanced up at the sail with a huge grin.

"I hope this wind lasts," he said. "I'm not looking forward to rowing again."

"I think it will last as long as it needs to," Darian said with a smile as he made his way back to the rudder. "It's following the command of its master."

Ethan stared at Darian for a few moments with a confused look. He then smiled as he made sense of what the elf had said. His countenance then changed, and he looked down at Traven accusingly.

"Why didn't you do that an hour ago?"

"I forgot I could," Traven replied back honestly.

"Well let's try hard not to forget again," Ethan announced seriously, trying to look stern.

Traven quickly stopped the wind and made it blow in the opposite direction. The boat stopped almost instantly, knocking Ethan off his feet. Darian burst out laughing as Traven started the wind blowing in the correct direction again. Jorb joined in the laughter as Ethan pushed himself up off the floor of the boat. He tried to look angry but was soon laughing with everyone else.

Luckily, Traven only had to sustain the wind for about an hour before the natural wind picked back up. He wasn't sure how much longer he could have held the ambience. By the time he was done, he was drenched with perspiration and felt completely drained. He gladly accepted the water and food that Darian offered him. The elf had kept a sharp eye on him the entire time and had regularly brought him water and nuts.

"Did you know that I see a faint glow around you when you wield the ambience?' Darian said.

"Really?" Traven asked after finishing his drink of water. "I knew that wielders could see auras around other wielders and judge their strength from it, but I didn't know that elves could see it."

"I don't see the glow all the time like a wielder would," he said. "I just see the faint glow when you are actually wielding the ambience. I never noticed it before. It's very faint. At first I thought my eyes were playing tricks on me."

Traven took another drink from the water skin, trying to hold it steady with his shaking hands so it wouldn't spill.

"How do you feel?" Darian asked, noticing the shaking of Traven's hands.

"I'm fine," Traven replied. "I just need some rest. Wielding the ambience for so long completely drained me."

"May I offer a suggestion?"

"Sure," Traven said. "And you don't have to ask me before suggesting something. Just tell me whatever you want to."

"Thank you," Darian said with a nod of his head. "I think it is unwise for you to wield the ambience to the point where it completely drains you. Do you have a headache?"

"Yes," Traven replied. It wasn't very bad, but there was a slight pounding right behind his eyes.

"If you receive a headache from wielding the ambience, you have wielded too much of it. It isn't healthy to wield more than you have strength for. Not only does your body have to restore its strength, it then also has to fix the damage you caused to it. You should stop wielding the ambience at the first sign of any headache. Your body will be able to regain its strength much faster if it doesn't have to repair any self inflicted damage."

After offering his advice Darian rose and moved back to take control of the rudder once again. Traven closed his eyes and leaned back to rest, hoping the throbbing wouldn't last very long. What Darian had told him made sense. He would try to manage his use of the ambience more carefully. The slight flapping of the wind in the sail and the soft rolling of the waves helped him to relax. It wasn't long before he dropped off to sleep.

22

Traven woke up an hour or two later. Not much had changed except for the position of the sun. It was now behind the boat instead of in front of it. Luckily, there was still a stiff breeze and the boat was sailing along speedily towards its destination. He was starving and helped himself to the meal that he had slept through. While he ate, he listened cheerily as Jorb and Ethan teased him about his lack of stamina and strange sleeping habits. His headache was gone, and that was all that really mattered to him at the moment.

The wind died down a little as the day wore on, coming and going in spurts. Traven helped keep the ship moving swiftly during the lulls in the wind by creating wind of his own. However, he was careful not to overexert himself like he had earlier. Fortunately, the wind would always pick back up fairly quickly, allowing him numerous breaks in between wielding the ambience.

Soon the sun was low on the horizon, almost touching the water behind them. They ate dinner and enjoyed the brilliant sunset over the water. Jorb said they had to be getting close. They had kept up a good speed the entire day with Traven's help.

"Land ho!" Darian announced with a smile.

Jorb and Ethan eagerly searched the eastern horizon. Both squinted but couldn't see any sign of the coast.

"Are you sure?" Jorb asked.

Darian pretended to not even hear the question. Traven glanced out over the water. He could see a strip of land on the eastern horizon as well. The sight was welcome indeed. He breathed a sigh of relief, knowing that they would reach the coast before night set in.

"I see it too," Traven chimed in.

Jorb and Ethan glanced back at the horizon and then looked at each other and shrugged their shoulders. Traven shared a knowing smile with Darian. A little later, they were close enough that the two human guardians could see the coast as well. Darian guided the ship in a slightly southeastern direction towards a small cove. Traven was so excited to get back on land that he added to the wind to help them reach the coast faster.

As the boat slipped into the cove, Jorb and Ethan hopped out and splashed into the water up to their waists. They helped pull the boat up onto the beach as far as they could. Traven and Darian then jumped out on the beach and helped pull the boat up a little further. They soon had the horses and all of their supplies unloaded. They then heaved the boat all the way out of the water and secured it in a small cave that was a short distance inland.

"We just leave it here?" Traven asked.

"Yes," Jorb replied. "Our home village is the closest anyone is to here, and it is about ten miles to the south. No one really ventures north of the village. There's nothing up here but dirt and wild beasts."

As soon as the boat had been taken care of, they all mounted their horses and headed eastward with Ethan taking the lead.

"I thought your village was to the south," Traven said. "Aren't we going to stop there for the night?" Ethan and Jorb exchanged wistful glances.

"As much as we'd like to," Ethan began, "it's better that we don't. We made an oath to serve at the keep for twenty years. If we see our homes and those we left, it will be harder for us to give it all up again and return to the keep. Jorb and I decided it would be easier for us to keep our oaths if we stay away from our village. We'll reach the town of Arcad in a few days and can restock our supplies there."

Traven would have liked to see the small fishing village that the human guardians came from. It would be fascinating to see what type of people would continue keeping the promise of providing the keep with guardians for so many hundreds of years. However, he understood that it might be hard for Ethan and Jorb to see their homes and have to leave immediately. He supposed that Ethan was correct, and it was best to bypass the village.

After traveling for a short distance through the growing darkness, the group stopped for the night. They started setting up camp at the base of a small cliff. Behind the cliff, dry mountains rose up, blocking the bottom half of the sky. They had been traveling at the base of the Parched Mountains ever since they left the coast.

"Are you sure you want to camp so close to the mountains?" Jorb asked Ethan.

"Sure," the other guardian replied. "We have a wielder and an elf with us. What have we to fear?"

"I guess you're right," Jorb said glancing northward at the mountains. "But it still makes me a little nervous to sleep so near them. I probably won't sleep very well."

"What's wrong with camping by the mountains?" Traven asked as they continued to set up camp. He glanced up into the mountains. They seemed desolate and devoid of anything but dirt and rocks.

"He's just scared of the mountain beasts," Ethan said dismissively.

"You would be too if you'd ever seen one," Jorb replied defensively. "They really do live in these mountains. Multiple people have seen them."

"What kind of mountain beasts?" Traven asked curiously.

"Some people don't believe in them," Jorb said giving Ethan a sharp look. "But they are definitely up in these mountains. They aren't seen very often. Though, every once in a while someone gets a glimpse of them. They have skin like blood, glowing yellow eyes, and sharp fangs. I saw one when I was a little kid."

"He thinks he saw one," Ethan cut in.

"I know I saw one," Jorb stated firmly. "And no one can deny how many people have disappeared in these mountains. Most people that venture too near these mountains never return."

"That is the truth," Ethan agreed. "These mountains are dangerous."

"It sounds like galdaks to me," Darian said, joining in the conversation. "They have red skin and their eyes do glow yellow. I didn't realize there were any this far west."

"See," Jorb said. "Darian believes me."

"But galdaks haven't been seen for hundreds of years," Ethan responded.

"Neither have elves," Darian stated, "except for the guardians. And I can personally guarantee that there are plenty of elves still alive."

"Wait," Traven said. "What's a galdak?" Everyone else seemed to know but him.

"Galdaks are another near human race like the elves," Darian said. "They are bigger than the average human and have thick red skin. They dwell in the caves of the mountains. No one is really sure how many of them there are. Centuries ago they used to interact with humans. Then there was a really bad drought and a famine in the land. When the galdaks ventured from their mountain homes in search of food, the humans refused to share any of their food with them.

"A huge war erupted between the two races. The galdaks, frustrated with the humans for allowing them to starve, began to destroy the human villages in the north. The humans gathered together a huge army and drove the galdaks back to the mountains. The humans were so upset over the villages that had been destroyed and the people that had been killed that they didn't stop pursuing the monsters. Even after the galdaks had been driven to the Parched Mountains, the human army continued to hunt them and drive them northward into the Barren Lands until they had killed all they could find.

"The galdaks haven't been seen or heard of much since then. However, some did escape into the caves of the mountains. They have been spotted by the elves from time to time."

Traven sat quietly, taking it all in. He glanced at the mountains to the north, wondering if there were any galdaks nearby.

"Are there any other races I don't know about?" he asked.

"No," Darian said chuckling. "As far as I know, the humans, elves, and galdaks are the only sentient races in the land. Now if we want to get an early start tomorrow, I suggest we finish setting up camp and go to sleep."

They all agreed and quickly finished setting up camp. Despite the talk of galdaks, they were all tired from the long day and were soon all asleep. The night passed without incident, and they were up and heading east before the sun rose.

Over the next several days, they covered a lot of ground. They arose early each morning, traveled all day, and stopped after dark. Traven wanted to reach Candus as fast as they could, and he was happy with the progress they were making. He learned more about the galdaks and about the elves, though Darian wasn't very forthcoming about his own people. He would answer specific questions that Traven asked, but he wouldn't offer up anything extra.

Traven spent the majority of each day continuing to practice wielding the ambience from his saddle. At first he mostly worked on the defensive shields that Eldridge had taught him right before he had left. He could soon create the shields easily, without much thought. He practiced making them different sizes and different shapes.

He also spent a lot of time thinking of how he could use the ambience to repel different types of attacks. When he arrived at the battlefront, he wanted to be prepared for whatever he might have to face. He wanted to be ready to repel arrows and javelins as well as fire and lightning.

One of the things he enjoyed practicing the most was bending light to make things invisible. It took him a whole day of practicing to finally be able to get it completely right. At first he could only blur things, but by the end of the day he could make them completely disappear. He had fun over the next few days making himself disappear at random times and making other various objects disappear.

They arrived at the mining town of Arcad after a few days and restocked their supplies. Darian stayed outside of the town to avoid anyone seeing that he was an elf. Traven offered to make him invisible so he could come along with them, but Darian declined. He said he wasn't quite ready to be in a whole town of humans yet.

Arcad was an even rougher sort of town than Jatz had been. Luckily, no one was brave enough to attack three armed men. Traven was once again thankful for the presence of the guardians. He looked at the several inns they passed longingly. As much as he would have liked to stay in the town overnight, he knew that it was more important for them to continue on as swiftly as they could.

Once they left Arcad, they were able to begin following the well traveled highway that would stretch all the way to Candus. The highway made traveling a lot easier, and they began to cover more ground each day.

Traven continued having visions at night of the crown and the absence of the princess. He would always wake with the same anxious feeling and the pull to get to her as soon as he could. Every night he would scree up the princess to verify that she was still okay. The nightly routine helped him to sleep better, until he would have another one of his visions.

He wouldn't only check on the princess and the position of the Royal Army daily, but he would also check on his own party's current position. It allowed him to have a very good feel for how far they had traveled and how much longer it would take them to reach their destination. Screeing allowed him to pick landmarks and set goals for the day's ride more accurately than a map would ever allow.

On the tenth night after they had left the keep, Traven walked a short distance from their campfire and once again called up the image of the princess. He had discovered about a week into the journey that he could actually call up the image of the princess without having to search for her like he had originally done. He wasn't sure how he was able to do it, but it made checking on her safety much easier.

The thin layer of water in the dish sprang to life as he stared down at it. He was anxious to see the princess once again and relaxed as the image came into focus. She was no longer in the army camp but in a grand dining hall. There were amazing dishes of food all around her, and the hall was full of elaborately dressed people and brilliant colors. She must have finally reached Candus.

He wasn't sure what the celebration was for. Perhaps they were celebrating the arrival of the army, but he doubted they would be doing such a thing before the battle. It did appear that the princess and her fiancé, the commander general, were the center of attention. They both had spots next to each other at the front of the giant dining hall.

Traven's eyes wandered back to the dazzling image of the princess. She looked as stunning and beautiful as he had ever seen her. A delighted smile danced across her lips in between her bites of food, her hair was done up intricately, and her gown seemed to sparkle. Traven smiled at her beauty for several moments and then with a conscious effort let her image fade away.

He was delighted to see she had reached Candus safely. She would be staying in the palace there and should be safe until he arrived. However, he still wasn't sure what he was going to tell her when he got to Candus. He knew he couldn't just approach her and tell her that she was missing from his dreams and he was worried for her safety. She would think he was crazy.

Another problem was that he couldn't deny that his feelings for her had grown over the last couple of weeks. He tried to tell himself that he was only doing his duty as a soldier in the Royal Army. He was just worried about the safety of the future High Queen of Kalia. There was nothing personal involved. However, no matter how many times he tried to tell himself that, he knew his feelings for her went beyond those of a loyal subject. He tried to fight his attraction to her but couldn't seem to.

He supposed it was his visions that had caused the connection. The deep feelings that stemmed from them were too strong to ignore. Every night when he called up her image in the screeing dish, he found it harder and harder to let her image fade away. Seeing her alive and well was one of the things he looked forward to the most every day. He wouldn't have worried about it so much if she wasn't royalty and engaged to be married.

He knew he had no right to feel anything deeper for her than loyalty as one of her subjects. He hoped that when he finally reached Candus and found her safe, the feelings of urgency to protect her would go away. Perhaps once those feelings disappeared, he would be able to get his own emotions under control.

Of course, he still had the problem of how to approach her when he arrived. At first he had thought that he could discreetly keep a watch on her from a distance. However, he wondered if he would be able to stop the threat to her if he wasn't nearby. He didn't want the hasty journey to end with her death because he was too afraid to tell her the truth. He had decided that perhaps it would be best for him to offer his service as one of her guards. He could also leave the guardians as guards in his place if he had to leave the princess to join the fast approaching battle.

He shook his head with a sigh. He pulled up a new image in the screeing dish and checked on their progress. It looked as if they could reach Candus within about eight days. At least he would have until then to figure out the best course of action to follow when they arrived. He supposed it would probably be a good idea to share his dilemma with the guardians and get their advice.

He let the image of their whereabouts fade, picked up the dish, and walked back towards the fire. All three guardians had already settled down for the night and were preparing to sleep. He supposed he could ask their opinions the next day during the ride. He unrolled his bedroll and settled down as well. They had been riding hard, and he had been practicing the ambience extensively during the day. He closed his eyes, hoping that he wouldn't have any visions, but secretly hoping that if he did, the princess would return to them.

23

Kalista raised her glass and clinked it against Gavin's raised glass.

"To us," she said, repeating the words Gavin had just spoken. She took a sip of the sweet drink and savored it. She then set her glass down and looked over the room once again. Most of the people who had come to the engagement feast had already filed out of the dining hall. The last few were finishing up their dessert and readying to head home for the night.

The Baron and Baroness of Candus sat to Gavin and Kalista's left, beaming at their son and soon-to-be daughter-in-law. They had thrown a wonderful feast, and Kalista was grateful for it. She had to confess that what her fiancé had said about a wonderful dinner when they reached Candus was true. The food had been varied and exquisite. It had no doubt been enhanced even more by the recent lack of variety and taste in her meals, but it would have been considered grand under any circumstances.

Baron Mikel had left the army encamped near the opening of the Pass of Banshi and had arrived in Candus that very afternoon. He had said that he would not be absent for the arrival of his future daughter-in-law. Kalista had been pleasantly surprised to find both of Gavin's parents waiting for their arrival.

The first things she had done after being greeted by the baron and baroness were settle into her sleeping chambers and take a steaming hot bath to cleanse herself of the grime of traveling. It had felt wonderful. She had then taken a short nap in a comfortable bed. When she woke up an hour later, she had prepared for the feast.

Her servants had said that she looked radiant and stunning, and by the look on Gavin's face when he arrived to escort her to the feast, he had agreed. The engagement feast had been grand with ten courses. Between each course musicians had performed, and just before the two dessert courses there had even been jugglers and acrobats. It had been delightful and charming.

She glanced over at Gavin and knew from the light in his eyes that he had enjoyed the evening as much as she had. As soon as the last guests walked out through the large double doors, Gavin rose to his feet and stretched.

"That was wonderful," he said to his parents. "Thank you so much."

Kalista echoed his comments and praised them for such a great celebration.

"We couldn't let your arrival in Candus pass without welcoming you," the baron said with a smile. "I wish we had more time to spend together. I guess we will just have to wait until after we have beaten back the Balthan Army. After our victory, we will have plenty of time to get to know one another better."

Kalista hoped that the battle would be over quickly. She would have time to spend with the baroness over the next week or two, but she doubted she would be able to enjoy it. She knew she would be worried about Gavin and his safety until he returned to her. She wanted to stay up and talk, making her time with Gavin last as long as she could, but she knew that it was more important for him and the baron to get a good night's rest.

"I'm exhausted," she announced. "The long march and the excitement of today's celebration has left me drained."

"Shall I escort you to your chambers?" Gavin asked.

"Yes," she replied. She then turned to his parents. "Thank you once again for such a delightful party. If you will excuse me?"

The baron rose to his feet and bowed as the baroness wished her sweet dreams. Kalista took Gavin's offered arm and let him lead her back to her room. When they arrived at her chambers, she allowed him to kiss her hand before she quickly slipped inside the room.

She let out a sigh as she listened to his slow steps head down the hallway. She wasn't sure how she was going to survive with him marching away from her and towards battle the next morning. She would worry and miss him every day until he returned. She wished there was some way that he wouldn't have to be away from her for so long.

An idea suddenly came to her. Did she really need to say goodbye to him the next morning? Why couldn't she accompany him to the camp? She had traveled with the army all the way from Calyn. Why shouldn't she continue traveling with them until they reached their final destination? The plan had been for her to stay in Candus during the battle, but the battle shouldn't begin for another week.

She hoped that Gavin wouldn't object. He had been fine with her accompanying the army thus far. She did not see any reason for him to worry as long as she was safely on her way back to Candus before the battle began. Perhaps he would even be excited that she was willing to stay by his side all the way to the army's main camp.

She hurriedly got ready for bed. She needed to get to sleep soon so she could arise as early as she needed to. She would have to quickly get all of her supplies together in the morning so that she could accompany Gavin when he left. She lay down on the comfortable bed with excitement instead of worry. She wouldn't have to say goodbye yet. She had found a way to delay the sad farewell for several more days.

Kalista arose early the next morning. She commanded her servants to prepare the necessary things as she finished getting ready for the day. Before the sun had risen, she was completely prepared. She knew that the troops had been told to be ready to march with the rising of the sun. She made her way to the courtyard where she was supposed to bid Gavin farewell. When she reached the courtyard, she was pleased to see that he had not yet arrived.

She sat down on a sculpted stone bench to wait for him. She was excited to tell him that she was coming along and they would not have to be parted for a few more days. When he walked into the courtyard a short time later, she could see the surprise clearly written on his face. She hopped up with open arms to greet him.

"Surprise," she said.

"Why are you dressed in your traveling clothes?" he asked. "I thought you would be sick of them by now."

"Oh I am," she said with a grin. "But how else would I dress if I'm planning on traveling?"

"What do you mean?" Gavin said with a concerned look. "You're not heading back to Calyn are you?"

"Of course not," she replied. "I'm going to the pass with you and the army!"

First Gavin's face took on a look of surprise. Then it became stern. His eyes narrowed, and he frowned.

"You are doing no such thing," he stated firmly. "Your place is here, safe in the palace, not anywhere near the battle."

"Oh, I will return here before the battle starts," she replied.

"No," Gavin said firmly. "You will remain here."

Kalista stared back at her fiancé's determined face. Did he really think he could tell her what to do? From the look on his face, she could see that he did.

"I am not asking for your permission," she stated back just as firmly. "I am informing you that I will be joining you on the march to the pass."

"No you will not," he said again. "There is no reason for you to-"

"Stop right there," she said, cutting him off. "You cannot give me orders. You forget your place. We are not married yet, and I am still your princess and you my subject. You will do as I say!"

Her statement and the authority with which she said it caused her fiancé to pause. She could see the conflicting emotions in his face. He took several deep breaths before continuing on. This time he moved forward more cautiously and with a different tone.

"Kalista," he began as he took her hands in his, "it's not that I don't want you to accompany me. I am going to miss you dearly over the next couple of weeks and would love nothing more than to have you by my side. However, the most important thing to me is your safety. I want you to stay here so that you will be safe and no harm will come to you. Will you please remain here in the palace?"

She stared back at him. She could hardly believe it. She had affirmatively stated that she would do as she wished, and yet Gavin was still trying to convince her to stay. Did he think she hadn't thought through her decision? Did he think she needed him to tell her what was best? She would not give in, no matter how hard he tried to get her to. She was going and that was that.

"I appreciate your concern," she said curtly. "But I have already made up my mind on the matter. I will be joining you as you head for the pass. When we reach the army's encampment at the opening of the pass, I will then wish you good luck and return to the palace. I will be safely on my way long before the battle begins." Gavin opened his mouth as if to say something, but she cut him off. "That is my final decision."

Her fiancé stared back at her with firm shoulders for a few moments before they slumped. She inwardly smiled. He had finally admitted defeat.

"As you wish," he said. "Do you have what you need? The sun is almost up."

"Everything is ready," she replied. "Now if you would please escort me to the stables, we can mount our horses and begin the march."

Gavin offered her his arm, and they walked from the courtyard towards the stables. By the time they reached the stables and mounted their horses, she was calm and feeling better. She had expected him to be excited about her coming along, not mad. However, she did understand his concern and was thankful that he cared for her safety so much. She turned to him with a smile as they led their horses around to the front of the palace. He smiled back at her.

"I am glad to have you with me a few more days," he said. "I am only concerned for your welfare. Will you promise me that you will turn back as soon as we reach the opening of the pass?"

"Of course I will," she said with a smile. "Wasn't that my plan after all?" Gavin just shook his head and chuckled.

They were soon around the palace. The Baron Mikel gave his son and Kalista a strange look as they rode up to him but didn't say anything. He glanced between the two, raised his eyebrows, and said that they should be on their way. All three, along with a procession of flag bearers and guards, rode out of the front of the city.

The Royal Army was ready and waiting just outside the city walls. Once the three of them made it to the front of the column, Baron Mikel gave the signal to begin the march. The trumpets sounded just as the sun peeked over the eastern horizon, and the army began marching directly towards it. After riding in silence for the first ten minutes, Baron Mikel turned to Gavin.

"Scouts reported this morning that the Balthan Army was camped at the eastern side of the pass five days ago," he said.

"Then the battle has already begun?" Gavin asked worriedly. It was only a five day march through the pass. Was it possible that the Balthan Army had already made it through and entered Kalia? "You should be there to lead the army."

"I have very capable generals under me," the baron replied. "And I don't believe the battle has begun yet."

"Why do you say that?" Gavin inquired.

"Our scouts set off an avalanche near the eastern opening when they saw the Balthan Army approaching," he said with a smile. "Apparently it was quite an impressive one. The scouts don't expect the route to be passable for a week or so. We determined that waiting until the last minute to create the avalanche would give us the best chance of disrupting the Balthan Army's plans. We should have plenty of time to join your troops with the rest of the Kalian Army before the pass is clear enough for an army to traverse."

"I see," Gavin said with a smile. "It looks as though your scouts have bought us plenty of time to prepare for the invasion. Congratulations!"

"I do have several tricks up my sleeves," the baron said. "We wanted the Bathan Army to clearly understand how we feel about them crossing into Kalia."

Kalista smiled as father and son continued to discuss the details and timing of the eventual invasion. She was glad that the baron had the foresight to stall the Balthan Army long enough to allow the Kalian reserves to fortify the Kalian Army's position. Hopefully the extra time would help give their army an even greater advantage over the Balthans.

Kalista felt a slight breeze at her back and looked around. She could have sworn that she had just heard someone whispering near her ear. However, no one was near her but Gavin and his father, and they were both still talking excitedly to one another. She shook her head and looked forward once again.

Another breeze made the stray bits of hair around her face flutter. She heard the same whispering sound again but looking around saw that, just as before, no one was near. What was going on? She hadn't been able to make out any words, but she was certain that she was indeed hearing whispers.

She kept her face turned around as she searched the nearest of her guards wondering if any of them were whispering. All were silent and appeared lost in their own thoughts. As she was about to turn forward, a stronger breeze gusted against her face.

". . . careful . . ."

Kalista's eyes widened with amazement. There was no mistaking it this time. Not one of her guards had moved his mouth, yet she had faintly heard the word 'careful'. She searched the skies but saw nothing unusual. It was as though the whisper had been carried on the wind. No one else seemed to have noticed anything out of the ordinary.

She turned around and looked forward towards the sun. What had the whisper been? Where had the message come from? Was it simply a message or was it a warning? She strained her ears to hear anything else, but the only sounds were those of the army making its way eastward.

After awhile she began to wonder if she really had heard anything at all. Perhaps it was merely her mind playing tricks on her. She settled back into her saddle as comfortably as she could and returned to listening to Gavin and his father discussing how they hoped the battle would turn out. Kalista would be delighted if the battle would be as easy to win as the two hoped.

* * * * *

"Do you think she heard it?" Darian asked as Traven stepped back from the screeing dish.

"I think she heard something," he replied. "I just hope she got the message and takes it to heart. What is she thinking leaving Candus and heading to the battlefront?"

Darian shrugged in response. Traven picked up the small water dish and after dumping out the water, hastily packed it away. They needed to get moving, and he had spent long enough trying to get a warning to the princess.

He had woken up this morning from a particularly disturbing vision. The princess had finally returned to his dreams. Unfortunately, it had not been the return he had hoped for. The vision had been of the Princess Kalista's funeral. He had stood over her lifeless body and wept with the crown of Kalia nestled on his head. He had woken with tears in his eyes and an overwhelming sense of sorrow.

The feelings of sorrow and loss had been so strong that he had decided to call up an image of the princess. He needed to see her safe in the palace. He feared that her return to his visions signaled something important. When he called up her image, he had been dismayed to find her not safe in the palace, but riding towards the pass with the rest of the army. He had decided that perhaps he could send her a warning.

He had attempted for the first time to send a message further than he could physically see. He had used the screeing dish to guide his message all the way to the princess. He had lost hold of the particle container several times before he was finally able to guide it all the way to her. It had taken longer than he thought it would to guide it so far. He had finally been able to deliver the simple message, 'Please be careful'. He hoped that it had been beneficial and not just a waste of time.

Perhaps the closer he got to the princess, the easier it would be for him to send another message. He quickly mounted Pennon, and they were once again hurrying down the road towards Candus. They needed to be swifter and travel longer each day if they hoped to reach the princess in time. Her heading towards the pass would make it that much harder for him to reach her and protect her.

A strange prickling sensation suddenly passed over him, making him shiver. Someone was watching him. He scanned the empty countryside, looking for the source of his discomfort. All was empty and quiet, but the feeling didn't go away. He suddenly remembered what the keeper had told him and cast a quick shield of invisibility above him and the guardians.

The feeling instantly vanished. Traven frowned. It seemed as though the wielder leading the Balthan Army knew about him and where he was. He would have to be more careful going forward. At least he now knew what feeling to be weary of. He left the shield above his group for about five minutes before letting it drop. Fortunately, the feeling didn't return.

He shook his head with frustration. Not only could he not get the image of the lifeless body of the princess out of his mind, he now had to worry about being tracked by the Balthan wielder. At least the threat was still distant. For now, he just hoped he could reach the princess in time.

24

Kadrak sat on his horse at the opening of the pass, staring forward at the immense pile of snow blocking his army from advancing into Kalia. He had camped at the base of the mountains with his army for the last five days in hopes that the snow would melt on its own. Unfortunately, the weather had been less than cooperative. A cold spell had set in, and very little snow had melted at all. The situation wasn't any better than it had been when his army had first arrived at the pass.

The Royal Kalian Army had done well. The avalanche they had orchestrated had effectively stopped Kadrak's army. He knew that the second group of soldiers would now have time to join the ones already camped at the western edge of the pass before he could attack them. He had watched from his screeing dish as they had left Candus earlier that morning. Not only would the full Kalian Army be in place to oppose him, but he had also seen that the Kalian wielder was heading towards the battle as well.

He had seen the pinprick of light indicating another wielder while he was screeing. However, as he had closed in on the wielder, the growing spot of light had suddenly vanished. The young boy must have learned how to shield himself. Kadrak wondered what the boy had been doing in the desert and what he was now trying to hide. Luckily, the young wielder was at least ten days away from the pass, if not more.

Whatever surprise the young wielder might have for him, he would face it when the time came. He wasn't overly concerned. He still had hope that the young wielder would never reach the battle.

However, if the boy did reach the pass, he would rather not face the wielder and the Kalian Army at the same time. As soon as he had finished screeing, he had decided on what must be done. That was why he was sitting at the mouth of the pass, staring at the enormous mountain of snow blocking his way.

He was tired of waiting on nature to allow him to march to victory. He had waited long enough for the snow to melt. It was now time for him to take action. It was time for him to clear the pass himself.

Kadrak raised his hands above his head and concentrated. Time froze, and the air thickened. Behind him, his army stood frozen in silence, intently watching their leader. They would be reminded once again of his unmatched power. The air began to swirl far overhead. It continued to swirl faster and faster.

Time and sound rushed back as fireballs began to rain down from the sky. The snow hissed as each fireball slammed into the mountain of snow. As the fireballs continued raining down, he focused the light of the sun at the front of the snow. He slowly eased the beam of light and heat forward along the base of the pass, creating a narrow path directly through the center of the snow. As soon as the beam reached the end of the avalanche, he let it disappear along with the fireballs

He took a deep breath and steadied himself as he admired his handiwork. The mountain of snow had been reduced, and there was now a clear path straight through the center of it. It was not as wide as he would have liked, but he didn't have the strength left to enlarge it. It would be wide enough for the supply wagons to pass through, and that was all that was necessary.

Kadrak raised his fist in the air. A thunderous cheer rose up from behind, washing over him. He smiled. His troops were ready and anxious for battle. When he had commanded that they assemble and prepare to march this morning, he was sure there were plenty who were confused and wondering if their leader had lost his mind. Everyone had known that the pass was still blocked.

It had been impassable, until faced with his power. Even nature could not stand against him. He basked in the cheers and adoration of his army for several more moments before dropping his fist. He immediately gripped his mount's reins tightly and booted him. As his horse leapt forward, the cheers of his army increased as they too surged forward with exuberance.

Kadrak led the way through the narrow path he had cut through the snow. Walls of snow and ice rose several stories on both sides. He studied them out of the corner of his eyes, making sure that they would hold. Luckily the snow was compacted enough that it shouldn't be a problem. The only drawback was the muddy ground underneath his horse's hooves.

With effort, he kept himself perfectly straight in the saddle as he led his troops along the narrow path. It had been wise for him to wield the ambience from his saddle instead of dismounting first. He had used so much of the ambience that it had left him incredibly weakened. He might not have been able to pull himself up into the saddle if he had worked his show of power from the ground.

He tried to ignore the twinge of a headache that had set in and stayed alert in case there were any enemies nearby. Thankfully, he didn't sense anyone ahead. He took another deep breath and closed his eyes. It was cold with the snow rising on both sides, but the cold was welcome. It helped to cool his overheated body.

As soon as he was past the avalanche, the path opened back up. While the tall mountains on the north and south kept him in shadow, there was plenty of space for the army to spread back out and march in their normal formations. He signaled for Gilrod to move to his side. His second in command hurried to fulfill his master's wish and was soon riding next to Kadrak.

"What do you wish, Master?" Gilrod asked.

Kadrak smiled. While another perhaps would have heaped praises on him for his magnificent show of power, Gilrod was always ready to serve him. Gilrod knew of his distaste for false flattery.

"Can you figure out a way to collapse the snow banks and seal the pass off once all of the troops have passed through?" Kadrak asked.

Gilrod hid his surprise well. He looked back at the narrow path through the avalanche and thought for a moment. He then turned back.

"Yes," he replied. "I think I could manage to collapse it and block off any chance for retreat."

Kadrak smiled. Gilrod had quickly figured out the reason for the request. He didn't care how Gilrod accomplished the task. He just wanted to know he could do it and was willing to do it.

"May I ask a question?" Gilrod said carefully.

"You may," he replied.

"While I will not go against your command, I would like to point out that not only will blocking the path prevent our soldiers from retreating, it will also prevent us from receiving any supplies or reinforcements," he paused for a second before continuing on. "I don't doubt we will be victorious, but we currently only have enough supplies to last for about ten days. If the battle doesn't go according to plan, I think it's prudent to have other options."

Kadrak stared back at the cunning man. He had said that he would do as he was commanded to, but he also had expressed that he didn't agree with the command. Gilrod was loyal, but he wasn't a fool. He understood the implications of a trapped army running out of food and supplies. What the man didn't know was that galdak warriors would be in place to reinforce the army if needed. The battle would be won in a timely manner, one way or another.

"I can guarantee that we will win the battle before our supplies run out," Kadrak stated confidently. "You know most of what goes on, but you don't know everything," he said, reminding Gilrod of his place. "If a retreat ever was necessary, I could clear a path back out of the pass, just as I did earlier. However, that will not be necessary. I want my troops to think their only way out is through the Kalian Army. I want them to think the only chance to restock supplies is through a quick and decisive victory. I want them to fight ferociously."

"You are wise and powerful," Gilrod said. "I will complete the task you assigned and let it be known that there is no path for retreating."

"You must remember that I am not a fool Gilrod. I am confident, but I am not foolish. I do have a backup plan if necessary, but I hope the troops will have plenty of motivation to end the battle in a timely manner."

Gilrod bowed deeply and headed back towards the opening of the path that Kadrak had cleared. Kadrak continued forward at the head of the army, riding alone once again. The army marched behind him, unaware that soon they would have no chance to desert or retreat. They would be surprised when they discovered that the pass was blocked but wouldn't be able to do anything about it.

That's how he wanted it. They would realize that their only hope for survival was through victory. He knew that the Kalian Army would prove to be a tougher foe than any he had yet faced. There were many troops, and they were very disciplined. If the battle was difficult, he didn't want any of his own troops to have the option to retreat or sneak away. They would have to fight for their very lives, just as he wanted them to.

* * * * *

Gilrod waited next to the opening that led through the snow. He watched as the troops filed through and then formed back up in their ranks. He also counted all of the supply wagons carefully as they passed.

It wouldn't be too hard to do what Kadrak had asked him to do. However, he was still leery of doing it. He knew of Kadrak's immense power, but he also knew that his leader had limits. The most recent display of his power had truly been awe inspiring, but he had seen how much it had drained Kadrak. The wielder couldn't defeat the entire Kalian Army by himself, no matter how powerful he was.

He supposed Kadrak knew what he was doing. He had said that he had something planned in case they weren't able to win the battle quickly. Gilrod didn't know what it was but assumed it had something to do with the wielder's trips back and forth to the mountains near Beking.

He had never been able to discover what exactly his master did on the trips. He knew better than to try and have him followed, but it was obvious that he was meeting with someone. Who that was, Gilrod didn't know. He had sent spies to search the area but none of them had found anything. A couple had even disappeared.

Kadrak had often returned from his trips with precious stones. Gilrod wondered if he had contact with a secretive smuggling ring. Perhaps he had placed assassins in Kalia. Regardless of what he had done, it was a secret that Gilrod hadn't discovered as of yet. He didn't like that. He made it his business to uncover secrets and know everything that was going on. He would discover this secret sooner or later. Perhaps if he continued serving Kadrak faithfully, the wielder might even come right out and tell him.

Gilrod turned his attention back to the task at hand. The last of the supply wagons finished making it into the pass. All appeared exactly as he had recalled earlier. The supplies would last about ten or eleven days. It would take the army five days to traverse the entire pass and leave the mountains behind. The army would be able to fight for six days at the most before the supplies ran out. He hoped that would be enough time for them to win the battle.

He grabbed one of his spies from the ranks of soldiers passing him and explained the situation. He needed someone he trusted on the other side of the avalanche. He also needed someone to take care of the extra supplies from Beking that would be arriving in two days. Once the spy understood what was needed, he waited patiently at Gilrod's side until the last of the troops had passed. He then slipped into the narrow path and sprinted back towards Beking.

Gilrod gathered about twenty soldiers from the rear of the army and gave them their orders. They retrieved the necessary equipment and began to fulfill Kadrak's command. Gilrod took a deep breath. He hoped the wielder truly did know what he was doing.

* * * * *

Kadrak smiled at the sudden sound in the distance. He could hear the snow collapsing down on the path, filling it in. A murmur slowly made its way up the ranks of soldiers as word passed of what had happened. He didn't mind the talk. He wanted all of them aware of what had just happened and what it meant. He was sure Gilrod had helped to start the message that was quickly being shared from soldier to soldier. All of the troops would soon understand the importance of winning the coming battle quickly and decisively.

He turned his attention from the troops to the tall mountains looming on either side of him. He wondered if the galdak warriors were already in place at the far end of the pass. The avalanche wouldn't have affected them at all. Shaman Azulk had assured him that the warriors would be in place in time. He supposed they had used tunnels. He wondered how many miles of tunnels truly existed through the mountains and how far they extended.

It would be advantageous to know how far the tunnels reached. He'd have to ask Azulk about it the next time he met with him. He would like to know where he could move the galdak warriors to and how fast he could move them there.

He continued riding in silence, taking in the magnificent beauty of the towering mountains. The immense mountains made one feel small, almost insignificant. However, Kadrak knew that he was not insignificant. He, like the mountains, towered over those around him. His power left others in awe. His power no doubt left others feeling insignificant. The Kalian Army would soon learn to fear his power.

25

In the distance, Traven could clearly make out the edge of the forest. They would reach it sometime in the next few hours. He was excited to be back amongst the trees. He hadn't been within a forest since he left his grandparent's home the previous fall. There was something comforting to him about being surrounded by trees. He wasn't sure if it was just the memory of his childhood, but for some reason he longed to be in the woods again.

He was also excited because Candus lay at the other side of the forest. The forest was huge and would take days to pass through, but it was an important landmark on their path to the princess. He looked back at the guardians and saw that Darian was also looking longingly at the line that marked the edge of the forest. It was close enough now that the human guardians could see it as well.

"We'll be in the forest soon," Darian said happily.

"I don't know why you sound so excited," Jorb said in reply. "That forest is full of nothing but trees and wolves."

"That shows how much you know," Darian said with a wry smile. "The forest holds many secrets. There is much more than just trees and wolves."

Traven wondered what the elf meant by secrets. He supposed that the thick foliage in the forests could easily hide many things. He also thought he understood the elf's excitement. All of the stories he had been told of elves as a child always referred to the creatures as coming out of the woods and disappearing back into the woods once they had completed their mischievous deeds. Perhaps Darian had grown up in the woods like he had.

Traven watched eagerly as they rode closer and closer to the edge of the forest. He soon realized that this forest was different than the one he had grown up in. The trees grew closer together and were much larger. The landscape didn't ease from the open grasslands they had been riding through into a forest. Rather, there was a very distinct line where the grasslands ended and the forest began.

After awhile they finally reached the edge of the forest. The road veered to the north and soon the edge of the forest was to the south of them. He knew from screeing that eventually the path would lead directly into the forest and cut straight through it towards Candus.

Jorb and Ethan kept casting worried glances to their right at the edge of the forest. It was obvious that the dense foliage made them uncomfortable. Riding next to the edge of the forest, Traven could see why. The trees were close enough together that their branches blocked out most light. The interior of the forest seemed unusually dark. For those who were used to being out in the open all of the time, he supposed that the forest would feel oppressive.

They paused at midday just before entering the forest and had lunch. Darian seemed in better spirits than he had been the entire trip, while both Jorb and Ethan seemed about as downcast as he had ever seen them. As soon as they were done eating, Darian eagerly took the lead and led them down the road and straight into the forest. The thick trees soon made a wall on either side of the road. The thick branches that stretched over head blocked out most of the light and bathed the four of them in shadows. Behind him, Jorb and Ethan rode in a depressed silence.

"The forest isn't that bad," Traven said to the two human guardians. "Did you guys know I used to be a woodcutter?"

"Maybe you could get your axe out and chop some of these trees down," Jorb said. "Then maybe we would be able to see the sky again."

After traveling through the dark forest for much of the afternoon, Traven began to understand the two human guardians' depression. Shafts of sunlight rarely penetrated through the dense foliage, and the air was still and somewhat stale. He didn't mind it nearly as much as they did, but could understand what they disliked about it.

Darian, on the other hand, seemed happier than ever. He kept looking around with a smile as he studied the trees and the birds that flitted amongst the branches. He didn't seem to mind the darkness at all. He supposed that the elf's enhanced vision allowed him to see much farther in the dark than the other guardians could.

Traven realized it was the same with him. His eyes pierced the darkness, and he could see deep into the forest. However, Jorb and Ethan probably could only see shadows. They continued on until the shadowed path began to get darker. As the darkness deepened, they decided that it would be best to set up camp. They wouldn't have the benefit of any moonlight or starlight underneath the thick canopy of branches.

Darian set off to gather some dead branches to make a campfire while the others took care of the horses and set up camp. They made their camp just off the side of the rode in a small clearing between numerous tree trunks. Darian returned quickly and started a fire.

"I will gather some more wood," he said after starting the fire. "We will want the fire blazing all night. This forest really is full of wolves."

Traven followed the elf into the darkness and helped gather more wood. If the forest was full of wolves, he'd rather not run out of wood in the middle of the night. He and Darian brought back several armfuls of wood before deciding that the pile they had accumulated was large enough to keep the fire burning brightly through the night.

As soon as everything was settled and the fire was blazing, they all sat down to eat. The flickering flames of the fire danced through the shadows creating a very eerie background for their nightly meal. Traven wondered how many wolves there really were in this part of the forest and whether or not any would come close to the camp. He hadn't seen or heard anything but birds since they had entered the forest. As soon as Ethan was finished with his meal, he stood up and tossed a few more logs onto the fire.

"I don't know how you two are so calm," Ethan said as he looked across the fire at Traven and Darian. "Jorb and I don't like it when we can't see more than a few feet in any direction. Does it really not bother you?"

Darian began laughing as he leapt to his feet and disappeared amongst the trees. Ethan watched him go and shook his head with disbelief.

"The elf's lost his mind," he said as he stared into the dark forest where Darian had disappeared.

The laughs soon vanished and all was silent once again. Traven wondered what Darian was up to. He wasn't worried for the elf. He knew he could see fine in the darkness and take care of himself, but he didn't think it was wise for anyone to be roaming the dark forest alone if there were wolves nearby.

He cleared his mind and reached out with his senses. He was soon able to locate the elf, and he tried hard to keep a straight face. Darian was slowly circling the camp and sneaking up near the side where Ethan was standing. Ethan and Jorb were still staring at the spot where Darian had disappeared, straining their ears for any sound of him

"Bwahhhh!" the elf shouted as he leapt out of the dark forest and into the light of the fire directly behind Ethan. Ethan almost fell over as he spun around with his sword whipping out of his scabbard and his eyes wide with fear.

Darian fell to the ground laughing as Ethan worked to slow his breathing and control his anger. Jorb had been as surprised as Ethan and was also working to slow his racing heart. Traven joined Darian in laughing.

"I can't believe you just. . ." Ethan sputtered. He took several deep breaths and continued on. "You're lucky I didn't put my blade through you!"

Darian just kept laughing. Jorb was soon chuckling as well, and eventually Ethan sheathed his sword and shook his head. Traven watched with amusement as Darian finally stopped laughing and apologized to his fellow guardians. Both accepted the apology but told Darian if he ever did something like that again, he would regret it.

They all settled back down around the fire, finished their food, and cleaned up. After sharing a few stories, they were all ready to sleep. As they began discussing whether or not they needed to worry about wolves, Darian got a worried look on his face and stared at the edge of the camp as though he was trying to hear something.

"Stop it Darian," Jorb said. "Don't you think your earlier stunt scared us enough?"

"Quiet," Darian said sharply. "Something isn't right."

Ethan was about to say something, but Traven motioned for him to keep silent. Something was suddenly making him feel uneasy as well. He closed his eyes and reached out with his senses. All was completely still outside of their camp, but the uneasy feeling didn't go away. He concentrated harder and tried to sense further into the surrounding forest.

The only things he could sense were the large trees and several large boulders to the north. He was about to ask Darian what he thought, when one of the boulders suddenly moved. He opened his eyes in surprise. It obviously wasn't a boulder. It was still a good distance from their camp, but it had moved in their direction. It was motionless once again, and he couldn't tell what it was.

"There's something fairly large in that direction," he said pointing to the north. "I don't know what it is, but it seems too big to be a wolf."

"Could it be a bear?" Jorb asked.

"No," Darian said quietly. "Something's wrong. It doesn't feel natural."

Traven had to agree with the elf. Something definitely didn't feel right about the situation. He concentrated on the large mound in the distance. Every so often it would move ever so slightly in the direction of their camp. As it slowly got closer, he was able to judge its size and shape more accurately. It had to be at least ten feet tall. It had four legs, pointed ears, and a long tail.

"I'm not sure what it is," he said. "But it's carefully making its way towards us, and it's at least ten feet tall. It reminds me of a cat stalking a mouse. I think we should be ready in case it attacks."

All four of them drew their swords as they stared northward into the shadows. Whatever the beast was, it was still a safe distance from the camp. He wondered if it was just creeping closer for a look. He doubted an animal would get too close to the fire.

"Do you think it will actually attack?" he asked Darian.

"I'm not sure," the elf replied. "If it reminds you of a cat stalking its prey, I think it would be unwise to rule out the possibility that it's stalking us. How far away is it?"

"I'm not sure," Traven replied as he tried to gauge the distance. "It's about eight trees away now, and it's still coming closer."

Suddenly he felt a disturbance to his right. He whipped around, and time froze. An arrow, pointing directly at his face lay frozen in mid air a foot away. He created a wedge of ice with a razor thin edge directly in front of the dark pointed tip of the long wooden arrow and pulled it into reality. Time returned as the arrow split in two. Each half flew by on either side of his head, ruffling his hair. All three guardians stared in shock as the two pieces whistled by and harmlessly disappeared into the dark.

The slight distraction was all that the beast needed to clear the distance between itself and the camp in three fluid bounds. It flew into the light of the fire with sharp teeth bared and razor claws extended. Darian and Ethan dove out of the way, but Jorb was too slow. Traven watched with horror as the giant, catlike beast slammed into the guardian and knocked him backwards into the woods with incredible force. The two other guardians were instantly back on their feet with swords ready.

Traven was about to join them when he felt a disturbance to his right once again. He dove to the ground as another arrow pierced the air where his head had been. He popped back up and ducked into the shadows of the forest. He would have to leave the beast to the guardians. Whoever was shooting the arrows had to be stopped. Two more arrows whizzed towards him in quick succession. He jumped behind a tree and let his eyes adjust to the darkness. He could hear the growling and hissing of the beast as the guardians fought to bring it down. He turned his attention from the beast and let his senses range eastward, searching for the hidden threat.

He located the assailant almost instantly. He wasn't standing still but quickly making his way to the south. Traven left the protection of the tree trunk and took off after the man. It was hard for him to see in the dark shadows of the forest, but there was just enough light for his enhanced vision to pick out a clear path. He weaved in and out amongst the thick tree trunks, quickly gaining on his attacker.

Out of instinct, he dropped to the ground just as another arrow whizzed by overhead. He lay completely still on the ground and listened. In the distance he could hear the struggle still continuing back at the camp. In front of him all was silent. The assailant had stopped and was probably ready to send another arrow his way.

He stared forward, straining his eyes for any sign of movement. The man couldn't be far away if he had been able to shoot an arrow so close to him in the dark. He realized how close he had come to being killed several times already. Whoever the assailant was, he was good, and he wanted Traven dead.

He knew he needed to be more careful. He slowly got up and into a crouch. He shut out the sounds of fighting coming from the camp and concentrated on the task at hand. It seemed that if he didn't kill his attacker first, the unknown man would kill him. He wished that he had a bow with him. It would be hard to get close enough to the man to do anything if the attacker continued shooting arrows his way. It would be much easier if he could attack the assailant from a distance.

He reached out with his senses and located the man. He was about five trees in front of him. Traven slowly crept behind a trunk and stood up silently. He carefully looked around the edge of the trunk and stared at the tree where he knew the man was hiding. He patiently waited and watched. After a few moments the assailant quickly and silently moved from the shelter of one trunk to another.

He wished for a bow once again. He could tell from the quick and silent movements of his attacker that the man was skilled and deadly. He wasn't sure how close he wanted to get to the man. It finally donned on him that he didn't need to get close, and he didn't need a bow. He was a wielder. He had innumerable weapons at his disposal in the air all around him.

Changing his frame of thinking, he instantly recognized the particles in the air around him and what would be easiest to create. Earlier he had created a wedge of ice to split the arrow because he had recognized instinctively that the cold, damp air of the forest was full of the particles he needed to quickly form ice. He supposed ice would work best.

He was afraid if he used lightning or a fireball he would give away his position and accidentally set the forest on fire. However, if he created a spear of ice, he could send it silently through the dark forest and surprise his attacker.

All went silent and still as he envisioned the thin spear of ice in the air at his side. He made sure it was perfectly straight with a sharp, deadly tip. He then pulled it to the border of reality and patiently waited for his assailant to move once again. He didn't have to wait very long.

As the man quickly moved towards another trunk, Traven yanked the ice spear into existence and sent it flying towards the unidentified attacker with incredible speed. It slammed into the man, knocking him off of his feet and throwing him to the ground. The man lay silently and completely still on the bare forest floor.

Traven carefully made his way towards the man. He wasn't sure where the ice spear had hit him and whether or not the blow had truly been fatal. He quickly formed a small particle shield between himself and the still body just in case. His precaution paid off as a blade flashed through the air and bounced off his shield with a dull thud. He quickly leapt onto his attacker, pinning him down and laying the edge of his own blade at the man's throat. The man glared up at him with a sneer.

"I should have known better than to take an assignment to kill a wielder," he wheezed. He then began coughing weakly.

Traven glanced down and saw that the ice spear had taken the man in his side. His labored breathing and unfocused eyes were clear indicators that the blow would prove fatal. The man let out a few more coughs before his body went rigid and lifeless. He stared down at him wondering who he was, and who had sent him.

His silent thoughts were interrupted as he heard a scream in the distance. He suddenly remembered the beast back at the camp. He leapt off of the lifeless attacker and ran towards the small clearing, gathering the power of the ambience around him.

* * * * *

    Darian stared up at the giant beast. He had never seen anything like it in his entire life. While it resembled a mountain cat, it was obviously something much worse. It was easily ten feet tall and instead of fur had dull grey scales covering its entire body. It had huge claws and teeth, and its eyes shone a brilliant red. It looked like something out of a nightmare.

    He studied the beast, looking for an opportunity to strike. Ethan was on the other side, and the beast was trying to keep an eye on both of them at the same time. Ethan suddenly feigned an attack, and the beast turned towards him. Darian saw his chance and took it. He leapt towards the back of the monster with his sword flashing. His sword bit into the creature's back but left only a small scratch.

    He jumped backwards as the beast swung a clawed hand at him and let out a snarl. The creature's natural layer of armor would make things difficult. Darian kept his sword firmly between himself and the beast. He decided that he might as well attack it straight on. Hopefully that would give Ethan the opportunity to do some damage from behind.

    Darian made a few swipes with his sword, trying to keep the creature's attention. The beast took another swipe at him. After dodging the monster's claws, he sliced the back of its arm. The creature screamed in pain and jumped at him with jagged teeth bared. He dodged the attack and jumped to the side.

    Ethan took the opportunity to attack the beast from behind. He jumped forward, his sword flashing back and forth. He landed several strokes before the creature reached back and took a swipe at him. He wasn't able to get out of the way fast enough and was caught by the beasts' claws across his midsection. Darian watched with a grimace as the beast heaved Ethan into the forest with deadly force.

Now it was just him left to face the beast alone. He gritted his teeth and stared back into the glowing eyes of the monster. It had sustained multiple cuts but didn't appear to be weakened at all. He wasn't sure if he could outrun it or not but decided it wasn't worth trying. Where would be the honor in fleeing from a difficult opponent? If he was quick enough, he could keep wounding the beast without getting mauled by its claws. Eventually all of the slashes would weaken the beast.

He carefully danced about the monster, jumping in for a quick strike and then jumping back just as quickly out of the reach of its claws. The beast soon had multiple cuts on its arms and legs, but none of them seemed to bother it much. Darian knew that he needed to find an unprotected spot on its body if he was going to do any real damage. He concluded that the only accessible spots that weren't covered in the thick scales were the beast's eyes and mouth. However, he knew it would be extremely difficult to get within range to strike at the beast's face while avoiding its teeth and claws.

He lay a few more strikes on the creature's legs before he lunged forward and slashed across its face. The beast screamed with rage and surged forward. Darian dove to the side but wasn't fast enough to escape unscathed. A single claw caught his thigh, slashing it open. He propped himself up using his good leg and prepared for the beast's next attack. He could feel the blood spilling from the deep wound on his thigh and knew he wouldn't be able to fight much longer.

The monster hissed at him as it crouched, readying itself to leap towards him once again. Darian had the satisfaction of seeing that one of the beast's eyes was closed tight with an angry slash across it. He would do his best to slash the beasts other eye when it attacked. If he didn't survive, at least he could limit the creature's ability to harm anyone else. He tensed as the beast prepared to leap. He was ready for it.

He suddenly felt a wave of heat as a huge fireball flew past his right side and slammed directly into the face of the beast. The creature reared up on its hind legs, roaring in agony. Almost instantly a large, gleaming spear flashed through the air past him and embedded itself into the creature's exposed stomach. The beast fell back onto all four feet, still roaring. Two more fireballs flew past and slammed into the monster in rapid succession.

The beast screamed as it took several tentative steps forward. A large ball of ice flew through the air and took the monster directly in the face. The dazed beast turned and tried to run off into the forest but collapsed after a single bound. The spear had apparently penetrated deep enough to do much more damage than any of the sword wounds. The monster tried to rise but collapsed back to the ground and went still.

Darian fell on his side, exhausted from the fight and the loss of so much blood. He glanced down at his mangled leg and cringed. He ripped his eyes away from the deep wound and glanced backwards into the shadows of the trees where the fireballs, spear, and ball of ice had come from. He could see Traven hurrying towards him. His master had saved his life. He had chosen well. His last thought as he began to lose consciousness was that he hoped he could still be of service to his master with only one good leg.

26

Traven knelt down over Darian's body, breathing heavily. The elf had collapsed just before he had reached him. The only wound he could see was a giant gash across Darian's left thigh. It looked like the elf had lost a significant amount of blood from the grotesque wound. He cut off a piece of cloth from Darian's pant leg and wadded it up. He then firmly pushed it against the gash hoping to slow the bleeding. He glanced around the camp but saw no sign of Jorb or Ethan.

He looked back down at Darian's wound and decided that he would try to use the healing stone on it. Hopefully he would be able to do enough to stop the bleeding and help the elf's leg to begin to heal. He pulled the deep orange stone out of his pocket and held it directly over the deep gash. He then did as Eldridge had instructed him.

He first concentrated on the types of particles that swirled around the might stone. He pulled the same combination of particles from the forest air all around him and directed them into the stone, feeding it with energy. The stone instantly began to glow a brilliant white. He continued to pull the correct combination of particles into the stone, keeping it glowing.

As the stone continued filling with energy, Traven felt his own being drained. However, the drain of his strength was secondary to the amazement he felt as he watched the gash begin to get smaller. He stared in awe as the giant gash continued to shrink. He felt a headache beginning and knew he should stop feeding the stone with energy but continued on regardless. He wanted to know if it was possible to completely heal the wound. He fought through the pain in his head and continued to feed the stone as the wound grew to a thin line and then disappeared altogether.

He immediately let go of the ambience and dropped his hand to the ground to keep himself from falling over. He watched as the stone faded back to its normal color and then closed his eyes with a grimace. His head was pounding, and he had almost blacked out. He probably should have stopped earlier, but he felt that it was more important to heal Darian as much as he possibly could than to prevent himself from getting a severe headache.

He rested for a few moments and then unsteadily got to his feet. He draped a blanket over Darian and looked around. He needed to see if he could find Jorb and Ethan. The last he had seen of them was when the beast had knocked Jorb into the woods. He wondered if the guardian was still where the beast had knocked him. He left the light of the fire and searched the woods in the general vicinity where he believed the guardian would have landed.

It didn't take him long to find Jorb's body. He was laying face down at the base of a large tree. At first it looked as though he was perfectly fine. There didn't appear to be any injuries, but when Traven touched him to roll him over he felt no warmth. Upon closer inspection he found that he wasn't breathing, and there was no sign of life. He wondered if he should try and use the healing stone but knew that Jorb was past healing. He also knew he didn't have the strength left to use the stone effectively.

He stood up numbly and searched the surrounding area for Ethan. He soon located the other guardian's body. He was only several trees over. Traven began walking towards him but stopped before he reached him. It was painfully obvious that Ethan hadn't survived the fight with the beast. A wave of nausea passed over him, and he had to brace himself against the trunk of a tree to stop from falling over.

He squeezed his eyes shut and tried to hold back the tears. Both had died trying to protect him. They would have been safe, happy, and alive at Faldor's Keep if he hadn't brought them with him. Now the guilt of both of their deaths lay at his feet. He didn't have the strength left to bury them now and would have to wait until the morning. He flinched as a howl split the night air in the distance. Luckily, it was only the sound of a normal wolf.

He realized that if he left the bodies in the woods, they would most likely be gone by morning. He gathered what little strength he had left and slowly dragged each of the guardians' bodies back into the camp near the fire. He then piled most of the remaining wood onto the fire and collapsed. He hoped that the wolves would stay away during the night, because he didn't know if he would have the strength to put up much of a fight if they didn't.

* * * * *

Darian slowly opened his eyes and yawned. The first light of dawn was just beginning to chase away the shadows in the forest. He sat up carefully, blinking his eyes. The fire was low but still burning. To the left of the fire he could see Traven soundly asleep. Across the fire he could make out the bodies of his two fellow guardians. Both were completely still and neither one appeared to have any life in him. He bowed his head in respect. He hadn't really expected that either would have survived the vicious blows that were inflicted by the beast. At least both had died with honor, facing the monstrous creature that had attacked them.

He was grateful to still be alive after the ordeal. However, with only one good leg, he wondered if it really was better to be alive. He was afraid that the damage that had been done would leave him lame in his left leg. Perhaps in time it would heal to the point where he would only have a slight limp, but he knew his skills as a warrior would never be the same.

There was a definite chill in the air, and he decided that he should put an extra branch or two on the fire. He carefully shifted his weight to crawl over and add some more wood to the fire. Surprisingly, he didn't feel any pain or soreness in his left thigh. He wondered if the damage was even more extensive than he had at first thought. He should be feeling at least some type of ache. He flexed his left leg and paused in surprise. He could feel his leg just fine, yet there was no pain.

He glanced down at the blanket that still covered him from the waist down. He wondered if Traven had given him some type of drug to numb the pain. He took a deep breath and worked up the courage to take a look at the damage in the faint morning light. He would have to face it sooner or later, so why not face it now?

He pulled off the blanket and stared at his thigh in complete amazement. It took him a moment to shake off the shock and fully process what he was seeing. He pulled up his torn pant leg and probed his thigh. While there was a huge tear in his pant leg and plenty of dried blood, there was absolutely no other sign of the wound. There wasn't even the slightest mark on his skin where the massive slash had been.

He shook his head, trying to clear it. Had he somehow imagined the injury? He knew he hadn't. The tear and dried blood was proof of that. He turned and stared at the sleeping form of his master with an ever growing sense of awe and devotion. He had saved his life the night before but had then done even more. He had healed him and made him whole!

*****

Traven awoke with a start. His dreams had been full of death. Instead of only seeing the lifeless body of the princess, as had been the case recently, he had seen the lifeless bodies of many others. Among them were the two guardians who had already died.

He glanced around the camp and found it completely empty. He jumped up with a start, worried that the wolves had taken the bodies. He calmed down as he noticed that the fire had been added to and the blanket he had put on Darian was folded. He assumed the elf must have taken the bodies of the guardians out of the camp. He could hear what sounded like someone digging in the distance. He followed the sound and soon found Darian at the base of an enormous tree. The elf was finishing scooping dirt back into a large hole.

Traven stood at the edge of the grave in silence. He watched as Darian finished covering the grave with the rest of the dirt. Soon there was a small mound that served as the only memorial of the two guardians that lay buried at the base of the tree. Darian took a step back from the mound and made several smooth motions with his arms. He then ended by holding his palms upwards towards the sky and bowing his head.

"It is done," the elf said as he turned to face Traven. "Their bodies have returned to the earth and their spirits have returned to the sky."

Traven bowed his own head in respect to the deceased and thanked Darian for taking care of their bodies. He was still weak and didn't think he would have had the strength to dig the grave.

"You gave me your strength," Darian replied. "You healed my leg and restored my hope. I can only repay you by doing all that I can in your service."

"You don't owe me anything," Traven said.

"Yes I do," the elf replied. "Master Wielder, I swore to serve you. Yet to this point you have done far more for me than I have done for you. Please forgive my weakness."

"You don't have anything to apologize for," he said. "If you hadn't kept that creature at bay, there's no way I could've stopped the assassin. I think the whole attack was my fault anyway. They were both sent to kill me. The deaths of the guardians are my fault."

"Don't be foolish," Darian replied. "You aren't responsible for their deaths. They chose to be guardians, and they chose to guard you on this journey. It is unwise to carry around more burdens than you need to."

Traven followed as the elf left the grave behind and made his way back to the camp. He supposed that Darian was right, but he still felt partially responsible for the deaths of his two companions. They skirted the spot where the slain beast lay. It appeared that even though it was already dead, the wolves hadn't come near it. He wondered where such a monster had come from. Upon returning to camp, they ate breakfast, loaded up their gear, and mounted their horses.

"You're right," Darian said suddenly. "They were after you."

"Why do you say that?" he asked

"I searched the assassin this morning and found this."

Darian pulled a dark red stone from his pocket and tossed it to Traven. It changed color to a brighter red as it got closer to him and landed in his hand. He stared at it. It was one of the seeker stones. It dawned on him that the first time he had seen a seeker stone it was also in the hands of an assassin. The kidnapper in Calyn had been sent for him before he even knew that he was a wielder. How many more assassins would be sent to kill him? How many others close to him would die?

"We need to hurry," Traven said. "It's late, and we need to ride hard if we're going to close the ground between us and the princess."

Darian nodded and snatched the stone from the air as Traven tossed it back to him. They were soon on their way at a quick pace. The large trees of the forest flew past them throughout the day. Occasionally a shaft of sunlight would flit over their bodies, illuminating them, before they were back in the perpetual twilight of the forest.

The next few days passed in a blur of shadowy trees, patches of light, and silence. They didn't talk much. Not because they were uncomfortable, but because they were lost in their own thoughts.

Traven couldn't stop thinking of the princess and his visions. He felt like he couldn't reach her fast enough. Every morning when he woke he felt the urgency stronger than ever. He often wondered why out of all the people in the land, it was the Princess Kalista that his visions told him to protect. Why was it so important that he protect her?

He also thought a lot about what he might do when he reached the princess and the battlefront. The recent attack had given him an opportunity to use the ambience in combat. He was beginning to realize how useful it would be but also how inept in using it he still was. He had almost been killed several times by the assassin's arrows before he had remembered to create a shield. He hoped that by the time they arrived, he would be proficient enough to help the Royal Army defeat the Wielder Kadrak and his army.

From screeing he knew that the battle would begin long before Darian and he reached the battlefront. The Balthan Army was getting close to where the Kalian Army had made camp at the mouth of the pass, and he supposed the battle would begin soon. He hoped that by traveling so hard, Darian and he would reach the frontlines in time to help. He also hoped that the princess would soon turn back to Candus. The reinforcements were closing in on the battlefront as well, and it looked as though they would reach it about the same time as the Balthan Army. Hopefully, someone would have enough sense to send her back to Candus soon.

Traven wasn't sure what Darian was thinking about. While the elf had at first seemed happier to be amongst the trees of the forest, he now seemed melancholy. He spent much of the day just staring north into the trees as they continued swiftly down the highway. On the morning of the fourth day since the attack, he decided to ask Darian what was wrong. The elf seemed to glance northward between every bite of food.

"Why do you keep staring northward?" he asked.

"You've noticed?" the elf said sheepishly.

It had been so obvious that Traven almost laughed at the question. Instead he just nodded. Darian pointed northward and slightly to the west.

"In that direction stands Mount Morian," he said. "The forest at the base of the mount is where I am from. It is the ancient home of all elves. It is where my family lives and where I grew up."

Staring northward into the thick forest, Traven could see why no one ever stumbled upon the elves. He couldn't imagine why anyone would want to search through the forest. It was strange to think of how many people had traveled this highway without the slightest idea of what these woods truly hid.

"How many elves live there?" he asked.

"Tens of thousands," Darian replied. "There are multiple elf havens throughout the forest. I grew up in the Morian Haven, the largest and the capitol haven of the elves."

"How far into the woods is it?"

"About a two day journey. During my time at the keep, I often looked forward to returning. I dreamt of marrying an elvish maiden and perhaps even raising an elfling. Now I suppose those dreams have gone away. I now follow a different dream."

"What do you mean by that?" Traven asked.

"I am devoted to you," the elf replied. "I no longer have my own dreams. My life is to serve you."

Traven was reminded once again of their strange arrangement. He often forgot that Darian was technically his servant. The elf was noble, independent, and wise. It made it difficult to view him as a servant. He hadn't realized before that the elf had been willing to give up his future dreams in order to serve him. Perhaps he would one day be able to convince the elf that he could honorably leave his service and fulfill his own dreams.

"Maybe we'll have to visit your haven once the battle is over," Traven suggested. Darian instantly turned pale. "What's wrong?"

"I don't know if that would be a good idea," the elf said. "Elves are very private and wouldn't necessarily welcome a human in their midst, even if he were a wielder."

"Well perhaps you can visit by yourself once the battle is over," he suggested.

"I can't do that," Darian said shaking his head. "My devotion to you prevents me from leaving you."

"What if I commanded you to visit your haven?" Traven asked. He was curious to hear the elf's response.

"I would have to go if it was a direct command," Darian replied with a wry smile. "However, I would be unwelcome. By tattooing your markings on my honor tattoo, I have sealed my fate to that of yours. The elves would scorn me and cast me out for either deserting you or failing to protect you."

Traven now understood just how much Darian had given up when he swore his devotion to him. He hoped that he would be able to repay the elf. He didn't feel right having the elf's fate determined by what he did or didn't do. However, he had to admit that it was comforting to know that Darian would stand by him no matter what.

They finished breakfast and headed east once again. They kept up their quick pace, only stopping to rest the horses periodically. They had also found that by switching between their mounts and the mounts of the two deceased guardians, the horses were able to keep up a much faster pace. By nightfall they were getting close to the edge of the forest. From there it would only be a half day's ride to Candus.

When they stopped for the night, Traven pulled out his dish to scree while Darian started a fire and made dinner. He not only wanted to check on their progress, but more than anything he wanted to check on the safety of the princess. He set the dish filled with water on the ground behind a large trunk, knelt down in front of it, and gathered the ambience around him.

First he pulled up an image of their current position. He was happy to see they were indeed close to the edge of the forest and would be able to reach Candus the following day. He then moved the image towards the pass and saw that the reinforcements had arrived there to join the main body of the army. Further to the east he could see the campfires of the invading army not far into the pass. The battle would most likely commence the next day.

He quickly pulled up an image of the princess. He frowned. She was still with the army. What was she doing? He could see that she was talking to Commander General Gavin. Looking around her, he saw that there was a contingent of royal guards mounted and waiting. He suddenly realized what was going on as the princess wrapped her arms around the commander general and kissed him. They were saying their goodbyes. He let the image disappear as he blushed.

The battle would start in the morning, and he was still a good five days away. At least the princess would be gone before the battle commenced. He dumped out the water and walked over to the fire. Hopefully they would meet up with the princess in a few days and easily be able to keep her safe until the battle was over. With the princess heading away from the battle accompanied by twenty royal guards, he hoped his nightly dreams would be more peaceful.

27

Kalista sadly stepped away from Gavin's arms. She had known this moment would eventually come, but she had hoped that it wouldn't come so soon. When they had set out from Candus, they had thought that the troops would have plenty of time to reach the opening of the pass and spend several days preparing for the attack. The march from Candus had taken five days, and the weather had been pleasant. She had not only enjoyed the extra time with Gavin, but had also enjoyed the time to get to know her future father-in-law better.

She had known that they would reach the main camp of the Royal Army the night of the fifth day, but she had planned on staying for a day while the troops were integrated and finished preparing for the upcoming attack. However, plans had dramatically changed earlier in the day. The scouts had appeared early that morning with the surprising news that the Balthan Army had somehow gotten past the avalanche and would be within striking range as early as that night.

Gavin had tried to send her back to Candus once again, but she had refused. She saw no reason not to accompany him to the camp. After another argument like the previous one they had in Candus, her fiancé had given in. She had convinced him that she would stay far from any danger. However, he had made her promise that she would turn back to Candus as soon as they reached the encampment. The army had marched in double time and reached the main body of the army that evening.

The scouts had updated them that the Balthan Army was indeed almost all the way through the pass. They had stopped not far from the opening and were setting up their camp for the night. The scouts expected that the battle would begin the next morning. After a quick dinner, Gavin had insisted that she keep her promise and leave for Candus immediately. She knew that it was time for her to go, but it didn't make leaving her future husband any easier. She gave him one last smile of encouragement and mounted her horse. From the top of her horse, she blew him a kiss and turned and rode away.

As she started back down the highway towards Candus, she began to worry for his safety. She couldn't believe that it was already the eve of the battle. She kept telling herself that he would be safe at the back of the army, directing its movements and tactics from the command area. She would have to believe that, or else she knew she would go crazy with worry.

Kalista stared forward as her horse carried her away from her beloved and towards safety. She was accompanied by her servants and twenty royal guards, yet she felt all alone without Gavin nearby. She took a deep breath and tried to calm her feelings of worry. He would be fine, and she would be fine. She tried to imagine the not far off day when Gavin would ride triumphant into the city, and they could move forward with their wedding plans.

* * * * *

Gavin watched as his beautiful future bride rode away from the army camp. He was sad to be apart from her but glad that she would be safely on her way to Candus before the battle commenced. He hadn't realized how stubborn she could be and was glad that she had kept her promise to leave as soon as they reached the camp. He watched her ride away until she eventually disappeared from view in the distance.

He then took a deep breath and headed towards the command tent. The battle would most likely begin in the morning and much needed to be discussed. His long strides soon brought him to the entrance of the large tent. It sat on a slight rise that offered an unobstructed view of the large area that sloped slightly down towards the mouth of the pass. The two guards at the entrance saluted and moved to the side.

He ducked inside the tent and looked around. It appeared that he was the last one to arrive. He took the last available chair at the base of the table. His two generals, Blaize and Kelt, were already seated at his right. His father sat at the head of the table with his two generals to his right. All five had been studying the map when he entered.

The huge table in the center of the room was almost completely covered by the large map. It accurately depicted in detail the area where the battle would occur. The map covered from just west of the camp all the way to a day's journey into the pass. The map was covered with small figurines that represented the different units within the Royal Army. There were also figurines of a different color to represent the rogue Balthan Army.

"Now that we are all here," his father began, "let's discuss the current position of the Balthan Army. Our scouts report that the army has set up camp for the night here," he said as he pointed to a spot just inside the entrance of the mountain pass. "It appears they have no intention of attacking until tomorrow. We'll keep a sharp eye on them in case they try any trickery, but I believe they will wait for tomorrow. They have been marching hard for the last five days and most likely want to rest before the battle begins.

"This is the current position of our troops," he said, bringing everyone's focus back to the figurines representing the Royal Army. "General Handel will explain how we will position ourselves in the morning to prepare for the attack."

Gavin watched intently as General Handel explained how the troops would form up at the first sign of the enemy approaching. He detailed which groups would be positioned where, and which groups would most likely take the brunt of the initial attack. Gavin carefully made mental notes of everything the general was saying. He could see that his two generals were paying close attention as well.

The defensive strategy was sound. If the Balthan Army thought that the Kalian Army would crumple when attacked by the Balthan wielder, they were mistaken. The troops all knew what to expect from the wielder Kadrak. If he attacked first, as had been the case in the previous battles, the Kalian troops had been commanded to remain completely still. When the Balthan Army's soldiers attacked, the Kalian troops would not be scattered or disorganized. They would remain firm in their positions and be ready to repel the attacking soldiers.

When all of the positions and strategies had been explained thoroughly, General Handel stopped speaking and answered the other generals' questions. When everyone confirmed that they understood what was to happen in the morning, Baron Mikel once again took over. He rose from his chair and pounded his fist against the map.

"We will be immovable," he said loudly. "With the arrival of our reinforcements today, we have half again as many troops as the opposing army. There is no reason for us to budge one inch. We will stand firm in the face of the wielder Kadrak. If he thinks he can defeat us by himself, he is greatly mistaken. We will not wilt when faced with death. We will show this wielder that there is no place for him in our grand country!"

As soon as his father was done with his speech, all of the generals reaffirmed their commitment and left to finish making the necessary preparations for the morning. Gavin remained in the tent with his father, looking at the map once again. While all of the generals had seen battle before, this was a first for him. His stomach was in knots at the thought of what the morning would bring.

"How are you feeling?" his father asked with a smile.

"Honestly?" Gavin said. "I feel a little sick."

"That's normal," the baron said with a smile. "There is always a certain amount of excitement and nerves on the eve of a battle." He walked over to him and put a hand on his shoulder. "A battle is never something one looks forward to. However, you are intelligent, brave, and disciplined. You will do just fine, and your troops will respect and follow your commands. We will show the Balthan Army tomorrow that we cannot be defeated."

Gavin thanked his father and left the tent. He stood in the cool night air and looked towards the pass. Towering mountains ran north and south from the narrow pass uninterrupted as far as the eye could see. Nothing marred the flat landscape that stretched out before him except the highway that wound down the rise and disappeared into the pass. All was quiet in the large field in front of him. It seemed strange that with the coming of the sun, the field would soon be full of troops awaiting battle.

He pictured in his mind where the attacking army would come from and where his troops would be waiting in defense. He ran over the different scenarios of what might occur as he stared out over the empty field. He wanted to run through all of the scenarios again but decided it would be best if he got some sleep. The coming day would be long and stressful. It would be much better if he was rested and had a clear mind.

He entered his tent and prepared to sleep. As he lay down on his cot, he tried to clear his mind of the worries that kept running through it. He would have plenty of time to worry about the battle in the morning. He closed his eyes and pictured the princess. A smile crept across his face. She was the reason he was fighting. Her memory would give him strength. He would make sure that the Balthan Army never posed any threat to her or her kingdom.

* * * * *

Kalista looked up at the stars. They had ridden for several hours before finally stopping, and she was exhausted. She knew she could have avoided the late night ride if she would have turned around earlier, but she didn't regret her decision to see Gavin all the way to the camp. It had been worth the extra hours she had been able to spend with him before leaving.

She gazed one last time up into the night sky and ducked into her tent. She needed to get to sleep. They would be breaking camp and leaving early in the morning. She had promised Gavin that she would get as far from the battle as she could before it started. She supposed that if they left early enough, she would be over half a day's journey towards Candus before the battle broke.

She quickly got ready and lay down for the night. She wondered how Gavin was feeling right now. She knew him well enough to know that he would have a hard time sleeping tonight. He would most likely be running through everything he had been taught about battle tactics over and over again in his head. She hoped that he was not too worried about the impending battle. She knew that he would do fine and be a great leader, but it was his first battle.

As she lay staring up at the roof of her tent, she wondered how much sleep she would be getting. She couldn't deny that she was worried for Gavin's safety. She reminded herself that he would be safely away from the front lines of the battle. He was not a common soldier. He was the commander general and would be directing his troops from the command hill. There would be numerous soldiers between him and the actual fighting.

She turned over in her bed and tried to get comfortable but couldn't. She felt somewhat exposed and vulnerable even though she had twenty royal guards with her. She had grown used to traveling with the large contingent of troops and having Gavin's tent nearby. She knew there was nothing to worry about, but she wished that she had someone she knew to comfort her.

She knew she wouldn't have Gavin nearby until the battle was over. Her servants were familiar but gave her no sense of protection. She longed to have her father nearby or someone else who was strong and caring to comfort her. Her guards would protect her with their lives, but she didn't really know any of them.

She sighed and turned over once again. She knew she would eventually fall asleep, but she couldn't get the thought of the impending battle out of her head. She hoped once again that Gavin would stay safely away from the fighting. As far as she knew, he had never seen death up close.

She shivered as she thought back to her own abduction earlier in the spring. She had seen death and it had shaken her terribly. The ordeal still gave her nightmares. If the young soldier Traven hadn't been there to save her, she would have been killed.

She smiled at the thought of the brave young soldier. She wondered once again how he was doing and if he had been able to find what he was looking for. She wondered where he was. She supposed it was possible that he had already completed his search and had joined with the main group of soldiers. She wondered if he would be facing death in the morning as well.

She suddenly felt worried for him. He would not be far removed from the fighting like Gavin. The young soldier could even be on the front lines. The thought of him dying bothered her almost as much as thinking about Gavin being killed. The other troops were just troops to her, but the young soldier Traven had a name and a face imprinted in her mind. He had comforted her and risked his life to save her when no one else could.

Kalista shook the thoughts of him from her mind. She had enough to worry about without thinking of him. At least he was an expert swordsman and would be able to defend himself. She hoped that if the fighting were to ever reach Gavin, all of his practice would pay off and he would be able to defend himself as well.

She finally reached the point where she physically couldn't stay awake any longer, and she dropped off to sleep. Her sleep was restless with memories of her kidnapping and dreams of battle. She awoke with a start when her chamber maid gently shook her shoulder. She calmed her breathing as she realized who it was at her bedside.

"Begging your pardon, Princess, but it is dawn."

Kalista let out a quiet groan and sat up. She felt like she hadn't slept at all. She hurriedly donned her riding clothes and the small party was soon once again on its way down the road towards Candus. It would be a while before the sun rose, and she wished she was still asleep. However, she had promised that she would rise early and head towards Candus before the battle started, and she wouldn't break her promise.

She glanced back over her shoulder and stared eastward down the road. She hoped that all would go well with the impending battle and that Gavin would remain safe. She knew that the next week would feel like the longest week of her life as she waited for news of his safety.

28

    Kadrak threw back the flaps of his tent and walked out into the cool morning air with a grin. Today would be a great day. He had gotten a solid night's sleep and was feeling wonderful. He looked out over the encampment. His troops were finishing their morning rations and preparing for the coming battle. Armor clinked and echoed off the tall mountains that rose on either side of the camp. The sky was clear and blue. It was a good day to conquer.

    He strode through the camp exuding confidence. He made his way past his troops and met Gilrod at the western edge of the camp. Gilrod was holding the reins to his stallion and patiently waiting for him. Kadrak took the reins and swung up onto his magnificent horse. From his perch on top of the stallion, he could see the entire camp sprawled out behind him. Soon all of the troops would be in their ranks and ready to march.

    He looked forward towards the opening of the pass in the distance. It would take less than an hour to march the rest of the way to the opening. He knew that the Kalian Army was camped just outside the pass upon a small rise. There was no doubt they were aware of the position of the Balthan Army as well. They would think they were ready for the attack, but they had never faced a wielder before.

    He knew that the Kalian Army outnumbered his own, but he was confident that his powers would make up for any disadvantage his troops might have. He also had his secret contingent of galdak warriors waiting nearby. If he needed them, they would be ready to turn the tide of the battle. However, he assumed that their help wouldn't be necessary. When the Kalian soldiers saw what he could do, they would break and his army would be able to rout them.

He took a deep breath of the fresh mountain air and smiled. He waited patiently as his troops formed up ranks behind him. When everyone was in place, Gilrod joined him, and he began leading the army towards the opening of the pass. Kadrak kept the pace slow and deliberate. He wanted his troops fresh and ready when the battle finally commenced.

As they neared the mouth of the pass, Kadrak heard a sharp whistle. Immediately, four arrows came rushing towards him. He smiled as all four arrows burst into flames and dropped harmlessly a good ten feet away from him on both sides. He quickly located the four shooters and four bolts of lightning struck the surrounding mountains. His bolts were perfectly placed, and without delay four bodies rolled down the sides of the pass and came to a rest at the edges of the trail. He shook his head with a smile. He supposed he couldn't blame the Kalian Army for trying.

Once they were out of the pass, the troops spread out into their formations. Across the large field, the Kalian Army was in place and waiting for them. He had to admit that the sight of the Royal Army was impressive. All had matching uniforms, shields, and weapons, and they covered the entire rise that led up from the field at the mouth of the pass. His own troops lacked the polished armor and matching uniforms of the Kalian Army, but they were ready for battle just the same.

Kadrak sat upon his stallion at the head of his army and signaled for his messenger to gallop forward and deliver his demands. No one could say that he attacked without first giving his enemies the option to submit to his will. No one could say that he was not a benevolent leader.

* * * * *

"Is he serious?" the baron said as he finished reading the message that had just been delivered. He chuckled and looked at his generals. "The Wielder Kadrak wants to give us the opportunity to surrender," he announced. "All we have to do is accept him as our new king and join our troops with his army. What do you say?"

Gavin joined with the other generals in laughing and suggesting what kind of counter offer they should send. A message was soon written and sent back to the Balthan Army. Gavin watched as the messenger quickly rode back to the invading army. His stomach was still in knots, and he hadn't slept much the night before. However, he did feel better about their prospects in the bright light of the early morning.

From the command area at the top of the rise, it was easy to see that their own troops far outnumbered those of the Balthan Army. While the opposing army's troops were formed up in loose, slightly disorganized looking formations, his own troops were perfectly consistent in tight formations. It appeared the only hope of the invading army truly was the wielder Kadrak who was at their lead.

It was unfortunate that the archers hidden at the mouth of the pass hadn't been able to bring down the leader and instigator of the conflict. He wondered if they had been able to escape or if they had been killed. He assumed the latter. It was unfortunate because they had been some of the best archers in the army. He wondered how the wielder had avoided their arrows.

He watched as the messenger delivered their reply. Perhaps they would soon find out just what the wielder was capable of. Gavin steeled himself. There was a palpable sense of anxiety and anticipation in the air. Everyone knew that the battle was about to commence.

* * * * *

Kadrak crumpled up the counter offer and let it fall to the ground. He had known that the Kalians wouldn't accept his offer, but when it was all over, he wanted them to remember that he had given them a chance to avoid the destruction that he was about to rain down on them.

He took off his cloak and tossed it to Gilrod. It wasn't as cold outside of the pass, and as soon as he began working the ambience his body would be plenty warm. He led his stallion a short distance away from his troops and out into the open field. He was still far out of the range of the Kalian archers, but close enough for them to see who it was that would defeat them. He stared defiantly at the large army standing solidly in his way and raised his arms to the sky. He concentrated and with a smile began his attack.

Numerous small balls of fire appeared in the clear sky above the Kalian troops and began falling towards the earth. He kept them falling until he had created over a hundred. He then dropped his arms and watched as the last of them crashed into the ranks of the army. He surveyed the effects of the barrage. It appeared he had struck several troops but most had merely hid behind their shields to avoid the fire. The troops were surprisingly still all standing firm in their tight formations.

Kadrak stared back at the disciplined troops with a grin. It appeared that he would need to be a little more forceful. He raised his hands into the air once again and concentrated. Let them try to hide behind their shields again. He smirked as the air began to buzz and crackle.

* * * * *

Blaize sat upon his horse at the top of the rise. His troops were on the left flank of the army. It felt strange for him to be watching from the back instead of being down in the midst of the troops. He watched with satisfaction as his troops stood firm and refused to budge as balls of fire rained down on them from the clear sky.

The wielder Kadrak truly had a power that he didn't understand. It had been awe inspiring. He glanced to the other leaders near him to judge their reactions to the display of power. Some were wide eyed while others watched impassively as the rain of fire ended. He glanced back at his troops, happy to see that they had effectively used their shields to block the fireballs. If that was the best the wielder could muster, he wouldn't be much of a factor in the battle.

As if in answer to his thoughts, the wielder raised his hands towards the sky once again. Blaize looked on as the air began to crackle. Suddenly, bolts of lightning appeared out of thin air and began to slam down into the middle of the army. Bolt after bolt slammed into the ranks. He watched with a cringe as soldiers were seared in place or their bodies were launched into the air by the force of the explosions. Apparently the wielder had only been testing the army with the fireballs.

Several of the troops began to panic and run, but the majority stayed firm and brave in the face of such an unexplainable attack. Blaize steadied his horse as a bolt of lightning struck not far below where all of the generals were watching from. He turned and found Commander General Gavin looking very pale. The young commander was obviously terrified, but to his credit, he kept his horse still and stood his ground.

The barrage of lightning bolts continued for several minutes. The previously quiet morning was marred by the loud claps of thunder and the dull explosions that accompanied the lightning. There were also cries of surprise and anguish from the soldiers who happened to be in the bolts' way. Blaize looked on helplessly at the destruction. He now understood why the Balthan cities had fallen so quickly.

The bolts finally stopped and an eerie quiet once again settled over the field of battle. The bolts had caused many fatalities but not nearly enough to hamper the large army. The soldiers remained firm, apprehensively waiting what might come next.

Blaize's eyes were drawn back to the sky above the army. A small ball of fire appeared and began to spin. It grew larger and got brighter as it spun. When it was roughly the size of a horse it stopped spinning. It hung silently in the air for several moments before dropping straight down. The soldiers underneath the falling ball of bright fire quickly brought their shields up.

He watched with amazement as the ball of fire fell straight through the soldiers' shields and slammed into the ground. Nothing was left where the soldiers had previously been. As if the dropping of the ball of fire had been a signal, the Balthan Army erupted with yells and charged forward. Fortunately, no more balls of the spinning fire appeared nor bolts of lightning. It seemed to Blaize that the barrage of magic attacks had come to an end for now and the physical battle would now take center stage.

He quickly surveyed his troops and was pleased to see that despite the wielder's attacks, they were firmly in their formations and ready for the onslaught. He watched as the Balthan Army covered the open space between the two armies and crashed into the frontlines of the Kalian Royal Army. It was as if a quiver rippled through the entire army at the impact, but the Kalian Army held firm.

Blaize shook away the astonishment from the wielder's attacks and focused on the details of the battle that was erupting before his eyes. The Balthan Army pulled back and attacked several different times throughout the morning but had no success in breaking through the frontlines. The Kalian soldiers were strong and disciplined and didn't budge in the face of the multiple attacks.

At one point around midday, the opposing army surged against the left flank. Blaize quickly commanded a few adjustments and reinforced his side with some of his cavalry. The Balthans were pushed back once again, losing any advantage they had gained in the brief surge. By mid afternoon it became apparent that nothing much would be decided by the end of the day. It was evident that the Kalian's wouldn't be beaten easily. What was left to be seen was if the Balthan Army would ever be able to push them from their position.

By the time the sun dipped below the horizon, the Balthans were trudging away from the field back into the pass. Blaize took stock of the casualties from the day and was pleased to find that the day appeared to be a victory for their army. It was obvious that the Balthans hadn't gained any ground. What would truly determine whether the day could be considered a victory for Kalia was how many actual casualties there had been.

Blaize watched as his own troops began ascending the rise and heading back to the camp. They looked tired from the long day of fighting but were mostly upbeat. He doubted the Balthan soldiers were feeling anything but frustration. He knew that both of their previous attacks had ended in victory for them in less than a day. They would find no such success here. He hoped that the soldiers would be discouraged enough after another day or two that they would just turn around and head back to Balthus.

He watched as the last of the Balthan soldiers disappeared into the pass. He gave the battlefield one last sweep before turning, walking to the command tent, and ducking inside. He took a seat at the command table and waited patiently for the reports to trickle in of casualty numbers on both sides. It soon became apparent that the day had indeed ended in a victory. The Balthan Army had lost nearly double the number of soldiers that they had lost.

Aside from the initial show of power from the Balthan wielder, the battle had played out as had been expected. The less disciplined and less skilled Balthan Army had fallen before the trained soldiers of the Kalian Army. If the casualty ratio held steady, the Balthans would have no choice but to turn back after another couple of days.

Blaize wondered why the wielder hadn't continued to rain his destruction down on them throughout the day. Obviously there were limits to the wielder's power, but he found it hard to believe that the wielder Kadrak would have brought a smaller army against them without the ability to do more than had been done today. He suspected the next day wouldn't be as easy for the Kalians.

They would need to be prepared for what the wielder might unleash the coming day. He supposed that Kadrak may have thought that his show of power would be enough to sway the battle more than it had. From the reports they had received on Kadrak, he knew that the wielder wouldn't make the same mistake again. He had some ideas of what he would do if he had the same powers as the wielder. When all of the generals were present and the reports had finished coming in, he was prepared to offer his opinion on how to prepare for the coming day's battle.

*****

Kadrak was anything but happy with the results of the day's battle. Not only had the Kalians stood firm against his barrage of elemental attacks, but his own army had not fought as if they even cared to win the battle. Apparently his troops needed to be reminded that their supplies would only last so long and that they were trapped in the pass.

He pulled up in front of his tent and dropped from his stallion. He angrily tossed the reins to one of his servants and ducked inside. As frustrated as he was with his troops, he was also frustrated with himself. He had wasted too much energy with his initial attacks. The barrage of fireballs, lightning, and the ball of liquid fire had left him drained and had little effect on the Kalians. It had shown them his power but had not caused the same frantic reactions as it had in the Balthan cities he had previously conquered.

He could have used the ambience to do more damage later in the day but had wanted to see how his soldiers would do on their own. It was obvious that his troops wouldn't be able to defeat the Kalian Army without his help. In fact, it appeared that they would be easily defeated. He shook his head in frustration and waited for Gilrod to arrive and report in detail on the outcome of the battle.

While he waited, he devised a new plan of attack for the second day's battle. Now that he had already shown the Kalians some of what he was capable of, he would use the ambience sparingly in conjunction with planned attacks and maneuvers. He would first target the Kalian Army's archers and remove them from the battle. He would then strike simultaneously with the soldiers' attacks, amplifying their potency. He supposed that the combined effort would be enough to turn the tide of the battle.

The unfortunate truth was that the battle would not end quickly. Even with his new plan, it would take several days to weaken the Kalian Army to the point where they would be able to gain the advantage to win a decisive victory. He didn't want to wait several more days. He wanted the battle to end swiftly.

However, he knew that the only way to accomplish that would be to unleash the hidden galdak warriors upon the Kalians. He was still uncertain that he wanted to reveal his secret army. He didn't know how much he could trust the galdaks, and he didn't know how his own troops would respond. He was tempted to signal the galdaks the next morning but knew it would be best for him to wait just a little longer.

He would wait. There were enough supplies left to test his new battle plan. If the results weren't as good as he hoped, he would then signal his hidden warriors. One way or another, he would defeat the Royal Kalian Army within the next several days.

29

Kalista stared up at the deep blue sky overhead. Several birds soared through the air in large, lazy circles. Everything seemed so peaceful. It was hard to imagine the destruction and death that was most certainly occurring only a two day's journey behind her.

She turned her focus back to the road and stared forward. In three more days she would be in Candus again, back in a safe, comfortable palace. As good as it sounded, she felt guilty to be heading towards it while her future husband battled against an invading army behind her. She assumed that the battle was nearing the end of its second full day of fighting. However, no messengers had passed them yet to bring word of how the battle was proceeding.

The last two days had passed slowly. She hadn't felt like talking to her servants much, and it was improper for her to talk at length with any of her guards. It had been two days of almost complete silence. The weather had been good, for which she was grateful, but each day had seemed to last forever. One would think after traveling so far already, a day of traveling wouldn't seem so long. However, she supposed that given her current company and the worry she felt for Gavin, it made sense that the days felt longer.

The sun was soon directly in front of them, making it hard to see. She kept her eyes down on the ground and let her guards worry about what was ahead. Another day had passed and still no word of the battle. She began to worry that somehow the battle had gone worse than planned. She wondered why a messenger hadn't been sent yet.

"Pull up and take defensive positions!" the head guard commanded.

Kalista's previous thoughts disappeared as she looked around to see what the problem was. The guards reformed around her facing eastward. Were they really about to be attacked? Her heart started racing at the thought. She stood up in her stirrups to see what was happening. It soon became apparent that there was only a single rider racing towards them from the east. As the rider drew closer, the royal markings of his uniform announced him as a messenger from the Kalian Army.

The news she had been waiting for was finally arriving. She hoped it was good news and everything was proceeding according to plan for Gavin and the Kalian Royal Army. She resisted the urge to move in the direction of the messenger in order to hear what he had to say. The man soon reached their group and pulled up. He quickly gave his report to the head guard and then hurried past them on his way to Candus.

"Proceed," the head guard announced.

They were soon formed up in their normal positions and riding westward. She tried to wait patiently, but when the head guard didn't immediately come to her to report, she signaled for his presence.

"Yes your highness," he said as he slowly came to her side.

"What did the messenger report?" she demanded.

"He reported on the first day of battle," the guard replied.

"Repeat his message to me," she stated firmly. It irritated her that the head guard was being so difficult. He had to know of her interest in the status of the battle.

"He said the battle was going as planned. The Royal Army was able to easily repel the attack of the Balthan Army." Kalista let out a sigh of relief as the guard continued. "There were casualties, but more on the Balthan side than on our own. If the Balthans aren't able to mount a better offensive, there won't be any difficulties in stopping them and soundly defeating their army."

"What of the Balthan wielder?" she asked.

"The messenger reported that he is quite powerful, but it appears he does have certain limits. He began the battle by calling down fire, lightning, and something else that was incredibly hot from the sky. A number of our troops were killed in the assault, but after the initial onslaught the wielder didn't attack the rest of the day. The generals aren't sure why but hope that it's because the magical attacks take so much of his energy."

"Was there anything else?"

"No," the lead guard answered. "All of the generals and commanders were untouched by the attacks and are hopeful that the conflict will end quickly."

Kalista dismissed the guard and went back to riding alone in silence. She felt as if a great load had been lifted from her shoulders. Gavin was okay and the battle was proceeding in their favor. She was deeply grateful for the good news. Tonight she would be able to sleep a little better.

The remainder of the day's ride passed by a little more swiftly. Camp was set up, dinner was served, and she did indeed sleep better than she had the past few nights. When the sun rose, she was back in the saddle heading for Candus. The morning passed quickly, but by the time the sun was directly overhead, she was anxious for a report on the events of the second day of battle. It didn't seem like the evening could come fast enough.

Fortunately, she didn't have to wait until evening. Just after lunch another messenger was spotted racing towards them from the east. She thought it strange that he had reached them so early in the day. She had expected that the messages would be delivered at increasingly longer intervals since she was constantly getting further from the battle. Perhaps the first messenger had just been riding slower than the second. She waited as the messenger reached them and delivered his report to the head guard. He was then past them, racing towards Candus.

Kalista could tell from the guards' reaction to the message that it wasn't as favorable as the message from the previous day. She braced herself as the lead guard immediately made his way over to her and delivered the report.

"The second day of battle did not go nearly as well as the first," he stated. "Our army is still in control and in position, but they sustained almost three times the number of casualties that they did on the first day."

"What happened?" she asked with concern.

"The second day's attacks by the Balthan Army were better coordinated and carried out," the lead guard said with a frown. "Apparently the Balthan wielder would strike using his powers at a specific point in our troops' ranks. His soldiers would then surge forward at the exact point where our ranks had been weakened. By the time our troops could recover and reorganize, the Balthans would already be deep into our defenses. The coordinated attacks almost broke all the way through our defenses several times, but they were all eventually repelled. The Balthans sustained a significant number of casualties in the attacks but not nearly as many as our own troops."

Kalista quietly turned the information over in her mind. If the Royal Army wasn't able to find a way to better defend against these types of attacks, the Balthan Army would eventually overrun them. With such a shift in the outcome of day two, she hoped that the current day would allow the Kalian Army to turn the tide back in their favor.

"Do you think our army will be able to adjust?" she asked the lead guard.

"I assume they've already devised a strategy to better combat the coordinated attacks of the Balthans. However, I don't know how much can really be done. The main problem is that the Balthan wielder appears to be able to strike anywhere in the ranks anytime he wishes. The only true way to fully combat the coordinated attacks would be to kill the wielder."

"How far is the range of the wielder's attacks?" she asked as a troubling thought occurred to her. The guard had said that the wielder could strike anywhere.

"It must be quite far," he answered. "Yesterday he lit the command tent on fire."

"Why didn't you mention that earlier?" Kalista almost screamed. What if something had happened to Gavin?

"Don't worry," the guard said in a calming voice. "None of the generals were hurt."

She heard the last statement, but it didn't calm her. If the wielder had struck at the command tent once, he could do it again. Gavin wasn't safe. Even at the back of the army with thousands of soldiers between him and the enemy, her fiancé could be struck down by one of the wielder's attacks.

She had to get back to him. He would be too prideful to hide from the danger. She would have to convince him somehow to get away from the fighting. She wasn't sure what she could do, but she had to try. She couldn't keep worrying everyday whether or not her future husband would be killed by the Balthan wielder, leaving her alone and hopeless. She had to act. She turned her horse and began riding back towards the battle.

"Your highness," the lead guard said as he caught up to her. "What are you doing?"

"I'm returning to my fiancé," she replied as if it wasn't a big deal.

"I cannot let you do that," the guard said as he grabbed her horse's reins and stopped her.

"Excuse me," she said firmly as she gave the man an icy stare. "Who are you to tell me what I can and cannot do? Do you presume you can tell the High Princess of Kalia what she can and cannot do?"

The lead guard's firm exterior quivered slightly at the question. She could tell that the statement had caused an inner conflict in the man.

"I can't just let you ride back into danger," he said. "I have sworn to protect you at all costs."

"What are you going to do if I refuse to comply?" she asked. "Will you tie me up and haul me to Candus like a prisoner?"

The guard was left speechless. He was aware that he wasn't allowed to touch her. He could say whatever he wanted to her and risk simply being discharged, but if he touched her he could face being put to death. She knew that she had him. He would not stop her. She watched as his face grew a dark shade of red. He was obviously very frustrated, but he held his tongue.

"I am returning to my fiancé," she stated. "If you have sworn to protect me, then I would suggest you accompany me and make sure no harm comes to me."

Having made her decision and ending any arguments, Kalista nudged her horse forward. She saw several of the soldiers give each other frustrated looks, and she heard rumblings of discontent behind her. However, not one of them tried to stop her. They formed up in their normal ranks and accompanied her down the road back towards the pass and the armies. She let out a sigh of relief. At least she was headed towards Gavin. She now only had to think of a way to get him to safety when she arrived near the battle field.

By nightfall they had more than covered the distance they had traveled previously in the day. She hoped if they maintained the quicker pace throughout the next day, they would be able to reach the battle sometime during its fifth day. Hopefully that would be soon enough for her to accomplish her goal of getting Gavin to safety. She finally pulled up and told her servants and her guards to make camp.

She stayed on her horse as they complied and went about setting up the camp. A light breeze blew past her, ruffling the loose strands of her hair. She gazed towards the east and hoped once again that Gavin had survived through another day of battle.

". . . careful . . . Princess . . ."

Kalista jerked around to see who had sneaked up on her but saw no one. Everyone was busily setting up the camp and taking care of the horses. Another breeze caressed her face.

". . . please . . . turn . . . back . . ."

She stared into the starry night sky. It was as before, but the words were so much stronger and clearer. There was no mistaking them, but she had no idea where they were coming from. It appeared they were coming out of thin air.

". . . wait . . . for . . . me . . ."

For some reason the whispers in the night air reminded her of a young soldier. There was something about them that reminded her of Traven. The comfort he had given her during her abduction had been firmly imprinted on her. She shook her head in confusion. If not for the sense of softness, earnestness, and familiarity of the sound, she would have been scared out of her wits by the words. As it was, she nervously wondered what was happening. How was it possible for someone to send a message on the wind? Should she listen to it and do as it said?

She shook her head once again. Why was she even considering doing what a disembodied voice was suggesting? She was almost certain that it was no trick of her imagination. She was definitely hearing something real. When she had heard it before, it had been so soft that she had wondered whether her mind was playing tricks on her. This time it had been distinct and clear. Was it the voice of her dead ancestors? Was it some trick of an enemy? She didn't know, but she knew better than to follow its pleadings.

She dismounted her horse and entered her tent. She had soon eaten dinner and retired for the night. As she lay in the dark she once again reflected on the whispers of the wind. She knew the voice on the wind should scare her and worry her, but for some reason she longed to hear it again.

*****

"It appears she heard it," Darian said as he stood next to Traven's side.

"I know," Traven replied as he let the image of the princess disappear from the screeing dish. "Though, I doubt it will do any good. Who would follow what a voice out of thin air told them to do?"

"You should just be thankful she wasn't so scared that she fell off her horse," the elf said. "Do you remember the time you whispered on the wind to me and the other guardians in the field?"

He smiled at the memory. They had all jumped at the sudden sound out of thin air. It had been hilarious to see the confusion and worry on the faces of the guardians. He dumped the water from the dish and put it away. They needed to get to sleep so they could get an early start in the morning.

Before screeing the princess, he had called up an image of the battle. It appeared that things weren't going very well for the Kalian Army. They were still holding firm in their position on the rise, but their numbers were dwindling. From the sections of scorched grass and holes in the ground, he knew that the Balthan wielder was actively involved in the attacks. He hoped that he would be able to do something to counter him when he arrived at the battlefield.

When he had then screed the princess, he had found her farther from Candus and traveling in the direction of the battle. He didn't know what she and her guards were thinking. Why would they be heading towards the fighting? He shook his head in frustration. He was so close, and yet now he didn't think there was any way he could catch up to her before she arrived at the battlefield.

His shoulders slumped. What more could he do? He began to worry that perhaps he couldn't change what his dreams were telling him. Perhaps no matter what he did the princess would end up dying. He quivered at the thought. Darian reached over and put his hand on his shoulder.

"You've done what you can," the elf said. "You've warned the princess, and we're traveling as fast as we can. Don't lose hope. The most important thing to do right now is to get a good night's sleep. We'll start early tomorrow and see if we can catch her."

Traven was thankful for the encouragement. He shook off his dismal thoughts and prepared to sleep. Maybe if they started early enough each day and rode hard enough, they could catch up to the princess before she reached the battlefield. He stared up at the starry night sky. They had left the confines of the forest and passed Candus the previous day. It was strange sleeping under an open sky once again.

He was eventually able to clear his mind and fall asleep, but his sleep was not restful. That night he dreamed of arriving at the edge of the battlefield. Upon his head sat the crown of Kalia and at his feet lay a wasteland of death. In the center of the wasteland, he could distinctly make out the lifeless form of the princess.

30

The time had arrived. As much as Kadrak had hoped to avoid this moment, he knew that to wait any longer could be disastrous to his campaign. The last four days of fighting had been intense and tiring. After the horrible first day of battle, his army had slowly been chipping away at the larger Kalian Army. Another few days and his army would be able to break through and overrun the Kalians. However, they didn't have a few more days. They had reached the end of their supplies.

He stood at the mouth of the pass with his army stretched out anxiously behind him. They were prepared and ready to win the battle today. They all knew that there wasn't any food left. If they wanted to eat the next day, they would have to overrun the Kalians and take their supplies.

It had become evident to him the previous day that it would come to this. He had stopped his attacks with the ambience in the early afternoon so that he could rest and regain his full strength for today. He was anxious and ready as well. The battle had already lasted too long, and his army had suffered too many casualties. He wondered if it had been wise to wait until now to call in his reinforcements. He shook his head and firmed his jaw. He wouldn't second guess himself. He had made the decision to wait, and it had been the right decision. Now the correct decision was to wait no longer.

He glanced at the mountains to the north as he raised his hands in the air. As soon as the galdak warriors responded to his call, he would send his troops in immediately and unleash a fierce attack of his own. The Kalian Army would buckle and break in the face of the three coordinated attacks. The battle would be over by midday. It was time.

A fireball sprung from Kadrak's outstretched hands and shot straight up into the sky. It was followed by two more in quick succession. He watched as all three reached their peaks high in the sky and disappeared one after the other. He paused for several moments and then summoned a giant lightning bolt. It came crashing down on the northern flank of the Kalian Army, pinpointing where the galdak warriors were to attack.

He watched the mountains, eager for a first glimpse of the mighty warriors. The Kalian Army had no idea what he had just signaled. His own soldiers didn't even know the significance of what he had just done. Only Gilrod was aware of the hidden warriors. Kadrak had shared the secret with his second in command the previous night so Gilrod would be prepared to send the proper message to the Balthan soldiers when the time was right.

Several more moments passed without any sign of the warriors. He shifted on his mount. Perhaps he had misjudged how long it would take them to respond. He waited patiently, but still no signs of the galdaks appeared. Was it possible they had missed his signal?

He raised his hands in the air to repeat the signal but stopped before wasting any more energy. He let his hands fall to his sides as anger flashed across his face. There was no chance his signal could have been missed. The galdak warriors would have been watching anxiously for the opportunity to unleash their pent up fury on the humans. The answer to why they hadn't come was simple. Shaman Azulk had lied to him. He hadn't sent warriors to help. The devious old galdak had purposely deceived him.

Kadrak took several deep breaths. The shaman would pay for his insolence. The elderly galdak would regret the day that he crossed the great Wielder Kadrak. He took several more deep breaths, trying to calm the anger and rage that welled up inside of him. Shaman Azulk would pay, but first the current battle needed to be won. He quickly thought through his options. There would be no reinforcements, but the battle needed to be won today nonetheless.

If his army was going to win the battle, it would be up to him. He alone possessed the power necessary to decide the outcome. He quickly changed his plan of attack as his army sat silently behind him, waiting for their instructions. He would have to strike at the Kalian Army with great force but with careful wisdom as well. He couldn't afford to waste any more of his energy. He turned to Gilrod who was still inspecting the mountains to the north.

"It looks like there will have to be a change of plans," he stated with a hint of anger still showing in his voice. "It appears we've been betrayed. We'll have to win this battle on our own."

He quickly gave Gilrod his new instructions. His second in command listened to the new strategy and hurried to relay the battle plan to the rest of the army. Kadrak waited patiently for the instructions to be passed to everyone. While he waited, he stared at the Kalian Army across the empty battlefield.

The last four days of fighting had been intense, but today's battle would be unlike any the world had ever seen. He pulled out a shallow screeing dish and unstopped his water skin. He carefully poured out just enough water to cover the bottom of the dish. He then called up an image of the Kalian Army in order to get a closer view. He surveyed the enemy's ranks and made mental notes of their positions. He located the generals and smiled.

Today he would strike where he could do the most damage. He would cause as much confusion as he could amongst the Kalians and then drive his army directly through the center of their ranks. Once they had broken through, they would double back on the Kalian soldiers and attack from both the front and the rear. He would keep up his barrage of elemental attacks, and the Kalian Army would crumble.

Gilrod returned to his side and confirmed that the battle plan had been relayed to everyone. His army was ready to attack and claim their victory. Kadrak glanced back over his soldiers and made himself glow. They needed to be reminded that they wouldn't be fighting the Kalians alone. They had a master wielder at their head. He raised his fist into the air and his soldiers cheered. The time had come. Today victory would be theirs.

* * * * *

General Blaize stared at the mouth of the pass from his position at the top of the rise. Earlier the Balthan wielder had sent three fireballs straight up into the sky. He had then sent a bolt of lightning thundering down into the middle of Blaize's troops. The wielder hadn't done anything else since.

He wasn't sure what the point of the show of power had been. At first he thought the Balthan wielder must be signaling something, but when nothing happened, he questioned what it could possibly mean.

The last three days had been rough for the army. They had suffered numerous casualties. It had been frustrating trying to defend against the wielder's attacks. They had worked out a system to reinforce spots quickly, but they could only do so much against the unexpected.

It had become obvious over the last few days that if they stuck with their plan to only fight defensively, the Balthans would slowly continue to deplete their army. Today they would employ a much different strategy. They would attack. They had lined up in the same formations as previously so as not to give any hint of their intentions to the Balthans. Once the battle began, about half of the army, including his troops, would surge forward and attack.

They would no longer sit back and allow the Balthan wielder to continue decimating their army from a safe distance. Today they would bring the battle to him. They knew that if they were able to take him out of the battle, they could easily defeat the Balthan Army. The troops were aware of the dangers of attacking the wielder directly, but they preferred it to sitting around and waiting for a lightning bolt to come crashing down on them.

Blaize checked his bindings and weapons. Today he wouldn't just be directing his troops from the rear. Today he would be riding into battle with them. It was now a waiting game. As soon as the Balthan Army made their attack, the Kalians would counterattack and hope to catch them off guard. If they were able to knock the wielder Kadrak out of the battle, they hoped to end the war today.

A cheer broke out across the battlefield. He watched as the Balthan Army surged past their leader and headed across the empty field. He took a deep breath. It was almost time. He gave the other generals a nod and moved towards the northern flank of the army. As soon as the Balthans engaged the waiting troops, he would sweep around their side with his cavalry.

Lightning began crashing down across the front ranks of the Kalian Army. The wielder was at it again. After the initial strikes across the front, the lightning bolts raced right up the center of the army all the way to the rear. But the strikes didn't stop when they reached the rear of the army; they intensified. Blaize wheeled around with worry. The wielder was deliberately targeting the commanders. He had never seen such an intense barrage of lightning bolts. He quickly averted his eyes from the blinding flashes.

After several moments the bolts left the top of the rise and raced back down the center of the army. His eyes darted across the area where he had been only moments before. Several of the generals who had been knocked down were climbing back to their feet in a daze. However, it appeared that a few would never be rising again. It appeared that among the dead was their leader,

Baron Mikel. The Commander General Gavin was kneeling beside the still form of his father. He was looking around frantically and his face was a pale white.

He hoped the young man could pull himself together quickly. Commander General Gavin was now in charge of the entire army. Blaize was tempted to return and help sort out the mess, but the Balthan soldiers were already beginning to crash into the front lines. He would have to trust the other generals and their second-in-commands to lead the army from the rear.

He had a more important responsibility. The mission he had volunteered for was critical to the army's success. He booted his horse and galloped the rest of the way to his soldiers. The time had come. Today there would be an all out battle.

* * * * *

Kadrak smiled. His barrage of lightning bolts had done exactly what he needed them to. The Kalian Army was left weak in the center and his troops were driving deep into their midst. He was also sure that he had killed several of the Kalian generals. The successful strike at the commanders had weakened the Kalians even more and would cause confusion and fear.

Today he would have his decisive victory. His smile grew larger as he sent another volley of lightning bolts slamming into the center of the Kalian Army, just ahead of his attacking troops. He would clear the way for them to cut all the way to the rear of the Kalian Army.

"Master," Gilrod said urgently.

"What?" Kadrak said with annoyance as he looked over at the man.

Gilrod was pointing to the northwest with a concerned expression. Kadrak looked where he was pointing and growled. A large group of Kalian cavalry had broken away from the main body and were racing around the right flank of his army. It appeared that they were heading for him. He redirected his lightning bolts towards the cavalry. There were too many soldiers for him to stop by himself, but at least he could slow them down.

"Have several battalions pull back and defend me," he commanded. "Our only hope to win today is if I'm allowed to stay on the offensive."

He watched as Gilrod quickly gave the commands. His soldiers were soon pulling back from the right side of the battle and moving to place themselves solidly between the oncoming Kalian cavalry and himself. He growled in frustration. It appeared that the Kalians had finally decided there only hope to win the battle was to directly attack him.

The new strategy of his enemies would definitely cause problems. It would cause him to have to divide his attention and strength between both attacking and defending. By pulling part of his troops back to defend him, it would also make it much harder for the rest of the troops to break through the Kalian defenses.

He peered across the field of battle, wondering if the Kalians had any other surprises. He soon found that a huge group of foot soldiers was marching around the left flank of his army. He quickly pointed them out to Gilrod. It was obvious that the fight truly was being brought to him. He thought of pulling back more of his troops but decided against it. He had to leave enough on the offensive to follow through with his plan.

He scowled and began raining lightning down in the center of the Kalian Army once again. His troops were now almost half way through. He still had plenty of time before the foot soldiers would get close to him.

"Let them come," he stated angrily. "I will make them pay!"

* * * * *

Several bolts of lightning struck near Blaize, throwing up clumps of dirt all around him. He gritted his teeth and continued riding hard. Behind him thundered half of the Kalian cavalry. The Balthan wielder was obviously now aware of their presence. Fortunately, there were too many for him to stop them. The cavalry continued around the edge of the Balthan soldiers as the Balthans began to fall back into a defensive position around their leader.

Blaize smiled. Apparently the wielder really couldn't stop them on his own. The pullback in troops would allow the rest of the Kalian Army to focus on repelling the main offensive in their center. He also knew that on the other side of the battle, a large contingent of foot soldiers was making its way around the flank and heading towards the wielder. If they could divide the wielder's attention in enough different places, hopefully Kadrak wouldn't be able to do enough damage to determine the outcome of the day's battle.

He concentrated and brought his focus back to the task at hand. His cavalry would soon be in the thick of the battle. He veered right and set a course directly into the center of the waiting Balthan soldiers. He laid low on his steed as he raced towards battle. The wind whistled in his ears and stung his eyes as he closed in.

He could make out the Balthan wielder in the distance above the heads of the ranks of nervous foot soldiers. The wielder was the target of their attack. The foot soldiers were merely obstacles in the way. He braced himself for the impact and whipped out his swords. The blades had been waiting patiently for four days to see action. Their wait was over.

31

Kalista saw the smoke rising above the battlefield long before she heard the cries. As soon as she saw the smoke, she picked up her pace. She wondered why there was so much of it coming from the battle. The lead guard tried multiple times to convince her to turn around, but she kept refusing. She had come this far and was not about to stop now.

As she got closer she began to faintly hear the sounds of battle. At first it was just the dull sound of commotion but soon it turned into sounds of clashing metal, cries of battle, cries of anger, and cries of pain. She faltered in her resolve for a moment. The sounds reminded her of what lay ahead. Perhaps she really didn't want to go all the way.

However, her fears were soon overpowered by her concern for Gavin. She had to find him and convince him to stay out of harm's way. She continued along the road that led straight towards the smoke and the sounds of battle. The army's camp soon came into view. Her guards became more alert and tightened their positions around her. The camp seemed eerily silent as they approached it. They carefully made their way through the empty camp.

Ahead of them the highway slowly rose until it disappeared over the slight rise where she remembered the command area being located. As they reached the base of the small rise, two of her guards broke away and ascended the hill while the rest of them remained. Kalista waited anxiously for their return. She hoped all was going well and that she would be able to easily approach the command area and fulfill her purpose. The two guards were soon on their way back down towards them.

"It's utter chaos on the battlefield," one of them said quickly. "There's no command area left to speak of. The entire top of the rise is covered in scorch marks and gouges."

Her heart missed a beat. No command area left? Was she already too late? She needed to see Gavin and know he was safe. If he wasn't in the command area, how was she going to find him?

"Our troops have abandoned their defensive positions, and the battle is raging all over the field in several different large groups of soldiers. I'm not sure what's going on."

"Is it safe to go up on the rise?" Kalista asked. The guard who had been speaking looked at her for a few moments before answering.

"All of the fighting is taking place below the rise and out on the field towards the mouth of the pass," he replied. "I think you can probably take a quick look without any harm coming our way."

The guard, having made his assessment, nodded to the head guard and moved back to his place. Kalista motioned for the head guard to lead them to the top of the rise. He shook his head in disapproval but complied with her request. She took a deep breath as they reached the top, steadying herself for what she might witness.

The sounds and sights of battle assaulted her senses as her party crested the small rise. The clanking of swords and shields was much louder. The cries of rage and pain were much sharper. The acrid smell of smoke stung her nose. The stench of burnt hair and flesh was almost overpowering. Motionless bodies, many of which appeared to have been burned, littered the rise all the way down to the field of battle. Kalista quickly covered her nose with the back of her hand. The sight and smell were almost more than she could handle, but she willed herself to stay detached and aloof.

She looked out from her vantage point on the top of the rise and surveyed the battle in the light of the late morning sun. The field, from the eastern base of the rise all the way to the opening of the mountain pass, seemed covered with large groups of both Kalian and Balthan soldiers. She was glad to see that there appeared to be more soldiers with the Royal Kalian Army uniform than the mismatched uniforms of the Balthan Army.

Although there appeared to be numerous pockets of heavy fighting throughout the field, one spot in particular drew her attention. Towards the far end of the field, near the opening of the pass, she could see infrequent bursts of fire emanating from an individual that sat alone in the center of a large ring of battling soldiers. It could only be one person, the Wielder Kadrak.

She glanced around the charred command area. There was no doubt the destruction had been caused by him. She was grateful that although there were several bodies at the top of the rise, none belonged to Gavin. She tried searching the field below for a glimpse of him but soon decided it would be impossible to locate him among the chaos of battle. She would be forced to anxiously wait until the end of the day to verify that he was safe and convince him to stay out of harm's way.

Her attention was drawn back to the Balthan wielder in the distance as a bright bolt of lightning struck into the center of a group of Kalian soldiers. Somehow he needed to be stopped. It appeared that only foot soldiers and cavalry were trying to get to him. She wondered where all of the archers were. It would be difficult for a soldier to break through the Balthan ranks surrounding the wielder, but a well placed arrow could easily put an end to the man.

If she were close enough, she could do it herself. The thought lingered in her consciousness. Why couldn't she get close enough to do it? She surveyed the field of battle once again. If she skirted the battle and snuck up from the north, she thought she might be able to get close enough to take a shot at the wielder without getting too close to any of the Balthan soldiers. She turned to the lead guard and mentioned the idea.

"Are you crazy?" he replied. "While I admit that your idea has merit to it, there is no way that you will be getting any closer to the battle than you are now. I have gone along with your wishes until now only because we are still a safe distance from the fighting. We should now return to the army's camp and wait for the battle to end."

"You just admitted the merit of my plan," she said. "And yet you refuse to act on it. Would you pass up the opportunity to stop the wielder and save the lives of countless Kalian soldiers?"

"If any of my men were skilled with the bow, perhaps the chance of bringing down the wielder would be worth it. However, they are all swordsmen. Besides, we are here to protect you, not fight in the battle."

"I could make the shot," she said confidently. "I just need your guards to continue protecting me while I do it."

"Let's stop this nonsense," the lead guard said firmly. "You've seen the battle, but you'll have to wait until tonight to see your fiancé. You will now move off of this rise and return to the camp."

Kalista stared as the guard turned his horse and began heading back towards the camp without a backwards glance. Did he really think he could tell her what to do? She glanced at the other guards angrily as they began to follow. How dare they? She did not have to follow them. They had to follow her!

She clenched her fists tightly on her reins and took a deep breath. She realized she was being irrational. The guards were merely trying to do their duty. She glanced over the battlefield with anxiety. How many soldiers were giving their lives for their country? How many would never return home to their families? They were willing to sacrifice their lives for those they loved.

She scanned the field again, hoping that she would somehow be able to pick out Gavin. He was willing to sacrifice his life for her, could she do any less? She turned from the raging battle and looked around the rise. She soon located an abandoned bow and some discarded arrows. She glanced from the guards to the battlefield below.

Fear welled up inside of her. She turned her horse as if to follow the guards but veered along the top of the ridge as if inspecting something. She got down from her horse and quickly grabbed the bow and two arrows. She then hopped back on her mount as her heart began pounding.

She flashed a nervous grin at the surprised guards and raced off down the rise towards the battle. Behind her she could hear the guards yelling for her to stop, but she paid them no heed. As terrified as she felt, she had made her decision. She would risk her life in order to save those she loved.

The guards would have no choice but to follow her and protect her. She headed for the north as she made her way down the rise at an angle. She didn't want to be anywhere near the battling soldiers.

When she reached the base of the rise, she glanced back over her shoulder. All twenty guards were giving chase. She slowed down slightly so they could catch up. However, she didn't slow down too much. She was afraid if she went too slow or stopped, the guards would try to force her away from the battle.

She turned her attention from the guards to where she was heading. Her adrenaline was pumping and her stomach was in knots. She couldn't believe that she was actually planning on taking a shot at the Balthan wielder. What was she doing? A princess did not ride into battle.

This wasn't an archery match. It was a war. She could be killed. The thought was almost enough to cause her to stop her horse and turn around. Maybe this wasn't such a good idea after all.

The guards finally caught up to her. She spurred her mount to move faster to keep any of them from getting in front of her. She took a deep breath and tried to forget about the danger. Her idea seemed slightly less dangerous with the royal guards flanking her.

She would be careful. As long as they stayed a safe distance from the battling soldiers they should be fine. They were on horses while most of the Balthans were on foot. If any moved in their direction, they could easily outrun them. She gave the battling soldiers a wide birth. Wide enough that she hoped her small party of twenty guards wouldn't even be noticed.

She continued around the battle until she was directly north of where she had seen the wielder. It was hard for her to tell from her lower vantage whether or not he was in the same position, but she supposed he likely hadn't moved much. She pulled up her horse and studied the empty field between her and the large clump of soldiers battling around the wielder.

"I underestimated you Princess," the lead guard said as he pulled up next to her. His face was flushed with excitement. "I can see that you won't be deterred in this endeavor. I can't believe I am considering going along with this, but may I offer a suggestion?"

"Proceed," she replied as she pulled the bow over her head and inspected it. It was much larger than her own bow, but she thought she could manage it. The positive thing about its size was it would allow her to shoot farther.

"I think we'll have a better chance of getting closer without being noticed if we continue a little farther before we cut south towards the wielder." He pointed at the foothills of the mountains. "If we ride all the way to the foothills and then work our way south, I think we can use the rise and fall of the land to conceal ourselves. We also might have a better chance at surprising the wielder if we attack from slightly behind him."

Kalista supposed the lead guard was right. They would be safer in the foothills. Since it appeared that he was now willowing to help her, she decided to let him lead the way once again.

"I agree," she replied. "Lead the way."

They continued forward at a quick pace until they reached the foothills. They then worked their way south towards the opening of the pass at a slower pace, staying in the lower parts of the hills to keep out of sight as much as possible. Kalista became more nervous as they got closer to the battling soldiers, but it appeared that as of yet no one was paying them any attention. The lead guard finally pulled up when they were still a safe distance from the edge of the fighting soldiers.

"How close do you think you need to be?" he asked her. "I could lose my life for letting you go through with this and don't want you any closer than is absolutely necessary."

She glanced towards the large group of soldiers. She was quite certain she could hit the edge of them from her current position. However, she would need to be able to shoot into the center of the group where the wielder was. She would also need to be high enough to see him. She looked around at the small hills between her and the soldiers.

"If we can get to that hill," she said while pointing, "I think I will be able to take a clear shot."

The lead guard glanced at the hill and then at the nearest battling soldiers. He glanced back and forth several times, judging the distance. He turned and looked her directly in the eye.

"Can you really take an accurate shot from that distance? I don't want to get any closer, but I also don't want to draw attention to us if there really isn't any chance of success."

"I've never shot with this bow before," she answered honestly. "But I am almost certain that I will be able to get a good shot at the wielder from that hill."

"Perhaps you should take a practice shot or two first," the lead guard suggested. "If you can shoot as well as you claim, we'll try our luck."

"I only have two arrows," she replied. "I'll need both of them."

The lead guard smiled as he motioned one of the other guards forward. The second guard pulled out a full quiver of arrows and handed them to her.

"Just because none of my guards are skilled archers doesn't mean that we aren't equipped with bows and arrows," he said.

Kalista accepted the quiver and slid off her horse. She pulled out an arrow and fitted it to her bow. It was difficult for her to pull all the way back on the string but she managed. She picked a small tree in the foothills of the mountains and let the arrow fly. She smiled as it glanced off the side of the trunk. She pulled out another arrow and embedded it in the bark of the trunk. She followed it with one more to be certain that she had the feel of the bow.

She turned as the third arrow lodged itself in the trunk near the second one. All of the guards were staring with wide eyes. Apparently they hadn't thought she was really that skilled with a bow.

"I am ready," she stated. "Let's get this over with before I realize how crazy it is."

"It's definitely crazy," the lead guard said nervously. "But now that I've seen how skilled you are, I think we might actually have a chance. I think it's best that we continue to the hill on foot. That way we will be able to keep out of sight until we reach the top."

He quickly gave commands to the other guards as to who was to stay with the horses and who was to continue on. Kalista took a deep breath as she began to creep towards the small hill with eight guards surrounding her. She wondered if her rash idea would really end up working. Could she really bring down the Balthan wielder?

They were soon at the base of the hill. The lead guard slowly crept to its crest and slid out on top of it, flat on his stomach. He remained motionless for a few moments before sliding backwards off the top and descending.

"The wielder's easy enough to pick out," he said after he reached the bottom. "No one is near him. He's a little further away than the tree was but not much. Are you ready?"

"As ready as I'll ever be," she replied.

Her stomach was full of butterflies at the thought of what she was about to do. She had never shot at a person before. She tried to calm her nerves by taking several deep breaths. She closed her eyes and imagined that she was back in the fields outside of Calyn hunting snow lions. The wielder was nothing but a snow lion.

"We'll creep up to just below the top with you Princess," the lead guard said. "Signal us when you're ready, and we'll all climb up on top together. I would suggest taking your shot as quickly as you can while still being accurate. We'll want to get off the hill and back to the horses as fast as possible."

Kalista nodded in understanding. She took one last calming breath and began creeping up the hill. She stopped just below the top and readied herself to take the shot. She pulled out an arrow and strung it. She closed her eyes and tried to drown out the sounds of battle coming from the other side of the hill. She went through in her mind exactly what she would do. She would let three arrows fly in quick succession and hope that at least one of them would find its target.

It was time. She signaled the guards and leapt in unison with them to the top of the hill. She immediately located the Balthan wielder, stood up straight, and let her first arrow fly. Two more followed in quick succession before the first had even reached its intended target. She dropped to the ground and watched anxiously as the arrows zipped through the air towards the wielder.

* * * * *

Kadrak let loose another lightning bolt and frowned. The day had not proceeded how he had hoped it would, and he was beginning to tire. The surprise counter attack by the Kalians had been fierce. He had been forced to spend the majority of the morning using his powers to defend his army instead of using them offensively.

His troops had broken through the Kalian Army eventually and forced them down from the rise. They now battled on equal ground. For that he was thankful. His morning attack had also killed several of the Kalian Army's commanders and left them slightly disorganized. He believed his army was gaining the upper hand with his continual support, but he feared that if he rested the Kalians would take control back.

He suddenly sensed a disturbance in the air near him. Time froze as he located the three arrows, one after another, pointing towards him. All three burst into flames and fell harmlessly to the ground several spans away from him. He growled in anger. Apparently the Kalians hadn't learned their lesson yet.

He quickly located the source of the arrows. A handful of soldiers lay flat against the ground at the top of a nearby hill. Did they think they could shoot at him and get away with it? Did they think they could hide? He focused on the hill and snarled. They would pay.

* * * * *

Kalista gaped in surprise as all three of her arrows burst into flames and fell harmlessly to the ground before reaching the wielder. She had underestimated him. Before she had time to think of anything else, she felt a buzzing in the air and her hair stood on end.

There was a blinding flash of light and a loud crack. Suddenly she was flying through the air.

    She grunted as she came crashing to the ground. Dazed and confused, she lay still for several moments. She then slowly pushed herself up and rolled over to her back. She stared up at the sky as her eyes tried to regain their focus. What had just happened? She blinked several times with her ears ringing. The sun appeared to be moving and growing larger. She blinked several times. As her eyes finally focused, she realized she wasn't looking at the sun but at a fireball that was falling rapidly down on top of her.

32

    Traven crested the rise and glanced out over the battlefield. A fierce battle was raging all the way down to the mouth of the pass. He disregarded the fighting soldiers and quickly picked out the princess and her guards. They were riding hard towards the foothills at a safe distance north of the battle. Where were they going? He shook his head in frustration.

    He had first caught sight of the princess when she was at the top of this very rise. He had thought she would stay put and he would be able to catch up to her at last. Instead, she had soon disappeared down the other side. It looked as though they would need to hurry in order to catch her. He turned to Darian with a shrug, and they both took off after the princess and her guards once again.

    As excited as he was to see her in person, it made him extremely nervous to see her so near the battle. He wouldn't feel comforted until he was at her side. He urged Pennon to go faster. He couldn't bear the thought of losing the princess because he hadn't been fast enough.

    He glanced at the battle raging to the south of him as he continued riding after the princess. It appeared chaotic and disorganized. He wondered where the commanders were. He hadn't seen any centralized location where the battle was being directed from. He hoped Blaize was okay. He would have to find him tonight when the fighting stopped.

    He turned his attention back to catching up with the princess. She and her guards had disappeared into the foothills near the pass. Pennon and Darian's horse continued thundering towards the hills.

He was so close to the princess and yet still too far away to keep her safe. They finally reached the edge of the foothills and pulled up.

"Where do you think she is?" he asked his elven companion.

"I'm not sure," Darian replied as he scanned the hills. "The only reason I can think of for them to go into the foothills is to hide."

"Why would they come to this side of the battlefield to hide?" Traven thought out loud. "They could have just turned around back at the rise."

"I think they are trying to get closer to the battle without being seen."

He followed the elf's gaze to where the foothills ended near the edge of what appeared to be the fiercest part of the fighting. A sick feeling came over him. What were the guards thinking? He booted Pennon and hurried along the edge of the foothills towards the fighting near the mouth of the pass. He kept an eye on the hills for any sign of movement.

The princess and her guards suddenly popped into view in the distance at the top of a small hill. He watched with surprise as the princess drew her bow and fired three arrows in a row towards the center of the large group of battling soldiers before she dropped to the ground. He wondered who she had been shooting at and why.

A bolt of lightning suddenly crashed down on the hill with tremendous force. He watched with horror as bodies were flung into the air.

"No!" he yelled as he continued racing towards the hill.

He was too late! As the dust settled he was able to pick out the body of the princess sprawled near the top of the hill. He gasped with relief as he saw her push herself up and roll over. She was still alive! His eyes narrowed as a fireball came arching over the battling soldiers and barreling down towards the princess.

Time froze. He quickly formed a shield above the princess' body. Time returned in a rush, and the fireball slammed into the shield and disappeared harmlessly several feet above her. He left the shield in place and hurried towards the base of the hill. When he reached it, he leapt from Pennon's back and raced up the incline to the princess' side. She was laying still upon the ground. He slipped his hand under her head and brushed the dirt from her cheek. Her eyes were closed and she was unresponsive, but she was breathing.

Darian hurried up the hill and joined him. They both looked up as another fireball came arching down towards them. The shield effectively blocked it just as it had the first. Traven glanced towards the field of battle to see where the attacks had come from. His eyes instantly locked upon the source.

In the center of the raging battle, an imposing man with flowing blond hair sat atop a horse staring towards them. A ring of empty field separated him from the soldiers battling nearby. A bright aura of golden light shown all around him. It was the Wielder Kadrak.

"Take her to safety," Traven said.

"What of you?" Darian replied. "I should stay by your side."

"No," he said firmly. "The Balthan wielder needs to be stopped, but I need to know the princess will be safe. Please take care of her."

"As you wish," the elf said as he took the princess from Traven and carefully scooped her up in his arms. "Be careful, Master."

Traven took one last long look at the unconscious princess before turning his attention fully to the wielder Kadrak. He focused and gathered his strength as Darian hurried down the slope and disappeared into the foothills. He rose to his feet and took a deep breath. He would need to be completely focused if he hoped to defeat the Balthan wielder.

He worked to calm himself, but the blood in his veins boiled. The wielder had hurt the princess. He had tried to kill her. Traven took another deep breath, trying to clear the raging emotion from his mind. The wielder had struck her with a lightning bolt. Traven would return the favor. Time slowed and the air thickened.

* * * * *

Kadrak stared across the battlefield to the small hill in the distance. The young wielder from Kalia stood atop it facing him. A shining, golden hued aura surrounded the boy, testifying of his power in the ambience. When the first fireball had exploded in the air harmlessly above the hill, Kadrak had been at a loss as to what had happened. He had sent another fireball with the same perplexing result. It became clear what was occurring when the boy had stood up.

Static abruptly filled the air around Kadrak. He immediately created a shield around him and his stallion. Almost instantly a giant lightning bolt crashed down into his shield and arced all around it to the ground. His horse danced around in surprise at the sudden bright light and dull boom of the bolt hitting the shield.

The boy had just attacked him! Did he think to challenge the mighty Kadrak? He growled and gathered his strength. He would teach the young wielder the true power of the ambience. The boy would be sorry that he had dared to challenge him.

Around him there was a sudden silence. The battling soldiers had all paused. They were staring towards him with wide eyes. They understood what had just happened. He had been attacked with magic. They followed Kadrak's smoldering stare and saw the lone figure standing tall upon the hill in the distance. He was dressed all in black. He was too far away for them to see many details, but it was obvious by his stance and posture that he was the source of the attack.

Kadrak gritted his teeth and sent a lightning bolt thundering down towards the young wielder in response. The lightning was effectively stopped by the boy's shield just as the fireballs had been.

Soldiers on both sides stared at the man in black who stood firm upon the hill, untouched by the lightning. They glanced between the two wielders and began to hurry out of the way. It was obvious a wielder's duel was about to take place, and they didn't want to be anywhere near it.

* * * * *

Traven stared back at the Balthan wielder. He obviously hadn't appreciated the lightning attack. Unfortunately, the wielder knew how to use a shield. He had expected as much but had thought it was worth a try. He watched from his perch on the hill as the soldiers from both armies began scrambling away from the Balthan wielder and hurrying out of the space between the two of them. It was clear they didn't want to be caught in any of the crossfire.

He waited anxiously for the Balthan wielder to attack again, but nothing happened. The wielder appeared content to wait for either the field around him to completely clear or for Traven to make the next move.

He wondered what his next move should be. It seemed strange to be facing an enemy with the ambience. Should he try and defeat his opponent with trickery or with brute force? He wished he knew how the Balthan compared to him in strength. It was obvious by the man's bright, golden aura that he was very strong. He wondered how his own aura of power looked to Kadrak.

After several more moments without additional attacks, Traven decided to move closer. He would rather be somewhere flat like the field where he could maneuver easier. He also hoped that by being closer to the Balthan wielder he might be able to identify a weakness more easily.

He took a few cautious steps forward. When nothing happened, he let his shield drop. He didn't want to waste any energy that he didn't have to. He continued down the hill carefully, keeping his eyes locked on the wielder and keeping his senses alert. When he reached the level battlefield, he continued forward slowly until he was within talking distance. He then stopped and planted his feet firmly. He wanted to be ready for anything that might happen.

"Let me introduce myself," the Balthan wielder said with a smile. "I am the Master Wielder Kadrak, Emperor of Balthus. Who might you be?"

Traven didn't let the man's pleasant persona distract him. He stayed completely alert, ready for whatever might be coming next.

"My name is Traven," he replied.

"You don't have to worry yet," Kadrak said with a chuckle. "I'd like to talk with you before we do anything rash. I have a few questions for you. May I?"

He stayed alert and ready as Kadrak slid from his horse and took several steps towards him.

"That's close enough," Traven said. "What do you want?"

"I want to know why you attacked me?" the Balthan wielder said as he came to a stop.

"You are an enemy to my country and my king," Traven replied.

"You may be a Kalian, Traven, but you're so much more than that. You are a wielder. There's no reason for you to serve any mere human king. As a wielder, you're far above that. Surely you must know this?"

He listened cautiously to what Kadrak was saying. It was true that he wondered where he fit in now that he was a wielder. He had contemplated the same thing when he was at Faldor's Keep and along the journey to reach this very battle. He still wasn't sure exactly where his place was. He knew that he wasn't a simple soldier anymore, but he also knew that his power didn't make it okay for him to do anything he felt like doing.

"Having power doesn't give you the right to do whatever you want," he replied.

"Yes it does," Kadrak answered. "Why can a shop owner tell his workers what to do? Why can a general command his soldiers? Why can a king dictate to his subjects what to do? Because they all have power." The Balthan wielder paused and smiled. "You have more power than any of them Traven."

While Kadrak's statements were true, he was implying that power was all that mattered. However, power wasn't all that mattered. Perhaps as a wielder Traven didn't really owe allegiance to any king, but he did feel an allegiance to those he loved. He would protect them from tyrants like Kadrak.

"You can join me on my quest to make a better world," Kadrak said. "You don't have to oppose me. We could do magnificent things together. You could have anything your heart desires."

"No," Traven replied. "I won't be a part of you killing innocent people."

"I don't kill innocents," Kadrak responded with a hint of anger creeping into his voice. "I only kill those who oppose me. Those who join me receive their just rewards. I could teach you so many things. In my years of study and practice I have learned to do things with the ambience that you can't even imagine. You could become my apprentice." He paused and smiled. "So what will it be? Will you join me or will you oppose me?"

Traven stared back at the Balthan wielder. The man really did believe he could do whatever he wanted because of his power. Traven didn't want to fight him. He was afraid that he couldn't beat someone who had been wielding the ambience for far longer than himself. However, he knew that he had to try to stop him. If he couldn't stop Kadrak, he wasn't sure there was anyone else that could. If nothing else, he could weaken the wielder to the point where the soldiers who were watching could overpower him with their numbers.

"I won't join you," he replied firmly.

"Then you oppose me," Kadrak said as his false smile disappeared. "So be it!"

Traven instantly created a shield as a blast of fire leapt from Kadrak's hands and exploded around him. He kept the shield firmly in place as a lightning bolt came crashing down with a deafening boom. The impact caused his shield to give slightly, but it held together.

Time slowed and the air thickened as he prepared to attack back. He quickly formed two lightning bolts shooting towards the wielder from different angles and pulled them into existence. The two struck Kadrak's shield simultaneously with immense force. He smiled as the Balthan wielder flinched at the impact. Apparently he wasn't as confident as he had pretended to be. He supposed this was the first time the Balthan had ever faced another wielder as well. It also seemed that Kadrak had been depleting his strength all morning. The realization gave Traven hope and courage.

His thoughts were interrupted as more lightning struck his shield. Bolt after bolt slammed into it, shaking him and weakening his barrier. He concentrated and kept the shield tight against the relentless strikes. After a continuous barrage of almost twenty bolts, the lightning finally stopped. He was relieved to find that he could keep the shield firm as long as he wanted to if his strength held up.

He wondered if the winner of the fight would be the one who had the most strength. Would one of them finally not have enough power left to keep his shield firmly in place? Traven concentrated and caused fire to burst forth all around the Balthan. He wondered if there was a way to weaken his shield. He focused as the flames continued raging along the outside of Kadrak's shield.

He suddenly realized that he could see the particles of his opponent's shield just the same as any of the particles in the air. He wondered if he could manipulate them as well. He focused and pulled on the particles at the front of the shield. They resisted but moved ever so slightly. He concentrated and yanked on them as hard as he could. They burst forward, leaving a gaping hole in the shield. Flames instantly rushed in on the Balthan wielder.

Kadrak's shield instantly disappeared and a burst of wind shot out all around him, extinguishing the flames. He glared at Traven with a look of both anger and surprise. A lightning bolt shot from the wielder's open hands and slammed straight into Traven's shield. The impact forced his shield several feet backwards. He leapt back with it, preventing the shield from hitting him and knocking him off his feet.

Apparently there were multiple ways to manipulate the shields. Traven sent a fierce stream of wind, flying directly into his opponent. It slammed against the Balthan's newly created shield. The force of the continuous stream of wind slowly pushed the shield backwards.

A fireball suddenly formed in the air above Traven. Just before it hit his shield, the top of the shield was ripped away. He let the rest of his shield disappear as he dove to the side. The fireball slammed into the ground where he had been standing, barely missing him. He wasn't the only one who had figured out that the shields could be manipulated. It now looked as though the winner would be determined by who was the quickest.

Traven let loose a barrage of fireballs in the direction of the Balthan and shredded the wielder's shield with barely a thought at the last possible second. Kadrak leapt to the side, but not before the first fireball grazed the sleeve of his arm, setting it on fire. The wielder quickly extinguished the flames, leaving a charred sleeve but no bodily damage.

Traven dove to the side as another bolt of lightning slammed down towards him. He created a shield as he came to his feet, just in time to deflect the fireball flying towards his head. He instantly sent a spear of ice flying back towards his attacker. Before the spear had even reached Kadrak, he called down three bolts of lightning in quick succession as well.

Kadrak had his shield up in time and deflected all four of the attacks. Before the Balthan had a chance to counter attack, Traven drenched the wielder's shield in water and quickly turned it to ice. He then quickly layered more and more ice around the shield.

He paused and took several deep breaths as he stared at the icy dome that contained his opponent. Traven's body was drenched in sweat, and he was beginning to tire. He wondered how long he would be able to continue wielding so much power. He hoped that Kadrak was being drained of his strength as well. He needed to figure out a combination of attacks that would catch the Balthan off guard.

He waited anxiously for Kadrak to break out of the dome of ice, but nothing happened. He wondered what the Balthan wielder was waiting for. He took the brief pause in the battle to quickly run through all that he had learned of the ambience from the Keeper Eldridge. He had now used lightning, fire, wind, water, and ice. The only other thing he had ever created was liquid fire, but he was afraid creating it would drain too much of his strength. If he attacked fiercely enough with a combination of everything else he knew, he wondered if he would be able to take the Balthan by surprise and overpower him.

His thoughts were interrupted as the ice dome shattered with an earsplitting boom. He quickly protected himself with a shield as glistening shards of ice flew towards him. As the pieces of ice began breaking against his shield, lightning leapt from Kadrak's outstretched hands and blasted into his shield. Bolt after bolt slammed into him, knocking the shield further backwards. Traven focused on maintaining the shield's strength as he moved backwards with each bolt's impact. Suddenly his shield was ripped apart. He was instantly enveloped in fire. He dove away from the burning heat as a lightning bolt came crashing to the ground. The force of the bolt's impact threw him forcefully into the ground. He rolled to his feet with a grunt and reformed his shield just in time to deflect several fireballs.

He quickly smothered the remaining flames on his burning clothes. The attack had left him with burns and bruises but no major injuries. He took several deep breaths as he stared at the Balthan wielder from within the safety of his shield. Kadrak stared back at him with a smirk. The lightning strike had been too close. If he had been a split second slower, the fight would have already ended. He didn't know how many more chances he would get. If he wanted to survive, he needed to end the fight now.

Traven exhaled deeply and fell into a trance of complete concentration. The world around him froze and all was silent. He no longer felt the stinging pain of the burns on his arms and face or the deep ache of the bruises on his side. He was beyond his physical body. He could sense every particle in the air around him and could sense the particles that were already beginning to move in response to Kadraks's commands. He drew upon the strength that welled up inside of him and began wielding the ambience like he never had before.

He formed multiple lightning bolts and sent them crashing down on his opponent. Before the bolts had even reached the wielder's shield, he formed multiple balls of ice and sent them flying as well. He followed them up with fireballs raining down from the sky, striking the Balthan's shield from different directions. He then began blasting at his opponent's shield with more lightning, first on the right side and then on the left. However, his furious barrage of attacks was only to disorient Kadrak.

While the bolts of lightning continued to strike, he began tearing at the wielder's shield. He left it in tact, but disturbed the shield enough to keep Kadrak's attention on maintaining its strength. While maintaining the two attacks simultaneously, he began to form his third and final piece of the assault, a large ball of ice. It was difficult to form the ice while continuing to send bolt after bolt of lightning and continuing to tear at the shield, but struggling, he managed to do it.

He carefully formed the sphere of ice high in the air directly above Kadrak. The strain began to wear at him as it grew larger and larger, but he persevered. When it finally reached the size of a small cottage, he could hold onto it no more. It slipped from his hold and began plummeting downwards, gaining momentum. Just before it reached the Balthan wielder's shield, Traven used the last of his strength to rip the shield apart.

Kadrak tried to recreate his shield, but there was no time. The giant ball of ice slammed down upon him and into the ground with an earth shaking thud. The quaking of the ground, along with the shock wave of air from the impact, knocked Traven off his feet. He tried to sit up, but his drained body was too exhausted. He stayed on his back, staring at the sky. A barely audible sigh of relief escaped his lips. He had survived.

33

Gilrod stared with awe and shock as the gargantuan ball of what appeared to be ice slammed into the ground, crushing his master under its massive weight. The ground shook with the force of the impact and a wave of air blasted through the ranks of soldiers watching from a distance.

Whoever the young man in black was, he had killed Gilrod's master. The mighty Wielder Kadrak had fallen. He watched as the young man in black struggled to get back on his feet but fell back and lay still. The power he had wielded had undoubtedly left him completely drained. He must have used every last ounce of his strength in his relentless attack against Kadrak. The Kalian wielder had defeated the most powerful man in the world, yet now he lay weak and defenseless.

Gilrod's eyes took on an evil gleam. The Balthan Army had no chance of winning if the Kalian wielder was left alive. Without Kadrak, they would be decimated by the wielder in black and the Kalian Army. He would not allow that to happen. He had tasted victory and power like he never had before, and he wouldn't give them up without a fight.

He burst from the crowd of soldiers who were still staring in wonder at the giant ball of ice. Their minds were still numb from the epic battle they had just witnessed. His mind was not. His legs carried him swiftly towards the body of the wielder in black. He held his sword at the ready as he closed in on the still form. The young man wouldn't survive to celebrate his victory over Kadrak.

* * * * *

Blaize stared with amazement as the midday sun glinted off the giant ball of ice in the distance. He could hardly believe what his own eyes had just witnessed. He had recognized Traven almost instantly when his young friend had appeared on the hill and challenged the Balthan wielder. His initial surprise had soon been replaced with fear and concern for his friend's life.

He had tensely watched the confrontation from his saddle. When the Balthan wielder had spoken with Traven, Blaize had strained to hear the conversation but was too far away to make out the words. The thick band of soldiers between him and the open field surrounding the two wielders had kept him back. The intense battle of magic that had ensued had left him speechless.

He had soon realized that Traven had somehow grown to be a master wielder over the last couple of months. He had no idea how it had happened, but it was obvious that his young friend was as skilled in the ambience as the Balthan wielder.

He had watched anxiously as the battle continued. When Traven had been engulfed in flames his heart had almost stopped, and when the young man had reappeared and launched such a ferocious counterattack, his heart had leaped. In the end, his heart had sung at his friend's victory.

He turned his attention from the glistening monument of ice and stared at the still form of Traven. The fight must have exhausted him. A flash of movement from the edge of the inner ring of soldiers caught his eye. An enemy soldier was running towards Traven with his sword bared.

Blaize instinctively reached for his war crescents. He groaned as his hands came up empty. He had used them both earlier in the battle. He tried to shove his way through the thick ring of soldiers but realized it would be impossible to get to Traven's side in time. He watched with despair as the enemy soldier closed in on Traven. There was nothing he could do!

His eyes widened as three arrows suddenly sprouted from the attacking soldier's chest. The man came crashing to the ground several feet short of reaching Traven's body. He quickly looked around for the shooter and located him. A tall, cloaked man stood on the same hill where Traven had first appeared with a bow in his hand. The cloaked figure quickly threw the bow over his shoulder and raced down the hill with surprising grace and quickness. He swiftly covered the open ground between the hill and Traven. When he reached the young man's body, he whipped out his sword and took a defensive position.

Blaize had no idea who the cloaked man was but was immensely thankful for his quick action. The man's defensive stance reminded him that although the Balthan wielder was no more, the battle wasn't over. There was still much to be done. Blaize quickly tied a rallying flag to the end of one of his swords and began waving it in the air as his voice boomed out in the silence.

"To me! To me!"

He smiled as the Kalian soldiers began regrouping and rallying around him. Traven's victory had destroyed the Balthan Army's most powerful weapon. Now it was up to the Kalian soldiers to finish the battle and defeat the remaining Balthan troops.

* * * * *

Traven slowly pushed himself into a sitting position and looked up at Darian. The elf had startled him when he had jumped over him moments before. Darian had his sword out and was surveying the soldiers at the edge of the empty field. Not far from him lay a Balthan soldier, riddled with arrows. Where had he come from? He turned back to the elf.

"Why aren't you with the princess?" he asked weakly.

"She's safe," Darian replied with a smile. "I'm just fulfilling my duty to keep you alive. Can you stand?"

"With some help," he replied. He took Darian's outstretched hand and let the elf pull him to his feet. He tried to stand on his own but wavered. His legs felt like jelly and his head was pounding. Darian pulled his arm up over his shoulder and allowed Traven to lean on him.

"I would suggest getting off the field of battle as quickly as we can," the elf said. "I don't think the Balthans are very happy with you right now."

He glanced around at the staring Balthan soldiers and saw that many did indeed have looks of hatred directed at him. The dead soldier near him took on a whole new meaning. Darian really had just saved his life. A wave of deep gratitude toward the elf washed over him.

"I think you're right," he agreed. "Let's get out of here."

He half walked, half stumbled as Darian led him back to the foothills. In the distance he could hear Kalian battle cries. Soon the battlefield was in commotion once again. The battle wasn't over yet. Luckily, none of the Balthan soldiers were brave enough to come after him. Darian quickly led him into the hills without any incidents.

"Thanks," Traven said once they were safely in the foothills. "I believe you just saved my life."

"That's what I live for," Darian said as he flashed a grin. "It's nice to know that I'm good for more than just errands."

He returned the elf's smile. He was reminded of how fortunate he was to have the elven warrior as his devoted servant. However, Darian was much more than a servant. He was a true friend. Traven leaned heavily against him as the elf led him deeper into the foothills.

The sounds of battle were soon muted by the tall hills at the base of the mountains. They turned a corner at the bottom of a hill and ran into six royal guards, all with their swords drawn. They apparently recognized Darian and stepped aside, letting the two of them pass.

Traven spotted the Princess Kalista immediately. She lay under a small tree at the base of a steep incline. Another eight royal guards were near her. A couple had burns and dirt on their uniforms, but the majority looked as though they hadn't seen any action yet.

Darian led him over to the princess. She was sleeping, but her breathing was quick and shallow. Her delicate face was marred by a puffy, blackened eye and her hair was clumped with blood and dirt. She also had bad burns on the left side of her body. She was alive, but she was hurt badly.

Tears brimmed in Traven's eyes. He hated seeing her in such a state, but he was relieved to see her safe and alive. In the end, he had reached her in time. His hand involuntarily reached out and brushed a stray piece of hair from her soft cheek. He realized what he was doing and jerked his hand away. He then carefully pulled out the healing stone from one of his pockets and held it just above Kalista's left side. Darian placed a hand on his shoulder.

"Is this wise?" the elf whispered in his ear. "You barely have the strength to walk."

"I have to do what I can for her," Traven replied. "I still have a little strength left."

He wasn't sure how much healing he would actually be able to do, but he wanted to ease the princess' suffering as much as he could. He concentrated and began feeding the stone. It started to glow with a white light that grew brighter and brighter. His pounding headache became excruciating. He pulled more energy out of himself and continued feeding the stone. His vision soon began to blur. He decided he better stop, but it was already too late. He slumped down and all went black.

34

Kalista gazed down at the sleeping form of the young soldier Traven. He lay on a cot in one of the soldier's tents. Despite the burns on him and the scrapes and bruises on his face, he appeared calm and content as he slept. His face looked surprisingly serene. She wondered what the young man might be dreaming about after such an intense battle.

It was hard for her to believe all that she had been told upon waking up. Apparently Traven had showed up just in time and saved her life. His mysterious cloaked companion had carried her safely back to the royal guards who had been waiting. While she lay unconscious, Traven had fought the Balthan wielder in an epic battle of magic and ultimately defeated him.

He had then made his way back to her side, healed her injuries, and lost consciousness. She still could not believe that she had been completely healed. She remembered the lightning blast that had scorched her and sent her flying through the air. She remembered slamming into the ground and then passing out right before being burned by a fireball. When she had woken up, she wasn't even sore.

It was hard for her to think of Traven as a wielder. It did explain how he had saved her from the serpent, but it was difficult to think of the nice young man as possessing such great power. She supposed it was hard for her to imagine anyone wielding such power.

She glanced from Traven towards the cloaked man that waited in the corner. She couldn't make out his face, but she could tell he was watching her every move. He made her nervous but not in a threatening way. No one knew anything about him except that he wouldn't lower his hood and he wouldn't leave Traven's side. She turned her attention back to her rescuer.

She wished she could do something for his burns and bruises. He would be in pain when he woke up. She was once again inadvertently the cause of his injuries. She would find a way to repay him. This was the second time he had saved her life. She would properly thank him when they returned to Candus. She reached down and squeezed his hand. A small smile flitted across his face as he shifted position on the narrow cot. She couldn't help but smile back. Kalista suddenly remembered that the cloaked man was still watching and pulled back her hand in embarrassment.

She gave her rescuer one last look and then ducked out of his tent. She hurried through the night air towards where she would be eating dinner with Gavin. As she walked, she rubbed her hand against the folds of her dress, trying in vain to get rid of the warm, tingling feeling left over from holding Traven's hand.

* * * * *

Traven sat upon the ornately gilded throne. The crown of Kalia rested comfortably on his head. A silver armband with a bright green stone was clasped tightly around his left bicep. At his side stood the beautiful Princess Kalista. He smiled as she laid her hand comfortingly on his shoulder. She was alive and safe. Things were how they were supposed to be. He felt calm and relaxed for the first time in over a month.

It made him slightly uncomfortable to be alone with the princess, but it also felt right. The strange thing was that he couldn't remember how he had gotten on the throne or why the crown was on his head. Maybe the princess could tell him how he had gotten there. He turned to ask her, but she stopped him by putting her finger gently against his mouth.

He stared back into her mesmerizing eyes as she pulled her finger away from his lips. She then reached down and grabbed his hand. The feel of her soft hand around his, sent a jolt of energy up his arm and throughout his entire being. He smiled back at her and reached towards her with his other hand. However, she quickly pulled away and hurried towards the door. Where was she going? He tried to stand up to follow her but couldn't. He struggled against the invisible barrier and finally sat up.

*****

Traven looked around in confusion for a moment. Where was he? He felt a presence near him and turned to see Darian standing off to the side. He was on a cot in a dimly lit tent. He closed his eyes against the pounding in his head and lay back down with a groan.

"You just missed her," Darian said.

"Who?" he asked groggily.

"The Princess Kalista. She just left."

He smiled as he remembered the feel of her hand wrapped around his in the dream. It was too bad he hadn't awakened before she left. He involuntarily opened and closed his hand at the memory.

"She held your hand," the elf stated.

"What?" Traven said as he sat up and opened his eyes. How could Darian know of his dream? "How did you know that?"

"I was standing right here," Darian replied with amusement in his voice. "I saw everything she did while she was here visiting you. Maybe you better lay back down and rest."

It took a moment for him to realize what the elf meant. The princess had actually held his hand in real life. Now he wished even more he had been awake sooner.

"Did she say anything?" he asked excitedly.

"Why would she say anything?" the elf responded. "You were asleep." He chuckled as Traven put his hands to his head and lay back down with a grimace. "She did stare at you for quite awhile. Almost for as long as you stare at her in your screeing dish."

"How long have I been asleep?" Traven asked as he quickly changed the subject.

"Since this afternoon when you passed out," Darian replied with more than a hint of amusement still in his voice. "The sun went down about an hour ago. You slept right through the surrender and the end of the battle."

"What happened?"

"After you defeated the Balthan wielder, the Kalian Army rallied and increased their attack against the invading army. Without the wielder at their lead, the Balthans lost heart and surrendered after only a few hours. It quickly became apparent that without him, they couldn't hope to prevail."

"So the war is over?"

"Yes," replied Darian. "And the Kalians recognize they have you to thank for it. You'll need to be very careful. By defeating the Balthan wielder you have become a very important person."

He knew Darian was probably right. He didn't want all the extra attention, but he knew it would be impossible to avoid it after his public battle with the wielder. Too many people had seen what he was capable of doing. He wondered if he should just sneak away and return to Faldor's Keep. He did know how to make himself invisible. As appealing as the idea was, he needed to find out if Blaize was okay and wanted to meet with the princess in person before leaving.

If the vision he had just had before waking was any indication of the princess' safety, he could leave her and head back to the keep. However, after so many days of worrying for her safety, he needed to wait a few more nights to confirm that she wasn't in danger any more. He tried to pretend that this was his main reason for staying, but deep down he knew it was more than that. After having his thoughts and emotions affected by dreams of the princess for so long, he wanted to be around her for awhile. He needed to clear up his feelings before leaving.

"You know what Darian?" he said as he reflected on his current emotions. "It's gone."

"What's gone?" the elf asked.

"The feelings of foreboding, depression, and loss. Every day since the princess first disappeared from my dreams, I've had those feelings linger with me. Now they're gone," he said with a smile.

"So you must be feeling great," Darian observed.

"Other than the fact that my burns sting, my side aches, and I have a pounding headache, sure I feel wonderful."

"I warned you about healing the princess," Darian replied. "The headache was your choice."

"Yes, but it was worth it," he replied.

"You should probably stay down and sleep it off," the elf suggested. "You pushed your body too far today. If I hadn't been there, you'd be dead. You would do well to remember that in the future."

"I know," Traven replied. He lay in silence for a few moments, resting. He then opened his eyes and sat back up. "Do you know what I need more than sleep right now?"

"What?"

"Food. I'm starving!"

Epilogue

"You look fine," Darian said with a chuckle.

Traven kept looking at his reflection in the wash basin and tried to smooth his hair down. He was wearing a clean set of his black clothes. He had washed the dirt and dried blood from his face, but there was nothing he could do about the bruise and scratches.

"It's just breakfast," the elf said. "You're not the only one that will be there with the princess."

He shrugged at Darian's comments. He just wanted to look presentable. He was happy that a full meal and a good night's rest had taken most of his headache away. His dreams had also been peaceful once again. He had been awakened this morning with the invitation to join the commanders and the princess for a midmorning breakfast.

He doubted he would have the chance to speak to the Princess Kalista at breakfast, but at least he would see her. He hoped he might even have the chance to ask her whether or not she had clearly heard the messages he had sent her on the wind. He glanced in the wash basin again. He decided he looked as good as he was going to and straightened up.

"You're sure you just want to wait here?" he asked Darian.

"I think it's best if no one finds out I'm an elf," Darian replied. "Besides, too many of you humans in one place makes me uncomfortable."

Traven smiled and left the tent. He was still a little weak but felt a lot better than he had the night before. As he walked through the camp towards the top of the rise, he realized that Darian had been right. He was definitely known to the soldiers now. He felt their stares and heard their whispers as he passed. A few even cheered for him, but others hurried to get out of his way. He didn't recognize any of them and wondered how his soldier friends had fared in the battle. He hoped they were all okay.

He had been relieved earlier in the morning to find out from Darian that Blaize was still alive and well. He was looking forward to seeing him at the breakfast. He finished making his way up the rise, trying to ignore the stares. He could see where the canopy had been set up for the meal, and he slowly made his way over to it.

There was a long table under the canopy with all of the chairs on the west side of it, so that everyone would be eating facing out over the battlefield. Several men were already seated. He saw that Blaize was among them and quickened his pace to greet his large friend. Blaize jumped up as soon as he saw him and wrapped him in a big bear hug.

"It's good to see you," Blaize said happily. "We'll have to catch up later today. I have a feeling you've had an interesting time since we parted ways in Calyn."

"You probably won't believe half of it," Traven replied with a smile. "I'm glad you're still in one piece. The battle looked pretty fierce when I arrived yesterday."

"Well, you know me. I just sat back and directed the soldiers from a safe distance."

"I'm sure," he replied. He knew that Blaize wouldn't have remained out of the fighting for long. He imagined the large warrior had been right in the middle of the most intense part of the battle.

"We'll talk more later," Blaize said. "We better take our seats. The commander general and the princess will be here soon." Blaize paused and then took on a very serious tone. "Don't forget your manners around royalty."

Traven rolled his eyes at his friend. Blaize apparently hadn't forgotten the first time they had run into the princess in the barracks. He tried to keep a straight face, but they were both soon laughing quietly. It had been funny. He grabbed the chair to Blaize's left and began to sit down, but the warrior general stopped him.

"That seat is reserved for Commander General Gavin," Blaize said. "I believe you're to sit on the other side of the princess two seats over." Blaize winked at him and took his seat.

Traven moved over to the chair Blaize had indicated and took a seat next to a commander he didn't recognize. The man had been watching him closely ever since he arrived. The commander nodded to him but didn't say anything.

Traven watched as two more commanders arrived and took their places at the ends of the table. There were now five commanders present and only two seats left in the middle of the table between him and Blaize. He stared blankly out over the battlefield as he waited anxiously for the princess to arrive. He was surprised that he would actually be sitting next to her. Maybe he would have a chance to talk with her.

He rose along with the commanders when the princess arrived with the commander general. Once the two of them were seated, he sat back down. He took a deep breath and tried to steady his nerves. The last time he had seen her she had been unconscious. The time before that he had been bedridden in the palace, recovering after being unconscious. It was strange to be with her in a public gathering. He wanted to say something to her but wasn't sure if his social position even allowed it. Fortunately, the commander general spoke up, ending the few moments of silence that had seemed to last forever.

"I would like to welcome all of you to this victory breakfast," Commander General Gavin announced. "You have all received invitations because of your key roles in making the Kalian Royal Army's victory possible. You will all have positions of honor in the victory parade when we reach Candus, but the princess and I wanted to thank you now as well."

The commander general then stood up and walked around to the front of the table. He gazed out over the field of battle for a few moments before turning and addressing everyone. His voice was slightly shaky as he began but grew firmer as he continued.

"First let us hold a moment of silence to recognize the sacrifices of those soldiers who gave their lives in protecting our grand country. There were casualties from the highest of our officers down to our newest soldiers. Let us respect their sacrifices before we move on."

Traven joined the others in a moment of quiet contemplation and respect. He had learned earlier in the morning that the Baron of Candus had been killed. He felt sympathetic towards what the commander general must be feeling. He knew what it felt like to lose one's father. He also wondered once again if any of his soldier friends were among the dead. He hoped they had somehow all survived.

"Now, let us look forward and honor those who were key in our victory," Gavin said, breaking the silence.

Traven allowed his mind to wander as the commander general began to list the accomplishments of the commanders at the table one by one. While they were receiving recognition for their heroics and being promoted, he was thinking of what to say to the princess if he ever got the chance to talk with her. It was almost more than he could stand to not look over at her while she was sitting so close to him. He could smell her sweet perfume and hear her soft breathing. As real as his visions seemed, they were nothing compared to physically being in her presence. His thoughts were pulled away from the princess by the mention of Blaize's name.

"I also want to congratulate General Blaize on his inspiring leadership during battle. If it were not for him leading such a ferocious attack with the cavalry yesterday, we wouldn't have defeated the Balthan Army as easily as we did. His quick thinking and firm leadership throughout the five day battle proved invaluable." Gavin paused and took a deep breath. "For your service Blaize, you will be promoted to take my position as Commander General of the Kalian Army."

He could hardly believe the honor Blaize had just received. He joined in applauding his friend and mentor. Now only the High King and Gavin ranked higher than Blaize in leading the army. Blaize graciously accepted his new appointment.

"And finally," Gavin continued. "I would like to thank the one that made our victory possible. The one who has saved the life of my future wife, not once, but twice. The one who defeated the Wielder Kadrak single-handedly. I would like to thank the Master Wielder Traven."

He blushed slightly as the rest of those in attendance applauded him. He nodded back to Gavin. From the corner of his eye he could see the princess looking toward him with a smile.

"I would promote you to a higher position in the army, but I can think of none higher than your own title of Master Wielder. I thank you for the great service you provided your country and the people of many lands in ridding the world of the tyrant Kadrak." Gavin then paused and looked up and down the table. "You will all receive your proper rewards and insignia when we reach Candus. For now, let us eat and enjoy our victory."

They all applauded as Gavin made his way back around the table and took his seat next to the princess. Servants arrived almost immediately and began serving a delicious breakfast. Traven was surprised at the fare and wondered where it had come from. He hadn't known that the army traveled with such delicacies. He joined with everyone else in eating the food, but he didn't really taste it. His mind was on other things.

"Traven."

He turned from his troubled thoughts as he heard the sweet caress of his name fall from the princess' lips. He responded by doing what he had wanted to do ever since she'd sat down next to him. He turned and looked at her.

"Yes, Princess," he replied.

"You don't have to call me that," she said with a smile. "Call me Kalista. I think we've been through enough together to be on a first name basis."

"If you wish," he said, surprised that the princess wanted him to use her first name.

"I do," she answered. "I wanted to thank you for saving my life again. You're probably getting tired of it, but I'm thankful you keep doing it."

"It does keep me busy," he said with a grin. They both laughed. He was glad to find that she was easier to talk to than he had remembered.

"I also wanted to thank you for healing me," she continued. "It's amazing what they say you can do."

"It was nothing," he replied modestly.

"No, it was amazing. I can't believe you created that out of thin air," Kalista said as she pointed towards the large sphere of ice at the far end of the battlefield. It was smaller than it had been, but it was still there. "You've been doing amazing things ever since I first met you."

As he stared back into her sincere eyes, his stomach did a somersault. It made him feel great to be so close to her. He wished he didn't enjoy it so much. She was engaged to Gavin and would be married soon. He needed to find a way to stop thinking about her. He jerked back as she reached up towards his face. What was she doing?

"Hold still," Kalista said as she continued reaching forward and carefully touched his bruised cheek. "That looks like it hurts. Why don't you heal yourself like you healed me?"

"It's not that bad," he replied uncomfortably. "I guess I probably could try to heal myself, but I've never done it before."

Behind her, Gavin turned from talking to Blaize. Kalista pulled her hand back from his cheek, and Gavin immediately took her hand in his. Traven could still feel her fingertips tingling against his cheek and a spark of jealousy flashed through him as he watched the two hold hands. He needed to stop thinking of her as anything other than the next High Queen of Kalia.

"So, Traven," Gavin said, "will you be staying with us in Candus?"

"I'm not sure," he answered. "There are things I still need to take care of."

"Surely you can rest in Candus for a couple of weeks," Kalista chimed in. "You must be as tired of traveling as we are."

Although he knew he should refuse the offer, he couldn't turn down a personal invitation from the princess. He supposed it would be nice to rest in comfort for a little while before making the journey back to Faldor's Keep.

"I guess you're right," he replied. "It would be nice to rest before continuing on."

"Great," Gavin said. "We'll have one of the special guest suites at the palace given to you. You're welcome to stay there as long as you wish. We know we can never repay you for all that you've done, but we'll do what we can."

"Thank you," Traven said. "I'd be honored to stay at the palace."

"We'll have to talk more later," Kalista said. "I want to know where your map led you."

She then turned from him and began talking with her fiancé. Traven let out a sigh as he finished his breakfast. He looked forward to speaking with her again but also knew that any conversation with Kalista would be bittersweet. He didn't know if it was more painful to be near her and know they could never really be friends or be far away and never see her again.

The meal was soon over. Gavin thanked them all for coming and left with the princess taking a hold of his arm. After the couple was out of sight, Traven stood and walked over to where Blaize was standing. He followed the newly appointed commander general's gaze out over the battlefield and to the large sphere of ice.

"You know, Traven," Blaize began, "I'd have never imagined when we first met that we'd end up where we are now. I'm the commander general of the most powerful army in the land, and you're a master wielder of the ambience. How'd we get here?"

"Long days in the saddle and rough nights sleeping on the ground," he replied. Blaize looked at him with a raised eyebrow.

"That sounds like something I'd say."

"I learned from the best," Traven said with a smile.

"I hope you do remember what I've taught you," Blaize said seriously. "With all your new power, you'll need to be careful of what you do."

"Don't worry, Blaize," he said. "I'm the same as I've always been."

"I hope so," the grizzled warrior said. He was quiet for a few moments as he continued staring at the large sphere of ice. Traven wondered what his friend was thinking. He didn't want his new power to change their relationship.

"So," Blaize finally said, "I hope you haven't given up your sword work now that you can blast others away with who knows what."

"I still practice every day," he replied with a smile.

"Really," Blaize said as he gave him a calculating glance. "Then I guess you wouldn't mind sparring with me today."

"I'd love to," Traven replied. "But I might not be easy on you this time."

"That sounds like a challenge," the warrior stated as he turned to face him.

"It is!"

* * * * *

Shaman Azulk looked out over the desolate battlefield from his position high in the mountains. Even in the dark of night he could clearly make out the last remnants of the sphere of ice that had crushed Kadrak and turned the tide of the battle. He had enjoyed watching the pitiful humans fight amongst themselves. The Balthans had been defeated, and the Kalians had marched victoriously to the west earlier in the day. Both armies had been weakened by Kadrak's selfish quest for power.

The time had now arrived for Azulk to call his warriors into battle. Not to gain power but to eliminate the human race. The humans had tried to destroy his ancestors hundreds of years ago, and now it was time for the galdaks to destroy them. The humans had enjoyed hundreds of years as masters of the land. Now it was time for a new race, a stronger race.

The humans wouldn't last very long. Their only hope for survival was the young human wielder who had shown up to defeat Kadrak. A low rumble gurgled in his throat. It had been entertaining to watch as the two wielders battled. He supposed the arrogant wielder Kadrak had never imagined that the young man would defeat him.

Kadrak hadn't known how his aura of power compared to the young wielder's aura. If he had realized that the young man's aura had been shining brighter than his own, he would have been more cautious. Kadrak's arrogance had led to his death.

Azulk had no doubt the young wielder could eventually grow to be incredibly powerful, perhaps even more powerful than himself. However, the young wielder would never have a chance to grow to his full potential. Azulk would personally make sure of it.

He looked down at the remnants of the Balthan Army camping in the pass. They would be the first to feel the wrath of the galdaks. From there he would split his army, sending half back towards the human country of Balthus. He would lead the rest of his army to face the young wielder and the soldiers of the Kalian Army. They would then work their way south, destroying all in their path.

He stretched his creaking bones and readied himself. It was time for him to let loose the call. His people were anxious and ready. They had been waiting for centuries. He cleared his throat and took a deep breath. He then let loose the loudest scream he could muster. The blood curdling sound echoed off the silent mountains.

He smiled and gazed up at the starry sky. He had finally done it. The call had been given. There was a short period of intense silence after the otherworldly sound. Then the silence was once again shattered. The night was soon full of galdak screams as his people responded to the call of their shaman and leader.

The screams expanded and spread north through the tunnels of the mountains as the message raced to every galdak. The call spread like wildfire on a dry summer plain. No matter how far away a galdak's burrow was, they would all know it was time. They would stream towards him from the far reaches of the Parched Mountains. By the following night, there would be plenty of warriors to begin exacting their revenge. Others would continue to flow towards him, reinforcing his army. Tomorrow the domination of the galdaks would begin.

Look for the final book of the *Wielder Trilogy*.
Coming Fall 2012.

About the Author

T.B. Christensen is an accountant and a dreamer in his late 20's. He has a wonderful wife and two darling children. He grew up in the hot desert and now lives in the cold mountains. You can learn more about T.B. Christensen and his current and future books by visiting his blog at http://www.tbchristensen.blogspot.com/.

Printed in Great Britain
by Amazon.co.uk, Ltd.,
Marston Gate.